Of One Heart

COMMEMORATIVE EDITION

CROWNS & KILTS: THE ST. BRIAC FAMILY
BOOK TWO

CYNTHIA WRIGHT

OLIVERHEBERBOOKS

Originally published 1984 by Ballantine Books

Cover artist: John Ennis

Originally published 1986 by Ballantine Books as **A Battle for Love**

Excerpt from **Abducted at the Altar** © 2018 by Cynthia Challed

Published by Oliver-Heber Books

0 9 8 7 6 5 4 3 2 1

- *Dedication* -

*For Kathy D'Huy—with thanks for wonderful memories,
including our trip to England to research this novel.*

Foreword

Dear Readers,

I am delighted to bring you this commemorative edition of OF ONE HEART with its original 1986 cover painted by the great John Ennis. Isn't it gorgeous? In those pre-internet and pre-photoshop days, every historical romance featured a cover painting created from scratch. This one is, I think, a work of art.

I wrote Andrew and Micheline's story in response to reader requests after YOU & NO OTHER was published in 1984. Thomas and Aimée are back as friends of

Micheline, but OF ONE HEART can certainly be read alone.

Andrew Weston, Marquess of Sandhurst, is one of my very favorite heroes! He was inspired by the British actor, Anthony Andrews, whom some of you may remember from the fantastic 1982 film version of The Scarlet Pimpernel. If you would like to catch up with Andrew and Micheline and see how they are enjoying married life, they return as supporting characters in QUEST OF THE HIGHLANDER, published in 2020. Also, Andrew became such a reader favorite that I created a look-alike descendant, Geoffrey Weston, in THE DUKE AND THE COWGIRL, a personal favorite among the books I've written.

Thank you so much for choosing this special edition of OF ONE HEART. I hope you enjoy it and go on to read the other books in the Crowns & Kilts series. You're invited to join my Cynthia Wright

Rakes + Readers group on Facebook and leave me a comment.

As always, I send my warmest wishes and thanks,

Cynthia

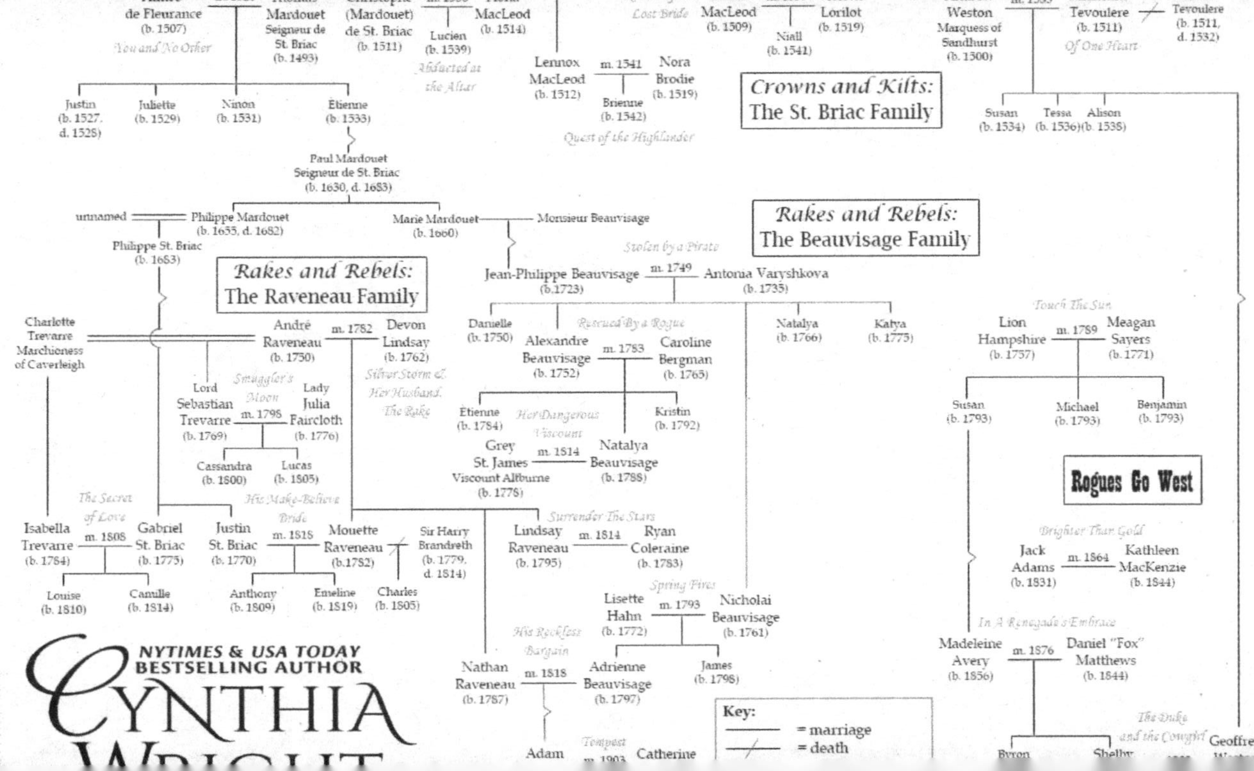

Crowns and Kilts:
The St. Briac Family

Rakes and Rebels:
The Raveneau Family

Rakes and Rebels:
The Beauvisage Family

Rogues Go West

NYTIMES & USA TODAY
BESTSELLING AUTHOR
CYNTHIA WRIGHT

Aimée de Fleurance (b. 1507)
m. 1526
Thomas Mardouet Seigneur de St. Briac (b. 1493)
You and No Other
Christophe (Mardouet) de St. Briac (b. 1511)
m. 1538
Fiona MacLeod (b. 1514)
Lucien (b. 1539)
Abducted at the Altar
Lennox MacLeod (b. 1512)
m. 1541
Nora Brodie (b. 1519)
Brienne (b. 1542)
Quest of the Highlander
Return of the Lost Bride
Ciaran MacLeod (b. 1509)
m. 1539
Violette Lorilot (b. 1519)
Niall (b. 1541)
Andrew Weston Marquess of Sandhurst (b. 1500)
m. 1533
Michelle Tevoulere (b. 1511)
Of One Heart
Bernard Tevoulere (b. 1511, d. 1532)

Justin (b. 1527, d. 1528)
Juliette (b. 1529)
Ninon (b. 1531)
Étienne (b. 1533)
Susan (b. 1534)
Tessa (b. 1536)
Alison (b. 1538)

Paul Mardouet Seigneur de St. Briac (b. 1630, d. 1683)

unnamed
Philippe Mardouet (b. 1655, d. 1682)
Philippe St. Briac (b. 1683)
Marie Mardouet (b. 1660)
Monsieur Beauvisage
Stolen by a Pirate
Jean-Philippe Beauvisage (b. 1723)
m. 1749
Antonia Varyshkova (b. 1735)

Charlotte Trevarre Marchioness of Caverleigh

André Raveneau (b. 1750)
m. 1782
Devon Lindsay (b. 1762)
Smuggler's Moon
Silver Storm & Her Husband, The Rake

Lord Sebastian Trevarre (b. 1769)
m. 1798
Lady Julia Faircloth (b. 1776)

Danielle (b. 1750)
Rescued By a Rogue
Alexandre Beauvisage (b. 1752)
m. 1783
Caroline Bergman (b. 1765)
Natalya (b. 1766)
Katya (b. 1775)

Touch The Sun
Lion Hampshire (b. 1757)
m. 1789
Meagan Sayers (b. 1771)

Cassandra (b. 1800)
Lucas (b. 1805)

Étienne (b. 1784)
Her Dangerous Viscount
Kristin (b. 1792)
Grey St. James Viscount Altburne (b. 1778)
m. 1814
Natalya Beauvisage (b. 1788)

Susan (b. 1793)
Michael (b. 1793)
Benjamin (b. 1793)

The Secret of Love
Isabella Trevarre (b. 1784)
m. 1808
Gabriel St. Briac (b. 1775)
Justin St. Briac (b. 1770)
His Make-Believe Bride
m. 1818
Mouette Raveneau (b. 1782)
Sir Harry Brandreth (b. 1779, d. 1814)
Surrender The Stars
Lindsay Raveneau (b. 1795)
m. 1814
Ryan Coleraine (b. 1783)

Rogues Go West
Brighter Than Gold
Jack Adams (b. 1831)
m. 1864
Kathleen MacKenzie (b. 1844)

Louise (b. 1810)
Camille (b. 1814)
Anthony (b. 1809)
Emeline (b. 1819)
Charles (b. 1805)

Spring Fires
Lisette Hahn (b. 1772)
m. 1793
Nicholai Beauvisage (b. 1761)

His Reckless Bargain
Nathan Raveneau (b. 1787)
m. 1818
Adrienne Beauvisage (b. 1797)
James (b. 1798)

In A Renegade's Embrace
Madeleine Avery (b. 1856)
m. 1876
Daniel "Fox" Matthews (b. 1844)

The Duke and the Cowgirl
Byron
Shelby
Geoffrey

Tempest
Adam
m. 1903
Catherine

Key:
= marriage
= death

Prologue

And wilt thou leave me thus,
And have no more pity
Of her that loveth thee?
Helas! thy cruelty!
And wilt thou leave me thus?
Say nay! say nay!

— SIR THOMAS WYATT
(1503-1542)

AMBOISE, FRANCE, SEPTEMBER 10, 1532

"BERNARD TEVOULÈRE PITTED against Arnaud Guerre in the tournament!" exclaimed Aimée de St. Briac to her husband. "Everyone knows of Bernard's affair with Elise Guerre. It's madness for him to joust against her husband!"

Thomas Mardouet, seigneur de St. Briac, drew off his helm and took a chair beside his wife in the gallery of the king's château at Amboise. Below them was spread the courtyard, where a day-long tournament was in progress. St. Briac had just finished his own joust, teamed with King François against two of their other childhood friends. This was all harmless fun and exercise as far as Thomas was concerned, but Aimée did have a point about Bernard Tevoulère and Arnaud Guerre.

As they waited for the two men to take their places on the field, St. Briac's penetrating turquoise eyes gazed southward over the dreamy Loire River that lay far below King François's magnificent château. As boys, he and the king had played at jousting here. Now they were men but their friendship endured and so did the games.

Other games—the inevitable feuds and intrigues that permeated so large a court—hadn't changed either. Thomas and Aimée spent most of their time at their château, happiest in that world fashioned around their children, home, and vineyards. However, these visits to court were necessary. King François missed his old friend, and it did Aimée good to socialize, but there were drawbacks. The most current example was the joust they would soon witness between the feckless Bernard Tevoulère and his enraged rival, Arnaud Guerre.

"I saw Bernard while preparing for my own match," St. Briac told Aimée softly, running a hand through his damp hair. "He's deteriorated sharply since our last visit to court. His new life as chevalier to the king has only weakened his character. He was drinking wine and boasting about the fact that he's to fight his mistress's husband..."

The king had come into the gallery, magnificent in his black and gold armor, and silence reigned until he had taken his place to oversee the remainder of the tournament. Aimée waited and worried.

Bernard Tevoulère was married to her dearest friend, Micheline. They'd met when Aimée had traveled south, babies in tow, to visit her parents near Angoulême. During the few short years of their friendship, Aimée had returned to Angoulême to see Micheline as much as to reunite her children with their grandparents. When Bernard had become bored with country life and began to spend more time at court, Micheline remained behind in Angoulême.

"Poor Micheline!" Aimée whispered to Thomas. "It infuriates me to think of her, living alone while he cavorts at court! What a fool he is! Married to the finest woman in France, and yet he leads a double life. I'd almost sympathize with Arnaud Guerre in this joust, if I didn't know how much Bernard means to Micheline—"

"Micheline's led a sheltered life," St. Briac replied quietly. "And Bernard has changed, *miette.*"

"Tragically!"

Thomas reached out to caress his wife's glossy black curls. "Bernard must have been flawed from the beginning; these circumstances have merely exposed his weaknesses. If the man had any honor, he'd realize what's truly important in life and bind himself to the lady he's blessed to call his wife."

A series of trumpet blasts announced the next contest. Bernard Tevoulère and Arnaud Guerre rode onto the field, pausing before the gallery to salute the king. Bernard, who was neither as tall nor as powerfully built as his opponent, lifted his visor and grinned confidently. While Elise Guerre stood to extend her hand to her husband, Bernard chuckled audibly and received a sharp glance from the king.

Moments later the two men on horseback were in position at opposite ends of the lists. Another clarion call signaled the first charge, which proved to be routine as lances struck shields and the horses reared back in reaction to the blows.

Aimée told herself that there was nothing to worry about. This was only a game, after all, not a fight to the death. Still, she couldn't help remembering another joust on this very field when an enemy of Thomas's had tried to kill him... and there was something about Guerre's bearing that sent a cold chill down her spine. Silently Aimée closed her eyes and began to pray.

She heard the trumpet, the charge of the horses, a loud crash, and then surprised gasps and cries of alarm from the assembled throng.

"Sangdieu!" hissed St. Briac. "Guerre struck at Tevoulère's helm!"

Filled with dread, Aimée opened her eyes to discover Bernard lying on the field, his head bent at an unnatural angle, while Arnaud Guerre remained on his horse, staring dispassionately at the body of his vanquished rival.

Part One

Well, fools must strike on the rebound.
While ladies volley in the air;
Collecting dues *Love* roams around;
All *Faith* is violated there.
Be hugs and kisses ne'er so rare.
Join hounds, arms, hawks and lovers'
    gains.
For all, at last, make mortals swear:
"For one short joy a thousand pains!"

– FRANÇOIS VILLON 1431-?

One

ANGOULÊME, FRANCE, SEPTEMBER, 1532

SOFT LATE-AFTERNOON SUNLIGHT filtered through the abundant green woods east of Angoulême as Micheline Tevoulère cantered home astride her huge white stallion, Gustave. She was the picture of beauty in a pale yellow gown that set off her luminous eyes, which were the color of the spring's first French irises. Lifting her face, she tasted the wind, curling brandy-hued tresses flying free in her wake.

Approaching the modest stone manor house where she had lived since her marriage four years earlier, Micheline felt a familiar shadow steal over her heart. She loved this place, but it hardly seemed a home with Bernard away so much at court. Dismounting outside the stables, she handed Gustave's reins over to the groom and then noticed the other horses in stalls that were usually empty.

"The seigneur and madame de St. Briac arrived this past hour, madame," the boy explained.

A radiant smile lit Micheline's countenance. "What

a wonderful surprise!" Gathering the books she'd brought back from her father's house, she raced toward the manor's rear entrance.

Aimée was there to greet her. They embraced warmly, then continued into the spacious flower-filled kitchen, where Micheline set her books on a long oak table and turned to beam at her friend.

"I cannot believe my eyes! It's as if you dropped from heaven, *cherie!* I'm so sorry I wasn't here when you arrived. I went to take a pie to Papa, then stayed to search his library for something I hadn't read more than twice before. With Bernard away so much, I'd be lost without books." She paused, shaking her head in renewed disbelief. "It's absolutely marvelous to see you! You're just what I've needed, Aimée."

The older woman heard the hint of melancholy in her friend's voice, and her heart ached in response. "I've missed you, too, Micheline. Thomas has taken our daughters to see my parents, so we have plenty of time for a long talk over a glass of wine."

Aimée took a chair and watched as Micheline poured Burgundy wine into pewter goblets. She was so lovely and unspoiled, so filled with intelligence and heart-melting warmth. Aimée thought, not for the first time, that all these gifts were wasted in the seclusion of the Angoulême woods. When Bernard and Micheline first married, it seemed a promising union. Micheline's mother was dead, her father bluff and distant, her brother moved to Normandy; only Bernard appeared to nourish the lonely young girl's heart. As an adolescent he had been her best friend, teaching her to ride, to swim, and, eventually, to kiss. By the time they wed, at seventeen, Micheline felt as certain of Bernard as she was of the sunrise. Who could have foreseen that he would turn faithless as he grew into true manhood?

Micheline set the goblets on the table and took the hand that Aimée stretched out to her.

"Do you remember when we first met?" Aimée asked softly.

"Yes—of course! It was just before Bernard pledged himself as a knight to King François and went off with the army to Italy. You'd come south with Juliette soon after her birth, and stayed for a month. I don't know how I should have endured Bernard's departure without you. You are my most cherished friend, Aimée! You came into my life just as I was learning that I couldn't rely on Bernard alone to fill my days."

"And you know how dearly I love you in return," Aimée replied softly, tears stinging her eyes. "It's important to have friends outside of one's marriage—and to nurture other interests, as you have done."

"*Alors,*" Micheline murmured, dropping her eyes. "I have always had solitary passions, like these books. I thought when I married Bernard that he would share these things with me. Something... happened to him, though. When he first went away, I told myself that he was helping France. I told myself that his wanderlust would fade. But when he came home, and we conceived a child, he rushed back to court!"

"I remember, *cherie*," Aimée whispered. "I was here when you lost the baby."

"How many times have you been here with me when Bernard has been away? When he finally did return home, he seemed almost relieved about the baby. I don't think he was ready to become a father."

"Perhaps that was the case." Aimée nodded. "And how do you feel now?"

"I *miss* him! Desperately!" A starry tear clung to her thick lashes. "I'm confused. Sometimes, I feel that we are almost strangers, but when he's away, it's the

Bernard of years past that I continue to yearn for. I gave him my heart when we were so young! That is the man I wait for. Do you think he will ever come back to me?"

"I believe that the man you married still lives, and always will, in your heart. And I think that he would have returned to you, in time... but that's no longer possible." Aimée crouched beside her friend's chair and gathered her into her arms. "Bernard won't be coming home. He was killed, accidentally, in a tournament at Amboise."

Micheline's exquisite face went white with shock and disbelief. "No! *No! Mère de Dieu!* It cannot be!"

Holding her near, Aimée stroked her hair. "I'm here, dearest. You won't be alone. Thomas must accompany the king to meetings with Henry VIII at Calais and Boulogne. You will come home to Château du Soleil with me until he returns. We'll take care of each other, *cherie.*"

Two

ST. BRIAC-SUR-LOIRE, FRANCE, NOVEMBER, 1532

IT WAS a chilly but sparkling afternoon when St. Briac returned home from the month-long meetings between King François I and Henry VIII in Calais and Boulogne. As he rode up the long, curving road to his ancestral château, a smile played over his mouth in anticipation of the reunion with his family.

Château du Soleil shone in the sunlight, a marvel of soaring white towers against the backdrop of the dark forest of Chinon. It was a castle of fairy-tale proportions but it hadn't seemed enchanted to him until the day he brought Aimée there as his bride. Now, accompanied by a groom and his wizened manservant, Gaspard Lefait, he dismounted before a courtyard that commanded a stunning view of the meandering Loire River. Dusting off the buttery suede doublet that accentuated his tanned, rakishly handsome face, St. Briac headed for the arched stone doorway. All his senses ached for Aimée.

"Thomas! You're home!"

He tried not to betray his disappointment when his

aunt, Fanchette, hurried from the gallery to welcome him. "It's good to see you, *ma tante*." He hugged her well-cushioned body. "It feels as if I've been away forever."

Thomas smiled down at the woman who had run his household since the death of his mother more than twenty years ago. She had raised his brother, Christophe, from infancy, and remained even after Aimée became mistress of Château du Soleil. The two women lived together in harmony.

"I'm missing my wife," St. Briac said frankly. "Where is she?"

"She and Micheline went for a walk in the woods, but I expect they'll be back soon. Don't fidget, Thomas! It's time you learned patience!"

"You needn't talk to me as if I were Christophe, old woman," he teased. "Even he is grown now and at the university. When will you realize that we are men?"

"Probably never," Fanchette responded dryly.

St. Briac walked into the gallery and began to pace, but soon the sound of a commotion upstairs intruded on his thoughts of Aimée. Fanchette stood off to one side and tried not to chuckle as she watched her nephew stop and incline his head.

"Has your lust for your wife caused you to forget your daughters, monseigneur?" she wondered. "'Twould seem that they have arisen from their naps...."

"Forget them?" he scoffed. "You insult me!" Striding to the foot of the curving staircase, St. Briac called, *"Mes anges!* Come down and give kisses to your poor papa!"

His shouts were met with distant squeals of excitement followed by the patter of little feet, and then the sight of two rosy-cheeked faces on the top step.

"Papa! Papa!"

St. Briac ascended and caught them up in his strong arms before they managed to clamber down three steps. Amid much hugging, giggling, and kissing, he gloried in the scent of their sleepy toddlers' skin, the silky texture of their curly hair, and their eyes that sparkled with excitement and love for their adored papa.

Though Juliette was three years old and Ninon nearly two, they still seemed to be babies to St. Briac. They expressed their thoughts clearly these days, yet their little bodies were dimpled, their faces round and sweet-smelling, and he could still easily fit a daughter in the crook of each arm.

Sometimes Thomas thought about the first child born to him and Aimée. Justin would have been deep into his sixth year now. There were moments when he imagined how his son might look and act had he lived. St. Briac could picture him laughing, running in the sunlight with a puppy, and then he'd force the thoughts away. Justin's death, after a year of life, had been a tragedy, but it had brought Thomas and Aimée closer together than ever. And time had brought these two rosy-cheeked little fairy princesses. The pain of Justin's loss made Thomas appreciate his daughters all the more. Aimée still longed ardently for another son, but Thomas felt no void. His heart was full.

"Papa," Juliette implored, "promise not to leave us ever again! We missed you frightfully!"

Ninon nodded solemn agreement, her chin quivering as if she might cry. "Promise, Papa!"

"We'll be together for a long time," he said, smiling. "And if I do have to go away again, for a bit, you know I will always come home to you and your maman."

"Where *is* Maman?" Juliette demanded.

St. Briac turned his head to gaze out the tall gallery windows. "I wish I *knew*," he murmured in response.

* * *

Out in the woods, Micheline and Aimée tramped over a carpet of rusty leaves, each lost in thought.

"Thomas is due to return soon, isn't he?" Micheline queried, reading her friend's mind. "You must be missing him terribly."

"Well, yes, of course...." Aimée was very conscious of Micheline's continued grief, and although she had missed Thomas desperately, part of her had been glad to devote all her attention to her friend. Surely the sight of Thomas, who could not conceal his love for his wife, would have daily sprinkled salt over Micheline's wound. Two months had passed since Bernard's death and only lately had Aimée seen Micheline smile, and even laugh, with any sign of true pleasure... and now Thomas was coming home. What effect would that have on Micheline's progress?

"My dear friend," Micheline said, stopping to take Aimée's hand, "please do not hide your feelings on my account. I'm very happy for you and Thomas."

"*Cherie*, it is so unfair that you should have to bear such terrible grief!" Aimée exclaimed, hugging her near. "I wish that I could take away your sadness."

"I fear that only time, and God, can do that. I know you understand my meaning after losing your little Justin. And you *have* helped, Aimée, by bringing me here to be with you." She paused, then continued gently. "But your husband is coming home. You must return your attention to him and your children... and I should go back to Angoulême before winter."

"*No!*" Aimée exclaimed. "You must not even think of that yet!" Seeing that Micheline would not be so easily dissuaded, she took her friend's arm. "Let us talk of this another time. The girls will be waking from naps, and you promised to teach the cook your recipe for braised wild boar with red wine. Tante Fanchette has been anticipating it so—she'll scold us terribly if we're late!"

Micheline smiled and yielded. Emerging from the forest, the two friends paused to appreciate the beauty that lay below them. The autumn sun danced over the vine-covered hillocks, down to the peaked towers of Château du Soleil and the luminous Loire River that swirled lazily in the distance.

For a moment Micheline forgot her heartache. The beauty of the day and the love of her friend warmed her heart. Life seemed sweet.

As they approached the château, Aimée's step quickened. "This may sound silly, but I've learned to trust my instincts. I think Thomas may be home!"

Micheline felt a queer mixture of emotions when they entered the château's great hall and discovered St. Briac sitting in a carved chair near the window, a daughter on each knee. The three of them were engaged in private conversation, heads bent. Juliette held fast to her father's big hand and kissed it repeatedly.

Aimée watched in silence, glowing, then spoke up at last. "Poor Maman! No kisses for *her*! No one even cares that she's here!"

"Oh, Maman!" cried Ninon, instantly sympathetic.

Laughing, St. Briac crossed the room carrying his daughters and Aimée met them halfway. The little family hugged while Micheline stood in the doorway, her own heart swelling with bittersweet emotions.

At length she called, "Ninon! Juliette! I'm going to cook a wild boar. Won't you come and help me? He has very long tusks!"

The girls squealed and Thomas set them down. As

they hurried across the floor, he grinned at Micheline and gave her a fleeting wink.

"Greetings, madame," he called to her as his arms stole around Aimée's waist. "And many thanks."

Three

MICHELINE RETIRED EARLY that night to her tower chamber with a book of poetry by François Villon. Propped against a bolster, she gazed out at the full moon that poured its light across the bed. A candle burned on the table next to her, but she had no heart for reading. It would be so much more convenient, she thought, if cheery surroundings and loving friends were enough to make one happy, but it seemed that moods could not be shaped quite so easily. No matter how many distractions she had, her mind went around and around of its own accord, taking the past apart and putting it together again in an effort to make sense of it, then fretting over the future.

Putting aside her book, Micheline blew out the candle and stared into the silver-blue moonlight. Sleep, she told herself. However, when her eyes closed, she saw images of Thomas, Aimée, and their two cherubs. How fortunate they were! It seemed that any chance of her own for such contentment had died with Bernard.

Micheline tossed this way and that in the cool darkness while memories and questions swirled round and round inside her. Finally, throwing off her covers, she put on a robe and went into the corridor. The château was quiet now. Tears burned her eyes as she descended the curving stairway to the moon-silvered gallery. Was there no escape from the pain that had seemingly had attached itself to her very soul?

* * *

The château was not as quiet as it appeared. Upstairs, Thomas and Aimée had just indulged in a long, shared bath. She was now sitting up in bed, naked under the covers, while Thomas combed out her long raven curls.

"I'm too tired to listen to the serious side of the king's meetings with Henry the Eighth," Aimée murmured with a yawn. "Save the details of the treaties and subterfuge for tomorrow... but do tell me about Anne Boleyn! Is she very beautiful? Do you suppose Henry will actually *marry* her?"

"Beautiful? No. But there is a... quality about the lady that some men might find attractive. François certainly seemed taken with her—he gave her a diamond worth fifteen thousand ecus. As for her chances to become queen of England, Henry recently made her Marquess of Pembroke, so I would wager in her favor. He's besotted; there's no doubt."

"Do you think the French court life impressed them? Were the entertainments fine?"

St. Briac shrugged, laid the comb aside, and began to caress his wife's shoulders. "Fine enough," he replied absently. "Bear-baiting, and a rather bizarre wrestling contest between Englishmen and French priests... and, of course, the usual balls and masques. François left Queen Eleanor at Fontainebleau, so he was free to partner Anne Boleyn in the dances."

Although Aimée was frankly aroused by her husband's increasingly intimate caresses, she could not resist the opening he'd provided for another avenue of conversation.

"So… the court is in residence at Fontainebleau? How I have longed to be there myself lately!"

St. Briac blinked in surprise, but did not waver in his own course of action. Drawing Aimée into his arms, he kissed her throat with warm lips. "I thought that you desired only to spend weeks on end here with me! Before I left for Calais, you could talk of nothing else except the son you intended to conceive before Christmas."

His fingertips were drawing fiery patterns on her breasts. It took every ounce of control Aimée possessed to continue the conversation. "I do still want to conceive a son, but right now there is a more urgent matter that demands my immediate attention."

"Impossible, *miette*," he murmured absently.

"You've been so busy stealing kisses from me and playing with the babies that you've scarcely had time to notice. I'm talking about darling Micheline!"

"My love, I have the utmost sympathy for Micheline's plight, and I hope that she will stay with us until she feels better, but I fail to see what this has to do with the two of us making a baby!"

Aimée tried to ignore St. Briac's waning patience with the conversation. "Your good wishes for Micheline are admirable, but I have realized that we, as her friends, must play a more *active* role in her recovery."

Thomas lay back on his pillow. "I hate to say it, but all the signs point to one of your notorious *plans.*"

"How well you know me!" she teased. "We must think of Micheline. You and I have everything that she does not, and a whole lifetime ahead of us in which to enjoy our blessings."

"And how do you propose to obtain our sort of blessings for Micheline?"

"Fontainebleau is the remedy!"

At this St. Briac gave her an incredulous stare. "*Fontainebleau?!* Surely you jest! A few months at court are more apt to corrupt than bless the unspoiled Micheline!"

"Not if we are there to watch over her!" She leaned toward him excitedly. "She is not ready to think of marriage yet. All I really want for her is to *live* again! At Fontainebleau, she is bound to feel a spark of interest. You don't understand how desperately melancholy Micheline has been since Bernard's death. She thinks her life is over!"

"Nonsense."

"I know you have not forgotten what we suffered after little Justin's death. Unspeakable grief! But at least we had each other. If we do nothing to help our friend, who knows how long it will take before something or someone comes along to make her take an interest in life again?"

She had said the one thing that could make his heart clench in empathy. "You're determined about this, aren't you?"

A tide of love swept over her as she heard the surrender in his voice. Wrapping her arms around him, she said, "Part of the reason I feel so strongly about this is that I'm certain Micheline has never been truly fulfilled in life or love before."

"That's a safe assumption considering the character of her husband. I've never been one to speak ill of the dead, but frankly Micheline is well rid of Tevoulère."

"We must be very careful to keep the truth about Bernard from her. It would destroy her! She nurtures an illusion that he was meant to be her mate for life."

St. Briac made a noise that succinctly expressed his opinion on that subject.

"And yet," Aimée continued, "I feel that even Micheline realizes, deep inside, that her marriage was not all it could have been. Bernard was the only man she's ever known. She simply doesn't know what she's been missing."

"I doubt that she'll make that discovery at court."

"Perhaps not, but she'll have entertaining distractions. She's like a wounded fawn, Thomas. First she has to heal and learn to enjoy the simplest pleasures; it may be quite some time before she's ready to think of love."

"I yield, my lady." St. Briac smiled, kissing his wife's hair. "We shall go to Fontainebleau for the winter, at least. Do you suppose, though, that in the meantime—"

Aimée turned her face up to joyously receive his kiss. He tasted the sweet secrets of her mouth and drew her closer to feel her softness against his hardness. "How I missed you, *miette*," he whispered.

She gloried in the hot swirling spiral of passion, giving herself over to it as St. Briac's mouth burned her throat and then found her breasts. Now that the matter of Micheline was resolved for the moment, Aimée could concentrate on her husband. He was, she believed, the most splendid man in France.

* * *

It was long past midnight when Thomas fell asleep. Aimée listened to his heartbeat, wide awake, dozens of plans circling busily in her mind. Gradually her sixth sense told her that Micheline might be awake as well.

St. Briac's long, elegant fingers were curved around her waist, keeping her near even in sleep. His fatigue from the arduous journey home was such, however, that he didn't stir when Aimée lifted his hand and crept out of bed. Donning a velvet robe, she lifted the latch and tiptoed out into the dark corridor.

Micheline sat near the bottom of the curving white marble stairway, leaning against a baluster fashioned of black wrought-iron grapevines. The moonlight was brighter than ever, flooding the gallery through the tall windows that opened onto the courtyard. Aimée approached Micheline carefully. She was so still that she seemed unaware of her friend's presence, but then, as Aimée drew near, she whispered gently, "Has the moon kept you awake as well, Aimée?"

"In part... the moon and thoughts of you." Aimée perched beside her.

"I'm sorry. Don't worry about me. You should be giving your attention to your family."

"I have love enough for all of you," she replied warmly. "Will you tell me why you are still awake?"

"I try to sleep, but Bernard is in my dreams. It's very hard."

"I have some news that might cheer you up," Aimée said.

"I would be so grateful!" replied Micheline earnestly. "I long for escape from this melancholy. It is like being lost in the woods, endlessly..."

"Perhaps my news will provide a way out. Thomas and I have decided to join the court at Fontainebleau for the winter, and we insist that you accompany us. You've never been to court, have you?"

"No." Micheline had always thought that she wouldn't enjoy court life, but deep inside her she realized that had only been her way of hiding her disappointment when Bernard did not invite her to accompany him.

"It's all quite gay!" Aimée declared brightly. "There

is so much to do. You'll have new gowns and new friends.... There will be little time for sadness. I know it will be good for you."

She stared out to the moon-drenched courtyard. "Perhaps you're right. Perhaps it would be the best thing for me." She paused, then turned to search her friend's face with eloquent iris-blue eyes.

Aimée reached out to touch Micheline's cheek, her own eyes swimming with tears. "It won't be easy, but if you have courage, you'll discover pleasure in living again."

"Do you truly believe it is possible?"

"Absolutely! I can't promise that you'll find your proper path at Fontainebleau, but I am *convinced* that it exists—and at its end lies happiness and fulfillment that you have yet to even imagine.

CHÂTEAU DE FONTAINEBLEAU, DECEMBER, 1532

LATE-AFTERNOON SUN GILDED the great trees of the forest. Oak, hornbeam, wide-girthed chestnut, and birch had shed their autumn finery to begin the long rest through winter. Naked gray branches arched toward the sky, impervious even to the thundering hooves of horses, packs of tired hounds, and fine-looking gentlemen riders returning from yet another successful hunt.

Bursting from the forest, the hunting party made for the palace gates, above which shone imposing high-roofed sandstone pavilions set in rhythmical order, their ornaments, pilasters, and capitals decorated with François I's bold F.

The king's horse galloped first through the gateway, hooves clattering over the cobbles of the magnificent Oval Courtyard. As grooms rushed forward to relieve the men of their horses, the king stole a private word with his old friend St. Briac.

"That was a fine hunt, *mon ami*, but I am dusty. Let us have a cold plunge before we sup."

St. Briac had been craving the company of his wife, but one look at the bold, determined profile of the king made him sigh inwardly and reply, "I am at your service, sire." To guard their three-decade-old friendship, Thomas had never accepted favors or rank from François, yet one did not refuse the king when he made requests in a certain tone of voice.

They walked leisurely across the cobbled courtyard toward the arched doorway that would lead them into the new *appartements des bains*. The Château de Fontainebleau was in the midst of a series of elaborate transformations. Ever since the king had decided to spend more time near Paris, this hunting lodge had been the focus of dramatic changes. For several years it had been noisy and dirty, filled with scaffolding and workmen, but slowly the grand new Fontainebleau was emerging.

A new wing had been added to the keep which so far housed the king's dreamed-of baths. Upstairs a long, splendid gallery was being constructed, and François had already begun to recruit the finest artists from Italy to ensure its perfection. He was extolling the virtues of Rosso and Primaticcio to Thomas when a familiar figure appeared on the stairway next to the *appartements des bains.*

"You go on, Thomas," the king murmured. "I'd like a word with Madame Tevoulère."

St. Briac arched an eyebrow, but left his friend alone to greet Micheline.

When she reached the bottom step, François exclaimed as if surprised, "If it isn't the loveliest lady in all France! How do you fare this afternoon, madame?"

"Very well, Your Majesty." Micheline flushed slightly

and dropped her eyes. Clad in a simple gown of dark blue silk which was properly modest for a widow, she nonetheless felt his hazel eyes sweep the curves of her body. Eager for distraction, she produced a book from the folds of the cloak she carried. "I hope you won't mind, sire. I took you at your word and borrowed this from your splendid library. I thought I might read in the garden."

"Mind? Have I not told you that all I have is yours for the taking?" François smiled at his own subtle wit, then leaned forward to read the title of the volume Micheline had chosen. "*Roman de la Rose!* An inspired choice. 'Twill do you good to read of romance. I've worried that you might have forgotten such pleasures!"

Micheline hardly knew how to reply. When the king reached for her hand and kissed it, the uneasy flush in her cheeks intensified. "I mustn't keep you from your bath, sire. *Au revoir.*"

François watched as Micheline walked under the archway leading to the elaborate gardens. The sight of her hair, gleaming in the sunlight, and the gentle sway of her hips made him sigh. Finally he turned and went to join Thomas inside the bathing room. Quickly the two men shed their soiled garments and walked down the flight of wooden steps that led to the great square pool. It was five feet deep, with two spouts that provided hot and cold water. Priceless paintings and statuary decorated the perimeter of the room.

"Ah!" exclaimed the king. "Could heaven itself be sweeter?"

St. Briac ducked his head under the water and emerged to shake the cool droplets from his hair. "I must agree, sire, that God Himself would doubtless be content here."

Servants appeared with jeweled goblets of strong red wine and plates filled with crusty bread, oysters from Cancale, strawberries from the king's greenhouses, and tempting little wedges of Auvergne cheese. The men, hungry after their exercise, ate contentedly.

"I feel that life is finally settling into place after the changes of recent years," François reflected.

St. Briac watched him plunge into the water and swim across the pool. Indeed, there had been changes. Two of the king's young sons, who had become hostages to Emperor Charles V in place of their father, had been ransomed in 1529 after three years. The negotiations for their release had been effected by two women, one of whom was Louise de Savoy, the king's mother. "The Ladies' Peace" had ended years of war, but in return for the safe return of his sons, François had to reconfirm his marriage by proxy to Charles V's sister Eleanor.

François had paused to rest against the gilded edge of the pool beside his friend.

"The death of my mother continues to grieve me," he said suddenly.

"Yes, sire. But it has only been a year, and she was your trusted advisor. You continue to adjust."

At length, François remarked more jauntily, "I do find myself intrigued with this subject of change. How boring life would be if nothing ever changed. Take women, for instance...."

Biting back a smile, St. Briac waited, knowing what was coming.

"Here at court," the king continued between bites of strawberry and cheese, "the women change like the seasons and most are forgotten. A few, however, stand out like roses in a field of daisies."

"Ah. Yes."

"One lady in particular..."

"Micheline?" he wondered innocently.

"*Oui*!" François averted his eyes, and took a long drink of wine. "Micheline has made an entrancing change in the court. Apparently you lust after your wife alone, my friend, but even you must admit that Madame Tevoulère is a female of exceptional loveliness." He sighed, smiling. "Most astonishing, however, is her *mind*. I can discuss even Roman history with Madame Tevoulère! My own complaint is that she continues to maintain a certain level of reserve when in my company. Could it be possible that she is immune to my charms?" He laughed at such a ludicrous notion, but his tone took on a low urgency. "Thomas, couldn't you speak to her? Assure her that I only wish to know her better?"

St. Briac's amusement waned. "Sire, if you imagine that I can intercede, I must dispel that notion. Aimee is trying to help Micheline recover from the shock of her husband's death, to learn to enjoy life again. She would not want her heart broken, even by her king."

"How can you suggest that I could harm so glorious a creature as Madame Tevoulère?"

"It might be a matter of circumstances more than intention, sire." Suddenly the water felt cold and tiresome and he longed to be elsewhere. "You know as well as I that you are married. For my Aimée, that would be obstacle enough, but there is also the matter of Anne d'Heilly, who has been your favorite for many years. It would not be an easy matter to displace her, even if you wanted to."

King François frowned, clearly displeased by his friend's words. Only from St. Briac would he tolerate such a conversation. Micheline seemed unobtainable, and for the King of France, such a challenge was virtually irresistible.

* * *

François was not the only person at Fontainebleau who contemplated Micheline Tevoulère. Even as he and St. Briac were talking, Anne d'Heilly sat at her writing table in her private chambers, worrying and planning. She was frankly scared. For years she had been secure in her position at court. The king might take other women, but they meant nothing; even this new queen, Eleanor, meant nothing to him. Why, François could scarcely bear to sleep with his own wife! Night after night he came to Anne instead.

She was proud, too, that he trusted her judgment. Since the death of Louise de Savoy, Anne had gradually replaced the king's mother as his advisor to the king. Anne d'Heilly had more power than any other woman in France. That very autumn François had taken her to Calais and Boulogne for the meetings with Henry VIII —while Queen Eleanor had remained behind.

Setting down her quill, Anne glanced distractedly at the pages she had just written, then rose to stare at herself in the mirror. Everyone said that each year increased her beauty, and she believed them. Fair curls brushed her brow while her wide eyes seemed bluer than ever. Her figure remained diminutive, its curves sweeter than they had been when she first met King François, at age seventeen.

"Micheline Tevoulère is no lovelier than I!" she whispered aloud.

That was the crux of her dilemma. Anne had instantly sensed the king's attraction to the newest member of his court, but after a fortnight's brooding she was no closer to finding a solution that she could effect on her own. Micheline did not appear to covet Anne's place as mistress to the king. In truth, she seem to have no interest in François at all beyond that of respectful subject. At last Anne had realized that this was the basis of the girl's appeal. Micheline Tevoulère was the first woman in years who was not his for the taking.

Anne knew now that the only solution was to remove Madame Tevoulère from the king's sight, from the court itself. Returning to her writing table, she thanked providence for allowing her to become friends with the king of England so recently. She dipped her quill into the ink and finished her letter by subtly reminding Henry VIII that she would repay any favor he might grant her. The English monarch was eager for François I to intercede with the pope regarding his divorce and impending marriage to Anne Boleyn.

"I am a romantic," she wrote Henry in closing, "and it warmed my heart to see the love between you and *your* Anne. I hope that the two of you can be married... and I shall do everything in my power to persuade my king to share my view if that happy event comes to pass."

* * *

As Anne d'Heilly was signing her name to the letter to Henry VIII, Micheline Tevoulère had been joined by Aimée in the gardens below, and they strolled aimlessly, unaware that others who wielded control were contemplating Micheline's future.

Even in December Fontainebleau was a place of unrivaled beauty. In winter the garden's hedges were clipped to form artful green tunnels that led into dormant flowerbeds, punctuated with urns and sculpture. Micheline did not regret coming here. The constant activity was a welcome change from the period of darkness following Bernard's death. During the day she rode or walked with Aimée or one of the other ladies of the court. Meals were events, attended by hundreds of people, and nearly every night there was entertainment of some sort. Lovely new gowns had been made for Micheline, and she enjoyed the warm admiration of nearly everyone she met—especially the men. However, in spite of the invitation in their eyes, she could not bring herself to respond. The thought of even being kissed by anyone but Bernard remained forbidden.

"I saw you talking to the handsome Chevalier d'Honfleur last night," Aimée ventured after a few minutes of companionable silence.

Micheline smiled and shrugged slightly, reading her friend's mind. "Guillaume is very nice," she allowed. "I agreed to go riding with him tomorrow."

"How nice." Aimée knew she should choose her words carefully, but, as usual, impulse overruled reason. "I would like to see you encourage someone, if only to *discourage* the king."

"What do you mean?" cried Micheline. "I cannot feel the slightest stirring of affection for any man I have met here, beyond that of simple friendship—including the king! Surely he is perceptive enough to realize that."

"I would guess that it is that challenge that intrigues him, *ma chére*. Don't fret, though. François is a gentleman at heart, though used to having his own way. You simply must continue to show only respect for him. Any encouragement at all would only heighten his desire... and determination."

Micheline paused to pick a sprig of mistletoe and gazed at it pensively. "I've begun to think that Bernard's death killed something within me. There are moments, when I talk to someone who is handsome, charming, and accomplished, and I marvel at the numbness in my heart." She met Aimée's concerned gaze with teary eyes. "I doubt I'll ever be attracted to a man again."

Aimée opened her mouth, then closed it, aching for her friend. She yearned to repair Micheline's heart, but lately she had realized that only God could perform such a miracle. Aimée could only wait and pray.

Five

LONDON, ENGLAND, FEBRUARY, 1533

DAWN HAD SCARCELY TINTED the eastern sky when the noise of the River Thames coming awake disturbed the slumber of Iris, Lady Dangerfield. She frowned slightly, still half-asleep, forgetting for the moment that she lay in the Marquess of Sandhurst's bed. His town house was fashionably situated on the Strand and overlooking the river, but this daily commotion on the water could become tiresome.

Iris opened one eye to find her bed partner still sleeping a few inches away. Clearly, Sandhurst was used to the clamor. Her irritation melted away as she gazed at him, lost in the spell he cast so effortlessly, even in his sleep.

Andrew Weston, Marquess of Sandhurst, would become one of the wealthiest men in Britain upon the death of his elderly father. Not only would the coveted title of Duke of Aylesbury be his, but also vast estates in Gloucestershire, and Aylesbury Castle in Yorkshire.

The mere thought of such riches and prestige made Iris ache inside, for she had married Timothy, Lord

Dangerfield barely two months before meeting Sandhurst at Hampton Court. She'd been satisfied with Timothy until then, but the instant she glimpsed that proud head across the garden and felt the heat of his compelling brown eyes even from a distance, Iris lusted for him. Then the Marquess of Sandhurst had slowly, casually, made his way to her side. When he reached out with strong, agile fingers to lift her hand to his mouth, she'd burned for him, nearly fainting.

That had been two years ago, and the force of her ardor seemed almost to amuse Andrew. He was fond of her, but Iris knew that even if Timothy should die Sandhurst would not marry her. He did not seem to want to be bound to anyone except himself. Naturally he would *have* to marry one day to produce an heir. Iris tried not to think about that. The idea of another woman having what she burned to possess was torture.

Longing to touch him now, she stared instead. Her gaze lingered on his tousled golden hair, which curled slightly against his brow and along the nape of his neck. Iris thought him the most splendid, masculine creature alive, and there were few women who would disagree with her. His face could have been sculpted, particularly the cheekbones and aristocratic nose. Just above his upper lip, on the left side, was a scar that cut down into the firmness of his mouth. This obvious flaw made him doubly captivating.

"My dear Iris," he murmured suddenly in a voice husky with sleep, "you are a woman of breeding. Were you never taught that it is rude to stare, especially at this uncivilized hour and at such length?"

There had not been even the flicker of an eyelash to betray his consciousness. Iris blushed, but whispered, "Forgive me, my lord. I only was staring because I could not touch...."

"Why not?" One side of Sandhurst's mouth quirked slightly, brown eyes opened lazily, and he was turning on his side to reach for her.

Even in winter his skin was golden brown against Iris's pale flesh. Leisurely he traced her breasts with one fingertip, smiling as he gathered her closer and breathed the scent of roses in her coppery hair.

"But... what about this uncivilized hour?" Iris somehow managed to tease, her breath already coming in little gasps.

"Perfectly fitting." Sandhurst kissed her then, before she could ponder his words. How convenient that she was always so hot and willing...

A loud, irritating tapping began on the bedchamber door. Impossible, he thought dimly. No servant could be so foolish. The racket continued until he finally lifted his head and shouted, "God's life, *stop that!*"

"Sandhurst? Are you awake? It's Rupert! I must speak to you!"

Rupert! What the hell was his illegitimate twit of a half brother doing in London—at his town house—at dawn?

"Don't you know what time it is? Go downstairs and have them bring you an egg or something. I'll join you after I've bathed and dressed."

"No, no, no!" Rupert's tone grew shrill. "I must speak to you *now*. I'm coming in!"

Furious by now, Sandhurst threw off the covers, bare feet meeting the chilly, rush-strewn floor. He yanked on his hose before throwing open the door.

"Be grateful I'm sparing your life, crackbrain!"

Across the chamber Iris clutched the thick covers against her chin and stared in shock. It wasn't often that Sandhurst lost his temper.

Now he was leading the slight, spindly younger man

to his dressing room. Rupert gaped openly in Iris's direction until he suddenly found himself closed in with his ominous-looking half brother.

"Don't be angry, I implore you!" he whined. "I've come to help you!"

Sandhurst took a deep breath before replying coldly, "Pray explain. *Quickly.*"

"The duke is here. Our father!"

"I appreciate the clarification," he said sarcastically. "Just tell me what the devil is going on!"

"Well, *well,* we were all settled in at Aylesbury Castle for the winter. Patience, my dear wife, and Father, who had a chill, and our younger sister. Cicely—"

"Rupert, I bloody *know* who lives at Aylesbury Castle! I am still a member of the family." It galled Sandhurst to be instructed by this stammering fool. If his own mother, the duchess, were still alive, Rupert Topping would never have managed to infiltrate the family. Five years ago Andrew's mother had died after an accidental fall, and the duke, ill and lonely in his castle, had allowed his old lover. Jane Topping, to take residence with the son she insisted was the duke's. Sandhurst, already estranged from his father, lived far to the south in London, and Cicely, at eight years of age, was not a fit companion for a crotchety old man. So Jane Topping made herself at home, while Rupert, then nineteen, treated his father as if he were God. After Jane, too, died, Rupert had stayed on, playing the dutiful son in the Marquess of Sandhurst's absence. Even the horse-faced Patience Topping, recruited as Rupert's wife last year from the village of Bubwith, had wormed her way into the family's bosom.

Lord Sandhurst's scorn for the entire situation that the duke had allowed to develop was almost surpassed by the repulsion he felt for his obsequious half brother.

As a consequence, Sandhurst stayed far away from his family and the already cool relationship with his father virtually disappeared.

"Oh, I *know* that you are one of the family, my lord!" Rupert was blubbering. "You'll never know how grateful I am—how *honored*—that I am your relative! I would do anything to help you, to bridge the gap between you and our father, to heal the wounds, to—"

Pained, he closed his eyes. "I perceive your meaning."

"Well, the thing is, I had a suspicion that Lady Dangerfield might be here, and I was afraid that our father's valet might come to your chambers to inform you of our visit. Kettlewell tells Father *everything*. He's almost like a spy!" Something in Sandhurst's eyes caused Rupert to get a grip on himself. "Well, that's getting ahead of the story. You see, this is what's happened. We were all settled in for the winter, as I told you, when King Henry sent word that he wanted to meet with Father at Whitehall. We had no idea what it was about, but the duke allowed all of us to accompany him. Cicely was especially eager for the chance to visit *you*!" He paused to nod cheerfully several times. "We arrived in London two days ago and went immediately to Whitehall. Exciting times, I don't mind telling you! Father met with the king, then last night he suddenly announced that we must come to your house at once. It was quite late when we arrived—you were, umm, asleep—and the servants saw us to our beds."

Now that the gist of the story was revealed, Sandhurst hated to prolong the interview, but curiosity got the better of him. "You are not exactly privy to the intimate details of my life, Rupert, so I wonder what led to your suspicion that Kettlewell might find Lady Dangerfield in my bed."

Rupert blushed and dropped his eyes. "Lord Dangerfield arrived back from a journey to Cornwall yesterday. As I understood the story, he went to his home, but his wife was absent. Then he—uh—visited the court at Whitehall, where he imbibed a rather injudicious amount of ale and told anyone who would listen that Lady Dangerfield was embroiled in an open affair with *you*, that she was doubtless in your bed as he spoke, that—"

"Am I to assume that you were one of those people who 'would listen'?"

"Only for your sake, Sandhurst!" Rupert assured him eagerly. "Only to help you!"

"I'm a grown man. I don't want your help." He turned away before reason fled entirely and he said something brutal. "Leave me now to bathe and dress. You may tell my father when he awakens that I will join him in his chambers."

Sandhurst returned to his own bedchamber to discover that Iris had gone back to sleep. Drawing back the covers, he lightly spanked her shapely bottom and sat down on the edge of the bed.

"You'll have to get up, I'm afraid." He spoke distractedly, staring out the leaded-glass windows. Snow swirled against the panes. "Didn't you tell me that your husband returns from Cornwall today?"

"Yes, but not until midday." Iris ran her fingertips down the long, tapering line of his back. "Come back to bed, my lord," she purred. "I'm still hungry."

"Save your appetite for Dangerfield. He's back, and he knows you weren't in *his* bed last night. I'd suggest that you dress and hurry home to appease him, if you still can...."

* * *

Joshua Finchley, faithful valet to the Marquess of Sandhurst, prepared a hot bath for his lordship, then laid out fresh clothing and took his leave. Unlike most noblemen, his master preferred to shave, bathe, and dress himself.

It was past eight when Sandhurst stepped into the corridor, clad in rich gray velvet. Puffs of white silk showed through the slashings of his doublet, which was sewn tight at his waist. A neat white fraise stood up against his golden-brown neck.

"Andrew!" cried a familiar female voice. He turned to find his sister, Cicely, running toward him, her face alight with love and excitement.

"Child," he murmured, and caught her up in his arms. "How you've grown."

"I'm almost a lady. I'm fourteen. A boy in Yorkshire has already asked for my hand!"

Sandhurst blinked, then smiled. "He was refused, I trust?"

"Of course, silly!" She stood on tiptoe, beaming up at him. Gleaming black curls framed her heart-shaped face which was dominated by beautiful sable-brown eyes. She was petite and slender, with gentle curves that he hadn't remembered... no longer a baby sister. "I've missed you so! How can you leave me up there with... *them* like this?" Cicely's voice had dropped to a whisper. She glanced down the hall toward Rupert and Patience, who appeared to be standing guard outside the duke's bedchamber.

"I'm not a fit guardian for a young lady," he replied with more than a twinge of guilt. If only their mother hadn't died, none of these problems would exist.

"Do you think it right that I'm being raised by—"

"My lord?" Rupert and Patience called in unison. "Your father awaits."

"I'm coming." He looked down at Cicely's earnest little face. "We'll talk about this later, all right?" Then, walking down the corridor toward the duke's bedchamber, Sandhurst could only feel a familiar rush of hostility. This was *his* house, after all, and he was thirty years old, yet other people continued to attempt to manipulate *his* life! They arrived without an invitation, ordering him about—

"Andrew? Andrew, where are you?" came the querulous voice of his father.

Lord Sandhurst paused for a moment and closed his eyes. Old instincts rose to the surface, but he pushed them back. He'd learned, years ago, that fighting with his father gained him nothing but frustration, though it had taken him many more years to perfect a more subtle approach. Opening his eyes, he practiced a smile on Rupert and Patience as he went through the doorway.

"Father, it is good to see you." Approaching the bed, Sandhurst extended his hand.

The Duke of Aylesbury wore an old nightgown faced with fox. He sat up in bed, propped against a mountain of pillows, his white hair combed back from his craggy face. In his youth the duke had looked not unlike his handsome son, but now his excellent bone structure served only to accentuate sunken cheeks and a sharp chin. His life had been bitter, made bitterer still by this rebellious son and heir who had the effrontery to smile at him and extend his hand in pretended affection.

"I'm too old for your games, Andrew. Sit down."

A muscle moved in his jaw. "I'd prefer to stand."

"I see no point in wasting time on aimless chatter," the duke continued. "I've come to tell you that you're going to be married. King Henry has found a wife for you, and I've agreed."

Six

"I MUST BE HEARING THINGS." Sandhurst's heart was in his throat. "I could have sworn I heard you say that you and King Henry had chosen a *wife* for me."

Apparently unable to resist the impulse to toy with his prey for a moment, the duke smiled. "You have only the king to thank on that score. All I have done is set the seal on his plans." Aylesbury's smile widened maliciously.

"Have I no say in this? No voice in my own destiny?" Somehow, he managed to sound calm, though the scar that cut through his upper lip had gone white.

The duke's smile faded. "You can say whatever you like, but I don't think you'll fight the will of the king the way you've always fought me. It is high time you learned that there are more important things than *your* wishes. You have never done the smallest thing to please me, your father, but you'll please me now whether you want to or not!" He let out a hoarse bark of laughter. "For years I've begged you to take an interest in my estates. I've longed to see you married, with sons of your own, before I die. I've encouraged you to make a place for yourself at court, but it seems that the most you could bother to do has been to waste your charm on Henry's favorite ladies. Even the future queen goes doe-eyed at the mention of your name! You're a *fool*, Andrew, and now you're going to pay for it!"

The old man was leaning forward, his face crimson as he railed at his son. For his own part, Sandhurst thought that he must be having a nightmare. Dimly he heard himself say, "Perhaps I've turned away from you because I sensed that your interest was not in me but in the family title. As the future duke it seemed that I was to be molded like a piece of clay, not a person."

"Bah! You needed a firm hand! You still do! If you wanted affection, you should have listened to me and taken a wife years ago. That's what a good woman is for." The duke smiled again, thinly. "You see, I'm doing you a favor! After your French bride begins warming your bed, you'll thank me! The chit probably won't even speak English, which'd be a blessing. If she can't talk to you, there will be just one thing for her to do—spread her legs!"

"This is utter madness," he muttered.

"Tell it to King Henry," the old man shot back.

"What if I were to do just that? I'm not some twelve-year-old who needs a marriage arranged for him."

"You don't seem to be able to arrange one on your own!"

"God's life, why should the king care about my marital state?"

The duke shrugged. "As I understand it, someone with power in the French court wants this girl disposed of—tidily, of course. A proper English husband who would take her to live across the Channel seemed the solution. Henry was glad to lend his aid because he needs assistance from King François in winning over the pope, more than ever now, I'd say, since there are rumors that he and Anne Boleyn were secretly married last month."

"But why was *I* chosen to be sacrificed?"

"Perhaps it was the will of God," the old man suggested with another malevolent smile. "Besides, you're an ideal candidate. You're an eligible, wealthy aristocrat, and the king would seem to have reasons of his own for wanting to see your wings clipped."

"And if I refuse to be a party to this madness? Will the king send me to the Tower and deprive me of my head?"

"Oh, no, we decided that the punishment should fit the crime. If you choose to rebel again, not only against me but the King of England, you'll lose your inheritance. Obviously no one can take your title away from you... and you will be Duke of Aylesbury when I die. But you would receive nothing else. Henry has agreed to make Rupert a baron this year, and upon my death all my wealth and estates would pass to him."

Sandhurst couldn't bear to look at his father any longer. Dazedly he walked to the window, every muscle in his body clenched. Yet through his rage he had to repress an urge to laugh wildly at the sheer lunacy of the situation.

"Your bride arrives in April. Her name is Micheline Tevoulère," the duke continued, his tone triumphant now. "You'll be married at Aylesbury Castle, of course, and King Henry has assured me that he intends to be present to join in the festive celebrations!"

* * *

A fire blazed in the winter parlor of Lord Sandhurst's town house, casting shadows that leaped and danced up the walls. On one side of the chamber his lordship presided over a table covered with the remains of supper. He was alone except for his friend Sir Jeremy Culpepper, who nibbled leftover bits of cheese, meat pie, and a fig someone had discarded after one bite.

"I still can't believe it," Sandhurst muttered. He'd lost count of the tankards of ale he'd consumed that day. Raising the latest, he took a long drink and sighed loudly.

"You've said that already," Jeremy complained. "Dozens of times. What's that little carcass on your dish? Quail? Did you pick it clean?"

Glancing heavenward, he pushed the plate across the table. "How can you eat at a time like this?"

"*I'm* not the one getting married to a stranger... from *France*," Culpepper replied cheerfully. "D'you suppose the chit speaks English at all? What'll you do if she can't learn?"

Leveling a deadly stare at his friend, Lord Sandhurst said, "If you find this amusing, you can go upstairs and have a few laughs with my father." He drank again, then added, "Besides, now that the shock's wearing off and I've had the day to think about it, I've decided not to participate in this farce."

Sir Jeremy Culpepper was a pudgy young man with curly blond hair, an unguarded tongue, and a tendency to flush when overcome by emotion. His cheeks were quite red now as he cried, "Be reasonable, old fellow! You'll be ruined if you refuse to go along with this plan of the king's! Not only will you be penniless, but you'll be shunned at court. Come to think of it, you'll be shunned by *everyone*!"

"Say no more," Sandhurst mocked. "You're scaring me."

"But how would you live?"

He felt himself relaxing, muscles untensing as a

smile tugged at the corners of his mouth. "I believe that I could make my own way rather well. You know, this house is mine. I bought it with profits from the horses I breed in Gloucestershire. I could sell it and buy another place in the country, then support myself with the horses." He paused, brightening. "The prospect of being out from under my father's thumb is rather appealing, actually."

"Look here, you've got to consider this matter carefully! You're talking about a decision that would affect not only your life but also the lives of your descendants. Just because you chafe under your father's admittedly overbearing efforts to dominate you, that's no reason to punish your offspring! He's an old man; he'll be dead soon. How will you feel then if you're breeding horses at some manor house while that ticklebrain *Rupert* is lord of Aylesbury Castle and the Sandhurst estates in Gloucestershire?! What will you tell your children? Don't raise that eyebrow at me! One day you'll have a family. How will your children feel when they grow up and *Rupert's* offspring own what's rightfully theirs?" Jeremy paused, breathing hard, then leaned forward to play his ace. "And what do you think your mother would say if she were here?"

Sandhurst wasn't smiling anymore. He closed his eyes and drained the tankard of ale. "I refuse to go like a lamb to the slaughter, Jeremy." He sighed. "My father would have a collar and a leash fitted for me, and I'd be angry for the rest of my life." After a brief pause, he added, "Even angrier than I am already."

"I know, I know. And you'd doubtless take it out on your poor little French wife, and then on your children," Culpepper fretted. He drank from his own tankard, brow furrowed in thought.

His lordship was thinking, too, turning the various

aspects of the situation over and over in his mind, yearning to discover a ray of light in the darkness.

"It's possible," Jeremy murmured doubtfully, "that the French might be a beauty. Perhaps she's even a bit of a rebel like you—maybe that's why they want to exile her!" Warming to his imaginings, he reached for a half-eaten sweetmeat on a distant plate and nibbled on it happily while continuing, "You might take one look at her and fall desperately in love!"

"It's more probable that Mademoiselle Tevoulère is a plain, shy fourteen-year-old with spots..." He rubbed the edge of his jaw, staring into space. "However... it might be prudent to investigate further before I make a decision."

Sir Jeremy Culpepper swallowed the sweetmeat and leaned across the table to grip his friend's forearm. "Yes! Yes! You're brilliant! That's the answer!" Then a shadow crossed his face as he dropped back into his chair. "But how can you *do* it?"

"I suppose I shall have to go to France. The girl's supposed to remain with the French court until the 'wedding' in April, so that would give me nearly two months."

"Do you propose to just present yourself to King François and announce that you've come to inspect Micheline Tevoulère before agreeing to the marriage?"

He laughed softly. "Obviously not. No, I'll have to pretend to be someone else."

"And why would a made-up person be welcome at court?"

"Ah, now there's the rub. Obviously I can't use my title to gain entrance, so I'll have to think of something else to offer." A genuine smile lit his face for the first time that day. "My canvases and brushes may be of use at last, Jeremy."

Culpepper had nearly forgotten that Sandhurst could paint. He'd shown talent as a youth and the duchess had sent him off to Florence to study for a year under the Italian masters. That had been a dozen years ago, at a time when she was as eager to separate him from his father as to nurture his artistic abilities.

"Are you any good at it?" Jeremy demanded bluntly, which elicited more low laughter from his friend.

"Actually I am. Hard to believe? You'll be even more surprised to learn that I still paint from time to time when I'm at Sandhurst Manor. Remember the portrait of Cicely in the hall?"

Jeremy stared in consternation. He'd always assumed that Holbein or one of the other artists favored at court had done the exquisite painting of Lord Sandhurst's sister which dominated the London house's great hall. "You're ribbing me," he muttered, then took a candlestick from the table and went out to investigate. In the lower righthand corner of the canvas he discovered a familiar *S*, barely a shade darker than the rose of Cicely's skirt.

A kitchen maid had come in to clear the table at last before retiring for the night, so Sandhurst didn't notice at first when his friend reentered the parlor. Jeremy stood clutching the candlestick, its flame accentuating the stunned expression on his face.

His mouth gaped open before he managed to exclaim hoarsely, "Unbelievable—incredible!"

"Come and sit down before you faint."

Jeremy staggered back to his chair. "Why didn't you say anything? I never imagined..."

"There was never a reason to talk about it. Now, however, my adequate talents may prove highly useful."

"If *I* could paint like that, I'd be boasting to anyone who'd listen! God's bones, Sandhurst, there's absolutely no question that you could pass yourself off as an artist at the French court! You've got charm and wit and extraordinary good looks to go with your talent. How could you fail?"

"You flatter me, but I do agree that the masquerade ought to succeed if I keep my wits about me." He indulged in wicked laughter as the plan fell into place. "It could almost be amusing to become acquainted with Micheline Tevoulère under such circumstances."

Beaming and nodding, Jeremy exclaimed, "'Zounds, I wish I could be there too!"

"But you *will* be there!" Sandhurst informed him smoothly. "You're coming with me. I'll need an extra pair of eyes and ears, not to mention a valet—you know, for appearance's sake. Finchley's perfectly capable of looking after my clothes, but he's not cut out for subterfuge. Besides, I don't want to involve him in all this. The less he knows, the better."

Jeremy's mouth hung open again, forgotten by its owner. "But—but—that is—I don't see how—" He fell silent, digesting his friend's speech, then narrowed his eyes suddenly. "Wait just a moment! You're saying that you expect me to be your *valet* while we're in France?!"

"Don't get into a huff, old fellow. I didn't mean to imply that you are my inferior in any way."

"Next door to it!"

"Look, you won't exactly *be* my valet; we'll just pretend that you are. It will be a role, like my role as a painter of portraits." Sandhurst arched a brow and grinned. "We'll both be commoners for a few weeks. It should be quite amusing!"

"This is all more your style than mine. What if we're found out? God's teeth, imagine the humiliation!"

"Jeremy, you know you wouldn't miss this adventure for the world, so why not spare us both the ordeal of this conversation and just capitulate?"

He sighed loudly. "All right then. I'll go."

"A toast, my friend!" Raising his tankard, he proclaimed, "To our adventure!"

"And its safe conclusion," muttered Jeremy. He drank deeply, Sandhurst's laughter echoing in his ears.

Seven

CHÂTEAU DE FONTAINEBLEAU, FEBRUARY, 1533

ANNE D'HEILLY stood in the king's magnificent oval bedchamber, waiting for him to return from the morning council meeting. She held the letter that had arrived from King Henry VIII the previous day, silently rehearsing her speech to François. If he guessed that she was behind this suddenly arranged marriage for Micheline Tevoulère, God only knew what would happen. Now that events had been set in motion in England, Anne was realizing just how great a risk she had taken. All that she had worked for years to attain might be lost if her king discovered her scheme.

Fretfully she went to the window and looked for François in the Oval Courtyard below. The sight that met her blue eyes replaced her doubts with a rush of consuming jealousy. Micheline had just strolled from the gardens through the Port Doree, while the king was entering the courtyard from his council chambers. Though surrounded by courtiers, he left them instantly and went to meet Micheline, who was looking lovely in the winter sunlight. Clad in a cloak of forest-green velvet trimmed with fox, she wore her warm auburn curls loose, spilling over her shoulders and down her back.

Anne burned at the sight of the genuine smile that lit her rivals's face as the king bent to kiss her hand. The girl had become his *friend,* gently rebuffing his advances over the weeks until he retreated and settled for what Micheline could offer. Anne knew, however, that he had not given up. The slow seduction of Micheline was a constant test for his patience and ingenuity.

Turning from the window, Anne paced from one end of the long oval chamber to the other until at last the outer door opened and the king appeared. Richly garbed in his usual black velvet cap, slashed doublet, and fur-trimmed cape, his vital presence seemed to fill the room.

"My dear Anne!" François exclaimed in surprise. "What are you doing here? I thought my daughters were to have their first Latin lesson this morning!"

"They are copying some phrases, sire, so I stole away to have a word with you in private." She went to him, her demure fraise looking like white rose petals beneath her cream and pink face. "Why don't you sit down and I'll bring you some wine?"

"Exactly what I had in mind. I've some dispatches to look at before mass, so I hope that your business is brief."

"I shall try," Anne promised. She placed a jeweled goblet of wine beside him on a table, then bent to bestow a few kisses, hoping to sweeten his mood. François smiled at her. Heartened, Anne took the chair opposite his and summoned her courage. "I received a very interesting letter from King Henry, sire."

François had leaned back in his carved walnut chair,

sipping his wine contentedly, but now he looked up in surprise. "Why would Henry write to you?"

"I wondered too, until I discovered that the letter had to do with a marriage he hopes to arrange. Perhaps he thought that I might be helpful regarding... affairs of the heart."

"What's this all about?"

"Do you know the Duke of Aylesbury? Or his son, the Marquess of Sandhurst?"

"I met the father some years ago, as I recall. I'm not acquainted with the son, but I've heard that he's a dashing sort. Unconventional and independent."

"Yes, and a constant source of concern to his father," Anne supplied, nodding. "Apparently the duke is dying, and he wants to see his son married, so he sought Henry's help and authority to bring that about."

"What can that possibly have to do with *you?*"

"It seems that Lord Sandhurst has a fondness for Frenchwomen, so his father thought that he would be more agreeable to the marriage if the bride were French... and beautiful and intelligent, of course!"

"Next you'll tell me that Henry suggested *your* name!" François's eyes twinkled, but there was a wary glint in them as well.

"Don't tease me!" Anne scolded with a giggle. "Just think of it, sire, a Frenchwoman in the English court... and soon an English duchess. Henry wrote that he believes such a marriage would strengthen the bonds of friendship between our two countries."

François pondered this for a moment. "It could be a good thing, certainly, from the standpoint of diplomacy, even though we do have the upper hand in that area these days."

"But it is always wise to plan for the future, sire," Anne said, her eyes wide with sincerity.

"That's true. Does Henry want you to find a bride for the Marquess of Sandhurst?"

"Not exactly. He already has one in mind." She took a deep breath, praying that she wouldn't make a fatal mistake in the series of lies she was about to tell. "It seems that one of those English visitors to Fontainebleau early last month returned home singing the praises of Madame Tevoulère."

"Micheline?" cried François, instantly suspicious.

"Yes, that's right." It took every ounce of Anne's control to keep her tone sweet and concerned when she longed to grab the goblet of wine and pour it over his head. "Apparently Henry is convinced that only Madame Tevoulère would be a proper candidate for Duchess of Aylesbury—and, sire, I must agree."

"*Why?*" wailed François. Then, remembering that his mistress had no inkling of the regard he felt for Madame Tevoulère, he struggled to appear more calm. "That is, she is still grieving. There must be someone else who would suit better."

"Don't you see that this would be the perfect solution for Micheline? Here in France she cannot forget her dead husband. Even six months after his death she continues to languish. However, new surroundings, a handsome new husband, wealth and position—all of these would mean a fresh start for Micheline. If we are her friends, we will do what is best for her."

Listening to Anne, the king flushed with guilt. "I suppose it would be selfish for us to deprive Micheline of such an opportunity," he murmured. "Very well. You may speak to her, and if she agrees, so shall I."

* * *

All through mass Anne d'Heilly pondered her next move. Her interview with the king had been a success, and though he had bade her speak to Micheline Tevoulère, Anne knew she must lay careful groundwork before that conversation could take place. She knew enough of the personality and character of her rival to realize that Micheline would never agree to an arranged marriage with a stranger, no matter how advantageous it might be. She was a romantic, or she wouldn't still be grieving for Bernard Tevoulère and rejecting the attentions of nearly every man at court, including the king himself.

The priest was speaking. In front of Anne, who sat with the two young princesses, François knelt beside Queen Eleanor. It was often the only time he spent with his wife in the course of an entire day and night. To the king's left were St. Briac and his family, and at the end of the row sat Micheline Tevoulère. Anne surreptitiously studied the face of the praying girl.

She's thinking of her dead husband, thought Anne. She still feels bound to him spiritually, and that's why she's unable to think of any other man.

Anne d'Heilly had known Bernard Tevoulère during his increasingly frequent stays with the court. As time had passed, his earnest shyness had seemed to melt away. He had gained confidence in proportion to his growing prowess as a knight, and then he'd begun an affair with one of the girls at court. Soon he was drinking too much and becoming arrogant. Still, there were always ladies at court willing to be entertained by Bernard, and gradually Anne had nearly forgotten that he had a wife at all... until the day Thomas and Aimée arrived at Fontainebleau with the exquisite, grieving Micheline Tevoulère in tow. The girl knew nothing of her dead husband's debauched behavior at court nor the facts of his ignominious death at the hands of a jealous husband. Everyone seemed to think that she needed protecting from the cruel realities of life.

Pondering all this, Anne began to realize what it might take to cause the idealistic Micheline to turn her back on the past and accept marriage to a stranger from England....

* * *

Dawn broke frosty and clear. Rising early, Micheline shared crusty bread, fruit, and milk with Aimée and her daughters. Then, shortly after eight o'clock, she donned her cloak, bade the others good-bye, and set off for what had become her habitual morning walk in the woods of Fontainebleau. Micheline loved the contrast between the pristine gray forest, all stark branches and carpeted with dead leaves that warmed and nourished the plant life through the winter, and the opulent artifice of the king's château—where few people or things were ever quite what they seemed.

Tramping now through the damp leaves, Micheline spied a great roebuck, gray now in winter to blend with the trees. His head was bent as he munched on some late breakfast, but he raised it instantly at the first sound of Micheline's approach. She stopped, smiling at him, and was gratified to realize that he trusted her. Calmly, he returned to the bit of green nourishment he'd discovered.

Often she felt more at home here in the forest than in the "civilized" court. Thomas and Aimée were wonderful and she'd come to like the king, but there seemed to be an invisible barrier between herself and nearly everyone else. Her heart was still with Bernard; even more here than at Château du Soleil, for he had spent time at Fontainebleau. Micheline often imagined him doing the things that she did now, speaking to the same people, inhabiting the same chambers.

Aimée tried to persuade her almost daily to try to look toward a new life, but Micheline had come to realize that she felt safer with her memories. Her instincts told her that it would be a mistake to seek her future in the court of Fontainebleau where values were different from hers. Micheline had learned to trust her heart, and it told her, over and over again, to be herself. Any changes would evolve naturally, inside her.

Rosy-cheeked and refreshed, Micheline emerged from the forest after more than an hour. She had brought a crust of bread and stopped now to feed the crumbs to the carp that darted about in the pond. When voices rose from the other side of a tall sculpted hedge, she stopped and held her breath.

"I am thoroughly fed up with the holier-than-thou behavior of Micheline Tevoulère!" a girl was complaining.

Micheline, though embarrassed, was about to show herself rather than go on eavesdropping, but an answering female voice brought her up short.

"Isn't everyone? We're all itching to tell her what her sainted Bernard was really like! Why, if she only knew..."

"That he'd made love to me?" giggled the first girl. "Why, it was months before I even knew he *had* a wife! The man was shameless!"

"And it wasn't only you, Felice, in case you've forgotten. From what I've heard, it sounds as if Bernard Tevoulère slept with half the women in the court!"

"And what about those naughty little games he liked to play in bed? The longer he was at court, the more outrageous he became."

"Certainly no one was surprised when Arnaud

Guerre dispatched him in that jousting match. Arnaud had murder in his eyes for weeks beforehand, but Bernard had become so cocky, he seemed to be daring Arnaud to do his worst!"

"Poor little Bernard," sighed Felice. "I confess I rather miss him! I'll never forget the time he brought a bowl of grapes into bed. I wonder what his prim little widow would say if she heard what he *did* with those grapes!"

The two women shared peals of wicked laughter.

Feeling as if she might retch right there, Micheline turned and bolted. Her skirts became tangled and she tripped, but picked herself up and ran on, back to the Château de Fontainebleau, which now loomed ahead of her like a hell on earth.

* * *

Unable to speak or even think, Micheline managed to suppress the urge to be ill as she rushed across the courtyard, her head bowed, past everyone who greeted her. The seigneur de St. Briac was one of these, and he stared after her, perplexed, before returning to his chambers to seek out his wife.

Micheline's rooms were modest but afforded a splendid view of the gardens behind the Oval Courtyard. She threw herself on the testered bed and tried not to think, but it was like trying to hold back a dam. Memories like heart-piercing arrows attacked her: Bernard's alternating coolness and uneasiness during his visits home, the awkward excuses he made to return sooner than planned to the court, the emotional distance she had felt between them when they were intimate... all of it made sense now.

Bernard's sudden death had left a wound that had

barely begun to heal. Now Micheline felt as though it had been ripped open wider than ever. She was unable to cry. Curled like a baby on the bed, she stared at the wall and wondered if she was dying. *Could* one die of a shattered heart?

"Micheline?" a voice called softly from the corridor. "It's Aimée. May I come in?"

She couldn't reply, and a moment later the door opened hesitantly. Through a fog Micheline saw Aimée approaching the bed, her expression concerned.

"What is it, *cherie*? Are you ill?" She sat down on the bed and stroked Micheline's hair. "Did someone say something to upset you?"

"I'll be fine. It's... nothing, really."

"You can tell me, you know," Aimée said gently. A suspicion spread within her like a dark stain. She knew about Bernard's increasingly blatant infidelities when he had been at court; in fact, Thomas had begun reminding her when voicing his own frustration over Micheline's devotion to her undeserving dead husband. Still, they could find no solution short of telling their friend the cruel truth, and that was out of the question. Now Aimée wondered if someone else had done just that.

"There's nothing to tell," Micheline struggled to sit up, then pasted on a wan smile. "I just felt a bit faint. Too much exercise, perhaps."

The chamber door had been left ajar and now it swung open. "Madame Tevoulère, may I have a few words with you?"

Aimée looked up in surprise to find Anne d'Heilly entering the room. Before she could protest, Micheline said numbly, "Oh, yes... Please sit down."

"*Merci!*" Smiling brightly, Anne took the chair next to the bed and scrutinized Micheline under lowered lashes. She was pleased with what she saw, wondering if François would be quite so enamored of this pale, pinched-looking girl.

For her part, Micheline was glad for the distraction —from her own consuming pain and Aimée's questions. She couldn't tell anyone what she'd learned, ever.

"I have something of great importance to discuss with you," Anne was saying kindly, "though it is rather *personal.*"

Aimée made no move to leave them alone, and Micheline merely murmured, "You may speak freely in front of Madame de St. Briac."

"Well, if you're sure." Anne straightened her skirts in annoyance. Why did Aimée have to be such a meddler? "The king himself has asked me to raise this matter with you, madame." She proceeded then to unfold the same tale that she had told François, dwelling on the Marquess of Sandhurst's attractive reputation, the beauty of England, and the fresh, bright future being offered to Micheline.

"Of course, it's an honor to have been chosen as the prospective bride to Lord Sandhurst. And, it's a chance to begin a whole new life, away from the... memories of the past." Anne paused to give her words time to sink in, then added brightly, "And, as I've doubtless mentioned, the marquess is said to be exceedingly handsome and charming. How fortuitous for *you* that he has a weakness for Frenchwomen!"

Aimée was thunderstruck. She would have spoken her mind immediately, but she was so certain that Micheline would veto these ridiculous marriage plans that she kept silent.

"Can you tell me when and where the wedding would take place, my lady?" Micheline queried instead. She looked rather dazed.

"Mais, oui!" exclaimed Anne. "You would go to England in April, and, as I understand it, King Henry himself intends to attend the ceremony at Aylesbury Castle, in Yorkshire. Of course, King François will see to it that you have everything you could possibly need before you leave France. We'll have such fun planning your wardrobe!"

Micheline sighed, and Aimée stared at her sharply, a sudden feeling of panic swelling with her. Before she could speak, though, Micheline said softly, "As you wish, then... I'll accept the marquess's invitation to become his wife."

Eight

FEBRUARY 21, 1533

DUSK WAS APPROACHING, heralded by a cold, penetrating wind. The forest of Fontainebleau seemed to close in on the two men on horseback.

"I don't like it, Sandhurst," complained Sir Jeremy Culpepper. "Not one bit. The whole place gives me chills."

Laugh lines crinkled the corners of Andrew's brown eyes. "Too late, my friend! There's no turning back. Besides, you'll feel different when you're sitting before a blazing fire with a cup of wine and a dish of hot supper."

"In the servants' kitchen!"

"Now, now," Sandhurst soothed, trying to smother his laughter. "You never know; they may send *me* there as well! I'm not at all certain where unknown painters rank in the hierarchy of a king's court."

"I've just got one thing to say!" Jeremy shoulted. "If I'm going to *lower* myself and pretend to be your lackey for the next few weeks, you'd bloody well better accomplish something to make it worthwhile. Don't raise your brows at me like that! I'm talking about the girl, and well you know it. If you don't fancy her, I'd appreciate it if you'd decide that right away so that we can be done with this foolishness and go home. My time is valuable, whether you appreciate that fact or not!" Jeremy's face was red long before he finished his tirade.

"Egad!" exclaimed Andrew, the barest quirk of his mouth betraying his amusement. "You're hungrier than I thought. And although that speech was very impressive, I can't promise to obey any of your commands." Gently he nudged his horse with his knees and, as it eased into a canter, glanced back in Jeremy's direction and added, "I must admit that I don't hold out much hope regarding the outcome of our undertaking."

"What!" Culpepper yelled in disbelief.

"I mean, what kind of woman would agree to marry a man she's never even seen? Not *my* sort, I fear."

* * *

As it turned out, a hot meal and several mugs of wine did go a long way toward improving Sir Jeremy Culpepper's outlook. He sat alone at the long scrubbed table in the kitchen, nearly oblivious to the pandemonium that surrounded him. Supper was being prepared for the king and his court, but the head cook had been sympathetic and hadn't made Jeremy wait for his. He found the *pain moullet,* a soft bread made with milk and butter, extremely soothing to his voracious appetite. The bread accompanied a steaming dish of rabbit stew flavored with green peas and carrots, and sprinkled with pomegranate seeds and fresh herbs. Jeremy had never eaten anything quite so flavorful in all his life.

In a different part of the château, Lord Sandhurst, now known as Andrew Selkirk, was standing in the long expanse of King François's unfinished gallery. The shell of it was complete, but the planned frescoes and carved paneling would take years. The king himself stood off to one side, reading a letter that had been sealed with the Marquess of Sandhurst's crest.

To His Majesty, the King of France:

The bearer of this letter is Andrew Selkirk, an accomplished painter who has created masterful portraits of members of my family. He brings you an example of his fine work, a likeness of my sister, Lady Cicely Weston.

It is my hope that you will give Selkirk a place at your court during his sojourn in France. Your Majesty's fine reputation as a patron of great artists leads me to believe that you will find Selkirk's visit an enriching one.

Most Respectfully,
Andrew Weston, Marquess of Sandhurst

François looked up from the sheet of parchment, scrutinizing the handsome man who waited nearby. "How do you like my new gallery, m'sieur?"

"I've just been admiring the portions of paneling that are completed, Your Majesty. Very impressive."

François found himself warming to the Englishman. "I understand that your king Henry uses much gilding in his houses, whereas I use little or none. I prefer timber finely wrought with diverse natural woods, such as ebony and brazil."

"I admire your taste, sire. I agree that these woods

are richer than gilding, and doubtless more durable as well."

"My sentiments exactly." The king beamed. "I bid you welcome to my court, M'sieur Selkirk. I think that we shall deal well together."

"Your Majesty is both kind and generous."

As they walked together through the gallery, François inquired casually, "The Marquess of Sandhurst is your patron?"

"I have made some paintings for him."

"May I ask your opinion of the man?"

"I am not really qualified to judge, sire," Andrew said.

"Please, I urge you to be frank. You see, Lord Sandhurst is betrothed to one of the ladies of my court, and I would see her happy."

"Betrothed, you say? Well, that's a surprise. In answer to your question, I can only say that it would be difficult for this lady not to be happy in a marriage with Lord Sandhurst. He has a great deal to offer! Perhaps it would be more to the point to wonder if this lady will make *him* happy."

François stared in consternation. "M'sieur, I can assure you that Micheline Tevoulère could make *any* man happy! She is a particular favorite of mine, and I confess that I am loath to relinquish her to your countryman." His hazel eyes were distant. "In fact, perhaps you should start your efforts here by painting her. I would like to be able to gaze at her likeness after she departs from France." The king stopped and met Andrew's neutral gaze. "There's no reason to tell her that you know Lord Sandhurst. In fact, the less said about him the better. I still entertain the hope that she may yet change her mind...."

"I shall be pleased to paint this lady's portrait, sire, and you can rely upon my discretion where his lordship is concerned," Andrew replied solemnly. Inwardly an urge to laugh aloud warred with consternation at François I's revelations. Was he to assume that Micheline Tevoulère was the king's mistress?

* * *

For days Aimée had appealed to Micheline to change her mind. The king would understand, she said. How could Micheline consider marriage to a stranger? One day her heart would heal and she would rediscover love, Aimée insisted. All her entreaties met with her friend's numb resolve.

"I am simply at my wit's end, Thomas!" Aimée was exclaiming as she stepped out of her bath and reached for the linen towels that had been warming in front of the fire.

"I've noticed," her husband remarked from the adjoining bedchamber. "Why don't you come in here and let me distract you?"

Laughing, Aimée did go in and sit naked on St. Briac's lap, kissing him deeply. He was half dressed for supper, and the sensation of her soft damp breasts against his bare chest made him forget all else.

"Thomas... please, we can't—"

"Indeed?" he murmured, holding her near as he blazed a trail with his mouth across one of Aimée's shoulders and down her tender inner arm. "According to whom?"

She shivered, frankly aroused as he tasted the sensitive bend of her arm. "According to me. For now, at least. After supper we'll have—" She paused, gasping. St. Briac's lips had found her wrist, and Aimée knew that next he would lift her hand and savor each finger. She knew, too, that he was well aware of the moist heat between her legs. One more moment and there would be no turning back. Clinging to the thought of Micheline, alone and vulnerable to the cattiness of the court ladies, Aimée wrenched free. "It's not that I don't *want* to, Thomas. I'm thinking of Micheline! You and I have the whole night ahead to romp in bed."

St. Briac let her go, reaching for his shirt instead. He was aware that there was a part of him that was jealous of all the attention his wife paid to Micheline Tevoulère, and it made him ashamed. Although he was fond of the girl himself, that same selfish part of him was secretly pleased that she was going away to England. Nothing that he and Aimée had tried to do for her seemed to have had much effect, and he wanted his wife back.

Still, guilt made St. Briac sigh and say, "It's all right. I understand. It's rather like being pushed aside at the crucial moment in bed because one of the babies is crying. I'm used to it." Aimée smiled warmly at him from the bureau, where she was removing undergarments, and that smile made him even more magnanimous. "I know your side of all this, *miette,* but what does Micheline have to say about it?"

"Oh, she says the same thing over and over again until I could scream!" Sparks seemed to flash from Aimée's green eyes. Tightening the delicate laces of her chemise, she reached almost angrily for her petticoats. "'There's nothing for me here,'" Aimée mimicked. "'I can't forget the past. At least in England I can attempt to begin a new life.' *That's* what she says!"

"Has it occurred to you that perhaps it *would* be the best solution? I'm surprised that you aren't more sympathetic to her plight, since you were once so desperate to escape your own lot that you ran away with the king's court train."

"That was different," Aimée retorted. "I was younger. I didn't have the opportunities and advantages that Micheline has—and I was being sold off in marriage to that horrible Armand Rovicette. *That's* a reason for me to sympathize with Micheline. What if this Lord Sandhurst is grotesque? Why, Micheline's life could be a nightmare! There is simply no reason for her to do something this foolhardy."

St. Briac watched his wife don a gown of emerald-green satin and went up behind her to lace the back. "My darling, I understand your feelings, but you must allow Micheline to make her own decisions. You of all people must understand how it would make her feel to be pressured, even by a loving friend like you."

The soft tenderness of his voice brought tears to Aimée's eyes and she buried her face in his fresh shirt-front. St. Briac's arms held her near as he stroked the tense length of her spine.

"Don't you see, Thomas," she choked at last, holding fast to her husband, *"this* is the most important reason why I don't want Micheline to go through with this plan. She has no idea what she's missed so far... and what she may forgo for a lifetime if she marries the Marquess of Sandhurst." Lifting her face, she gazed into her husband's eyes and said, "Love, real love, between a man and a woman is a miracle. Micheline must search for that miracle, not run to England!"

* * *

Micheline felt dazed and numb most of the time. It spared her the pain of introspective thought and protected her from memories.

Activity, though distracting, was often fraught with risks. Tonight, as she dressed for supper, Micheline wished fervently that she didn't have to go downstairs and mingle with the entire court. She lived in fear of hearing the voices from the carp pond, which would mean facing one of the women her husband had made love to. Sometimes, when the court gathered before meals to socialize, Micheline imagined that people were whispering about her. They all knew about Bernard, she realized now, and they must all think her a fool.

But it would be worse to stay in her chamber. So she bathed and dressed each evening and pinned up her curls in the current fashion, then went to supper with Thomas and Aimée, her head held high. Soon enough she would escape France and all its painful memories...

"Micheline, are you ready?"

It was the seigneur de St. Briac, calling gently at her door as he did every evening. Micheline paused to glance in the mirror, appraising the curls that framed her slightly pale yet lovely face, and the elegant gown of golden velvet that she wore. Sprinkled with tiny emeralds and topaz, it nipped in at her waist, while its deep square neckline flattered her bosom. She wore only one necklace, a band of emeralds at the base of her neck, plus earrings of topaz and emeralds that set off her cognac-hued hair to perfection.

"Yes, I'm ready," Micheline said, and opened the door with a convincing smile.

* * *

Sandhurst longed to lean against the elaborately carved chimney piece, but the juniper-scented fire kept him at bay. He was fully aware that Anne d'Heilly had been the king's favorite for years, but here she was, chatting and smiling at him from just a few inches away.

Glancing toward the sumptuously garbed men and women that were filling the hall, Andrew said, "I begin to regret the fact that I had no time to put on more appropriate clothing. I fear I shall be rudely conspicuous at supper."

"Not at all, m'sieur!" Anne laughed. Her eyes swept the fawn doublet and breeches that skimmed his masculine body more appealingly than any amount of velvets, jewels, and furs ever could. "You have just arrived; everyone will understand. Aside from that, you are an *artist*. Such people may dress as they please."

"You are very kind, my lady." Andrew smiled.

"Do, please, call me Anne...."

His attention had wandered, however, to the stairway at the far end of the hall. An attractive couple was descending, but it was the young lady behind them who caught his eye. Even from this distance he recognized the intelligence and sensitivity in her face and radiance of her eyes. In the torchlight, the lady's hair was a mixture of gold and fire, and though her gown was fine, Andrew found himself staring at the graceful curves hugged by the velvet.

"M'sieur!" Anne exclaimed, pretending to pout. "Have you forgotten me?"

"Hmm? Oh no, of course not." He gave her a distracted smild and inquired, "Can you tell me the name of the unaccompanied young lady who is at the bottom of the staircase?"

Anne narrowed her eyes at Micheline and demanded, "Why do you ask?"

"The lady has an interesting face. It's not as beautiful as yours, of course, but it might be a challenge to paint."

"Oh." She tried to decide if she'd been complimented. "Well, that is Micheline Tevoulère. She's betrothed to a countryman of yours—the Marquess of Sandhurst."

"Really!" Andrew exhaled slowly. "That's very interesting...."

Part Two

The knight knocked at the castle gate;
The lady marveled who was thereat.
To call the porter he would not bin;
The lady said he should not come in.
She asked him what was his name;
He said, "Desire, your man, Madame."
She said, "Desire, what do ye here?"
He said, "Madame, as your prisoner."

– WILLIAM CORNISH
14?-1523

Nine

BEFORE SANDHURST COULD CONTRIVE some means of meeting Micheline Tevoulère, the king came up to them and put a possessive arm around Anne's waist.

"I'm pleased to see that my Anne has been entertaining you." He smiled. Clad in cloth of silver, black velvet, diamonds, and ermine, François cut a splendidly royal figure. "We shall sup shortly, but first..." He scanned the crowd distractedly. "First I would like to introduce you to your first subject."

"Ah!" smiled Sandhurst, feigning surprise. "Very thoughtful of you, sire."

As if the king had sent a silent message, Micheline became visible among the chattering assemblage.

"Madame Tevoulère!" François called. The sound of his raised voice caused others to fall silent, and Micheline looked around immediately. "Will you join us?"

When she came smiling out of the crowd, Sandhurst thought that she was even more radiantly beautiful close up than she'd appeared to be on the distant stairway.

"How may I serve Your Majesty?" she inquired respectfully.

The king was satisfied that Micheline truly wanted to go to England and marry the Marquess of Sandhurst, but he hadn't liked the shadows that had appeared under her eyes and in her manner these past few days. Anne assured him that it was probably just a case of nerves, so François hoped now that the fresh new presence of this artist might lighten her mood.

"I would like you to meet a guest at our court, *ma chere,*" he told her kindly. "Allow me to present Andrew Selkirk, a gifted painter from England who has agreed to make some portraits while he is with us." Turning to Sandhurst, the king smiled. "M'sieur, you have the honor to meet Micheline Tevoulère, a true gem among the ladies of my court."

"It is a pleasure, m'sieur," Micheline murmured. For the first time in days she was conscious of something penetrating the fog that surrounded her: Andrew Selkirk's compelling gaze.

"The pleasure, I can assure you," he said smiling, "is all mine." Lifting her slim hand, Andrew pressed a kiss to her fingers, wondering at the sudden flutter of her pulse.

"Perhaps you would sit with M'sieur Selkirk when we sup," François was saying to Micheline. "Since he's just arrived, he knows no one else."

"Certainly, sire," she replied obediently. For some reason her cheeks felt flushed, and she glanced downward so that the stranger from England would not misunderstand.

* * *

The boards had been laid and the court wandered over to be seated. The sight was impressive. The huge hall was paneled in walnut and hung with panoramic tapestries depicting King François during various triumphant moments throughout his reign. Servants were lined up beneath the tapestries, holding flaming torches, wine vessels, and golden dishes. The sound of musical French voices filled the air as the splendidly garbed lords and ladies found their places.

Sandhurst took it all in with his usual casual curiosity. He'd supped with King Henry at various castles in England, so his sense of awe had melted away long ago. A servant poured wine into his silver goblet from a pewter vessel with a long spout. Sandhurst sipped it and turned to look at the girl everyone meant him to marry. She had placed her fingers on the stem of her goblet but did not lift it. Instead, she stared into the distance, seemingly at a torch on the far wall, her utterly beautiful blue-violet eyes filled with secrets.

"Will you raise your glass with me, mademoiselle?" he queried softly.

"Oh! Of course, m'sieur!" Hastily Micheline turned to meet his smile. "You will pardon me, I hope, if I seemed rude. I... haven't felt quite myself lately."

"Then let us drink to the rebirth of your high spirits."

She nodded and they lifted their goblets and sipped together. High spirits, she thought ironically. How long had it been since she had been acquainted with such pleasure?

"And now," Sandhurst continued, "I would like to make a more selfish toast—for luck."

This time she didn't have to remember to smile. "By all means, m'sieur."

"Will you drink with me to France?" Micheline had already raised her goblet, but he held up his hand. "Wait, there's more!"

"I didn't think that sounded particularly selfish," she heard herself remark lightly.

"That was just the preface!" Andrew laughed. "We must drink to a happy sojourn for *me* in France."

"Excellent," she approved.

The goblet had almost touched her lips when he added, "And to new friendships... for both of us."

She watched him drink then, raising his eyebrows at her over the rim of his goblet. Unaccountably her cheeks were warm again, but somehow she managed to sip her own wine.

Before Micheline could wonder if she was ill, distraction appeared, in the form of a peacock that was arriving at the table in full plumage. It was set down amid a flourish of trumpets and the applause of all present. The bird's beak was gilt, its tail-feathers spread brilliantly, and it rested on a mass of brown pastry painted green to represent a field. Eight banners of silk were arranged around the peacock, which towered above the other appointments of the table.

"Very impressive," Sandhurst murmured.

Detecting a note of satire in his voice, Micheline glanced over in surprise. A funny, unfamiliar bubble of delight rose inside her and Andrew gave her a fleeting wink. Truly flustered now, Micheline turned her attention to the food. Suddenly she felt as if she'd been dropped into some foreign place and filled with completely unknown sensations. Was she ill? It couldn't be Andrew Selkirk's fault; he'd done nothing except smile at her, converse in a friendly manner—and look at her in a way that made her suspect he could see into her very soul. The latter was a product of her imagination, Micheline decided now as she tasted the peacock. The man simply had quite magical eyes. Probably the old woman he bought his eggs from blushed when he smile at *her*. Charm could be a dangerous gift, especially for its recipients.

There was much more to eat besides the peacock. Micheline nibbled at sturgeon that had been cooked in parsley and vinegar then covered with powdered ginger, boar that had been grilled and larded with *foie gras,* tiny ortolans, and juicy breast of heron. The next course was a salad that consisted of raw greens mixed with vegetables and red poultry crests.

Conscious of the silence between her and Andrew Selkirk, Micheline inquired politely, "Does our food compare favorably with that in England, m'sieur?"

He drew his brows together in mock seriousness and replied, "Oh, yes, mademoiselle. Most favorably." Andrew leaned toward her conspiratorially. "Can you keep a secret?"

She nodded, her heart pounding.

"I've never eaten peacock. You'll think me a peasant but the truth is that I normally dine on only three courses." His eyes sparkled as he leaned closer. "Are you shocked?"

Micheline heard helpless feminine laughter. Was it hers? "No, m'sieur! And I will tell you a secret in return." The way he inclined his head in anticipation was so captivating that her heart seemed to skip a beat before she continued. "I am not accustomed to peacock either. I grew up near Angoulême, and though my father is seigneur of our village, we lived simply. After I married, my life was simpler still, and to be honest, I prefer it that way. I am only here at all because my dearest friend, Madame de St, Briac, thought that the excitement of court life would help to dispel..."

"Yes?" he prompted gently.

Though her eyes had clouded, she finished softly,

"My husband died this past summer, and I have been in pain of one sort or another ever since, it seems."

The Englishman blinked in surprise. "You are a widow! How very – unexpected. I am sorry, mademoiselle—or, I should say, madame—to hear of your loss, and for the carelessness of my first toast this evening." He put his hand over one of hers. "Take heart, though. You are young, with your whole life before you. One never knows what lies ahead."

Micheline, gripped by sadness a moment earlier, now felt a little flutter of hope as she looked at the hand that covered hers. Andrew Selkirk's skin was golden, even in winter. His hand was well-shaped, square, and strong, yet the fingers were long, and she had already noticed the particular deftness that marked their movements. More important, Micheline felt a warmth and energy that seemed to flow from his hand to hers.

A servant set a dish of Loire salmon sliced with eggs before her, and she freed her hand even as her heart beat madly.

"I—I appreciate your sentiments, m'sieur. *Merci*." She stabbed a morsel of salmon with her fork, a utensil that had been unknown to her before Fontainebleau, and gave him a weak smile.

"Madame..." he ventured at length, "you'll pardon me, I hope, if my curiosity has caused me to dare too much, but I have to ask."

"You may dare, m'sieur," she said, smiling.

"It may have been only a rumor that I heard, completely untrue, but I was under the impression that you were betrothed to the Marquess of Sandhurst."

"Oh." Her smile faded.

"I understood that you were going to England in April to be married to Lord Sandhurst," he pressed. "Am I mistaken?"

"No, no, you are not mistaken." Micheline held out her goblet to a passing wine squire, then drank of it, unable to meet his gaze. "However, I do not wish to discuss this matter with you, m'sieur."

"Hmm." Lifting his eyebrows, he gazed at his dish of salmon and eggs and sighed. "Well, I will respect your wishes, madame, but I like you, and we may become friends. You see, the king has requested that my first portrait in France be of you."

Micheline swiveled to stare at him, her mouth an O. "I don't understand." she finally exclaimed.

"His Majesty holds you in high esteem. It seems that if he cannot have you present in the flesh, he would at least keep your portrait as a reminder."

Hot blood suffused her cheeks again, and she looked away, only to discover not just François I but her friend Aimée staring at her from across the table. What was happening?

"Look," Andrew said gently, "we'll make a pact. Since we must spend a great deal of time together until the portrait is finished, I promise not to speak of your late husband or your betrothed unless you raise the subject first. How's that?"

Dishes of figs, dates, walnuts, red sugar plums, and pear pastry were being presented, along with a sweet dessert wine. Micheline selected a sugar plum and took a tiny bite, wondering at the affinity she felt for this stranger.

"All right, m'sieur," Micheline told him, thinking that she hardly had a choice, "I agree to your pact. And I am grateful for your friendship."

* * *

It was long past midnight when Sandhurst returned to the modest chamber he would share with his "valet," the erstwhile Sir Jeremy Culpepper. There had been entertainments after supper, mainly jugglers and tumblers who cavorted among the rushes and fresh herbs strewn over the tiled floor, but Andrew had not been greatly entertained. Anne d'Heilly had claimed him as soon as they left the table, holding his arm a bit too tightly as she led him around to meet other members of the court. Occasionally Sandhurst had caught a glimpse of Micheline through the crowd. She stood off to one side with a lovely, dark-haired girl, smiling absently as her friend acted very gay. When at last he was free, Andrew went to the place where Micheline had been. He made the acquaintance of the enchanting wife of the seigneur de St. Briac, who told him that Micheline had pleaded fatigue and gone to bed. They had talked for a bit, but in his disappointment Sandhurst was too distracted to notice the appraising way that Aimée stared at him. At length, as the revelry continued unabated, Sandhurst also excused himself.

Sighing now, he opened the door, half hoping that Jeremy would be asleep so that he could think.

"At *last!*" an annoyed voice exclaimed. "Where have you been?"

"I've been playing my part with the king and his court," Sandhurst replied shortly.

"Oh, *yes!* A real hardship, I'll warrant! You were forced to eat all that food I watched the cooks preparing... and drink all those fine wines! How was the *peacock?*"

He had to smile at that. "Adequate," he pronounced dryly. "Why are you in such a state?"

Jeremy sat up in his narrow bed, his cheeks crimson now. "Perhaps I can't sleep on this frightful straw mattress! Your bed doesn't have one, by the way. *You've* got goose down!"

Unlacing his shirt and doublet, Sandhurst couldn't resist lifting an eyebrow and saying reasonably, "Don't you think I deserve it?"

"Are you itching for a fight? I'd be glad to oblige you, solely on the basis of the name you christened me with when you presented me to the head chamberlain!"

His lips twitched as he sat down to pull off his boots. "You don't care for 'Jeremy Playfair'? I thought it had a rather honorable ring to it."

"Do you have any idea how many times I've been called 'Playfair' tonight?" shouted Culpepper. "It's driving me *mad!*"

"Have a care, Jeremy. You'll give yourself an attack." Tugging off the second boot, Sandhurst sighed. "I do miss Finchley at times like this. A man likes to be looked after at the end of a hard day."

"You push me too far, you know," Jeremy growled, looking about for a weapon. "Next you'll suggest that I play your valet in private as well as in public... and they'll find you smashed on the courtyard below our window!"

Laughing softly, Sandhurst bent to remove his fawn breeches and hose. Too tired to look for water to wash with, he drew back the covers on his bed and lay down with a contented sigh. "I'm having you on. You do know that, don't you?"

The color softened in Culpepper's cheeks as he muttered, "Yes. I suppose I do."

"I couldn't get through this masquerade without you."

The two men exchanged affectionate smiles. "I'm glad to be here... in a way," Jeremy allowed. "It'll be another adventure for us to laugh about later—and if it actually does any good, well, then..."

"I met her tonight. Micheline Tevoulère, I mean." Staring up at the plain green velvet tester, Sandhurst found that her name tasted sweet upon his tongue.

Suddenly ashamed of the time he'd wasted with his ridiculous outburst, Jeremy rose on an elbow to stare at his friend. *"And?"*

"It's a long story and I am exhausted. I'll tell you all of it tomorrow, but for now let's just say that the situation holds definite possibilities."

Ten

MARCH, 1533

"I CAN'T GO for my walk this morning," Micheline told Aimée as they finished a light *petit dejeuner*. Ninon had gone to sit in a corner, where she now rolled a tennis ball for their rambunctious new puppy. Her little rosebud mouth was smeared with honey and bread crumbs, so Aimée moistened a serviette and gave it to Juliette, who proudly went off to play mother.

"Why not?" Aimée returned a trifle absently, watching her daughters to be sure Juliette's ministrations didn't make Ninon cry.

"That Englishman is going to begin work on my portrait at eight-thirty." Micheline didn't know how she felt about the large amount of time she'd be spending with Andrew Selkirk. The man both tantalized and alarmed her. Most confusing was the realization that she wasn't alarmed because of anything he had said or done but because of her own reaction to him. All the previous day Micheline had avoided him, until, last evening, his chubby valet had brought her a message. In flawless French Andrew Selkirk had written to request that they meet this morning in the king's second antechamber to begin work on the portrait.

Micheline stood now to keep that appointment, brimming with a mixture of emotions, not the least of which was a pleasant sense of anticipation.

"This should be an exciting experience," Aimée said with a bright smile.

"Sitting still while someone paints me?"

"It's a *change* certainly. And the company of M'sieur Selkirk should prove highly diverting!" Aimée gave a mischievous laugh. "Is he not shockingly attractive?"

Micheline blushed. "You should be ashamed of yourself. You're married to the handsomest man at court! As for me, I have no interest in Andrew Selkirk or any other man, and well you know it."

"Don't forget the Marquess of Sandhurst," Aimée said recklessly.

The younger girl turned away to hide her flaming cheeks. "I'll be late. *Au revoir.*"

* * *

The king's second antechamber, located in the old keep, had recently been decorated with frescoes and stuccoes by the Italian artist Primaticcio, who was currently at work on the magnificent François I gallery.

At this hour the king was downstairs at his council meeting, so the huge square room was quiet. Micheline entered hesitantly, her eyes immediately finding Andrew Selkirk. He sat at a table that was covered with sheets of heavy paper, an inkhorn, and several white swan's quills. Sunlight poured through the massive windows, lightly gilding the Englishman's hair as he bent over one of the papers, appearing to write.

"*Bonjour,* m'sieur," Micheline said softly.

He looked up in surprise, then gave her a smile so disarming that her heart skipped. "It's good to see you, madame! You look lovely."

For a moment Micheline forgot to speak. She stood rooted to the spot, watching as he rose and came toward her. Andrew wore a doublet and breeches of unembellished moss-green velvet slashed to reveal hints of white linen, and fine leather boots. She realized that she should walk forward to meet him, but then it was too late. When he lifted her hand and kissed it with warm, firm lips, she had to resist the impulse to flee. Why did *this* man, who was little more than a stranger, have such an effect on her?

"You are well?" he was asking.

"Oh—yes! Of course!"

"Good." He smiled again and continued to hold her hand. The pressure of his fingers was light, but his hand felt very strong. "You look a trifle pale... and I thought I felt you tremble."

Her face was suddenly hot. Did he *know*? "I am fine, m'sieur."

"Ah, yes, I see the color in your cheeks now. I hope you didn't think me rude, but I asked only because sitting for a portrait can be surprisingly tiring. One of my subjects complained so loudly that I had to learn to paint while she talked, since she found it impossible to remain still." Andrew gestured with one hand for her to precede him across the chamber. "I hope you'll be comfortable in this chair."

Micheline found her nerves melting again under the spell of his easy charm. The chair he indicated was positioned so that the sun was at her back, warm and soothing.

"This will be fine," she assured him.

The Englishman walked over to his table and stared

at her for a moment, then returned to adjust the angle of the chair. "The light is very important," he explained. "Because it must be just right, we can work only in the early morning and late afternoon."

"Oh." Suddenly Micheline realized that she had uttered nothing but inanities since entering the room. Casting about for a topic she might raise, she heard herself ask, "Who was the lady you painted who was unable to remain both still and silent?"

He blinked. "She was only twelve years old at the time, but still qualifies as a lady, if only by title. My subject was Lady Cicely Weston... sister to the Marquess of Sandhurst."

"Oh!" Micheline said again. She opened her mouth, but no more words came out. Andrew Selkirk must know the Marquess of Sandhurst! Part of her wanted to ask a dozen questions, but stronger still was her apprehension about the possible answers. In truth, she simply didn't want to think about her future husband yet.

Andrew sat down behind his table, trying not to smile. He'd seen the surprise and curiosity in Micheline's wide eyes, and had recognized the panic too. She didn't *want* to know about the man she was to marry. Why not? Not for the first time, he wondered how and why the marriage had been sought in the first place.

"Where is your canvas, m'sieur?" Micheline queried, happy to change the subject. "And your paints, and—"

He held up his hand. "Not so fast. If we're to create a proper portrait, a few preparatory exercises must be performed."

"They must?" she echoed.

"Yes!" The lady was simply enchanting. Her manner was open yet laced with mystery, and her beauty was luminous. "I like to do a series of sketches first. Pen drawings. I'll work on those today, and if the results are satisfactory, we may be able to begin the actual portrait tomorrow."

"What are the drawings for?"

"They help me become accustomed to your face, body, and spirit." Micheline's sudden blush made him glance away out of kindness. Andrew picked up one of the swan's quills, dipped it into the inkhorn, and began to sketch her. "To create a portrait of any depth, it's important to develop a deeper understanding of the subject. Also, the drawings help me decide what the best design would be for the finished painting." As he became more involved in what he was doing, Sandhurst's sentences took on a disjointed quality. "The position of your body, the tilt of your head, the expression on your face, the most flattering style for your hair and gown— they're very important. Critical, in fact." He met her eyes and smiled briefly. "We'll look at the sketches together, if you'd like, and you can tell me if you have any thoughts about the way you want to look. It won't be just *any* portrait, after all."

"I know," Micheline broke in. "And I would be pleased to see the drawings when you finish, m'sieur. It's kind of you to offer."

"Not kind at all. At least half the credit for any painting must go to the subject, I believe. That's why I like to paint people. They can share more actively in the artistic process."

Aside from her heightened sensations in the presence of Andrew Selkirk, Micheline was now disconcerted by having to carry on a conversation with someone who rarely made eye contact with her. He'd be scrutinizing her hair or her neck or her nose while she spoke, so that she wasn't certain if he was listening, or else he was actively sketching, which made her feel as if she shouldn't speak at all.

After a long minute of silence Andrew laughed softly and met Micheline's eyes. "Don't be so stiff, madame! Relax. We are not in church, and I can assure you that there is nothing sacred about my work." The sight of her nervous, obedient smile only increased his amusement. "Why don't you talk to me. As I recall, you said that you grew up in Angoulême. Tell me about it."

Uneasily she said, "It's not a very exciting story, m'sieur. We lived some distance east of the town of Angoulême, in the country, near Nieuil. When I was a child, King François had a hunting lodge very near my family's château, but he wasn't there very often. I couldn't have been more than ten when he went off with the army to fight in Italy, and then, of course, he was held captive for over a year. He did visit after his return, and my parents attended a celebration at the hunting lodge, but soon after it became the property of a man named Grunn. Apparently he owned some land in the forest near Château de Chambord that the king coveted, so they made an exchange."

Sandhurst had given no indication that he heard her at all, but now he glanced up to remark dryly, "I see. What about *you?*"

"Well..." She faltered, blushing. "There's not a lot to tell. Because we lived in the country, I had a quiet childhood. My brother, Paul, was many years older and not very much company. I spent a great deal of time outdoors. I liked the woods—I still do. I love animals. My mother saw to it that I learned to read. We had a wonderful library. I think that my father likes books better than people, but at least the books became my friends as well." Micheline was relaxing now, gazing at a fresco rather than at Andrew as she continued. "As far back as I can remember, Bernard Tevoulère was my best *human* friend. He was a year older than I, and he taught me to

ride and swim and climb trees. He taught me everything. When I was twelve, he gave me one of his own
horses as a birthday gift." She smiled softly as she recounted the memory.

"You're fond of horses?"

"Oh, much more than that!" she declared. "I can't
tell you how I've missed my Gustave these past months.
He's getting old, but somehow that makes me love him
more than ever. I often think that horses are more
human than people."

Andrew's brows went up as he digested this. "I'm
inclined to agree with you, madame. But please, pardon
my interruption. I like this story about you much better
than the one about the king's hunting lodge."

His voice warmed her from a distance, encouraging
her to continue. Micheline hesitated for a moment, then
told herself that after this month she would probably
never see Andrew Selkirk again. Her confidences seemed
safe with him.

"Well, let's see..." She sighed, remembering what
must come next. "That twelfth birthday marked the end
of my childhood. The next year my mother died, and
Paul went away to Paris, leaving me alone with Papa. I
don't know what I would have done then without
Bernard. I had to take care of my father, who scarcely
spoke to me unless it was to ask for something. So
Bernard and I became closer than ever, and we had
grown up. I stayed with Papa as long as I could bear it,
then married Bernard when I was seventeen. We had
four years together."

A hand touched Micheline's wrist, then covered her
fingers. Her eyes swam with tears as she looked over to
find Andrew Selkirk sitting back on his heels next to the
chair.

"I'm sorry, Michelle." His voice was gentle. "I never

meant to cause you pain when I encouraged you to tell me about your past."

"Don't apologize. I feel better somehow. Sometimes here at Fontainebleau my old life seems like a dream. Taking to you about those years helped to make them real again."

He reached up with a forefinger and caught a tear that spilled onto Micheline's cheek. Staring into his deep brown eyes, she felt an inexplicable tremor at her core.

"The light's changing," Andrew said gently. "Why don't we borrow two of the king's horses and have a good long ride."

***

To Micheline the cold wind on her face and the strong, rhythmic movements of the horse provided the perfect tonic for her spirits. She and Andrew rode full out across the fields that skirted the dark forest, a bright midday sun beaming down on them to soften the chill in the air.

From time to time Sandhurst glanced over at Micheline, admiring her skill with an expert eye. It was clear that she rode well, and with great enthusiasm, but she also rode properly. There was an undeniable elegance in the motion of her body; she and the horse were one. The combination of abandon, feminine grace, and rapport between Micheline and her steed struck a chord within him. Horses were one of the great passions of his life. In the past he'd known women who had enjoyed riding, but they'd always pretended to *adore* it, hoping to win his favor. Unfortunately Sandhurst had an instinct for spotting artifice. He'd long ago given up hoping that a woman might simply be herself, for better or worse, and have faith in her own worth, without resorting to a lot of elaborate games.

"M'sieur!" Micheline called gaily over her shoulder. "Are you holding back to make me feel better?"

"I think you took the faster horse!" He laughed. Leaning forward so that his knees pressed hard against the stallion's sides, Sandhurst drew alongside Micheline, then slightly ahead. She was laughing, too, as they raced, and he felt a wave of pleasure at the sight of her curling auburn-gold hair, waving behind her like a banner. Micheline was clad all in rust-colored velvet. A soft velvet cap set with emeralds puffed sideways in the wind, and her gown was covered by a matching cloak trimmed in sable.

"Stop showing off!" she cried as he gradually passed her. Never one to lose without a fight, Micheline urged her steed forward faster, but it was not enough, and even in her frustration she had to admire his skill and masculine beauty as he rode.

The Englishman brought his horse slowly to a walk and waited for Micheline to reach them. "Let's have something to eat," he suggested, swinging down from the stallion's back.

Seeing a pond nearby where the horses could drink, she nodded breathlessly. He had walked over to help her down, and though she certainly didn't need his aid, she capitulated and slid down into his waiting arms. The sensation of his strong hands encircling her waist was pleasurably unsettling.

"I apologize," he said with a smile. "If I were a gentleman, I'd have let you win."

"Don't be ridiculous," Micheline said. "I certainly wouldn't have let *you* win if I could have helped it!"

"I know." He appeared pleased by this knowledge.

Together they took the bundles of food down from

behind his horse's saddle, then the two steeds wandered off to rest and drink at the pond.

Andrew, with Jeremy's help, had raided the château's kitchen while Micheline changed clothes for their ride. Her eyes widened now as he spread a cloth over the long grass and produced a slender, fragrant baguette, apricots and strawberries grown in the king's greenhouses near Paris, slices of young chicken and ham, a little rush basket of curdled Vincennes cheese, and a generous stoppered flask of wine. There were even cups, serviettes, knives, and butter.

"Oh, m'sieur, it is a feast!" Micheline exclaimed. Suddenly she was ravenous.

"Wait." Sandhurst held up a hand. "Before we eat, I want to settle something."

She paused in the act of tearing off a piece of bread and waited.

"Are we friends?"

"Why, yes... I think we are."

"Then kindly do me the favor of calling me Andrew."

"*D'accord*... Andrew. Will you call me Michelle?" She blushed under his warm regard and admitted, "I liked it when you said it earlier."

"I liked it too." He smiled. "And I would be honored."

* * *

They took a more direct route back to the château, through the forest of Fontainebleau. In another hour the light would be favorably soft, and Andrew was eager to return to his sketches.

"I'm glad that one of us knows the way," he remarked to Micheline as she rode ahead of him.

"I always use this path when I get so far from the château. It would be easy to become lost in these woods. It's wider, too, than the rest, so we can go faster."

A companionable silence reigned between them then. Andrew watched the path unfold ahead of them, but he was frequently distracted by Micheline's graceful form. His gaze wandered over the line of her back, admiring the fire of her tumbled curls and occasional glimpses of her lovely profile. Thus, he failed to notice a sharp turn in the path ahead. Micheline took it with barely a pause. An instant later there was a loud crashing sound that mingled with a woman's scream.

Sandhurst reined in his stallion in the midst of the turn in the path. The horse came to a stop just feet away from an enormous pile of cut birch trees. Swinging down, he found that the path's obstruction was waist-high. Micheline's gelding was on the other side, its saddle empty, prancing fitfully about while its rider lay crumpled on a bed of brown leaves.

He was at her side immediately. She was trying to sit up and he knelt to cradle her against him.

"Are you hurt? What happened?"

She blinked in confusion. "I feel so foolish. The horse—he's all right, isn't he? He made the jump—more alert than I—but it all happened so fast that I had no time to prepare. Suddenly I was falling..."

"Do you have any pain?"

Gingerly she flexed her arms and legs and moved her torso from side to side. "No, nothing's broken, I'm sure." Micheline looked up to give Andrew a reassuring smile, only to find him looking at her in a way that made her forget all else. Suddenly she was keenly aware of his hard thighs pressing against her, the strong fingers laced through her hair, the velvet-clad masculine chest that cast its shadow over her more delicate form.

"Michelle." His voice was husky.

Her heart was pounding as he turned her deftly in his arms. The instant her breasts met his hard chest, they tingled and sent a current of warmth through her body. Even during the most intimate moments of her marriage she had not experienced such intense, and unexpected, sensations. Without thinking she reached up and touched Andrew's face... and then he was kissing her.

His lips were warm, firm, practiced—gentle at first, tasting and savoring, then opening more forcefully as passions stirred and swelled. Micheline lost herself in the bliss of his utterly masculine embrace. He was harder, warmer, and more agile than Bernard had been, her senses confirmed. He kissed her now, long and hungrily, his thumb rubbing softly along her cheekbone. Micheline was hungry too. She strained against him, longing to be closer still, and then her horse stamped beside them, whinnying, and she broke free.

"It's only the horse," Andrew murmured in amusement. "He won't tell anyone."

Feeling his warm mouth on her throat, and the accompanying shiver that traveled down through her body, Micheline stiffened.

"Let me go."

He drew back in surprise, his brows raised.

"You mock me with your eyes," she accused him irrationally. "Loose me!"

Sandhurst sat back on his heels and held up his hands in surrender. "The last thing I was meant to do was 'mock you with my eyes,'" he protested. "What's amiss?"

She suddenly felt vulnerable and humiliated, lying there in the leaves. Struggling to her feet, Micheline cried, "You attempted to *use* me, m'sieur, like some kitchen wench, out here in the woods in broad daylight."

"I intended no such thing."

"You think that I am a loose woman because I have been married before, that I must now burn for the touch of a man, but I can assure you that I have not missed it at all."

He rose lithely, brushing leaves from his velvet doublet. In response to Micheline's outburst he glanced up and murmured satirically, "Indeed? Well, perhaps that's the problem. Perhaps you have been missing a man's touch all your life..."

"You flatter yourself," she interrupted, outraged. "In any case, I'd say that's a matter for my *husband* to consider, m'sieur. I am betrothed to another man, you know."

Sandhurst swung easily onto his horse, then coolly lifted both brows in a way that made her face burn.

"How quickly we forget...."

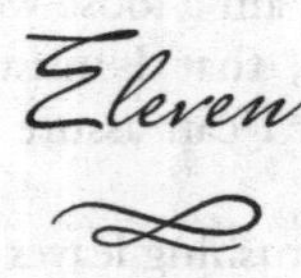

Eleven

ARRIVING BACK AT THE CHÂTEAU, Sandhurst turned to Micheline in the courtyard and told her flatly that he wouldn't be making any more sketches that afternoon. Then he went to the *appartements des bains* in an attempt to scrub and sweat away the edginess and desire that lingered from their encounter in the forest. Jeremy, summoned to bring fresh clothing, waited for his friend to dress, and the two of them walked back to their chamber together.

Sandhurst, his damp golden hair brushed back from his face, wore a brooding look that few people ever saw. Jeremy knew it well. A muscle moved in his friend's jaw and the scar above his mouth was almost white.

Hoping that a bit of humor might help, Jeremy ventured, "Is something wrong, master? Have I been lax in the performance of my duties?"

Without slowing his pace or looking over, he did smile slightly. "You're a twit."

Jeremy was unable to think of an appropriate response. Upon reaching their chamber, Sandhurst went to the table that sat before a window overlooking the courtyard.

"Make yourself useful, Jeremy, and take a look at these."

He walked over to find that his friend had spread fresh pen drawings across the table. "Is this—"

"Micheline. Yes."

"God's teeth, did you really do these?" he demanded in astonishment.

The sketches, though simple enough, were remarkably lifelike. The artist had conveyed a sense of depth and rounded grace emerging from the flat page, with a rain of parallel hatchings slanting from left to right across the paper in the shadowed areas. Culpepper could almost feel the delicate curves of Micheline's face: her high cheekbones, rather abbreviated nose, the tiny cleft in her chin, the sensual fullness of her lower lip, and the sweep of long lashes over eyes that were beautiful, intelligent, and somehow sad all at once. In contrast, her hair and shoulders were only suggested compared to the telling detail of her face.

"What do you think?" Sandhurst queried, not bothering with his friend's question.

"I think you're a genius!" Jeremy exclaimed. "I had no idea."

"That's not what I mean," Sandhurst said slowly, his own gaze fixed on the series of drawings. "What do you think about the lady?"

"Oh! Well, she's beautiful! I've caught glimpses of her here and there, and I'd say that you've captured her looks with extraordinary accuracy." He paused, remembering their conversation in London, and chuckled. "She's certainly a far sight from what we imagined in England! No fourteen-year-old with spots, or a fat widow that the king longs to banish! In fact, I heard last night that François rather fancies her himself. I was talking to one of Anne d'Heilly's maids, and she thinks the king's mistress might be responsible for finding an English husband for Madame Tevoulère. She was worried that the girl might eventually come out of mourning and respond to King François's advances...."

Sandhurst murmured, "Indeed? If that's the case, Anne may have complicated all our lives for nothing. It's doubtful that Micheline is capable of responding to *anyone's* advances."

"Oh!" Dumbfounded, Jeremy wondered if it was possible that the Marquess of Sandhurst could have just suffered his first rejection... at the hands of his betrothed. What irony! "Am I to assume that your outing in the woods took an unfavorable turn?"

He shot him a menacing look. "Oh, the meal was fine! I was beginning to rather *like* the chit! It was later, after she took a spill from her horse, and I, ah—comforted her. She liked it well enough for a while. Perhaps too much! At that point she began reminding me that she's betrothed to another man."

"But that's *you!* I should think you'd be pleased!"

"Well, I'm not." Sandhurst tossed down the drawing he'd been staring at and began pacing. "How would you like to be put off in favor of a *stranger?*"

Jeremy was becoming confused. "But that's you!" he repeated.

"Micheline doesn't know that."

"Why don't you just tell her and put an end to this madness? We can take her home to England with us and everyone will live happily ever after."

"Absolutely *not.*"

Shaking his head, Jeremy sat down on his meager bed. It all seemed perfectly simple to him.

"Have you decided, then, that you don't want to marry her?" he queried rather weakly.

"I'm certainly not in love with her, if that's what you mean."

"When did love become a prerequisite for marriage?"

"Perhaps it needn't be, but if I'm going to spend the rest of my life with one woman, it would be much more agreeable if we cared for each other."

"I don't mean to pry," said Jeremy, "but would you mind telling me what you're going to do? You won't tell the girl who you are, you're not in love with her, she's being loyal to a stranger that she doesn't know is you...."

"I haven't decided," Sandhurst muttered. "Perhaps I'll just wait for a bit and see what develops."

Jeremy nodded dolefully. His instincts suggested that his friend might risk everything to discover if Micheline Tevoulère would fall in love with a penniless artist and choose him over an English nobleman. He sighed miserably, wondering how long it would take for this situation to resolve itself one way or another.

"You needn't moan and carry on, because it won't do any good," Sandhurst said edgily. "After all, this is a matter of principle."

Jeremy managed a rather sickly nod. "I was afraid of that...."

* * *

Wisps of steam drifted upward as Micheline reclined in her bath. Extending a slender, shapely leg, she soaped it leisurely, enjoying the faint lily-of-the-valley fragrance that enveloped her. The water was very hot; in fact, the serving girls who had filled the tub had warned her against getting in too soon, but she welcomed the heat. How she wished she could wash away the memory of Andrew Selkirk's touch, but a slight, unsettling throb returned to her lips when she remembered his intoxicating kiss.

"Bon soir!" Aimée called from the corridor. "May I come in?"

"Yes, of course." Micheline smiled, thinking that her friend, always full of energy and conversation, would be a perfect distraction.

Aimée was already dressed for the evening. Her hair was swept up and studded with amethysts, and she wore a beautiful gown of lavender silk. "How was your day? Did you enjoy posing for the portrait?"

"Well enough, I suppose."

Aimée sat down in a *caquetoire*, a chair with a trapezoid-shaped seat and arms that bowed out to accommodate her voluminous skirts. Micheline's tone had suggested that she didn't wish to discuss the matter further, and now she appeared totally engrossed in washing her left arm.

Never one to be put off easily, Aimée persisted. "Were you posing for M'sieur Selkirk all day? I didn't see you once after breakfast!"

"He did sketches of me until the sun made the light too harsh," Micheline said carefully. "Then, we went riding for a while."

Aimée leaned forward in an effort to get a look at her friend's face. "That explains why you both were absent during the midday meal. Did you take a *dejeuner?*"

Micheline only nodded.

"What fun! You and M'sieur Selkirk would seem to be cultivating a friendship."

"It grows cold in this bath. Would you hand me the towels?"

She complied, adding, "Why don't you put on a nice warm robe and join me in some wine, *cherie*? I've a feeling it might do you good."

Micheline obeyed silently, taking a chair facing Aimée. For a long minute she didn't move, sipping the strong wine and gazing into the fire.

At length Aimée leaned closer and touched her hand. "I wish that you would tell me what is bothering you. Did that Englishman do something to offend you?" She had a sudden frightening vision of Selkirk forcing himself on Micheline in the woods. Please, God, not that!

Micheline began combing out her damp hair. "Andrew is not dishonorable, if that's what you mean," she said tentatively.

Aimée blinked when she heard her use Selkirk's Christian name. "Something happened. I can sense it. Micheline, you should talk to someone. It will help you to sort out your feelings." She was thinking, too, that they really knew very little about this English painter. Devastating good looks and charm were well enough, but could the man be trusted?

"You needn't be suspicious of him," Micheline said softly. "He has actually been very kind to me. He seems to genuinely like me. We had quite a nice day." She reached for her wine and sipped. "There's something about him that allows one to relax and speak quite freely. He encouraged me to talk while he drew me this morning, which made that time more enjoyable, and I found myself telling him all about my past. I felt that he was honestly interested in everything I said."

Aimee was alert. She'd never heard Micheline talk this way before. "Was your ride in the forest as nice as the morning had been?"

"Yes, for the most part. Andrew shares my love for horses, and we had a marvelous time racing across the meadows. Our meal was lovely. He'd brought all sorts of wonderful things from the kitchens! I can't remember the last time I had so much fun."

Seeing the dreamy look in her eyes, Aimée felt slightly sick. How could this have happened and *what* could be done about it? "You must tell me the rest, *cherie.* Something must have gone wrong; I could see it in your face earlier."

"It wasn't his fault. We were riding back to the château through the forest. I went ahead since I knew the way, and I suppose I wasn't paying attention. We came around a turn and there was an enormous pile of tree branches. My horse made the jump, but it was all so sudden that I flew off—"

"*Parbleu!*" Aimée exclaimed. "Are you hurt?"

"No, no. I must have fallen correctly, and the leaves were a cushion. But Andrew rushed to my aid, and he held me against him... and he kissed me."

"I knew it!"

"That's all, though. It was just a kiss. When I asked him to stop, he did."

She caught Micheline's gaze and held it. "And why did you ask him to stop?"

"Well, because it was wrong! I—I'm betrothed to another man!" Her cheeks were flushed.

"Are you certain there wasn't another reason?" Aimée asked gently.

Micheline closed her eyes and put her hands up to cool the heat in her face. "It's so difficult for me to even think this, let alone say it!" When she opened her eyes, they were brimming with tears. "Oh, Aimée, do you remember the day I told you I didn't think I would ever be attracted to another man again?"

"Andrew Selkirk has changed your mind, hasn't he? But, my dear, this man is a wandering painter! It's quite obvious that M'sieur Selkirk loves women and they love him. He may break hearts without intending to. Is he aware of your betrothal?"

Micheline nodded mutely, swallowing tears.

"And even if this did prove to be love for him, what kind of life would you have? Selkirk must travel to paint—he may not even *have* a home!"

"It's all beside the point. I've agreed to marry the Marquess of Sandhurst, and I intend to keep my word." Micheline spoke with careful control, determined not to cry. "What I am feeling about Andrew is just a temporary flight of fancy. From now on I will keep my emotions in check. It will be a test of my maturity."

Wincing slightly at her friend's speech, Aimée wondered, "But what if it's not a 'flight of fancy'? What if it's *love?*"

Micheline averted her eyes. "I don't want to fall in love. That's the reason I agreed to marry Lord Sandhurst. There's more pain than pleasure in love."

* * *

The court was sitting down to supper when Micheline Tevoulère entered the hall. The crowd was so large that no one remarked upon her tardiness. The seigneur de St. Briac made a place for her to his left and she gave him a bright smile.

Across the table Sandhurst watched Micheline while attempting to converse with Queen Eleanor, who sat beside him. He felt sorry for the naturally vivacious queen, who had entered into marriage with François with hopes that had been immediately dashed by Anne d'Heilly. Since her arrival in France three years ago, Eleanor had felt awkwardly out of place. Queen Claude had died in 1524, and Anne had been establishing her position at court since the king's return from captivity in Spain seven years ago. Eleanor had been used as a bargaining chip between her brother, Emperor Charles V, and François, and though she was now both queen and wife, her husband generally pretended she didn't exist. François did not even want children, since Claude had given him seven, five of whom still lived. A woman of great passion, Eleanor nearly always slept alone; and most of the power she should have had as queen had long ago been claimed by Anne d'Heilly.

"Are you married, M'sieur Selkirk?" the queen was inquiring in Spanish-accented French.

"No." He forced himself to stop glancing at Micheline and turned to smile at Eleanor. "My friends tell me that I'm growing old and should take a wife, however."

"How sad for the rest of us," she murmured, then put a bite of roasted lark into her mouth, regarding him as she chewed. Tonight the Englishman wore a doublet of slate-gray velvet that fit close to his tapering chest. Snowy-white linen showed through the slashings and made a pleated fraise against his tanned neck. The torch and candle light accentuated the sculpted contours of his face and the rakish scar above his mouth. Many of the courtiers had rings on every finger; Andrew Selkirk wore only a sapphire set in gold on the last finger of his left hand.

The queen asked, "How did you come by your scar, m'sieur?"

His brows flicked upward in mild surprise. "I took a spill from a very large horse when I was very small, Your Majesty. I'm told I fell right on my face, and a sharp stone inflicted this injury."

"And yet you wear no beard," she mused. "You know, my husband first grew a beard to cover some scars on his face, and now it seems that every man has followed suit."

"Shall I?" Andrew wondered, amused.

"Oh, no!" she cried. "It would be a crime to hide *your* face, m'sieur. And that scar is... dangerously appealing."

Hardly knowing how to react, he replied carefully, "You flatter me, Your Majesty." Sandhurst then turned his attention to the lark on his own dish, sighing inwardly. He was all too familiar with the queen's dreamy expression. The last thing he needed right now was the queen of France lusting after him.

Micheline, meanwhile, appeared not to notice Sandhurst or his plight. She was conversing with Robert de la Marck, seigneur de Florange, who sat to her left. Florange was as old a friend of the king's as St. Briac. Though over forty now, he was still known as the "Young Adventurer," and he loved women as much as ever. Tonight he basked in Micheline Tevoulère's beauty. Clad in a gown of rich blue velvet sprinkled with pearls and rubies, she wore more of the gems on thin gold chains about her neck and studded throughout her upswept curls.

"I shall miss you when you go to England, madame," Florange said frankly, sipping his wine.

"There will be another lady to take my place at court, monseigneur," she replied. Sweets were being served and Micheline took advantage of the slight interruption to glance down at Andrew as she reached for a cluster of grapes. The sight of Queen Eleanor's rapt expression while he spoke to her, gesturing with one hand, made Micheline's face burn.

"There are some ladies who cannot be replaced," Florange was saying wistfully. "A few years back, your friend Aimée was one of those special cases. She became betrothed to St. Briac before any of us had a chance, and now you have done the same!"

"You flatter me, monseigneur."

They chatted on until the last course, the *boute-hors,* consisting of wine and spices, had been served. People began rising from the table as jugglers and tumblers streamed into the hall. A dancing monkey capered about, behaving outrageously for the amusement of the court.

Before long a minstrel appeared, singing to the accompaniment of a harp. To Micheline's surprise, the king approached her and bade her dance with him. She seemed to have no choice and was happy that she was familiar with the *gaillarde,* a dance that consisted of advancing, bowing, and retiring in a pattern that conformed with the music.

"You are looking exceptionally beautiful tonight, *ma chere,* " François remarked with a wink.

"How kind you are, sire."

"I speak only the truth." He reached up to touch her hand and struck an attitude. "How is your portrait coming along?"

The mere thought of Andrew Selkirk made her blush, but she hoped that the king would assume that the rosemary-scented firelight was to blame. "M'sieur Selkirk has made only pen drawings thus far, sire, but I was able to look at them, and he appears to be very talented."

"The drawings resemble you?"

"In a flattering way, yes."

"Bon!" François beamed. "I can't say I'm surprised, however. He brought a painting of the Marquess of Sandhurst's sister to show as an example of his work, and it was splendid!"

Micheline was still digesting this information as the music ended. The king bowed; she curtsied and took his arm to return to the crowd. No sooner had they parted than Andrew Selkirk appeared before her and requested the next dance.

Micheline was about to refuse, but there was something in his deep brown eyes that gave her pause. "If you wish, m'sieur."

"I do wish."

The music began and at least two dozen couples milled into the middle of the hall. Sandhurst and Micheline came last and stood facing each other for rather a long time, their eyes locked. The music had begun and the other dancers had advanced, bowed, and retired once before Sandhurst made a move. When he did, he only stepped forward, touched her hand, and declared, "I want to talk to you. Alone."

Micheline blinked in surprise, then blushed. "That is not possible, m'sieur."

"What's amiss? I wish only a few moments of private conversation in the courtyard."

Caught in the spell of his eyes and the pressure of his hard male hand on hers, Micheline capitulated.

"*Alors,*" she whispered. What harm could there be in a few moments alone with Andrew Selkirk?

Twelve

IT WAS past midnight and the sky was black, covered by a ruffled blanket of silvery-blue clouds. The exit Sandhurst had chosen at random led into gardens rather than the courtyard, so they were alone together in a green tunnel of clipped hedges.

"Everyone was watching us leave," she whispered in distress. "I could feel their eyes on us."

"Why should you care? You're quitting France in a few weeks, aren't you?"

"*Oui*, m'sieur!" Micheline sounded upset and confused. If she took one step, their bodies would meet.

"Do you speak English?" Andrew asked suddenly.

"Of course," she replied in his native language. "And I am fluent in Spanish and German as well."

Her accent delighted him. Each word was quite clear, but all the same there was a French lilt in her English that was utterly appealing. Sandhurst laughed with pleasure.

"What was it you wanted to say to me, m'sieur?" she inquired sternly. "I hope I have not made a spectacle of myself before the entire court so that you could ask me if I know English."

He wanted to touch her, to press her soft body against his hard one, to taste her mouth, to open her gown... but all of these things were out of the question.

"I realize that I told you I would not speak of your betrothal to the Marquess of Sandhurst unless you raised the subject first, but the events of this afternoon compel me to break that promise." There was a passionate undercurrent in his voice. "I want to know how you can justify marrying a man you've never seen."

"Why does it concern you?"

"I do not care for games, Michelle. You and I are not strangers. Indeed, I have begun to feel that I know you, and the more I know, the harder it is for me to comprehend how this betrothal could have happened. You don't seem the sort of woman who would commit to wedding a stranger, regardless of his title or wealth."

Micheline turned from his gaze, her face in profile as she replied softly, "It does not matter if he is a stranger. Nor do I care for his title or wealth. Even if I were acquainted with Lord Sandhurst, I know now that I could not judge him, because believing you truly know another person is the mark of a fool... or a person in love." She glanced up into his eyes and gave him a sweet, rueful smile. "Perhaps people in love *are* fools, and in the future, I intend to be neither."

"You're quite disenchanted for so young a lady," Sandhurst murmured.

"I've lived more than most my age, and I like to think of myself as realistic now. I have lost my appetite for dreams."

"And for romance?"

"Yes." Micheline looked away again.

"Appetites have a way of returning," he remarked thoughtfully.

"I appreciate that bit of advice, m'sieur. I shall be on my guard."

Sandhurst reached out slowly and encircled her slim arm with his fingers. He felt her stiffen, her eyes still averted.

"Have you no *feelings,* madame?"

Stung, Micheline turned to retort, and found herself in his arms. What had passed between them that afternoon had done nothing to abate her yearning; in truth the taste had left her hungrier than ever. Micheline's efforts to keep such feelings at bay were quickly overturned and, like a butterfly in a net, she yielded to his strength.

Andrew's hands were touching her. One, on her back, seeming to burn through the velvet as he pressed her against his hard chest, and the other was at the nape of her neck, where his strong male fingers laced through her hair. She could feel the muscles in his arms flex against her softer flesh, and then his mouth captured her own.

Quel splendeur, Micheline thought. They kissed gently, over and over, learning the texture of each other's lips. When he kissed her more purposefully, his mouth opening on hers so that she could taste him, Micheline thought that her knees would give way if he were not holding her. Her bones seemed to melt, while an odd, exquisite heat began to radiate from the place between her legs. Bernard had *never* made her feel this way! Was Andrew Selkirk a sorcerer?

As she answered his kiss, her lips parting, he slid his hand caressingly down from her neck. How soft her throat was! Micheline's subtle fragrance drifted upward as he touched all five fingertips to the swell of her breast. She pressed nearer and he felt the tautness of her nipple through the velvet bodice. Her breast was lush and firm against his palm.

"Your heart is beating madly," Sandhurst whispered as he raised his head.

Micheline stared up at him with huge blue eyes, her cheeks flushed, lips rosy. Finally, as his mouth scorched the base of her neck once more, she gasped, "Oh... what am I doing?"

"You're feeling, Michelle," Andrew murmured.

Somehow she found herself on a stone bench farther into the garden. He was caressing her arms through the velvet of her gown, kissing her temples, her eyelids, her throat, her shoulders, and then the first curves of her breasts. They felt swollen, aching in the same way as her woman's place. Andrew was unlacing the front of her gown just a bit.

"You smell delicious," Micheline heard herself whisper as she buried her face in his gleaming hair.

"So do you, fondling," he returned, looking up with an engaging smile that melted her heart. "And you taste even better."

"*Sangdieu...*" She uttered St. Briac's favorite epithet when Sandhurst's mouth touched her suddenly bare breast. Liquid fire seemed to course through her veins, leaving showers of sparks in its wake. First he tenderly kissed the taut nipple, then circled it with the warm, moist tip of his tongue. Micheline felt faint. His hand moved to cup her other breast while he kissed the first hard peak in the way he had kissed her mouth.

Micheline had never dreamed of such arousal. She could feel Andrew's heart beating against her midsection, and suddenly she realized that he, too, was aroused. The thought of his manhood made her tremble with excitement.

"Selkirk!" It was the voice of St. Briac, calling from the château. "Are you out there?"

Micheline plummeted back to reality as they abruptly separated.

"Help me, m'sieur!" she cried frantically, fumbling with the laces on her gown.

"We aren't obliged to answer, you know," he told her in a low voice, his brown eyes searching her face.

"Yes, we must go back!" Her cheeks were flaming. "I am so embarrassed. What shall we say?"

"We don't have to explain to anyone, Michelle. You and I are adults." Her obvious humiliation bothered him, but he brushed her hands aside nonetheless and laced her bodice neatly.

"It's cold. We shouldn't have come outside at night!" She began to shiver all over.

Sandhurst blinked, but helped her up and put an arm around her. "I apologize, madame. It was thoughtless of me."

"No, no, I was foolish. I just didn't *think.*"

Glancing down at her, he saw the familiar distracted expression on her lovely face and knew that the barriers had gone up once again.

"You go inside. I'll explain to St. Briac."

She obeyed gratefully as they approached the château. Thomas made a tall, broad-shouldered silhouette against the windows, and Micheline was relieved to see that his expression was one of concern rather than anger.

"We began to walk, chatting about the portrait," Andrew was saying casually, "and forgot the time. Micheline finds that she's a bit chilled, so she's going in."

"*Au revoir,* gentlemen," she called over a shoulder, then the door closed behind her.

St. Briac stared after her. "You do know that the lady is betrothed."

"I'm reminded of that fact hourly, it seems. Was it

concern over Madame Tevoulère's honor that sent you in search of us?"

"No. I'm Micheline's friend, not her keeper. The king was speculating about your absence and I merely hoped to avert a problem. If François thought that you had designs on Madame, he'd banish you from court in an instant."

"Why? Because his own designs on her have been thwarted by the lady herself?"

St. Briac smiled with a trace of irony. "Perhaps. Micheline was all the more fascinating to the king because she was a challenge. He only agreed to this betrothal with the Marquess of Sandhurst because he'd become resigned to the fact that Micheline wouldn't yield to him... or to any other man. He's quite fond of her, so when she insisted that this was what she wanted, he agreed to it. I've seen him watch you with her tonight, though, and I assure you the king isn't about to let someone else succeed where he's failed."

"For some reason I thought that this betrothal was the king's own idea."

Thomas shook his head. "My wife told me that the request came from King Henry—and that Micheline was mentioned specifically. It seems that Lord Sandhurst has a weakness for Frenchwomen."

"*Really.*" Andrew smothered an urge to laugh. "And how did he happen to choose Madame Tevoulère?"

"There were some visitors from England at the court in January, and word has it that they returned home singing the praises of Madame Tevoulère."

"I see. That's very interesting."

"Well, it's none of my affair, and though I'm not certain I approve of this marriage, Micheline's mind seems to be made up. I'd hate to see her... hurt in the meantime."

"As you say, her mind is made up, and she strikes me as a singularly headstrong woman. It's highly unlikely that she'll be swept away by passion on my account, don't you think?" Sandhurst smiled wryly. "In any event, I like Madame Tevoulère. I have no intention of harming her. I hope that she'll be happy as much as you do."

St. Briac narrowed his eyes slightly in the moonlight. "I'm relieved to hear it."

"Now that we've settled all this, I'm ready to go back inside. I could use another cup of wine, followed by a long night's sleep."

* * *

The next morning the king went on a hunt with a few of his courtiers, including St. Briac. Usually a band of privy ladies joined the men periodically during these excursions, but this time cold weather prevented that. Three days without female company seemed like torture to François. He found himself thinking excessively of Micheline Tevoulère and brooding about the scene between her and Andrew Selkirk. The sight of them dancing together had elicited comments all around about the attractive pair they made, but the court had positively buzzed when the Englishman led Micheline out into the garden. What had they been doing for so long? If Selkirk imagined that Micheline was within his grasp, it was up to the king to set him right. It was hard enough for François to restrain himself, but it was easier somehow to accept defeat knowing that she would marry a stranger. He was not about to let some common painter turn her head.

The hunting party arrived back at Fontainebleau in the evening of the third day. The next morning, after his council meeting, François sent word to Andrew Selkirk that he would like to see him in the royal chamber immediately.

The message was carried two rooms away to the antechamber, where Sandhurst was at work on his portrait of Micheline. The light was perfect, soft and golden, and he was staring intently at his subject, brush in hand.

Since the night in the garden, Micheline had been distant, and Sandhurst had accepted her unspoken rules. He sensed that she was afraid of the feelings he'd stirred up in her. Further, he was honest enough to admit, if only to himself, that those feelings had been reciprocated.

These past three days they'd continued to converse, but not about personal matters. Occasionally they laughed together but broke off if the air grew too heavy with intimacy. That tension in the air was present all too often. At times all it took was an unexpected glance or smile and then Andrew and Micheline seemed to be touching across the room, both of them aching in silence because they were not.

When the page arrived with the note from King François, Sandhurst read it with a measure of surprise. He knew the king had just returned the previous night, and it was now barely nine in the morning. What was so important?

"It seems that your king wants to see me," he informed Micheline while wiping his hands on a rag. Turning to the page, he asked, "Shall I wash up first?"

"No, m'sieur. His Majesty bade me bring you immediately."

Sandhurst looked askance at Micheline and shrugged. "I've no idea what this is about, or how long it will take."

"I'll wait." She smiled. "I can study my painting for flaws."

"Since there aren't any," he parried with a laugh, "that should keep you well occupied."

He followed the page to the royal bedchamber, pausing momentarily in the doorway to admire the great oval room, with its antique borders, rich ceiling, and magnificent chimney.

"Ah, Monsieur Selkirk! There you are!" François rose from a carved walnut chair, smiling in greeting.

"At your service, Your Majesty," Andrew replied with a touch of satire, "if you'll tolerate my appearance." He gestured down at his paint-smudged shirt, which he wore without a doublet.

"Think nothing of it. I'm glad to see that you are hard at work. Sit down, won't you?"

Sandhurst took a chair opposite the king's. A servant brought them jewel-encrusted goblets of wine, then departed after a nod from the monarch.

The two men chatted briefly about the weather and the just-completed hunt, then François inquired about the progress on the portrait of Micheline.

"It's going quite well," Sandhurst replied carefully, watching the king over the rim of his goblet. "Madame Tevoulère is an ideal subject. Her face is not only beautiful; her spirit is beautiful as well. It is a challenge for me to capture both the inner and outer woman on canvas."

"You seem quite taken with the lady." François spoke casually, but his hazel eyes were slightly narrowed as he stroked his trim beard and waited for a response.

"What man would not be?"

"That's all very well, m'sieur, but I must ask you to keep your admiration to yourself. As you are well aware, Micheline is betrothed to one of your noblest countrymen."

"It's hardly a love match, sire," Andrew heard himself reply in an even, hard-edged voice.

"It is what Madame Tevoulère has chosen! Lord Sandhurst will one day be a duke. His reputation is unblemished. He is wealthy and can offer her a magnificent life."

He regarded his wine for a moment before glancing up to reply. "In short, the Marquess of Sandhurst is everything that I am not—including honorable, I take it."

"I do not wish to quarrel with you, Monsieur Selkirk. The truth is that I like you and I am highly respectful of your considerable talent. However, you *are* a commoner... and you are an artist. I've never known a painter who was constant. What could you offer a lady like Madame Tevoulère, even if she were within your grasp?"

"Love, perhaps?"

"Now, now, let us be serious!" François exclaimed with a hearty laugh. "We are both men. You can be frank with me! It's not Micheline you love, but the challenge. You're a free spirit. I'm certain that you have enjoyed the favors of highborn, beautiful, and frequently married females in your bed, but Micheline is not like them."

"I am aware of that, sire."

"If that is true, then you will keep your distance. This lady is vulnerable. Her heart is mending still after the death of her beloved husband. I am asking you to leave her in peace."

Sandhurst rose, well aware that it was rude to do so before the king dismissed him. "I appreciate your advice, sire, and in response I can only repeat what I have said to the seigneur de St. Briac. I have no intention of causing Madame Tevoulère further distress. I admire the lady very much and value her happiness."

François stood up, narrowing his eyes. "In that case,

you won't have a problem remembering your place. This is not a conversation I wish to repeat."

Sketching a bow, Andrew replied, "Nor do I, sire. If you'll excuse me, I will return to work."

"By all means. Good day, monsieur."

Alone again, the king slumped in his chair, sipping his wine. He sensed that he'd lost this battle of wits, but his opponent had prevailed so subtly that he couldn't really call him on it.

Across the room, the door to the queen's second antechamber was slightly ajar. On the other side Anne d'Heilly drew back and knit her brows thoughtfully. She was strongly attracted to Andrew Selkirk herself, but now it seemed advantageous to encourage his flirtation with Micheline.

If the girl ran off with a penniless artist, she would disgrace not only herself but her king as well, for he would have to explain to the jilted bridegroom. How furious François would be! Anne smiled and rubbed her delicate hands together. It really would be perfect. Such outrageous behavior would make Micheline's permanent absence from the French court an absolute certainty.

DRESSED all in pink and looking as sweet as a ripe strawberry, Anne d'Heilly sat at her writing table and stared out at the bank of pale gray clouds that rose above the white horizon. It was going to snow. Everyone said so. A huge storm was predicted—an oddity in France, but not an impossibility. The temperature was right, just below freezing, and there was an eerie stillness in the air outside, broken periodically by sudden gusts of wind. People were pointing most often to that thick layer of clouds and the lack of color in the sky. Those two signs meant snow, and lots of it.

Anne twisted her long necklace of pearls around a finger, thinking. A snowstorm could be used to bring Micheline Tevoulère and Andrew Selkirk together. The question was where—and how?

* * *

Thomas had gone riding with the king, so Aimée decided to test the waters and visit the antechamber where Micheline's portrait was in progress.

"May I enter?" she inquired hesitantly from the doorway.

Sandhurst made a sweeping gesture of welcome with one hand, a paintbrush between his fingers. "Do come in, madame. No doubt my subject is starved for the sight of any face but mine."

Clad in a gown of gold velvet parted in front to display a silken leaf-green petticoat, Micheline was looking especially lovely. There was not much sunlight this morning, yet her curls still gleamed softly, and she wore a contented smile.

"How good it is to see you!" Micheline rose to embrace her friend. "I called on you day before yesterday, but Suzette told me that Ninon wasn't well and that you were with her. Do tell me that my little angel is recovered!"

"Little hellion is more like it," Aimée laughed, returning Micheline's hug. How good it was to see her dear friend glowing, whatever the reason. "Ninon complained of a sore throat, and she sniffled for an hour or two, but I think she's stronger than her father. After a nap she ate ravenously and now is jumping up and down in our chambers in anticipation of the snow!"

"I'm glad to hear it! And I'm so glad you've come. I have missed you, Aimée."

"It's mutual, *cherie*. I decided that it was time to discover whether all these hours you've spent away from me have been worthwhile. May I see the portrait?"

Micheline glanced up. "Andrew?"

"Of course," he replied lightly.

Approaching the painter and his canvas, Aimée's eyes traveled lightly over Andrew Selkirk and she almost sighed aloud. Even in fawn breeches and a simple paint-smudged white shirt, he possessed that rare combination of splendid looks and charisma. Aimée couldn't help wondering what effect Andrew Selkirk must have on

Micheline, whose heart was like a budding flower that longed to open.

"What do you think?" her friend was asking.

"Just bear in mind that it's far from complete," Andrew interjected.

Aimée turned her attention from the two of them to the unfinished portrait. It was unmistakably Micheline who looked out from the canvas, her exquisite iris-blue eyes filled with longing and sadness. The rest of the face was perfectly Micheline, too, from the proud tilt of her chin with its tiny cleft to the sensuous curve of her lower lip to her abbreviated nose and elegant cheekbones. Aimée was transfixed.

"Parbleu!" she whispered. "It's extraordinary."

"Capturing Micheline on canvas has been a tremendous challenge for me," Andrew murmured as he studied the painting himself for the thousandth time. "Of course, it's impossible—"

"Oh, no, m'sieur, you have had astonishing success!"

"Isn't he talented?" Micheline chimed in. "Look at the background!" It consisted of muted trees that might have been those in the forest of Fontainebleau during springtime. A soft meadow receded from the figure of Micheline, leading to the trees, which were veiled in a thin mist. "Andrew used a technique called *sfumato* that he learned from a master who trained under Leonardo da Vinci."

Sandhurst elaborated rather absently. "The purpose is to create a dreamlike atmosphere, only for the background. It's thought that this allows the inmost nature of the true subject to be sensed more deeply. The contrast seems to work for Micheline... making her beauty and the radiance of her spirit that much more striking."

"I agree, m'sieur." Aimée nodded, staring up at him. Could Andrew Selkirk truly be in love with Micheline?

This painting, that seemed to reach inside her friend's soul, told her that the answer was yes. Aimée resolved to see the other portrait she'd heard that he had brought to Fontainebleau as a sample of his work, so that she might compare the two.

Meanwhile, Micheline had begun to blush. "How fortunate I am that Andrew was so well trained in Florence! He knows all manner of tricks to make me look more beautiful in this portrait than I could ever hope to be in life!"

The Englishman merely turned his head and stared at her with compelling brown eyes. "That's nonsense," he said softly. "No amount of training or talent could begin to do you justice, Michelle."

The currents of yearning in the room made Aimee wish she could disappear. "I should be going. My daughters will be looking for me."

Just then a page appeared with a message for Andrew. He broke Queen Eleanor's seal and scanned the words, his brow furrowing.

"The queen asks that Micheline and I meet her at her cottage in the woods. Apparently the king will be dining there as well, and they want to have a private meal with us to discuss our progress with the portrait." He looked up. "Rather odd, don't you think?"

"They may want you to paint the queen," ventured Micheline.

"That is possible..." acknowledged Aimée with a puzzled frown.

"I don't like the look of the sky. What if a snowstorm descends while we're off at this cottage?" he said.

"I've been to the queen's little retreat in the forest," Aimée reassured him. "It's nicer than most houses in France. Very cozy, with plenty of food and firewood. The king had it built deep in the woods, hoping that

Queen Eleanor would go there to meditate, leaving him alone with Anne, I suppose. At any rate, I can think of worse places to be snowbound, if it comes to that."

"If the king's there, I don't suppose we'd be snowbound long," added Micheline. "Besides, it sounds like a pleasant change to me. I'd enjoy the ride."

"Well then, we'll go." Sandhurst paused, adding wryly, "Not that we truly had a choice..."

* * *

By the time Andrew and Micheline set out for the queen's cottage, the snow had already begun to fall, swirling about them in gentle gusts that seemed quite harmless.

They rode the same horses as before, both riders bundled up against the elements. Micheline wore a hooded cloak of green velvet that was lined and trimmed with fox, while Andrew had changed into breeches, doublet, and a fur-lined jerkin of toasty brown velvet, all embroidered with fine golden thread. As she rode behind him through the lacy curtain of snow, Micheline thought that he looked positively royal. He sat gracefully erect in the saddle, exuding an easy confidence.

For a moment, she wished that Andrew Selkirk were the Marquess of Sandhurst instead of an itinerant painter. It was impossible that her betrothed, for all his noble blood, could be a better man. Micheline sighed softly, her breath making a puff in the frigid air, and reminded herself that it was all just as well. Love was a trap. Even Bernard, whom she had trusted and loved since childhood, could not be faithful. It would be even more dangerous to give one's heart to a man like Andrew, who could doubtless have any woman he chose.

As for the Marquess of Sandhurst, he must not

want love any more than she did. They would become friends, she hoped, and build a life together rooted in mutual respect. She would have children, friends, books, and of course there would be wonderful horses. It would be a comfortable, secure life, which was just what she longed for.

"Are you all right?" Andrew called, turning in his saddle to look back at her. "Warm enough?"

"Oh—oh, yes!" Her heart skipped at the sight of his tender smile. Snowflakes glinted like diamonds on his hair.

"Good. You were looking terribly serious."

"I was... just wondering what Queen Eleanor wants with us."

"Well, we'll find out soon enough. According to her directions, we are halfway there."

A minute later Sandhurst chose a right fork in the path, which led them deeper into the forest. After another half hour Micheline caught sight of a stone building through the trees and thickening snowfall.

The cottage appeared charming, as Aimée had promised, and there was a small stable in back stocked with hay, but there was no smoke coming from the chimneys. Sandhurst saw to the horses first then joined Micheline where she waited in front of the cottage.

"I don't think the queen has arrived yet," she said, looking puzzled.

"I suggest we find out." He knocked, but there was no response. "I suppose we should go inside and wait. Would that be ill-mannered?"

"I don't think that Queen Eleanor would expect us to stand on ceremony in this weather. She's a very nice person."

"I'm surprised that servants weren't sent ahead to start a fire and prepare things," Andrew remarked. He threw open the heavy wooden door and stood back to allow Micheline to enter first.

"Oh, isn't it pretty!" she exclaimed

What appeared from the outside to be little more than a well-tended peasant's cottage was a different matter inside. The walls were paneled in carved oak, and the floor, richly tiled in a pattern of red, blue, and ivory, was strewn with fresh herbs and dried rose petals. The furnishings were elegant pieces of oiled walnut, and included blue-upholstered chairs, a dresser filled with dishes, a long table bracketed by benches, and, on the far side of the room, a luxurious carved bed hung with blue and gold velvet curtains. Its deep goose-down tick was covered by a counterpane made of what appeared to be the pelts of white foxes.

There was plenty of dry wood stacked against the wall, and Sandhurst busied himself laying ample fires in both stone fireplaces. Micheline, meanwhile, was opening cupboard and dresser doors to discover all manner of fresh provisions. There were potatoes, apples, carrots, pomegranates, a large chunk of cured ham, eggs, a pitcher of sweet cream, a jar of sweetmeats and dried figs, several stoppered flasks of strong wine, and a dish of butter. In addition, Micheline found four newly killed pigeons hanging next to the back door.

"No one could starve to death here," she remarked, "but I don't see what the queen intends to serve us and the king for dinner."

"Perhaps her servants are bringing food from the château. It's obvious that they've been looking after this place. Those pigeons couldn't be more than a day old."

"Everything is quite fresh, especially in this temperature. The cream looks like it's straight from the cow." Micheline went over to the fire, removed her kid gloves, and held her hands out to the leaping flames. The cottage warmed quickly now that both fireplaces were ablaze. Out of the corner of her eye Micheline saw Andrew pause at the window and stare pensively out at the dense flurry of snowflakes. "Are you thinking that the queen may not be coming?"

"It *has* occurred to me," he replied. "If she has any sense, she'll remain at the château, and I don't doubt that the king has returned there himself after his ride. The snow's so thick you can scarcely see the trees."

Micheline went to stand beside him. Staring out at the swirls of white flakes that had already completely covered the leafy ground, she found herself acutely conscious of his nearness and the fact that they were alone together in this cottage. There was no one else nearby, nor was there even another chamber to escape to. A shiver of panicky excitement washed over her.

"What shall we do?" she wondered in a small voice.

"I wouldn't subject even the horses to this storm, let alone you," Andrew said flatly. "We've no choice but to stay here and hope that the weather clears." He looked over at Micheline, her eyes wide and cheeks flushed, and sighed. "In the meantime, I'm hungry. Let's prepare something hot to eat."

* * *

Two hours later, the snow was several inches deep, the queen had not arrived and seemingly never would, but the cottage was warm and fragrant. Andrew had plucked and cleaned the pigeons, then announced that *he* would cook them. Peeling potatoes, Micheline had watched dubiously as he shed his doublet and folded up his shirtsleeves. He'd proceeded to combine fresh herbs and bread crumbs, which he then mixed with egg and used to stuff the pigeons. These were placed in a pot with red wine, cloves, and ginger, plus a few scoops of snow, and now it all simmered invitingly over the fire beside Micheline's pot of potatoes and carrots.

Andrew brought cups of wine for the two of them, and they sat side by side in the walnut chairs, their stocking feet sharing the same stool near the hearth.

"Where did you learn to cook?" she asked.

He gave her a mysterious smile. "My mother taught me." Unwilling to lie to her, he realized nonetheless that she would accept this explanation, thinking that his beginnings must be humble. In truth, the Duchess of Aylesbury had been proper in every sense except for her penchant for dismissing the cook and taking over herself. As a little boy in Gloucestershire, Andrew had spent rainy afternoons helping his mother chop and mix ingredients, and now those times were treasured memories. The duchess had been happy and relaxed, enjoying the creation of a meal, and he had basked in her glow.

"You are very fortunate to have your mother. I can't tell you how much I miss mine."

"We are alike in that, Michelle. My mother died, too, five years ago."

"I'm sorry." Micheline gazed at him and it seemed that she could see his soul in the depths of his eyes. She wanted to put out her hand and caress his arm, feel the warmth of his skin. All afternoon she had been beset by sudden waves of happiness. Never in her life had she known such pleasure as she felt in Andrew's company, especially now that they were isolated from the rest of the world. Sipping her wine, Micheline found it astonishingly easy to shut out all the warning voices in her mind.

For his part, Sandhurst was making an effort to listen to his own conscience, but this situation sorely tried his powers of resistance. She sat within touching distance, guileless yet sensual, sipping her wine as if they had lived together for a lifetime. Firelight played over her hair, which spilled in long, loose curls over her shoulders but did not obscure the creamy curves of her breasts above the bodice of her gown. Farther down, green velvet tapered in to accentuate Micheline's waist. Sandhurst's eyes wandered to her trim ankles and slim feet while he imagined the rest.

She looked over with a dreamy smile. "This is nice, isn't it? I'm rather glad the queen didn't come. This cottage is a welcome change from the crowds and space of the château."

With an effort he forced himself to remember the issues at hand. Suddenly he sighed harshly and said, "Perhaps I'm slow, but I still don't understand why you are so determined to marry the Marquess of Sandhurst. Is there a reason why you don't *want* to love your husband?"

Micheline blinked as if he'd offended her. "Why should you mention that now?"

"What better time?" he shot back, suddenly needing to erect barriers between them.

"I don't believe there is any right time for questions such as yours, m'sieur!" Eyes flashing, she sat up straight in her chair. "Why should I reveal to you things even my dearest friends do not demand to know?"

His gaze softened. "I think you know the answer to that, Micheline."

She felt like sobbing. There was *something* between her and Andrew Selkirk, but whatever it was, it had no future. For this one day she would have liked to enjoy their relationship for its own sake. Why did he insist on asking questions that she could not answer? It was impossible for her to tell anyone about Bernard's infidelities; her heartache and humiliation were still too acute.

Staring at the fire, Micheline felt an abrupt surge of anger. This man had no right to demand that she bare her soul to him, and she had no obligation to tell him the truth..

"D'accord," Micheline said heatedly. "If you must know, the reason I cannot marry for love is because I cannot forget my dear husband Bernard. I shall love him through eternity, and thus it is impossible for me to give my heart to another man."

Andrew's brows flew up. "Really! Are you certain?"

Somehow, she managed to meet his intent gaze. "Absolutely."

"That's very touching, Micheline, but I don't believe it."

"How *very* unfortunate, m'sieur!" she exclaimed. "And now it is my turn to ask you a question."

"I can't wait," he said dryly.

"You told me the other night that you painted the sister of the Marquess of Sandhurst. Please tell me what you know about his lordship."

"Surely you don't expect me to sing the praises of my rival!"

"You and I are supposed to be friends, aren't we? I wasn't aware that you desired my hand in marriage."

He had to admire her nerve. Smiling, he murmured, "Now you know my secret."

"Do not tease me! I would appreciate it if you would simply be kind enough to answer my question."

Color stained her cheeks and her eyes sparkled in a way that Sandhurst found frankly arousing. So much passion was hidden within Micheline that even she was not aware of.

"You ought to find out these things for yourself before you pledge your heart, fondling," he said gently, "but I can tell you that Lord Sandhurst is not an ogre.

He's not old and fat and boring, if that's what's worrying you. As for his positive qualities... I'm not really qualified to list them."

"I see," she whispered.

Andrew rose then to check the pigeons. "They're almost ready," he announced, turning to find her gaze fastened on his body.

"Oh. I should prepare the apples. Then we'll eat."

"Yes," he murmured, suddenly ravenous for Micheline. "I suppose we shall."

Fourteen

DUSK WAS WRAPPING the cottage in a mauve embrace. Micheline looked out the leaded-glass windows as she put dishes and candles on the table and thought that the snowflakes looked like fluttering pink primroses against the twilit sky.

Andrew's pigeons were delicious and juicy in their sauce of red wine, complemented perfectly by potatoes with parsley and butter, baby carrots, and sautéed apples. Hungry as they were, both of them also craved this opportunity for relaxed conversation, and they spent most of the meal talking about books. Sandhurst was astonished to hear all that Micheline had read, and they discovered that they had many favorite books in common, since she was very familiar with English authors and poets.

"That was part of the reason I learned other languages," Micheline explained, her hair agleam in the candlelight. "Papa speaks and reads everything from Latin to German, so our library was filled with books in every language. I loved to read so much that once I'd exhausted every printed word of French, I begged him to help me with the others."

"How old were you?"

"Oh, still a child. I remember speaking English quite competently even before Maman died. I must have been seven or eight when I began exploring other languages." She paused, sipping her wine with a smile. "I think it's easier when one is very young, don't you?"

"Yes, and easier still for the child who has the desire to learn. Languages were forced on me by tyrannical schoolmasters, so naturally I hated every minute."

"How typically male," laughed Micheline. She wanted to ask him about his education, even about his childhood, but feared that he might be embarrassed to tell her. She assumed that Andrew's family was part of the lower class, and that he had raised himself this far by dint of hard work, innate intelligence, and talent. It was a pleasant surprise to hear that he had gone to school.

"I brought my parents considerable grief in that respect, I'm afraid," he was saying reflectively. "I never wanted to do what I was told; I always had a better plan. Now, of course, I'm grateful that an education was pressed on me against my will. If I'd never learned to speak French, I probably wouldn't be here, would I?" He gave her a smile across the candles, but his thoughts were far away, remembering the years he'd spent at Corpus Christi College at Oxford. So much of the time Sandhurst had rebelled against being told what to read, write, and learn, for he often had interests in any subject except those being taught at the moment. The rift between him and his father had widened dangerously during that period, since the duke had insisted that he stay. They had been on such bad terms when he finished at Oxford that his mother had arranged the year of art study in Florence. Now, after talking to Micheline, Sandhurst momentarily softened toward his father.

He'd been fortunate to have received so fine and extensive an education.

Micheline rose to cut wedges from a cylindrical Auvergne cheese. She arranged them on a plate with sweetmeats, then split a pomegranate and placed it in the center. At the table Andrew was pouring more wine for both of them, but he glanced up as she approached, noting the gentle sway of her hips. He envied the emerald that nestled warmly between her breasts, its delicate gold chain glinting in the firelight.

Micheline's cheeks warmed under his gaze, and suddenly she wondered how they would pass the hours that stretched before them.

"Do you play chess?" she asked abruptly.

Sensing the reason for her question, Sandhurst warred unsuccessfully with an amused smile. "Naturally, madame."

"I saw a lovely carved board and ivory pieces in the chest!" she exclaimed. "Would you care for a game?"

"Your whim is my command."

Micheline rushed to bring the board and pieces while Andrew casually selected a wedge of cheese. "I warn you," she declared, "I'm awfully good at this!"

"No doubt..." His eyes captured hers and held them until she blushed.

Before her marriage she had played so often with her father that she often won, but this was much different. The silence combined with Andrew's nearness to unnerve her. She found herself more aware of his fingers on the chess pieces than she was of their destination. He snacked on cheese and pomegranate seeds while she tried to concentrate on her moves, and Micheline couldn't resist the urge to study him under her lashes. Watching him rub a drop of red juice from his mouth with his fingertip, she felt a frightening surge of desire.

Occasionally he would look up, catching her in a moment of lust, and Micheline would stare at the board, her cheeks on fire. She was shocked at the longings of her own body. Still, these hours at the queen's cottage felt like an interlude out of time. With each passing minute she found it increasingly difficult to remember past and future, promises and responsibilities. The barriers she had so carefully built against Andrew in her mind and heart were melting away.

"Check." Andrew lightly moved his black knight to capture her queen.

Micheline was aghast. How could this have happened? She saw the board clearly for the first time and burned with embarrassment as she remembered her boast at the beginning of the game. Sipping her wine agitatedly, Micheline surveyed the possibilities. She tried to protect her king with her rook, but he was steps ahead of her.

"Bad luck, fondling," Sandhurst murmured with a rueful smile. One move of his bishop allowed him to tell her softly, "Mate."

Breathing anxiously, Micheline glanced down to see that her breasts were moving in rhythm with her heart. She attempted a cheerful smile. "It must have been all the excitement of the day. I just couldn't concentrate!"

"Perfectly understandable."

When he spoke in that low, masculine voice, tiny shivers of pleasurable panic ran over Micheline's nerves. Slowly, she looked up to find Andrew staring at her. Golden firelight played over his face, casting soft shadows and accentuating each chiseled feature. He looked at her with a warm, melting gaze that was both compelling and sensual.

"We shall have a rematch," she managed to whisper.

"Certainly, but not tonight. It's getting cold and that bed looks like the place to be."

"Why don't you put on your doublet? And your jerkin?"

"I can't sleep with clothes on," Sandhurst told her with a small, slightly wicked smile. "Besides, those furs on the bed look warm enough."

"I didn't mean in bed!"

"I know what you meant, Michelle." Lifting his cup of wine, he drained it. "Don't look so nervous. I have myself under control. Didn't I just prove it during our game of chess?"

What was going to happen? she wondered wildly. "Do you intend that we should sleep in the same bed, m'sieur?"

Sandhurst gave in to low, irrepressible laughter. "I don't see that we have a choice, madame." He arched a brow. "Shall we be formal? Would that make it easier for you?"

Feeling foolish, Micheline tried again. "You needn't mock me. It's just that—"

"Don't say it!" He held up his hand. "I know; you are betrothed to the dreaded Marquess of Sandhurst! Never fear, sweeting; your honor is safe with me. I won't trespass on your side of the bed unless you insist."

She straightened her back and replied primly, "In that case, we shall both sleep soundly."

Several irreverent replies danced on his tongue, but he managed to swallow them. Instead, he pushed back his chair. When he began to gather up their soiled dishes, Micheline waved him off.

"No, no, you cooked the pigeons. It's my turn to clean up. You're tired and cold; go along to bed."

Shaking his head and smiling, Sandhurst put a pot of melted snow over the fire so that she would have hot water to clean with, then crossed the room and began undressing. Micheline made a show of tidying up, but she couldn't resist sneaking a guilty sidelong glance in his direction.

Silhouetted in profile against the orange flames in the other fireplace, Andrew had removed his shirt and was now bending to shed his breeches. Micheline glimpsed broad shoulders and the play of muscles over his back and arms, but when a lean hip and the hard curve of a buttock became visible, she turned away in haste. A confusing whirlpool of feelings swirled within her—and at its vortex were acute excitement and shame.

* * *

Finally there was nothing left to do. The cottage was truly cold now. Every dish and pot had been scrubbed and put away. Across the room Andrew had closed the bed's velvet draperies and was presumably asleep within. Micheline put two more logs on the fire, then finished her cup of wine. It did nothing to slow her racing pulse.

At last Micheline approached the bed. She unlaced her gown, removed it, and laid it over the back of a nearby chair. Next came her petticoat. Few people wore clothing to bed, including Micheline, but the idea of sleeping naked beside Andrew Selkirk was too incredible to entertain. Still wearing a thin chemise, she parted the curtains, lifted the fur spread and the covers under it, and slid into bed with the utmost care. The velvet draperies shut out all light and evidence of the outside world. Micheline lay motionless, feeling Andrew's warmth in the bed and hearing his soft, rhythmic breathing. She was afraid to breathe herself, or make the slightest movement that might disturb him. For what seemed like hours she remained thus, thinking her heartbeat would never slow and sleep would never come.

* * *

Deep into the night Sandhurst dreamed that ripe breasts were touching his chest and a soft, shapely leg was sliding over his own hard limbs. Meanwhile a hand had crept around his bare waist.

"Mmmm." The voice's owner pressed her face against his shoulder and made another contented sleep sound.

His eyes opened to total darkness. Iris? he wondered fuzzily, then gradually remembered that he was not in England but in France, not in his own bed but—

Silky hair caressed Sandhurst's jaw. He held his breath and felt his heart jump. It was Micheline! Quickly he reminded himself that she was asleep. She had probably gotten cold and snuggled against him for warmth, completely unaware of what she was doing. Completely innocent, he repeated sternly, clenching his teeth against his own involuntary arousal. Micheline chose that moment to sigh, her breasts swelling against him through the thin stuff of her chemise, while her hand slipped down to Sandhurst's hip and brushed his fully hardened manhood for one life-stopping instant.

Smothering a hoarse moan, he turned slowly on his side to face her. Micheline nuzzled his chest. Tentatively he brought his hand up under the covers, softly cupped her breast, and felt the nipple harden against his palm. Micheline was raising her face, searching in the dark. Sandhurst needed no further encouragement. His open mouth closed over the delicious softness of her parted lips. After a moment she returned his kiss in earnest, matching his passion, and he gathered her into an intimate embrace.

Awakening, Micheline could see nothing in the blackness, but she knew immediately that this was no dream, and that it was a very real Andrew Selkirk who was kissing her with such ardent expertise. Resistance didn't occur to her. She cared for nothing except the ravenous hunger that seemed to consume both her body and soul. Now that she was in his strong arms, she didn't want to ever leave them.

Micheline wrapped her own arms tightly around him, glorying in the taut warmth of his skin and its intoxicatingly male scent. Desire mixed with violent emotion to make her shiver. When she put her tongue into his mouth, tasting and exploring with mounting eagerness, Sandhurst could feel her lips trembling. An elemental need much stronger than simple physical passion radiated from her body, and his heart swelled in response.

He found the ribbons of her chemise and deftly unlaced them, then lost patience and tore the delicate garment open to bare all of Micheline's enticingly curved body. Burying his face in the valley between her breasts, Andrew felt the wild beating of her heart and kissed the satiny flesh that covered it.

"How lovely you are," he murmured hoarsely.

Micheline sank her fingers into his hair, arching against the mouth that sought her aching nipple. A moan rose from the deepest part of her when his tongue burned the sensitive peak as he kissed her there, rhythmically, until a fire seemed to spread downward to rage between her legs.

Although Andrew lingered hungrily at her breasts, his right hand strayed lower, bestowing feather-light caresses over Micheline's slim legs, flat belly, and the curves of her hips. When, at length, he touched her intimately, he nearly groaned aloud. She was hot and slick, pressing upward against his exploring hand. For long minutes the world was reduced to her need and his deft fingers in the darkness as he brought her to a shuddering, shivering climax beyond anything she had ever imagined, and still he didn't stop touching her. Making little primitive panting sounds, her core throbbing, she searched for him.

Sandhurst thought he might die on the spot when Micheline's slim hand traveled over his hip and belly to find his pulsing erection. For a moment her fingers skittered away before making a bolder return. The initial shyness of her touch only heightened his agony. Never before had he known such exquisitely torturous arousal, not even with women a thousand times more experienced.

Barely able to contain himself, he kissed her shoulders, throat, ears, and eyelids before their mouths came together again and he turned her against the pillows.

Now her fingers were caressing the muscles of his back while he cupped her buttocks. Sandhurst's thick hardness tantalized Micheline's moist softness before he pushed into her, intending to be gentle but unable to hold back. Her hips arched upward in a shock of welcome, then met each thrust so that their bodies joined, over and over again. She was gasping against his mouth, her slender form tensing gradually in his embrace, and then she made an incoherent sound. The incredible sensation of Micheline's tautness contracting rhythmically around his manhood brought him to the brink.

"No," he moaned, but she pushed up against him again, drawing him in deeper still, and it was as if a dam had burst inside his soul. In the inky light there was just that moment of utter blinding release, their bodies fused, shuddering.

Pleasure swirled up over Micheline's body like waves breaking on the sand. Never in her life had she imagined such an experience. What had happened to her? How had Andrew done it? His face was buried now in her tumbled curls, their hearts thudding in unison. She loved the sensation of him still inside her, still pulsating in the afterglow.

"Oh, Michelle," he whispered, and let out a ragged sigh.

The hair that curled against his neck was damp when she touched it. Unable to speak, Micheline could answer only by turning her face to kiss Andrew's mouth. Even in the darkness she didn't have to search for it.

He was part of her now.

Fifteen

"HOW CAN you be so calm during a crisis?" Aimée demanded of her husband. "I'm worried sick!"

She was pacing to and fro in their bedchamber while little Ninon toddled determinedly in her wake.

"Watch that you don't trample the baby," St. Briac warned mildly. Seated by the window in a ray of soft dawn sunlight, he was braiding Juliette's chestnut hair. It was not yet seven o'clock, but they were all up and dressed, roused by Aimée, who had barely slept all night.

"What if they were lost in that blizzard," she cried now. "Micheline might have frozen to death for all we know!"

Thomas arched a dubious brow. "That's impossible, *miette*. She and Selkirk set out in the full light of day with a clear set of instructions to bring them to the queen's cottage. That man is more than capable of seeing to Micheline's safety, and in any case, I would say that she could have taken care of herself even without him."

"But it was all some sort of mistake! The queen told us herself last evening that she had never invited them to the cottage, nor was there any plan for François to go there!"

Gaspard Lefait, who had served impertinently and loyally as St. Briac's manservant for twenty years, entered at that moment, carrying a freshly laundered doublet. The sight of his master braiding Juliette's hair made him stop, wincing.

"Oh, monseigneur," he moaned. "What next?" With a heavy sigh he thought back to the days when he had followed St. Briac into battle and witnessed the seductions of the most desirable women in France. Since Aimée's appearance in his master's life, nothing had been the same.

St. Briac was laughing. "You're just jealous, windbag, because you haven't a pretty girl like my Juliette to sit on *your* lap!" Tying the last bow on her braids, he bent to kiss his daughter's rosy cheek, then lifted her down. She promptly went to Gaspard and raised her arms, thinking to console him.

The old man's heart melted. He handed the doublet over to St. Briac, then lifted the little girl into his arms. When she kissed his cheek, Gaspard blushed and cleared his throat. "Perhaps the children would enjoy it if I bundled them up and took them out to play in the snow," he suggested gruffly.

"That's very kind of you, Gaspard!" Aimée approved, while Ninon and Juliette squealed with excitement.

St. Briac only smiled, his turquoise eyes agleam with fond amusement.

When they were alone, Aimée began to pace again.

"I wish you would stop that," he complained. "Micheline is a grown woman! How would you have felt if someone had hovered so protectively over *you?*"

"I'm only worried about her safety."

He sighed. Setting down the doublet, he walked over and put his arms around his wife, then tipped up her chin and kissed her soundly. "You know what has happened as well as I. They've spent the night together in that cottage, which was the wisest thing the way the snow was coming down last night. There is always more than enough food there, and I'm sure they've been perfectly comfortable. The snow has stopped now. I've no doubts that they'll return this morning, but if they are not here by noon, I'll go to the cottage myself. Now do you feel better?"

Her green eyes were still worried. "Oh, I know that you're right...."

"It's not Micheline's safety from the storm that concerns you so much, is it, *miette?*"

She shook her head, then rested it against his broad chest. "No, I suppose not. I saw them together yesterday, I saw the way she looks at him. Oh, Thomas, what if—"

"They are both adults, Aimée. You can't live Micheline's life for her. I know it's hard, but you can't interfere. Besides, she's an intelligent girl."

"Who knows nothing about her own heart! I admit that I felt this betrothal to the Marquess of Sandhurst was a terrible mistake, but this—this romance, or whatever it is, with Andrew Selkirk may be even worse. What are the chances of him proposing marriage? And if he *did,* what could he offer her?"

"I'll agree that Micheline's life has become rather complicated of late, but you're going to have to let her resolve matters herself."

"I'm going to pay a visit to M'sieur Selkirk's manservant," Aimée said suddenly.

"What?"

"I want to see the portrait he brought from England. I told you how impressed I was by the way he had captured Micheline's spirit on canvas. If that quality is missing in this other painting, I'll feel better."

"Go, then, if it will set your mind at ease. I'll finish dressing and get something to eat." He cupped Aimée's little face in his hands and kissed her, wishing that she could spare him a fraction of the attention she lavished on Micheline.

* * *

Jeremy Culpepper chewed a bite of greengage plum and wondered what Sandhurst was up to now. He'd said the queen had invited him and Micheline to her cottage, but kitchen gossip had it that Queen Eleanor hadn't ever intended to leave Fontainebleau and was professing complete innocence about the note Andrew had received. No one really expected the couple to come back last night considering the snowstorm, but all the servants were buzzing about what the betrothed Madame Tevoulère might be doing alone in a secluded cottage with that dangerously attractive English painter.

A knock sounded at the door and Jeremy jumped. Sandhurst would never knock, and the only other person who might visit him was the amorous little saucemaker who liked to purr that she found him adorable. It was awfully early in the day for that sort of social call....

He opened the door to find the seigneur de St. Briac's pretty wife. God's toes! Jeremy thought. What if she's one of those married women who like a bit of diversion with the servants? Her husband's a giant!

"*Bonjour*, m'sieur," Aimée said warmly. "You are...?"

"Jeremy—uh—Playfair." He choked on the name, cursing Sandhurst silently. "How may I help you, my lady?" This really was *too* much. He had to not only claim that idiotic surname but also act the servant, as if he were no better than a dog she might deign to pat on the head.

"I know that this might sound odd, m'sieur, but I would appreciate it if you could show me the painting your master brought from England. I have admired the portrait he is making of Madame Tevoulère, and am curious to see more of his work."

Odd indeed, thought Jeremy, especially at seven in the morning!

"Come in, madame. I hope that you'll excuse the chamber's appearance—and my own. I didn't expect—"

"It is I who owe *you* an apology, M'sieur Playfair!" Aimée declared. "It is very early, and I came on a whim, hoping that you would pardon my rudeness."

Jeremy began to like the lady. She wasn't condescending in the least, and they chatted easily as he unrolled the canvas of Cicely Weston and propped it on the table by the window.

Aimée blinked. *"Parbleu!"*

"Quite beautiful, isn't it?" Culpepper said proudly. He wanted to give credit to Lord Sandhurst, then claim him as a friend and equal, but instead he had to continue, "Master Selkirk is extremely talented. I couldn't believe it myself when I first saw this. It's as if Lady Cicely Weston were here, alive in this chamber."

"Cicely... Weston?" Aimée was staring at the portrait, her spirits sinking. This manservant was right. If it had been love that brought Selkirk's painting of Micheline to life, then he must love this child as well. Her personality was revealed on the canvas, or so it seemed. Miss Weston appeared intelligent and willful in a charming way, and though she couldn't have been more than a dozen years old, her eyes were also filled with adoration.

Of course, they held none of the sensual overtones of Micheline's, but it was love all the same.

"Weston..." Aimée repeated absently. "That name sounds familiar."

"Lady Cicely is the sister of the Marquess of Sandhurst."

Never one to use devious means to gain information. Aimée decided to be frank with Selkirk's manservant. "M'sieur Playfair, are you aware that Micheline Tevoulère is betrothed to Lord Sandhurst?"

He swallowed visibly. "Yes, I have heard about that, madame."

"The lady is my dearest friend, and as you might imagine, I've been rather concerned about the fact that she and the marquess have never met."

"Perfectly understandable." Jeremy nodded.

"I hope, then, that you'll understand my curiosity as well when I ask if you know Lord Sandhurst at all. I'm eager to discover what sort of man he is."

"The marquess is a very fine man," he said, pulling at his collar as if it were too tight. "He is blessed with extraordinary good looks and intelligence. I doubt that there's a lady in Britain of marriageable age who wouldn't gladly take Madame Tevoulère's place. Don't waste time worrying that your friend has chosen ill. I don't think that there's the slightest chance that she'll be unhappy in this marriage—or that she won't love her husband."

Aimée thanked him, stole a last glance at the portrait of Lady Cicely Weston, and left Andrew Selkirk's chambers. Alone in the corridor, she leaned against a paneled wall and sighed in frustration. What in the *world* was the answer to this dilemma? Perhaps this situation wasn't fair to Micheline. How could she choose between Andrew Selkirk and a man she'd never seen? If

Playfair's words were true, Lord Sandhurst might be even more appealing than this impoverished painter! Was that possible?

* * *

Sunlight bright as melted butter poured through a gap in the bedhangings. Micheline awoke reluctantly, sensing that the hours out of time were at an end. Andrew lay facing her on his side, still sleeping, while she rested on her back, nestled close in his embrace. She gazed over at his face, tears stinging her eyes. Everything about him was excruciatingly dear to her. She adored his sleep-mussed hair, the laugh lines that crinkled around his eyes, the scar that set him apart from every other handsome man, and the fresh stubble of beard that glinted gold in the sunlight.

Andrew's hard-muscled right arm curved over her slim body, his fingertips resting lightly on the swell of Micheline's breast. She studied his fingers, which, though sturdier than one might expect of those of an artist, were handsomely shaped. And his sensitive gift for painting carried over to the way he used his hands, mouth, and entire body, in the act of love.

A sharp pain spread through Micheline's breast. She was so afraid now that daylight had invaded their private world. It did no good to lie here mooning over him, for her suffering would only be worse later. She had to leave the bed before Andrew woke. If he opened his eyes she might drown in them and never find her way out.

Slowly Micheline edged away. When his hand slid from her breast, he made a sound and rolled onto his back, freeing her completely. Quickly but carefully, she slipped to the edge of the bed. Her torn chemise was there. She took it with her as she emerged naked in the sunlit but chilly air of the cottage. The abrupt change from the scent of Andrew inside the bedhangings sent another sharp twinge through her heart.

Fiercely, Micheline told herself that the joys of the past night must last her a lifetime. There would be pain, but in the end the pain would be less, so she must not look back!

Repeating this litany to herself, Micheline donned her petticoat, gown, and stockings. Without a chemise she felt doubly conscious of her tender breasts and womanhood. She washed with the melted snow left from last night, then stirred the embers in the hearth and added wood. Soon the cottage felt warmer. Micheline sat down before the fire to brush her hair.

Across the room the curtains stirred on Andrew's side of the bed.

"Michelle! Come back," he moaned in mock agony.

She tried to steel her heart, wishing that she didn't have to talk to him just now... or look at him. What if he touched her?

"You must rise, Andrew," she said in as neutral a tone as she could manage. Walking over to the bed, Micheline drew back the draperies to let in a flood of sunshine. He still lay on his back, looking tanned and tempting against the white pillows. In defense against the bright light, his strong forearm came up to cover his eyes.

"It's cold," he complained. "Come back to bed."

As hot blood rushed to her face, Micheline wished that her cheeks would not invariably betray her. "Morning is passing, and everyone at Fontainebleau will be worried about us. We should go back now."

Her tone gave Sandhurst pause. Suddenly he was fully awake, sitting up and reaching for her hand.

"What's amiss, fondling?"

She perched on the edge of the bed, but averted her eyes from his penetrating gaze. "Nothing is wrong. The sun is out and we must be on our way before they come to search for us."

He ran his free hand through his hair and tried to think, but thought only confused the situation further. The truth was in his heart, what he felt and what he *knew* that Micheline felt. Shortly after dawn Sandhurst had awakened to discover her naked body curled trustingly against his own. The sight of her face, and the contented smile she wore even in sleep, had reassured him that all they had shared in the darkness had been very real. Micheline had looked as transformed as he felt, but now that she was awake, everything seemed changed.

"Look at me, Michelle."

She managed only a quick, painful glance. "You really must rise and dress now."

"Why are you acting as if you're afraid of me?"

"Don't talk nonsense." She tried to free her hand from his, but he held fast.

"Was last night nonsense?"

Micheline's blush deepened. "No, no—of course not. But... it was a mere interlude of pleasure. I am not ashamed of what I did, but you should understand that I do not care to dwell on it. Last night is gone, and I would like to put it behind me. What we did changed nothing."

"Indeed!" Muscles clenched in Sandhurst's jaw. "*You* are not changed?"

"I am betrothed to another man. That is what I must remember from now on."

"You've evaded my question, but I'll let it go for the moment. I have something to say to you and I will say it only once. Last night was much more than 'a mere interlude of pleasure' for me, and in spite of your protests, we both know the truth." Reaching out with his free hand, he lifted her chin and forced her to look at him.

Her heart thundering, Micheline whispered, "No. I..."

"Be brave and allow me to finish." There was no charm in his voice, only determination and an edge of anger. "Perhaps because I'm older and more jaded than you, I find myself quite stunned by the honest emotions that have grown within me since I first saw you on the staircase at Fontainebleau. Love's a precious commodity. I'd come to doubt its existence, but now I know better." He paused for a moment, searching her eyes. "I love you, Micheline, and I want you to be my wife."

Andrew's words had a violent effect on her. Trembling, she pulled free and turned away. "No! You must not say such things. It is impossible. We have to return to the château and pretend that none of this happened!"

He wanted to hold her and force her to tell him what was wrong, but sensed that it would do no good. "I've stated my case and I won't change my mind. If you should see the light and decide to choose love over wealth and nobility, you may come to me at any time before I leave Fontainebleau for England."

"You aren't leaving now?" She was unable to keep the panic from her voice.

"Oh, no, I'll have to stay long enough to at least complete your portrait." His voice held a sharp edge. "Don't say you'll miss me!"

"I'd hate to think I'd driven you away."

"Don't worry, madame."

When Andrew ripped back the covers and emerged naked from the bed, Micheline fled to the other side of the cottage. Pain suffused her body as she listened to him dress. She longed to cry but couldn't, longed to speak the truth but wouldn't.

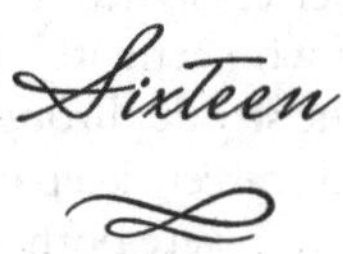

Sixteen

SANDHURST BURST into his chambers and slammed the heavy paneled door. Jeremy Culpepper, who had been napping peacefully on his friend's grander bed, jumped and let out a startled exclamation. To his even greater surprise, Andrew neither teased him nor pretended to dress him down for invading the testered bed in his absence. In fact, he didn't seem to even notice.

"Put on your boots and jerkin. We're going for a walk."

"Look here, Sandhurst, there's a lot of snow outside in case you haven't noticed!"

"That's why you'll need boots. Hurry up."

Jeremy blinked in consternation but did as he was told. Only when they were out in the courtyard did he dare speak again.

"Where were you all night? The court can talk of nothing else but you and that girl snowbound—"

"At the queen's cottage in the forest," he finished shortly.

"Queen Eleanor says that she never sent you a note, and the king insists that he had no plan to go there either. It wasn't some sort of scheme on your part to get Micheline Tevoulère alone, was it?"

"Jeremy, I have no patience for this mindless chatter. I did receive that letter signed by the queen, and it hardly matters now who sent it!" The long muscles in his legs were taut as he strode through the snow.

Culpepper could scarcely keep up.

"Well, as long as you were both safe—"

"Safe from what?" Sandhurst shouted, giving vent to his frustration now that they were away from the château. "The elements? I'd have had an easier time dealing with that cursed snowstorm!"

"Oh. I see." But he didn't see, and had no idea what to say next.

"She's a study in contradictions. First she tells me that people who love are fools, then turns around and says that the reason she's marrying a stranger is because she will love her dead husband through eternity!"

Assuming that "she" was Micheline Tevoulère, Jeremy trotted along beside his friend and chose what seemed a safe response. "The chit sounds confused!"

"Perhaps, but it's more than that. There's something she's not telling me!"

"Oh! What's that?"

"How do I know? She hasn't told me, you fool!" Sandhurst strode on into the forest, while Culpepper raced to keep up. Eventually his pace slowed. "I suppose I may as well tell you. I have reason to be certain that Micheline is in love with me."

"*Love!*" cried Jeremy. It was not a word he was accustomed to hearing from Sandhurst. If this French minx was in love, Andrew must be eager to flee.

"It gets worse," he continued with quiet amusement. "I'm in love with her as well."

Jeremy froze on the path. "I don't believe it!"

Turning to look at him, Sandhurst lifted his brows and smiled slightly. "It's the truth. It's as if fate caused my father and the two kings to bring us together."

"But—"

"You've chosen just the right word, my friend. *But* Micheline won't have me. She's determined to go through with this marriage to the Marquess of Sandhurst."

"But that's *you!*" was all Culpepper could reply, seemingly for the dozenth time since they'd arrived in France.

"Don't you see? That doesn't *matter*! Micheline has no idea that it's me, and she's choosing what amounts to a stranger over the man she loves. You'll think I've lost my mind, but I find myself quite resentful and jealous of the Marquess of Sandhurst."

"You're right about one thing, I *do* think you've gone mad. For God's sake, Sandhurst, just tell the girl the truth!"

"I cannot. If I told her now, and we married, that would be ever between us. I would always wonder if she loved me or my title more, and worry that I hadn't been good enough to win her on my own." He stared off into the distance. "No, I don't intend to tell her who I am. Either she will choose me for myself and for love, or there will be no marriage."

* * *

As March passed, Sandhurst's words to Jeremy in the forest seemed discouragingly prophetic. Work on the portrait of Micheline continued, but she was extremely reserved, avoiding his eyes, his touch, unnecessary conversation... in short, any form of personal contact. There were moments when he glimpsed something in her eyes

—pain, or fear perhaps—that made no sense to him. Why should Micheline fear him?

He could feel the strong currents of yearning that suffused the air whenever they were in the same room, and sensed that Micheline might capitulate if he were to hold her, kiss her, and demand that she admit the truth, but his pride was too great. Either she would come to him by choice, or not at all.

One sunny afternoon found Sandhurst seated on a stool in front of Micheline's portrait, studying her image pensively. He had dismissed her early, unable to concentrate in her presence. The painting was very good. Too good, perhaps. On canvas Micheline gazed at him in a way she never allowed herself to do these days. Her beautiful face glowed with the love she could not admit, and yet there was a hint of that sadness that baffled him so. Staring at the portrait, Sandhurst tried to decide if it was sadness, regret, or fear... or a combination of all three. Of course, the greater mystery was what *caused* so poignant a shadow on the face of someone so fresh and young. Micheline would have him believe that the culprit was grief for her dead husband, but all his instincts told him otherwise.

"*Excusez-moi*, m'sieur...."

Andrew turned his head to discover a young page standing in the doorway. "Yes, what is it?"

"His Majesty requests your presence in the royal bedchamber. If you'll follow me..."

Sighing heavily, Sandhurst rose. What could the king want this time? They'd already played cat-and-mouse after the night of the snowstorm. Since then, there certainly hadn't been anything between him and Micheline that would further arouse the monarch's suspicions!

"Ah, Selkirk!" François turned from the window to

greet the Englishman. "You're looking rather worse for wear! Sit down and have some wine."

"Thank you. Now that you mention it, I am tired. If this is about Micheline Tevoulère—"

"No, no, absolutely not!" The king took a chair and Andrew followed suit, then they both sipped goblets of strong Hungarian wine. "Ah, that's good. Revives the spirit, hmm?"

"Quite." He nodded dryly, wishing his own spirit could be revived so easily.

"As it happens, I am well pleased with your behavior regarding Madame Tevoulère these days. I know that you have been keeping your distance, and I appreciate how difficult that can be." François's brows went up over his hazel eyes for emphasis.

Sandhurst had guessed that the king had harbored feelings of his own for Micheline, but this near confession startled him. Instead of answering, he merely drank his wine and waited.

"I propose that we put Micheline out of our minds and turn our attention to more... receptive subjects. You may be aware that François Rabelais arrived here today. He is our rather astonishing monk who left the monastery to pursue all manner of things. Last year, as a physician, he dissected a corpse at Lyons, and now students have begun following his example. He has also written a book, called *Pantagruel,* and has come here now to bring me the first copy. The story sounds interesting... about the king of Utopia."

"Having read Sir Thomas More's book, I am familiar with the theme of Utopia," remarked Andrew. "And I have heard of your Rabelais as well. Quite a colorful character, isn't he?"

"Yes! I must say that court life has become rather boring of late, and Rabelais's appearance is a perfect curative. I never could bear March. We're all fed up with winter, itching to ride and hunt all day, and along comes Lent to make the month even more tedious. Forty days of *fish!*" The king rolled his eyes.

Sandhurst was beginning to wonder if the king had earlier been into the wine with Rabelais. "Yes, well..."

"We'll have another visitor soon that will cheer us all, including my children! When your king and I met this past autumn, we agreed that it would be a fine thing if his son were to come to the French court to be raised alongside my own boys. I received the happy news this morning that the Duke of Richmond will arrive in a week!"

Andrew went pale. The Duke of Richmond and Somerset was actually Henry Fitzroy, illegitimate son of Henry VIII and Bessie Blount. In the absence of other children, the king had bestowed two significant titles on the boy when he was only six. Now fourteen, the young duke had been introduced to the Marquess of Sandhurst on countless occasions, and Andrew knew that he would blurt out the truth immediately if they met at Fontainebleau.

"A week, you say?" he echoed.

"Yes. My own François is the same age as young Henry, so he especially is looking forward to his arrival. But enough about that. More wine?" A steward rushed to refill their goblets. "You are doubtless wondering why I wanted to see you?"

André nodded absently, his mind racing with the news about the Duke of Richmond.

"I understand that you are nearly finished with Madame Tevoulère's portrait. I had heard such marvelous things about it that I confess I went for a look myself last evening, and I found it breathtaking. Congratulations, monsieur."

"Thank you, sire."

"Mademoiselle d'Heilly has her heart set on being your next subject, but a different idea occurred to me today. How would you like to paint the incomparable Rabelais?"

"I realize, sire, that it is an honor to be asked, but unfortunately I shall have to return to England shortly."

"Shortly?" The king's brow gathered.

"Yes. Within the week…"

* * *

The next evening Micheline went down to the hall for supper, clad in a sumptuous gown of blue and white velvet, her flame-tinted hair cooled by a silvery crispinette. These meals had become an ordeal for her, since she was always aware of Andrew Selkirk's presence above all else.

Tonight was different. Boards were laid, as usual, on trestles, to make three extensive tables that ran lengthwise down the hall, while the king's table was placed horizontally at the head of the huge room. Ever since Andrew's arrival at court, he had been given a place among the privileged, but tonight Micheline glimpsed him sitting far away at one of the other three tables. Moreover, his place was filled by François Rabelais, who had chosen a seat next to Micheline.

The eccentric, charismatic genius from Chinon proved a perfect supper companion for Micheline. Although three years out of the monastery, he still wore his monkish cowl, but his attitude was anything but holy.

"Ah, my good September soup!" Rabelais cried gustily when the first goblet of wine was poured. "Drink up, madame. I taste the essence of violets in this wine. It is obviously a product of Chinon grapes!"

Spellbound at first, Micheline soon was completely distracted by the lively company of Rabelais. He had an opinion on everything. While she enjoyed a dish of sturgeon eggs and olives, Rabelais held forth on the subject of astrology. His tone was mocking, his choice of words humorous, and yet his points made sense.

Soon everyone at the table, including the king himself, was listening to the monk. No one was safe from his sharp, ingenious tongue. He gaily attacked the Sorbonne, various theologians and pompous scholars, and let his humor stray dangerously near the monarchy. His listeners laughed, albeit nervously through course after course. The torchlight seemed brighter than usual to Micheline, and once, when laughter seemed to come at her from every direction, she pushed back her plate, remembering the intimate evening she and Andrew had spent at the cottage in the woods.

"On what do you meditate, madame?" Rabelais inquired.

Pastries shaped like swans and white and vermilion sugar plums were being served along with a sweet German wine. More wine was poured, and the rest of the company lapsed into quieter conversation. Micheline smiled at the erstwhile monk.

"I often wonder why the things in life that give us the most pleasure are also the most complicated."

"Complicated by *whom?*"

"Other people, I suppose, and even by ourselves..."

"Madame, you are clearly intelligent. Let me tell you something that it has taken me most of my forty years to learn. There are all sorts of fools in this world. Don't be a fool yourself because you've allowed other people to exert pressure on your life. I've come to believe in freedom. We only have one life... and when it ends, we can only hope to go to the great perhaps. With that in mind, I've adopted a new motto."

Dancing bears and monkeys wearing hats and playing miniature harps were entertaining the court, but Micheline noticed none of this.

"Pray tell me, m'sieur, what is your motto?"

"*Faye ce que vouldras.*" Rabelais grinned, finishing his wine. "Do as you please."

* * *

By morning Micheline had taken ill. Aimée, who rushed to her bedside, watched in alarm as Micheline retched until she lay pale and exhausted. She could only pray that it was something her friend had eaten or a result of the strenuous festivities of the night before. There had been a great deal of toasting going on between Rabelais and Micheline.

Suzette, Aimée's maid, went to give Andrew the news, which he accepted skeptically. It seemed much more likely that Micheline merely wished to avoid him now that her presence was no longer necessary for the completion of the portrait.

Two more days passed. Sandhurst completed his painting and presented it to the king, who had been scarcely civil to him since he declined to remain at Fontainebleau at François's beck and call. The sight of the portrait did banish the monarch's ill temper, however, and he even called Anne d'Heilly in to view the masterpiece.

"*Magnifique!*" she exclaimed. "Why, Madame Tevoulère looks almost beautiful."

"I should hope so, since she is more than that in life," said Sandhurst.

Anne smiled at the Englishman. "Monsieur, have

you been to visit our poor Micheline? She has been desperately ill."

"Has she? I heard that she was not well, but I wasn't certain if it was serious."

"Oh, *mais oui!* Madame de St. Briac has feared for her life!"

Sandhurst looked sharply toward the king. "And your physician? What has he to say?"

"It is a digestive malady. I hardly think that the lady is fit to receive male visitors."

Observing the way François glared at his mistress, Sandhurst felt suspicious again. It seemed highly likely that all of this was merely a ruse to keep him from Micheline—at her own request.

"I would not want to disrupt Madame's recovery," Sandhurst said evenly. "If she is better before I leave Fontainebleau, I will see her then."

"Leave?" cried Anne. "When are you leaving?"

"Before the week is out, my lady. I have pressing business in England this April."

Anne sighed and murmured, "How sad for us. I do hope, though, that you will return to our court."

Sandhurst glanced up. "That is very unlikely, I fear."

MICHELINE WAS DREAMING OF
RABELAIS. His face, alternately whimsical, serious,
and laughing, advanced and retreated, telling her over
and over again, "You've only one life, and then comes
the great perhaps. Do as you please... do as *you* please..."

She awoke covered with a sheen of perspiration, her
eyes alert.

"Aimée, I must see M'sieur Rabelais."

"*Cherie,* you cannot! He left Fontainebleau two days
ago." Aimée pressed a cool cloth to Micheline's brow.
"Why on earth do you want to see *him?*"

"I hoped to seek his advice about love," she
whispered.

"What knowledge could Rabelais have on such a
topic? The man's a monk!"

"Yes," Micheline agreed as her stomach began to
gurgle in a familiar way, "but he seemed to know about
all of life...."

Aimée watched as her friend turned her face away
to stare out the window, her eyes filled with melancholy. It hurt Aimée to see her like this, but she told
herself that it would be better in the long run. An-

drew Selkirk was only an infatuation. Why, Selkirk's own manservant sang the praises of the Marquess of Sandhurst. What better recommendation could there be?

Micheline drifted back to sleep throughout the day, waking only to take periodic nourishment. She had been very ill and remained extremely weak. Remembering the horrors of the first day, Aimée could only thank God that her friend had lived.

In the evening Suzette came to relieve her mistress so that Aimée might sup with her family.

"You must call me if Madame Tevoulère becomes ill again," Aimée told her softly. "And she must be left alone to rest. If anyone calls, tell them she cannot yet have visitors."

"*Oui,* madame." Suzette nodded.

It was past eight o'clock when a knock sounded at the door. Micheline was sleeping fitfully, tossing and making sounds, but she did not awaken. Suzette went to answer the knock.

"I wish to see your mistress."

It was Andrew Selkirk, the Englishman who had kept every female servant on pins and needles since his arrival at Fontainebleau. Suzette had been married for over six years, but she was no exception. Blushing, she smiled dreamily up at Andrew.

"I wish I could oblige you, m'sieur, but I've orders that Madame must not have visitors."

Sandhurst was all too familiar with the maid's expression. Usually he was loath to take advantage of feminine weakness, but this case did seem to be special.

"You seem to be a girl of extraordinary beauty and understanding," he murmured, his brown eyes melting her defenses. "Couldn't you make an exception in my case? I'm certain that Madame Tevoulère would thank you for it. You see, I'm leaving Fontainebleau tomorrow, and this is my only opportunity to tell her good-bye."

"Oh... well... I suppose, in that case—" Suzette found that she could scarcely speak in his presence. "The thing is, she's asleep, and I don't know if it's wise-—"

"I promise to be careful, mademoiselle. I won't disturb her. If she doesn't awake, I'll leave quietly."

"*D'accord,*" Suzette replied weakly.

"I'll be only a moment." Sandhurst gave her a potent smile. "You'll trust me alone with Madame Tevoulère, won't you?"

The girl was still nodding when the door closed and she found herself alone in the corridor.

On the other side of the door, Sandhurst turned to behold Micheline lying in a great testered bed, looking extremely pale and small against the pillows. He was ashamed for ever suspecting that her illness might have been a lie, but his guilt was quickly replaced by concern. He crossed to the bed, perched on the edge, and took her limp fingers between his two tanned, strong hands.

"Fondling, can you hear me?"

After a moment Micheline blinked and smiled weakly. The dreams improve, she thought. How real he seems!

"I have to talk to you, Micheline. It's very important. Do you understand?"

She beamed at him and nodded slightly.

"I have to leave Fontainebleau tomorrow, but I couldn't go without seeing you. Have you reconsidered? Is there anything you want to say to me?"

His face swam before her. So many thoughts were tangled in her mind that she couldn't sort them out. Rabelais. Yes, that was what she wanted to tell Andrew.

"Do as you please," Micheline whispered, smiling.

"I see." A muscle flexed in his jaw. "Well, then, good-bye."

Her eyes were closed. "The... great perhaps..." she seemed to murmur.

"Quite." Sandhurst stood, then stared down at her lovely face for a long moment. *"Adieu,* Michelle."

* * *

That same night Sandhurst sought out Aimée de St. Briac, who assured him that Micheline was no longer in any danger. She was weak from the two long days of profound upset to her digestion and the king's physician had recommended these vast quantities of rest.

"Does he have any idea what caused this?" he asked, his brows knit with concern.

"The physician says it could only be something Micheline ate, but since everyone else at the table partook of the same foods, we are all quite mystified."

"Very odd indeed," he murmured.

"Was there something else, m'sieur? My daughters are waiting to be kissed good night."

"I should bid you farewell, madame. I return to England tomorrow."

Aimée felt a sharp pang of sadness. It was a shame that things couldn't have turned out differently. If only Andrew Selkirk were another sort of man...

"We shall miss you, m'sieur," she said sincerely. "I wish you good fortune."

Lifting her hand, Sandhurst kissed it lightly and managed to smile. "I return your sentiments. Good-bye, my lady. Kindly make my farewells to your family."

"I shall. *Au revoir,* m'sieur."

* * *

Lying warm and naked in the great testered bed, Aimée watched her husband undress by the firelight. In spite of her mixed feelings about Andrew Selkirk, now that he was leaving a burden seemed lifted from Aimée's shoulders. At least the conflict was ended. Micheline would *have* to marry the Marquess of Sandhurst, and some sixth sense told Aimée that all would be well. She could return her attention to Thomas, and this seemed a perfect time to begin.

"Mmm," she purred, "I've missed you."

"Have you!" St. Briac glanced over at his wife, his mouth flickering with amused surprise. "I'm shocked that you have time for such selfish emotions."

"If you are referring to my preoccupation with Micheline, I can happily report that matters seem to be resolving themselves without me. She is nearly good as new, and Andrew Selkirk leaves tomorrow for England. There's nothing left for me to worry about—at the moment at least!"

Thomas stopped in the act of unlacing his breeches. "Did you say that Selkirk is leaving?"

"That's right—in the morning. He asked me to tell you good-bye."

St. Briac reached for his shirt and put it back on. "I ought to speak to him before he goes."

"What! *Now?*"

He arched a brow, smiling. "Now you're getting a taste of what I've been enduring these past months."

"You're being hateful."

"Not at all. It's just that I happen to like Selkirk. I'd like to remind him that he had at least one friend here at Fontainebleau." Pulling on his doublet, St. Briac leaned across the bed and dropped a kiss on his wife's pouting lips. "It's time you learned patience, *miette*. You're much too spoiled."

In the doorway he glanced back and caught sight of a pillow flying from the bed. St. Briac dodged the missile just in time, and then the sound of his low laughter drifted back to Aimée from the other side of the door.

Thomas discovered Andrew Selkirk in his modest room, folding shirts and drinking wine.

"You ought to leave that to your manservant," St. Briac remarked.

"Oh, Playfair is off making a long farewell to a little saucemaker he's gotten to know rather well. In any case, I don't mind. The activity distracts me."

Thomas didn't need to ask what the Englishman needed to be distracted from. "Have you seen Micheline? Does she know you're leaving?"

"Yes on both counts." Andrew proffered a goblet of wine to St. Briac. "If you don't mind, I'd rather not discuss it."

When the shirts were folded and stacked, the two men took chairs in front of the fire. The flames leaped and danced, gilding Andrew's hair and handsome profile. They talked for a time about horses and England. At length, Thomas inquired, "Are you familiar with Paris? I can recommend excellent lodgings."

"I'd appreciate that. The last auberge where we lodged was sadly lacking." Ironically the Duke of Aylesbury owned a magnificent house in Paris, but Andrew had no intention of going there. He didn't want word to reach his father that he'd been in France at all. "We ate cold vegetables and hard bread on a greasy board and the wine was *piquette*. Playfair and I had to take turns sleeping to ensure the safety of our belongings. Needless to say, I shall be grateful for your recommendation."

"My sister, Nicole, is married to an artist named Michel Joubert. They live quite comfortably on the

Right Bank, and I can assure you that they would be more than happy to give you rooms for a night."

"But it would be too great an imposition! They've never met me."

"Trust me, my friend. My sister enjoys guests above all else. I will write a message for you to take to her. She will be delighted to welcome you—and equally delighted to hear all the news of my family."

"In that case, I am grateful."

The two men rose and shook hands. "It is late," said Thomas. "I'll say *adieu* now and wish you godspeed."

"I've enjoyed knowing you, my lord," replied Andrew.

"I have to tell you that I am sorry your story with Micheline could not have had a happier ending. I only hope that my wife is right and that Micheline will not have cause to regret her choice."

"My lady is for Lord Sandhurst?" Andrew inquired, his brows flicking upward.

"She heard that he is a paragon of manhood," Thomas replied with a trace of irony. "And I'm sure that if you care for Micheline, you also must wish her happiness in her marriage."

He went to the table and took up a quill to write a brief message to his sister. On another sheet of parchment he wrote her name and directions to help Andrew find the house.

"You should not look so angry," Thomas admonished when he put down the quill. "After all, the lady had already given her word to marry Lord Sandhurst before she ever met you!"

When Andrew spoke, there was an unmistakable edge of steel in his voice. "You're right, and I do hope that Micheline will be happy, but it *won't* be with the Marquess of Sandhurst. Of that much I'm certain."

"Why do you say that?" St. Briac asked in surprise.

"Forget it. I was just raving."

Andrew laughed then, but Thomas felt uneasy. After they exchanged farewells again and he took his leave, he walked only a few paces down the corridor before stopping. Raking a hand through his crisp hair, he ran the Englishman's words through his mind over and over. What could he have meant?

"Greetings, my lord!"

St. Briac looked up to see Jeremy Playfair, weaving slightly as he approached.

"Playfair!" he exclaimed softly, elated. The young man looked more than slightly intoxicated, which might prove helpful. Taking Jeremy by the arm, he drew him farther away from Andrew Selkirk's door. "I have something to ask you, and I must demand that you give me an honest answer."

Jeremy blinked. "Certainly, my lord! If I can!"

"A few minutes ago your master said that he wished that Micheline Tevoulère might be happy, but that it wouldn't be with the Marquess of Sandhurst. He emphasized that he was certain about that. What did he mean?"

"Why—why—it's because he don't intend to go through with the wedding!"

St. Briac's confusion grew. "Who doesn't?"

"Lord Sandhurst!" As soon as this was out, Jeremy's eyes bugged out, but Thomas was still in the dark.

"How would Andrew Selkirk know that?" An absurd notion occurred to him. "That is, unless..."

"I can't say another word, my lord! If he finds out, he'll have me drawn and quartered! I must go now."

St. Briac caught the young Englishman by the collar of his shirt. "Be easy, my friend. I give you my word that I will not betray your confidence."

"Do you swear? Swear that you won't tell a soul in all the world that it's been Sandhurst himself here at Fontainebleau!"

So there it was, a truth that left Thomas stunned. "I swear," he sighed.

"He meant no harm! The marriage was being forced on him by the king and the Duke of Aylesbury. He considered refusing outright, but the stakes were high, and so we thought it might be prudent to at least have a look at the chit. You see, I'm not Playfair, either; I'm Sir Jeremy Culpepper, Sandhurst's friend."

"I think I can guess the rest. Your friend fell in love with Micheline, and his pride was stung when she continued to choose a stranger over him. I can imagine how he must feel."

"Sandhurst's always been cynical about love and marriage, but now I think he'll never take a wife. A shame, isn't it?"

"Yes, M'sieur Culpepper, it is a shame. I must be off now. Thank you for your time."

"You won't forget?"

"My oath? Rest easy, m'sieur; my word is good."

* * *

Before Château de Fontainebleau awoke at six o'clock, Andrew and Jeremy mounted their horses and clattered over the moonlit Oval Courtyard.

"God's toes!" exclaimed Culpepper. "I don't know about you, but I shall be bloody glad to be back in England. France is well enough, I suppose, but there's no place like home."

Sandhurst looked up at Micheline's darkened windows and expelled a harsh sigh. "Indeed..."

* * *

It was not yet sunrise when Micheline awoke. She had tossed fitfully all night, not because of illness but because she was feeling herself again and had had enough sleep to last a lifetime.

As soon as the first pink streaks stained the eastern sky, Micheline roused Suzette and told her she wanted a bath. This was soon accomplished, and as she scrubbed herself in the *cuvé*, Micheline rehearsed every word that she would say to Andrew. All the time that she'd been sick, she had dreamt of him. Since her conversation with Rabelais, everything seemed to make sense. The monk's pronouncements had been unorthodox, yet perfectly suited to Micheline's problems. She had allowed silly fears and events from the past that had nothing to do with Andrew cloud her judgment. Rabelais was right. Micheline would only have one life, and now she was determined not to waste it. Andrew was everything Bernard couldn't be; his strength and tenderness emanated from a steel core, while Bernard had been innately weak. Now that Micheline's eyes were open, she knew that she would never compare the two men again.

Suzette fretted aloud as Micheline dressed, worrying that she should not have gotten up and that this sudden burst of energy might trigger a relapse. The younger girl placated her by nibbling on some bread and sliced orange, but she would not be persuaded to return to bed.

Finally, clad in a gown of buttery-yellow silk, her freshly washed curls spilling loose down her back, Micheline was ready. It was past seven now. Andrew would certainly be awake.

"There's someone I must see, Suzette. Don't worry —I'm not going outside!"

"But, madame, what if my mistress should come? What shall I say?"

"Aimée never leaves her own rooms until eight-thirty, but if she should appear before I return, simply tell her that you couldn't control me. Tell her I was incorrigible!" Laughing gaily, Micheline opened the door and came face to face with St. Briac.

"*Bonjour*, monseigneur!" she greeted him. "I've recovered!"

"So I see." His smile was distracted. "Micheline, I need to talk to you."

"Can it wait? I was on my way to speak to Andrew Selkirk."

"Save your breath, *cherie*. I hate to tell you, but he's left for England."

Part Three

Lord, what is this world's bliss,
That changeth as the moon?
My summer's day in lusty May
Is darked before the noon.
I hear you say farewell. Nay, nay,
We depart not so soon.
Why say ye so? Whither will ye go?
Alas! what have ye done?
All my welfare to sorrow and care
Should change, if ye were gone,
For in my mind of all mankind
I love but you alone.

"LEFT? BUT HOW CAN THAT BE?" The blood drained from Micheline's face as St. Briac led her over to a chair.

"He said that he told you good-bye, *ma petite.* Don't you remember? I had the feeling that he didn't want to think about whatever passed between you."

"I—I thought Andrew was here, but later it seemed that it must have been another dream. The physician gave me so many sleeping draughts that even when I felt I was awake, I was scarcely conscious. What could I have said to Andrew?"

St. Briac held tight to her trembling hands in an effort to calm her. "I don't know. Perhaps he expected you to change your mind about marrying him when you heard that he was leaving."

"Yes, I would have! I've thought and dreamed of nothing else for days."

"Are you certain, Micheline? I want you to be honest with me. Why did you refuse him in the first place?"

Something in Thomas's face gave her hope. Perhaps, if she told all to him, he would find a way to help her.

And so Suzette was sent from the chamber and Micheline spilled out the tale of her marriage to Bernard. She told of her adoration for the young man, of her implicit trust in him, and of the confusion she had felt when he began spending more and more of his time with the court.

"Bernard had been the one ray of sunshine in my life ever since Maman died, and now, looking back, I see how naive I was... and how hungry for love. Bernard seemed the answer to all my prayers. When he began to change, I couldn't face it. I was certain I must be at fault, so I tried harder than ever to be a good wife, hoping that he would want to stay with me in Angoulême."

"And instead he did the opposite," St. Briac said grimly.

"I told myself that all would be well... next month, or next season. There didn't seem to be any meaning to my life without Bernard. When I lost the baby, I felt that I had failed him."

Thomas reached out to wipe away the tear that spilled onto Micheline's cheek.

"You know how desolate I was when he died. Even after I came to court, I continued to grieve, but then..." she sobbed.

"Trust me, Micheline. I'll help you if I can."

She tried to smile through her tears. "I haven't been able to tell anyone, not even Aimée." Taking a deep breath, Micheline looked into St. Briac's kind eyes and repeated the story of Bernard's infidelities that she had heard in the garden. How long ago that seemed! She had been a different person then.

"It broke my heart. I felt robbed of my last shred of pride and my last illusion about my marriage. I didn't think I could ever feel the slightest attraction to any man again, let alone—"

"Fall in love?"

"Yes! And even after my love for Andrew became almost overwhelming, I tried to deny it. I was so afraid that giving in to my feelings would bring me even more heartache than I'd suffered because of Bernard."

"What changed your mind?"

"Many things... I suppose it was inevitable. I'd turned away from the truth in my marriage, but when it caught up with me, it had grown to drastic proportions. Deep inside, I probably knew from the first night I met Andrew that I would eventually have to surrender to my feelings. Love and fear have been struggling in my heart ever since... and, of course, the problem has been compounded by my betrothal to the Marquess of Sandhurst. I hid behind that commitment as long as I could." Micheline gave him a shaky smile. "Too long, it seems. Then I met François Rabelais. The things he said to me stirred up my deepest emotions and made me see the truth!"

"But then you were taken ill," St. Briac sighed. He rose to pace before the fireplace. "Are you really prepared to cast aside caution now?"

"I don't see it quite that way, monseigneur. Andrew is not Bernard. That, of course, was apparent from the start, but what I had a harder time realizing was that he would not repeat Bernard's behavior just because he is a man. While I was ill, I had a great deal of time to think about Andrew. He is very masculine, yet so tender, just the right mate for me. None of us knows what the future will bring, but for now I am resolved not to waste another day because I'm afraid to live."

"And it doesn't matter that he can't offer you wealth or nobility?"

Micheline laughed softly. "Of course not! He is

better than any nobleman. All I ask is to share his life—if he'll still have me."

Her eyes widened in silent appeal. St. Briac rubbed his bearded jaw and made a low sound of frustration, then returned to sit across from Micheline.

"Please," she implored, tears springing once more to her eyes, "say that you know where Andrew has gone! If I could not find him..." That thought was too terrible to articulate.

"As it happens, I do know—"

Micheline leaped nearly into his lap. "Oh, monseigneur, I love you!" she exclaimed, weeping and laughing at once. "Tell me, please, tell me!"

"I'll do better than that, *ma petite*. I'll take you to him myself, though God knows what Aimée will have to say about it." Thomas spared a sigh at the prospect of trying to explain to his wife without breaking his oath to Jeremy Culpepper. Then he rose and grinned at Micheline.

"Make haste, madame. We leave for Paris by midday!"

* * *

As it turned out, St. Briac was able to persuade Aimée that Micheline should be reunited with her true love, once she was convinced that her friend truly did love Andrew, but when he told her of that day's journey to Paris, she took a stand.

"I hope you do not entertain thoughts of leaving me behind, Thomas!"

"As a matter of fact, I do." He pretended to be busy selecting clean clothing for the journey.

"I'm going," she declared.

"You must stay and look after the babies. Besides, I shouldn't be away more than two days."

"Suzette can care for the girls, especially for so short a time. I will not be denied this adventure! What if something goes wrong? Micheline may need me! Besides, I want to visit Nicole. I miss her."

St. Briac tried to repress a smile as he thought back to the last time he had ordered her to stay behind like a good wife. Aimée had followed him to Paris anyway—pregnant and dressed as a boy.

"I may be lord of a village and all the surrounding lands, but I cannot master my own wife," he sighed.

Aimée crossed the room and stood on tiptoe, wrapping her arms around his neck. "Don't be silly. I shall be happy to allow you to master me—as soon as we're alone in bed tonight." After kissing him sensually, she added, "In Paris."

* * *

Micheline's final task before leaving Fontainebleau was to meet with King François in the royal bedchamber so that she might make her farewells. Thomas was there to back her up, but Micheline needed little support. With newfound confidence she stated her case to the king, expressed her gratitude for his hospitality and friendship, and told him that she hoped he would wish her well.

François's hazel eyes clouded as he beheld Micheline's radiance. If only... he thought. It was bitterly ironic to him that a penniless English painter had managed to succeed where he had failed, but a part of him realized that Micheline could never have been happy as a mistress— even to the king of France. Of course, François thought that Selkirk was unworthy, but to point that out would only alienate her. She was clearly in the throes of romance

—a condition that the king had learned was intense yet fleeting. He harbored a secret hope that she would come to her senses one day and return to the French court.

Summoning a regal smile, François murmured, "You deserve all the best in life, madame. My thanks to you for gracing my court." He pressed a lingering kiss to her hand. "I wish you joy."

Micheline was surprised to feel tears stinging her eyes. "I will never forget your kindness, sire, and I shall always remember my time here at Fontainebleau with great fondness."

She hurried off to the stables then, but St. Briac remained with his friend until she had disappeared from sight.

"I wouldn't worry about writing to Henry the Eighth just yet about this if I were you, sire," he advised. When François glanced over in surprise he added, "I mean... the outcome is still uncertain. Why not wait until I return from Paris and can make a full report."

Then Thomas took his leave and the king went to the window. Anne d'Heilly appeared, as if on cue, to console him, but as they watched the trio emerge from the stables and ride under the Porte Doree toward the forest, a satisfied smile curved her pretty mouth.

* * *

The day-long journey to Paris seemed endless to Micheline. The travelers rode northward over the broad King's Highway, which was paved and lined with majestic plane trees. During a midday pause at an auberge, where they rested the horses and partook of food, Micheline found that she couldn't swallow a bite. She was completely focused, body and soul, on reaching Andrew.

When at last Thomas, Aimée, and Micheline approached the walls and ramparts of Paris, the sky was violet. Soft, lacy snowflakes had begun to swirl down, dusting their hair.

"I'm so excited!" Micheline exclaimed. She sat up straighter on her horse, already aware of the energy of the city that lay beyond these three-hundred-year-old walls. "I've never been to Paris before."

Aimée beamed at her friend, remembering her own first visit to the city.

"At least the smell isn't quite so repulsive at this time of year," St. Briac allowed.

Of course, a large portion of Micheline's excitement was nervousness. She didn't really care that much about Paris; it was thrilling to be here because Andrew was somewhere within the city's walls. The road from Orleans, which passed Fontainebleau for the king's convenience, entered Paris through the Porte St. Jacques. As Micheline rode through the gates, she imagined Andrew doing the same a few hours earlier.

They made slow progress up the rue St. Jacques, which was crowded with carts, livestock, and students from the university. The latter occupied much of the Left Bank, a maze of colleges, spires, convents, and lecture halls, with the attending hostels, taverns, open-air book stalls, and shops of those engaged in the academic trades. Micheline had never imagined houses and buildings crowded so closely together, or such a labyrinth of narrow lanes.

"There is the Sorbonne," Aimée told her, pointing. "It was Thomas's college."

Micheline stared through the dimming twilight and sprinkling snowflakes. She saw a massive Gothic structure, with towers flanking the high arch of the main door, and a steeple rising above. Beyond were the shapes of many more buildings, and the figures of students and officials rushing to and fro over snowy cobbled pathways.

"I have heard about the Sorbonne from my father," she told St. Briac. "He said it was the finest college in the university, and that there is a Latin library with over one thousand volumes!"

"That's true." He nodded. "The Sorbonne has always been an excellent college, but I must give credit to King François for improving not only the Sorbonne but every college in the university. The curriculum has expanded, the professors receive salaries—"

"And now the king should decree that women may attend!" Aimée interjected.

Her husband smiled. "I agree in theory, *miette,* but I fear we won't live to see that happen... and unfortunately neither will our daughters."

Micheline thoughts were with Andrew. "Are we nearly there?" she queried.

"Patience. It's not far." St. Briac heard the urgent note in her voice and prayed silently that nothing would go amiss.

They turned left on the Quai St. Michel, which bordered the Seine. All along the river booksellers were closing up their stalls for the night. The Pont St. Michel took the trio across the Seine to the Ile de la Cite, the island that was the heart of Paris. Passing to the right of the dark pepper-pot towers of the Conciergerie prison, Aimée and Thomas exchanged glances, remembering the day they had risked their lives to rescue Georges Teverant from his condemned-prisoner's cell.

They were caught in a crush of horses and carts on the Pont au Change, the bridge that connected the Cite to the Right Bank. Micheline paid little notice. She gazed out over the Seine, which shimmered in the moonlight while snowflakes danced downward through the night sky to melt when they touched the water. Four-and-five-story houses huddled close along the riverbanks, their windows beginning to glow, one by one, with candlelight. After the sameness and solitude of Fontainebleau, Micheline felt happy to be in Paris.

When they emerged on the Right Bank, the light had gone, and she was left to her mixed feelings of apprehension and elation.

"I am so grateful to both of you for coming with me," she said after a time. "I never realized that Paris was such a tangle of streets!"

"We're your friends, *ma petite,*" St. Briac replied. "It's our pleasure to help you if we can." What he didn't say was that he had come not only to aid her in locating Andrew but also to bring her back to Fontainebleau if the Englishman had changed his mind, either about staying at Nicole's *or* wanting to marry Micheline.

He turned then into the narrow alleyway that led to the stables behind his sister's house. Even as they were dismounting, Michel Joubert came out of the rear door of the narrow four-story dwelling.

"Who is it?" he called.

"It's Thomas, Michel. I have Aimée with me—and a friend of ours."

They went to meet him in the light of the doorway. Michel was a dark-haired, slender man in his mid-thirties. Always an artist, he now taught painting at the university as well.

"How good it is to see you both!" he exclaimed, embracing them fondly. "Nicole will be ecstatic!"

"Michel, I'd like you to meet Micheline Tevoulère," St. Briac said, putting an arm around the girl.

Warm greetings were exchanged, and then they came into the kitchen. The first thing Micheline noticed was a tiny vase of crocuses on the long, bleached table. It prepared her for the charming beauty of Thomas's sister, who seemed not a bit surprised by this unexpected visit from her brother. Nicole Joubert looked very like St. Briac, in a feminine way. She was tall and graceful, with gleaming sable curls, bright blue eyes, and a merry air about her.

After introductions were made, they sat down at the table and accepted bowls of *galimfree,* a fricassee of poultry sprinkled with verjuice and sauced with spices. Even though they had eaten heartily at Barbizon that afternoon, Micheline found that she was suddenly quite ravenous.

"How good it is to see you all enjoying my cooking!" laughed Nicole. "Your friend, M'sieur Selkirk, ate with equal enthusiasm before he went out this evening."

St. Briac, sensing Micheline's questions, held his hand up to silence her. "So, Andrew arrived?"

"Mais, oui! He came this afternoon!" Nicole paused to give her brother a puzzled glance. "Didn't you know, *cherie?* I thought you sent him here!"

"I did. I only wondered if he would take my advice."

"Oh, absolutely. What a charming man—and so handsome! He almost made me regret my marriage!" She laughed then in a way that caused Michel to bend down to kiss her.

"Incorrigible wench," he murmured.

Micheline was hoping that all this activity would distract the Jouberts from her flaming cheeks, but Nicole missed nothing.

"Ah, Micheline! I see that I am not the only woman whom M'sieur Selkirk has charmed!" she teased.

"Darling sister, you have a busy mouth," St. Briac remarked.

"A family trait!" Nicole parried.

"What woman could be oblivious to Andrew Selkirk?" cried Aimée. "But, are we not in danger of being overheard?"

"Oh, no. M'sieur Selkirk and his manservant went out earlier, to a favorite tavern of theirs from years past. I had the feeling that he was longing to drown his sorrows. He'll doubtless be out late, and if a *fille de joie* gets her hands on him, he won't be back at all tonight!"

Aimée decided that it was time to take matters into her own hands.

"Thomas, don't you and Michel have some manly subject that you should discuss alone?"

"Yes! Now that you mention it, we do!" Having no idea at all what this subject might be, St. Briac led his brother-in-law off to the next room and closed the door.

Since Andrew Selkirk might return at any moment, Aimée decided that there was no time to be lost. Even though she knew nothing of his true identity, she described the situation to Nicole in a way that brought tears to the eyes of all three women. Nicole knew what it meant to marry for love rather than wealth or position, since she had done just that herself. Michel's career as an artist had had its twists and turns, but she had never regretted her decision.

"How wonderful for M'sieur Selkirk!" she declared, smiling approvingly at Micheline. "Since the moment he walked through the door, I have thought that he looked like a man in need of love."

"I mean to give it to him!" Micheline vowed. "In that way, we need each other. I never knew what a man's love truly meant until Andrew came into my life, but now that I've made this discovery, I realize that nothing else is really important."

Nicole wiped a tear from her cheek. "You've learned the most important lesson of all, *cherie*, and it cannot be taught, only experienced." She paused, gathering her thoughts for the more practical details of the current situation. "How shall we effect this reunion? I gather that M'sieur Selkirk may need to be persuaded that Micheline is in earnest."

Mentally Aimée counted the bedchambers in the Joubert household. "Perhaps all they need is an opportunity to be alone," she suggested.

Nicole laughed. "That may be unavoidable unless you wish to share a bed with Micheline while Thomas sleeps with Andrew. I've made a small chamber for Playfair, the manservant, in one of the hanging rooms built out over the street, but that's the last spare bed."

"Good!" Aimée proclaimed. "It's a perfect solution!"

Both women looked to Micheline for approval, and she managed to smile and nod in spite of the tremors that shook the pit of her stomach.

Nineteen

HAPPILY AIMÉE CRAWLED naked into bed beside her husband that night. The sensation of his arms drawing her near filled her with joy.

"Thomas...?"

His mouth was blazing a trail from her mouth to her breasts, tasting the sweetness of her skin and enjoying each inch of the journey.

"Mmm?" he managed to answer, then raised his head to inquire, "Is this any time for a conversation?"

"I only wanted to tell you that I had another reason for wanting to accompany you to Paris... and return to your sister's house." Happiness swelled Aimée's heart as she continued. "Do you remember what I told you the first time we came here? When we had to hide in the attic from Chauverge?"

He laughed and kissed the sensitive spot below her ear. "How could I forget? Never have I felt such a mixture of anger and exultation as I experienced that moment when you told me you were with child. Only *you* would dare to travel to Paris in that condition."

"In many ways, I have not changed, my darling," she

said, running her hands over the hard muscles of his back.

Suddenly St. Briac tensed, lifting himself up to stare at Aimée in the darkness. "You don't mean..."

"Yes." Nodding, she wrapped her arms around his neck and buried her face against his shoulder. "And it's a son this time. I can feel it."

"I can't believe it!" he shouted, not caring who heard him. "You rode all this way to Paris, when you *knew* that you were with child!"

"Shh." Aimée put a finger over his mouth and grinned when he bit it lightly. "Your son wouldn't want to be coddled. Besides, he'll need a head start to keep up with his sisters."

"What am I to do with you, *miette?*"

"I have an excellent suggestion, monseigneur."

* * *

In Andrew's darkened bedchamber across the hall, Micheline barely heard St. Briac's raised voice. She lay on the far side of the curtained bed, her thoughts occupied by Andrew Selkirk. Where was he? It was past midnight! When would he return? And when he did enter this chamber, what would happen?

She imagined women twined about him in the corner of a tavern. One would not need to be a *fille de joie* to lust after Andrew Selkirk! Perhaps he had gone home with a willing lady and would not even return to the Joubert house tonight!

At that moment the door swung open, revealing a familiar male silhouette, then closed. Micheline held her breath, heart pounding, as she watched Andrew strip away his clothing before the meager fireglow.

He is here! she thought joyfully before another sudden wave of fear washed over her. It had been days since she had been fully conscious in his presence, and in all that time Micheline had dreamed of nothing else. Still, now that Andrew was truly present, walking naked and splendid across the darkened room to clean his teeth and bathe his face in a basin of cold water, Micheline wished that the floor would open and swallow her up.

She wished that she were the kind of woman who could throw herself across his body when he got into the curtained bed, but she wasn't. Instead, Andrew slid between the covers and instantly sensed her presence. His first thought was that it must be the Jouberts' serving girl, Rosette, who had blushed, stammered, and finally tried to kiss him that afternoon.

Turning on his side, he touched a cheek that felt hauntingly familiar. "You really cannot stay. I'm sorry," he said gently.

Micheline was totally undone by his nearness. The sensation of his fingers against her cheek sent her in search of his mouth. No sooner had their lips met, Micheline's opening helplessly, than Sandhurst drew back.

"I must be dreaming!"

"I'd be tempted to agree, m'sieur, except I have dreamed so long of this moment that I cannot be confused."

"*Micheline?* Is it really you?"

Tears sprang to her eyes. "Yes. Yes! Of course it's me!"

"Just a moment. Don't move." He scrambled off the bed, felt for a candle on the table, lit it in the fireplace, and returned to hold the flame before her face.

The light illuminated his expression, too, and she smiled fondly at the sight of his eyes, wide with shock.

His mouth open, closed, then open again as he tried to find words. A lock of hair fell engagingly over his brow.

"How good it is to see you," she whispered. Impulse prompted her to lay her hand on the hard-muscled expanse of his chest. "You're warm. It's so hard to realize that this is not another dream."

Micheline's touch released a long-suppressed flood of yearning inside of him. He reached back to replace the candlestick on the table, then caught her up in his arms. His mouth slanted hungrily over hers, tasting and plundering, while Micheline matched his ardor. They were both naked, kneeling on the feather tick, their bodies pressed together. The soft curves of her breasts burned his hard chest, and farther down their hips met, Andrew's fully roused manhood hot against her belly and between her legs. Micheline's hands gloried in the rich texture of his hair and the breadth of his shoulders, while he ran his fingers down the elegant curve of her back before molding her buttocks and drawing her closer still.

Micheline was moaning, her breath warm in his mouth. Every fiber of her being craved the union of their bodies. As one, they fell back on the pillows and she arched her hips against him, aching until with one hard thrust he filled her. They moved together with a rhythmic urgency, breathing harshly, passion seeming to crackle in the air that surrounded their straining bodies.

Finally Micheline was jolted by a climax that swept out in wildly pulsating currents, down her thighs, over her breasts, even to the tips of her fingers and toes. Soon Sandhurst found his own release, and the two of them lay entwined in the aftermath, gasping for breath.

Slowly the storm receded and coherent thought seeped into his consciousness. He forced himself to withdraw from the addictive warmth of Micheline's body and lay on his back a few inches away from her.

"I cannot believe that I just did that! Damn!" he cursed.

"Andrew, what is it?" Micheline reached out to him in confusion.

"Don't touch me. For the past twenty-four hours I have steeled myself to live without you, told myself to forget you, tried to convince myself that I am strong enough to put all that was between us in the past and get on with my life. Tonight I went out with Jeremy and saw a few old friends, and even enjoyed myself for a moment or two. I was beginning to feel quite proud, thinking I might conquer heartache with the sheer force of my own will. Don't you find that amusing? I walked in here, found you, and the force of my will and all my resolutions went right out the bloody *window!*"

"Kindly allow me to explain."

"Yes, that's right, *explain*. Did you come here for one last good-bye, since you weren't in any condition to send me off properly last night?"

Stung, Micheline reached out and slapped him sharply, but Sandhurst caught her wrist in a punishing grip. "Spare me the dramatics, madame, and tell me what brings you to Paris... and to my bed."

Emotion boiled up within her and tears burned her eyes. "I—I came here to tell you that I love you. *I love you,* Andrew. You must believe me. I don't even remember talking to you last night. The king's physician kept giving me sleeping draughts, and after a while everything seemed a dream. When I awoke today, feeling well, and learned that you had left Fontainebleau, I had to come after you. I was wrong before, and I admit it. I want to marry you more than anything in the world... if you'll still have me."

Sandhurst rubbed both hands over his face, then folded them and pressed his mouth against the clenched knuckles. "Oh, God."

"Is that all you can say? Have you changed your mind?"

"Michelle, this is all well and good, but I can't just wipe out every word you've spoken in the past." He turned to stare at her through the shadows. "You were so adamant about choosing marriage to the Marquess of Sandhurst over my simpler but heartfelt proposal. What happened to your resolution never to love again... and your lifelong devotion to your dead husband? It's certainly gratifying to hear you say that you do love *me*, but how do I know that you won't reverse this position tomorrow, or next month?"

"I swear to you that I am sincere. I simply couldn't face my true feelings before."

"And why not?" The softness of his voice held a steely undercurrent. "Tell me, Michelle. I've seen that haunted look in your eyes. If you expect me to believe that you love me, you'll have to start by being honest."

"*Alors.* I will explain." She shivered in the darkness and Sandhurst relented and reached out to draw her into his embrace. Safe in the warm circle of his arms, Micheline rested her head against his chest and haltingly told her story.

She spared no detail, revealing all that St. Briac had heard that morning and more. Somehow, it was easier than she had expected. What had caused her such desperation in the past now seemed a fading memory.

"I see my marriage in a different light now," Micheline whispered at one point. "After I learned of Bernard's infidelities at court, and it dawned on me that I had been clinging to an illusion, I felt disgraced. Every time I thought of Bernard, and our marriage, a knife twisted in my heart. It wasn't until you came into my life that I saw the past clearly. Bernard brought me happiness when we were young but it was an immature love that we shared, and he changed as he grew older. I'm not bitter anymore about Bernard. I feel sad for his sake, but in my own case, I've grown up only these past few months, learning first of all to rely on myself, and then... what real love can mean."

Micheline went on to explain the stages she'd passed through before facing the truth about her love for Andrew, including the odd influence Rabelais had had on her. When her story was finished, ending with her journey to Paris with Thomas and Aimée, Micheline sighed with pleasure. "I feel so different, but I don't suppose I've really changed. Do you remember the day I told you that there were doors I'd kept shut inside of me?"

"I remember everything, fondling," Sandhurst replied, kissing her fragrant hair.

"I was afraid to open those doors, because I couldn't be certain what lay on the other side. As my love for you developed, courage came with it, and I couldn't hide any longer."

"What did you find on the other side?"

"Freedom. Freedom from the past and all the fears that were suffocating me. I feel as if I've shed a tremendous weight. My heart is light now, perhaps for the first time."

Andrew was silent for long minutes, lost in thought, until Micheline turned her face up to gaze at him.

"You haven't changed your mind, have you?"

"About loving you? Marrying you?" He smiled and kissed her tenderly. "No. No, I haven't changed my mind. I'm just digesting all of this. Why don't we get some sleep, and hopefully I'll have sorted out a few things by morning."

That wasn't quite what Micheline had hoped to hear, but it was difficult to worry when they snuggled down under the covers and she lay in Andrew's warm, strong embrace. Sleep seemed impossible, yet moments later she was breathing evenly, one slim hand curled around his forearm.

Sandhurst, meanwhile, stared into the darkness, thinking.

* * *

Micheline blinked against the sunlight that flooded the bedchamber.

"Good morrow, Michelle." Andrew sat in a carved chair near the bed. Washed, shaved, and dressed, he was eating an apple and looking exceedingly handsome.

"What time is it?" She rose on an elbow.

"Ten o'clock. Don't look so guilty! You must have needed the sleep." He, in turn, had needed the early morning to speak to St. Briac. Andrew had suspected that word of his true identity had slipped out, but the Frenchman had reassured him that he was the only person who knew. Most important, Micheline still thought Sandhurst was a painter named Selkirk. St. Briac swore that love alone had prompted her to travel to Paris in search of the man she meant to marry.

"What of you?" she was asking. "You claimed that you needed to sort things out. What have you decided?"

He moved to sit on the edge of the bed, offering her the apple, which she nibbled at solely because it was in his hand.

"I've decided to take you back to England with me, fondling. How could I refuse?"

"Oh, Andrew, I love you!" She reached up to trace the sculpted line of his cheekbone, and felt that she would die of happiness when he caught her hand and brought it over to his mouth.

"And I love you, Michelle." He kissed her sensitive palm. "I've never said that to another woman, nor have I even considered marriage in the past. I'm deadly serious now, though, and for that reason I want to put off our wedding until we're in England."

She looked stricken. "I don't understand."

"We're both rather besot at the moment, but we have to keep in mind that there's more to marriage than love." He paused, smiling ironically. "In truth, until I met you I wasn't even sure that love was necessary. The point is, I want you to see what your life will be like while you still can change your mind. There's a great deal you don't know about me."

"I know enough!" Micheline protested. "I know what kind of man you are."

"There's much more involved than that. England is quite different from France, and my usual life is different from the one I led at Fontainebleau."

"Andrew, I could be happy with you if we lived in a *hovel!*"

He had to laugh. "I appreciate that... and I can reassure you that my circumstances aren't that desperate, but all the same, I want you to see for yourself. I have relatives that even I have trouble tolerating—"

"I shall love them all," she vowed.

"I doubt that. I'm quite serious about this, so you would do well to save your breath. We'll go to England, you will see for yourself what lies in store for you if you marry me, and then, if you remain certain, we'll have the proper sort of wedding you deserve."

Micheline sighed, pretended to pout, then suddenly gave him a radiant smile unlike anything Sandhurst had seen before.

"I yield, my love," she said. "But can we depart for England without delay?"

Twenty

"IS this some sort of perverse jest on your part, Sandhurst?" Jeremy Culpepper demanded, his cheeks red with outrage and stuffed with the freshly baked bread he had been chewing.

"Shh!" Andrew laid a finger over his mouth and shook his head with mock severity. Drawing his friend into a corner of the kitchen, he whispered, "It's only for a few more days, old man! Just until we reach London."

"I don't believe it! The chit's followed you to Paris, begged to marry you after all, and still you won't tell her who you really are. Sometimes I think you continue this farce only because it amuses you to watch me humiliate myself answering to 'Playfair' and acting the part of your manservant."

"Jeremy, stop ranting." The spark of humor had gone from his eyes. "I have my reasons for not telling Micheline I'm the Marquess of Sandhurst, and I can assure you that they have nothing to do with you. Instead of complaining, why not look on the bright side? It's April. Spring's in the air, and we leave for England within the hour."

Pretty Therese Joubert, at ten the oldest of Nicole's

three children, came in then and he greeted her, glad for the interruption. She offered them some sweet butter to spread on the warm bread, which Jeremy accepted. It seemed that his appetite only increased when he was upset.

Sandhurst excused himself to check on the horses. Outside, he glanced up to the third-floor window that Micheline had flung open earlier to let in the sunshine. Last night's snow was only a memory; today was warm and fragrant with the promise of spring. Micheline was making final preparations for the journey to London while Aimée kept her company. It would be their last opportunity to talk for a long time to come.

Sighing, Andrew wondered once more if he was right not to divulge his true identity to Micheline yet. He told himself that he wanted her to have a chance to become accustomed to one thing at a time. So much had happened just in the last twenty-four hours. What if she had second thoughts as they traveled to England? It seemed better that she be given the opportunity to ease into her new life... or even to change her mind.

Sandhurst had other reasons that he was less willing to examine. Part of him still worried that Micheline might have acted on a romantic whim. It was difficult to forget all the things she had said to him during their weeks at Fontainebleau, and difficult to believe that the shadows were gone from her eyes forever. They were both new at love, and there was still a part of him that remained detached, watching in cynical disbelief. He, too, needed the next few days, before she learned that she was marrying the Marquess of Sandhurst after all, and not Selkirk the painter.

Besides, he had grown to like his new identity. He was in no hurry to reclaim his wealth, title, relatives... or past.

"For a man in love, you look altogether too serious," St. Briac remarked, coming up behind him.

Sandhurst mustered a faint smile. "My heart may be filled with joy, but my mind is overcrowded with worries."

"Will you take a piece of advice from an old married man?"

"Gratefully!"

"Listen to your heart if you begin to despair. You and Micheline have genuine love on your side. I've learned that problems which may seem insurmountable when they arise really can be sorted out, and later forgotten, if two people love each other enough. Have faith, and for God's sake, don't give up."

"It sounds as if you're sending me off to war," Andrew remarked sardonically.

"Believe me, war is far simpler than marriage... but nowhere near as much fun."

St. Briac's wry laughter was irresistible. Sandhurst joined in, clasping the Frenchman's hand. "I appreciate your sage advice... I think!"

* * *

A hearty midday meal was served in the Joubert kitchen, complete with several toasts to the future happiness of Andrew and Micheline and the health of the next St. Briac baby. Then, amid loud cries of *"Au revoir!"* and *"Bonne chance!"* Andrew, Jeremy, and Micheline rode out into the crowded street, bound for London.

They first had to reach Calais, which lay on the northernmost coast of France. Sandhurst's first thought had been to hire a coach, but Micheline would not hear of it. She loved nothing more than riding. On horseback they could reach Calais more quickly, and since the weather was fine, what was the point of a coach?

Once they were out of Paris, Andrew watched as she galloped ahead. She wore a ladylike habit of hyacinth-blue velvet, and her curls were protected from the wind by a pearl-studded gold crispinette and a velvet cap, but Micheline's manner was that of a free-spirited young girl.

"What a wonderful day!" she exclaimed, laughing as she looked back over a shoulder. "Don't dawdle, you two! We've a long way to go!"

Even from a distance he could see the sparkle in her eyes. "Dear God, I hope she won't feel obliged to change once she learns she's to be a marchioness," he murmured.

"What's that?" Culpepper asked, his own gaze riveted on Micheline.

"I said, hurry up! Have you no shame? Do you want to be left in the dust by a female?"

Sandhurst was laughing now himself, and urging his steed forward. The sun struck sparks on his hair as he drew alongside Micheline and reached out to briefly catch her hand.

"I am the happiest lady in France!" she proclaimed, beaming at the man she loved.

He arched a brow. "I only hope you will express corresponding sentiments when you are in England."

Micheline laughed. "How could I not? I shall be Madame Selkirk then!"

Behind them Jeremy Culpepper rolled his eyes and wondered if he'd ever see this coil unsnarled....

* * *

It had been dark for an hour when the three travelers stopped at a quiet auberge called the Levrette, near the village of Poix. The place appeared clean, which was a change from most inns, and the food smelled appetizing.

First, they ate in the common room. There was a rich *potage* served on pewter dishes covered with thick chunks of bread. Micheline ate as heartily as the men, enjoying the mixture of veal, beef, mutton, bacon, and vegetables. They drank strong sour wine from pewter cups, then Sandhurst bade the innkeeper show them their rooms. By then Micheline was glad to escape, for the stares of the other male guests, including two ruddy-cheeked monks, were making her nervous.

"Your chambers are at the end of the corridor, on the right." The innkeeper, carrying tankards of wine and ale to other guests, motioned vaguely with his bald head. "They're the only two I have that adjoin."

Sandhurst glanced back at Jeremy. "Go and see to the horses, won't you, Playfair?"

"But—" Color flared in his cheeks. "As you wish, *master!*"

Upstairs, Micheline followed right behind Andrew into the first room and put down her bag of possessions on the grander of two beds. When the straw tick made a crunching sound, she tried not to wince.

"A far cry from Fontainebleau," she said, smiling bravely, "but it won't matter as long as you're next to me."

Sandhurst crossed the chamber and opened a connecting door. "I appreciate the thought, but you'll be sleeping in here." Picking up her belongings, he disappeared through the doorway.

Surprise then embarrassment washed over her.

Slowly Micheline followed her betrothed into a smaller room with a clean and serviceable bed for one.

"I don't understand," she whispered.

"Last night was a mistake that I don't intend to repeat until we're married," he explained evenly. "It would be best if we didn't bind ourselves together with words —or acts—of love until... you are absolutely certain that you have made the right choice."

Her eyes were wide with confusion. "I have already made my choice. I want *you.*"

"You may have second thoughts after we arrive in London."

"What is wrong? Are you afraid that I'll meet the Marquess of Sandhurst and be led astray?" Micheline approached him and declared, "I don't want Lord Sandhurst! As far as I'm concerned, he can take his title and his wealth and go to the devil."

Andrew flinched slightly. When her small hands clasped his own, their eyes met and he opened his mouth. Whether he'd meant to speak or to kiss her, Micheline wasn't sure, for a moment later he was turning away.

"Sleep well, fondling. We have a long day ahead of us if we're to reach Calais by nightfall."

* * *

Micheline enjoyed the next day's ride, over countryside that was different from what she was used to. They passed through valleys that were already beginning to turn green. Farms and villages were set amid willow-hung canals, while wooded hills curved gently in the distance. Micheline wished that Jeremy would disappear and that she and Andrew could pause for a leisurely meal under one of the romantic-looking willow trees.

Instead, they ate quickly at a village tavern, then continued the long ride to Calais. Dusk was upon them when their destination appeared on the horizon, its towers and battlements seeming to rise straight out of the sea. The walls were broken by Lanterngate, the broad archway that led into a town Micheline found quite charming. The crowded, winding streets were lined with wooden houses with crow-step gables and pleasant gardens. After passing Our Lady Church, with its tall, graceful spire, and the cobbled marketplace, they stopped before the swinging sign of the Cross Keys tavern. Andrew dismounted before lifting Micheline down from her horse. She savored the sensation of his hands about her waist.

"Well," he said, "the worst is over. We'll sail at first light, and you can relax the rest of the way to London."

Relaxing wasn't exactly what Micheline longed to do, but there seemed little to be gained by arguing. Later that night she looked out the window of her solitary chamber, observing the shadowy ships that crowded the wharves along the foreshore. Moonlight played over their various shapes as they swayed in the glittering blue-black ocean, their pennants streaming in the wind.

Which one would carry her to England? And what waited for her there?

Micheline slept alone again, dreaming fitfully of Andrew, until her door opened in what seemed to be darkness and his voice urged her gently, "Dawn is breaking, Michelle, and we must sail with the tide."

An hour later she found herself on a trim, tastefully appointed yacht called the *Stargazer*. The waves were rather choppy under the lavender-gray sky, but the wind was with them. Once the sails were set, Andrew joined Micheline on deck. His normal good temper was returning now that they'd left France behind and England lay just a few hours away.

"Wherever did you get this magnificent craft?" queried Micheline.

Culpepper, in the act of tying off a line, shot a look at his friend.

"That's not important," Sandhurst said in a tone that was light and firm at once. "What is important is that we have a comfortable means of travel across the Channel. Do you know, I surprise myself, but I'll own that I'm happy to be returning to England!"

"Are you happy that I'm with you?" she asked, eager by now for some reassurance.

"Yes, of course I am." Seeing Micheline shiver in the sea air, he put an arm around her and held her close, then sought what seemed to be a safer topic. "I nearly forgot to tell you—St. Briac is going to send all of your clothes and other possessions on to London."

Micheline was surprised. She'd nearly forgotten the abundance of gowns, jewels, and accessories she'd accumulated in anticipation of her marriage to the Marquess of Sandhurst.

"That's nice, I suppose... though it's a relief to know I won't really need all of that once we're married. I truly will prefer a simpler life."

"I am contrite that I haven't even provided you with a maid."

"But, I don't miss that in the least! Playfair is acting as chaperon, isn't he? And after we're married, I'd much rather have you all to myself. Servants only get in the way. Why would I want a maid when I'll have a husband to brush my hair and unfasten my gowns?" Her expression was sensually radiant.

Sandhurst shut his eyes for a moment, wishing he didn't have to think at all. "Why don't you go below?

There's food and wine in the cabin, and you'll find a few books as well."

Although she would have preferred to stay with him, something in his eyes made her obey. When he took on that remote look, it worried her. Most perplexing was the fact that she couldn't explain to herself why he was keeping himself so distant. The possibility existed that he didn't really want to marry her, that she'd forced his hand with her blatant words and actions in his bed at the Jouberts'. That thought was enough to make her grateful for the distraction of books waiting below.

Rough seas lengthened the crossing, and it was dark when the yacht anchored at Dover. Andrew had decided that a hot supper at a small inn called the Hand-in-Hand would do them ail good, but afterward he intended to sail the remainder of the way up the Thames to London. As much as a part of him dreaded returning to his real life and telling Micheline the truth, he was eager to end his charade.

After supper they cast off under a bright full moon and charted a northeasterly course along the coastline toward the North Foreland, at which point they could turn west and sail directly for London. Micheline remained on deck for a time, wrapped in a heavy woolen cloak that she'd found in the cabin. It smelled tantalizingly of Andrew, and she wondered, not for the first time, how he had come by this yacht.

"You must be awfully cold," he remarked, glancing up from his charts.

"Only a bit." In truth, she felt better than she had since they'd left Paris. Andrew seemed more relaxed, and though everything that lay ahead was unknown, Micheline felt as if she were being borne into the future on the hands of fate. It seemed that whatever happened would be for the best.

He had crossed the deck and reached out to trace the line of her cheek. "We won't be in London until daybreak, fondling. The bunk in the main cabin is quite comfortable. Why don't you get some sleep?"

The sight of his handsome, moon-silvered face squeezed her heart with emotion. "I'll go on one condition."

"Name it." Andrew's smile flashed in the dark.

"Will you come with me and kiss me good night? I've been so lonely at bedtime...."

"All right, if you'll promise not to test my powers of endurance."

Happily she led the way below. In the cabin Andrew leaned against the bulkhead and tried not to look as Micheline stripped off her clothing swiftly, then climbed into the snug bunk, still wearing her chemise.

"Tuck me in," she said, beaming.

"It's time you learned the way we say things in England, my darling."

"Pray instruct me."

He leaned closer, his eyes warm as he tightened the covers around her slim body. "You see, I'm tucking you *up.*"

"I shall try to remember."

Sandhurst smiled in a way that melted her heart. He stroked her hair, which resembled dark cognac spilling over the pillow. "It won't matter what you say, Michelle. Everyone will love you... just as I do."

"Don't forget my good-night kiss."

He cupped her face in his golden-brown hands and bent toward her. She felt pleasantly dizzy when his parted lips gently touched her own, slowly savoring each taste and sensation for a long minute. She wanted to twine her arms about his neck and longed to feel the length of his body against hers, but remembered her promise.

Finally Sandhurst lifted his head and sighed. "I'd better go above before Jeremy crashes the *Stargazer* into Ramsgate."

Micheline whispered, *"Bon nuit, mon cher."*

He rose and walked away, but paused near the bulkhead to look back at her. "Good night, Michelle. Tomorrow will be an eventful day. Sleep well and remember... I love you."

* * *

Micheline awoke before dawn, filled with excitement. Having found a stoppered jug of fresh water, a basin, and a cube of castile soap, she washed and then donned clean undergarments and a gown of azure figured velvet, its low square bodice trimmed with pearls and gold lace. After she combed her long curls and tucked them into a golden crispinette, Micheline ventured from her cabin.

It was so quiet except for the sound of the river, and she had no idea where Andrew was, or where and whether he had slept during the night.

She found him on deck, looking rested and fresh. He wore a handsome doublet of tawny camlet that she had not seen before, and his hair was tousled in the breeze.

"Michelle! You're up early." Andrew crossed the deck to take her in his arms. "How beautiful you are."

Her only response was an incandescent smile. Sandhurst stared down at her, amazed by the magical glow that spread from her body to his, before bending to kiss her, wonderingly at first, and then more passionately, until Micheline's slim arms rounded his shoulders and her fingers tangled in his hair, pressing him closer still.

"Ah-hem!" Jeremy had to clear his throat repeatedly, in various noisy ways, before the couple seemed to notice him. "The Tower's in sight."

When Andrew released her, Micheline looked around curiously. A pale pink mist hovered over the Thames, but still she was able to make out the branching masts of vessels ahead on the river, and a forest of bare spires that rose above the endless maze of gabled rooftops.

London! They had arrived!

The closer they came, the more boats Micheline saw. The Thames was crowded, even at this hour, with vessels of every description.

"The city has such narrow streets that people would rather travel by water," Andrew explained.

"Look!" she exclaimed in delight, pointing at a trio of swans that passed the *Stargazer* in single file.

"You'll get used to them," he said, smiling, "and don't touch. They're fond of biting."

They sailed past the Tower, where the river ran through the bars of the Traitor's Gate, and soon approached London Bridge. There they dropped anchor, amid the larger trading ships, and before long Micheline found herself on a barge, being rowed through the rapids under the bridge in progress upriver.

When the barge drew up alongside a water gate that led to a splendid mansion of rose brick, Micheline was too awestruck by all she had seen to be surprised. This was obviously not Andrew's home, but only a means of reaching it, she reasoned. He handed her over to the first dry step while Jeremy dutifully paid the waterman.

Sandhurst was intending to sit with Micheline in the garden and tell her all, but his plan was spoiled by the appearance of one of his servants, who rushed down the steps to greet them as they came through the gate.

"Welcome home, my lord!" the boy cried enthusiastically. "We weren't sure if you'd ever come back!"

"Hello, Bartholomew," Sandhurst muttered, wincing when he heard the lad shout "Sir Jeremy" behind them.

Micheline's expression was confused. "Why does he call you 'my lord' and Playfair 'Sir Jeremy'?" The sight of his averted face sent a chill down her spine. "Andrew?"

"As it happens, I was just about to explain all that to you, Michelle." He led her over to a stone bench on the far side of the well-tended garden. The green shoots of daffodils and hyacinths were already poking up amid white, pink, and violet crocuses.

"Please, *do.*" Micheline exclaimed. "I have never been so puzzled. Whose house is this, and why are we here?"

Andrew stared out at the river, yet barely saw the fast-moving boats or the borough of Southwark on the south bank of the Thames. He sighed heavily, then turned to meet Micheline's urgent gaze.

"This house belongs to me, fondling, as does the *Stargazer.* Will you still love me if I tell you that I am not poor, but rich?"

"You know full well that I would love you in any condition, but I do not understand!"

"Wait. There's more. I have other revelations to share." He paused to let her absorb his words. "You should brace yourself."

She took a deep breath. "Continue."

"My name is not Selkirk, either, though it was my mother's name before she married. I don't make my living as a painter."

Micheline's head was spinning, and for a moment all she could think of was her discovery in December that Bernard had been a stranger all through their marriage, smiling and professing his love even as he deceived her.

"Sweet Michelle, it's time you knew the truth. I am Andrew Weston, Marquess of Sandhurst."

Twenty-One

"YOU'RE TEASING ME... aren't you?" Micheline whispered after a long moment of silence.

"You know I would not jest about something like this." Sandhurst took both her hands in his and found them cold as ice. "I know it's a shock, but I think that once you adjust to the idea, you'll find it quite agreeable."

"Agreeable?" she repeated weakly. "Should I rejoice that you have lied to me since the moment we met? Did everyone know? Were you all laughing at me behind my back?"

Closing his eyes for an instant, he sighed. "No one has laughed at you, fondling, and no one at Fontainebleau knew my true identity except Jeremy. I gather that St. Briac found out toward the end, but—"

"This must be a bad dream," Micheline said, pulling her hands free. "A few minutes ago I was so happy. I felt as if I were coming home, that London was embracing me, because I was with you and this was the place where we would make our life together. Now I learn that I don't know you at all. You're a stranger who has deceived me!"

"Of course you know me," Sandhurst protested. "The only difference is my surname. Michelle, I love you. Isn't that what counts?"

"How can I believe you?" Tears glistened in her beautiful eyes. "How can I believe anything you say, ever again?"

He raked a hand through his hair in desperation. "This isn't the place to discuss all of this, and there's a great deal that must be said. Let's go inside. You can see your rooms and freshen up, then we'll sit down and I'll try to explain how all this came about." Sandhurst gave her a hopeful smile, but Micheline dropped her eyes.

"*D'accord,*" she sighed. "I don't seem to have any choice, do I?"

As they walked side by side up the neat gravel pathways that led from the garden to a handsome arched doorway, Micheline kept her eyes averted from him.

Inside the great hall, with its carved paneling and beamed ceiling, an old woman and man waited to greet their master. The affection that shone in their eyes bolstered Andrew's spirits.

"Michelle, I'd like you to meet Throgmorton, my head steward, and Mistress Goodwyn, who runs Weston House for me." Smiling at the two servants, he explained, "This is Madame Micheline Tevoulère. She will be staying with us." He wanted to introduce her as his future wife, but couldn't be certain himself if that was still the case.

Mistress Goodwyn, a small, white-haired, rosy-cheeked woman, came forward first to embrace Andrew. Since she had been lady's maid to the Duchess of Aylesbury in her youth and had watched this boy come into the world, it was impossible for her to keep a respectful distance.

"Welcome home, my lord." She kissed his cheek. "I've been worried about you."

"I appreciate that, Nan. As you can see, I am quite well." He turned then to clasp Throgmorton's outstretched hand. The old man, who had been a page in the last duke's household, was stooped now and nearly bald, but his mind was as sharp as ever.

"We've missed you, my lord," he intoned, then allowed a warm smile to stretch over his wrinkled face. "It's good to see you home safe."

"Madame Tevoulère will need a lady's maid, Nan," Sandhurst remarked. "I was thinking of Mary. She seems a sweet girl."

"That's true, my lord, but she's had no training as a lady's maid."

"I don't mind," Micheline interjected in her perfect, lightly accented English. "I'm not used to having my very own maid, either, so we can learn together."

Mistress Goodwyn pursed her lips. "I'll tell the girl, then. She'll be over the moon, I'll warrant!"

"Would you show Madame Tevoulère to the rose room? And perhaps Bartholomew can take her belongings upstairs."

"Aye, my lord." They both nodded.

Micheline followed the old woman up a broad wooden staircase with splendidly carved newel posts, handrails, and balustrade. It was quite unlike the curving stone staircases in France.

"What a magnificent house," Micheline said to fill the silence.

"Oh, Weston House isn't much compared to Sandhurst Manor, or Aylesbury Castle for that matter, but it's much cozier. Lord Sandhurst bought it himself, you know, with his own earnings from the horses he breeds in Gloucestershire." Reaching the top step, Mistress Goodwyn turned back to look at the young Frenchwoman. "I've served the aristocracy all my life, madame, and Lord Sandhurst is the finest nobleman I've ever known."

"It would seem that he is fortunate to have you."

"Lord Andrew's a love. Even as a child he was a love. And so handsome! If only the duke weren't so mean-spirited... and if the duchess hadn't died, Lord Sandhurst would be a happy man today, just as he was happy as a child." Mistress Goodwyn led Micheline down the corridor, still talking. "That's not to say that he's *unhappy*, but these troubles with his father have cast a shadow over his life. I've always said that all Lord Andrew needs is the true love of a good woman, but he's slow to trust." She opened a paneled door and stepped aside so that Micheline could enter first.

Micheline could find no response to the housekeeper's speech, so instead she turned her attention to her spacious, charming room. The gardens and the distant river could be viewed through tall sparkling windows, a few of their diamond panes stained blue and rose. There was an enormous bed with carved posts, and the counterpane, curtains, and valance to the tester were all embroidered in rose and ivory. Pretty pale pink dried rosebuds were scattered among the fresh herbs on the floor.

"It's simply lovely," Micheline murmured.

"A lady's room," nodded Mistress Goodwyn. "It's usually used only when Lady Cicely comes to visit, which isn't often enough to suit me!" Shaking her head, she returned her attention to the visitor from France. "Are you here long?"

Micheline flushed. "I'm not certain, Mistress Goodwyn."

"Well, it's good to have a lady in the house!" she approved. "Would you like a bath?"

"That would be delightful."

"Is there anything else I can do to assist you, madame?"

"It would please me if you would call me Micheline."

The housekeeper blinked in surprise, then nodded. "As you wish—Micheline." Mistress Goodwyn's expression showed her curiosity about who this young lady might be, and why she was here.

* * *

Downstairs Sandhurst was served a frosty tankard of ale and seated himself in the winter parlor to consider what to say to Micheline. Jeremy had gone home, so at least he wasn't there to remind him of the coil he'd managed to ensnarl himself in. The more Andrew thought about it, the more dismal he felt. Why *should* Micheline ever trust him again? Especially in light of what she'd told him about her philandering husband, he could certainly see her point.

Perhaps a half hour had passed, during which he'd observed serving girls carrying buckets of steaming water upstairs for Micheline's bath, when Throgmorton appeared in the doorway.

"Lady Dangerfield is here to see you, my lord."

Before Sandhurst could tell him to send her away, Iris brushed past the steward and ran to kneel at Andrew's side.

Lifting his brows helplessly, he murmured, "That will be all, Throgmorton."

"Yes, my lord."

Iris buried her face in his lap. "Oh, my darling, you are home at last! I have come almost daily, praying that you would have returned, and now my prayers have been answered."

"I wasn't aware that you were on such intimate terms with God." His tone was dry.

She raised her head and regarded him through narrowed green eyes. "Are you not happy to see me? You left London without a word, which was exceedingly rude of you, but I have overlooked your bad manners. For nearly two months I haven't known if you were alive or dead. I've been frantic!"

"How is Timothy?" he wondered.

"What?"

"Timothy Dangerfield. Your husband." He reached for his tankard of ale, purposely avoiding her eyes.

"Why do you speak of him at such a moment?" She reached up, clinging to his soft doublet. "Have you not missed me, my lord? Have you not hungered for me as I hunger for you?"

"Iris... you are married to another man, and from what I heard in February, Timothy was growing weary of your infidelity. Perhaps it would be prudent for you to turn your attention to your marriage."

"I don't want Timothy!" Now she attempted to sit on his lap. "I want *you!*"

Sandhurst sighed. "There's no point in living in a fantasy world, Iris, which is exactly what you've been doing for the better part of four years. You are another man's wife."

She drew back and stared him. "That never bothered you before. When did you acquire scruples, my lord?"

He had to smile at that. "Something amazing has

happened. You see, I am in love for the first time in my life, and I hope to make that lady my wife."

"What nonsense!" she cried. "You, in *love*? Ridiculous. Next you'll tell me it's that French whore people are saying the duke is forcing you to marry."

His brows came together. "That's enough, Iris." He reached up to lift her off his lap. "You'd better leave."

"No. You are talking such foolishness only because you have been away so many weeks. After you're used to being home again, you'll want things the way they were!" She snuggled against him, searching for his lips, her arms twined like thin bands of steel around his neck.

As Sandhurst moved to separate their bodies, he saw Micheline stepping into the doorway. She wore an enchanting gown of yellow silk and her brandy-hued curls arranged over her shoulders. In the first instant she had been smiling tentatively, but then horror transformed her expression. Before Andrew could push Iris away and speak to her, she fled.

* * *

"Damn!"

Iris wondered at his curse. She, too, had seen the girl in the doorway and suddenly felt more curious than amorous. "Was that your lady love?" she inquired archly.

Out of patience, Sandhurst roughly set her away from him. "Don't you have somewhere to go?"

"I hope that the rumors I've been hearing aren't true! Don't tell me that you've given in to your father and mean to marry a stranger. I thought that you were a man!"

"Iris, I am asking you to leave." Muscles clenched in his jaw as he stood up. "If you must badger someone, go home and badger your husband. He's earned that honor, and perhaps it will cause him to believe you really care."

With that, Sandhurst strode out of the room, but his outrage ebbed halfway up the staircase. Now he would be dealing with Micheline, and this would be delicate work.

Arriving at her door, he knocked but there was no answer. "Michelle? Are you there?"

Her only response was a muffled sob. Sighing, he opened the door and beheld the woman he loved sitting on the embroidered counterpane, weeping as if her heart had broken.

"Please... leave me alone."

He took a deep breath and crossed to sit beside her on the bed. "I realize that what you saw downstairs just now looked rather incriminating, but I assure you that there is a logical explanation."

Micheline raised her tear-stained face. "I know how adept you men are at explaining such things. I've been all through this before, but the only difference is that my eyes are open now. I won't be made a fool of a second time—and I won't smile docilely while you make a mockery of my honest emotions."

"For God's sake, Micheline, I am *not* Bernard Tevoulère!"

"That's true. At least he told the truth about his *name* and his background, and he managed to refrain from engaging in passionate embraces with other women when he was in the same house with me." Her voice was bitter.

"Christ!" Sandhurst didn't know where to even begin. What had been complicated enough an hour ago was now a tangled mess.

"Do you know, after talking to your loyal Mistress

Goodwyn a while ago, I was prepared to listen to your story with an open mind," Micheline said. "That was what I went downstairs to tell you. Rather pathetic, isn't it? I suppose I must be one of those people who never learn. However, I don't need to have my nose rubbed in the truth. It's very clear now."

"And what is that?" he asked, sensing that he wouldn't like the answer.

"I cannot stay here. Obviously you have been playing some sort of game ever since the day you arrived in France. It wasn't enough to arrange a marriage with a stranger; you had to make me fall in love as well. I was right the first time, when I made up my mind to avoid love at all costs. I was right when I told Aimée that it brings more pain than pleasure. You've managed to make my worst nightmare a reality, Andrew."

"Now, that's enough." Sandhurst gripped her slim shoulders with strong hands. "You are wrong, Micheline. Why don't you give more credit to your instincts? You trusted me from the moment our eyes first met at Fontainebleau, and you were right."

She turned her face away, tears spilling onto his fingers. "Let me go."

"Not until you've listened to what I have to say." He sighed harshly. "Won't you look at me, fondling?"

"No," she whispered. "You'll cast some sort of spell on me with your eyes."

Andrew almost laughed at that. "Have it your way." He reached up to brush the back of his forefinger over her wet cheeks. "Please, do not cry."

The sensation of his tanned finger caressing her face filled Micheline with a bittersweet yearning. "I thought you had something to say, my lord."

"So I do, but I wish you wouldn't call me 'my lord.'" She did not answer, and kept her face averted, so Sandhurst plunged onward. "First I should tell you about Iris, or rather Lady Dangerfield. She is part of my past, and that is where I want her—in the past. I never loved her. Michelle, she is nothing compared to you! Perhaps her feelings were stronger than mine and that was what you saw today. I told her that I was in love for the first time in my life and that I mean to be married. When you walked in Iris was...endeavoring to change my mind, but I put her from me immediately."

There was such desperate honesty in his voice that Micheline's heart was swayed. "Assuming, for the moment, that I did believe you, what about this lady? How long has this *friendship* between you endured?"

"Oh, perhaps two years, but—"

"How could you be such a beast?" she accused. "That poor woman! How must she feel, if she has loved you so long and suddenly you turn up with a new choice for your wife?"

Sandhurst blinked. Was there no possible escape from this coil? "Iris couldn't have become my wife in any case, Michelle! She's married to another man."

Her mouth dropped open. "You speak of your adultery as if it will excuse all your other sins."

His patience, worn to shreds, tore at that moment. "Enough of this! Am I going to be held accountable for every mistake I ever made up to the night we met? Three nights ago in Paris you wept and begged me to understand why you said certain things and acted the way you did during our weeks at Fontainebleau. Because I love you, I listened to your story with not just an open mind but an open heart as well. I'm asking you now to put aside the pain Bernard caused you and judge me as a person. I want to tell you what brought me to Fontainebleau, and I ask you to remember that if I had not come under another name, we would not have met at all, for I would never have married a stranger."

Her lower lip trembled. "I suppose you will tell me next that your code of ethics would have prevented you from taking part in an arranged marriage."

"Unfair! Curb your tongue for a few minutes and attend me." Sandhurst rose to pace the sunlit room. "I'll not claim that my life had been tragic, but I have had my own reasons to distrust love. I never agonized over it. It simply never occurred to me that I could fall in love, and, frankly, I didn't care to. My mother died five years ago, but even when she was alive and I was young, there was no warmth between my parents. As for the duke, few people could surpass his talent for appearing singularly unlovable. And there are other family members who have helped to spur my desire for independence. I went away to Oxford at sixteen and have lived on my own ever since."

"What about the sister you painted who couldn't sit still?" Micheline wondered.

"Cicely?" He looked back, his features softening. "She's my one regret in my estrangement from my father. But this isn't the time to delve into my family relations. First things first." Andrew paused next to the bed. "I suppose that the walls I erected between myself and my father carried over into other areas. That's why my relationship with Lady Dangerfield was so convenient. It met certain of my needs, and yet I could remain detached."

"What made you seek this arranged marriage with me?" Micheline asked softly, puzzled.

"I didn't. The duke—my father—arrived here one day in February and announced the bloody thing to me! He and the king had made all the plans, and if I didn't go through with it, all the family estates and wealth would pass to my illegitimate twit of a half brother, Rupert Topping."

"But I was told that you had a weakness for Frenchwomen!"

Sandhurst smiled dryly. "I know. St. Briac mentioned that. Quite amusing. I, on the other hand, was told that someone in the French court wanted to get rid of you and had asked King Henry to find you an English husband. Enter my father, who had been nagging me to marry and provide him with an heir. I was caught like a rabbit in a trap."

"I don't understand! Why were we told different stories?"

"Who knows?" He shrugged. "My instincts tell me that Anne d'Heilly was behind the plan. The king's unrequited desire for you threatened her. Yet it hardly seems important now. Once the thing was agreed upon, it took on a life of its own." Sandhurst paused, staring out the window. "I struggled against the trap. I told my father to go to the devil and take King Henry with him. I didn't care if I lost my inheritance... until Jeremy reminded me that Rupert would have everything that would have gone to my children. He had a point. Odds were that I would marry one day, and I did want children. I couldn't agree to marry a stranger for that reason alone, though, so Jeremy and I hit on a compromise."

It all fell into place in Micheline's mind then. "You decided to go to France and have a look at me," she supplied.

Andrew smiled ruefully. "It seemed a great adventure at the time, and it was a perfect counter-strategy against my father." He dropped down beside her on the bed and lifted one of Micheline's delicate hands. "To be honest, I never expected anything to come of it. I half hoped I'd find you repulsive so that I would feel completely justified in spitting in the duke's face... and theoretically in the king's as well."

She felt the corners of her mouth turning up. "It didn't quite work out the way you planned, did it?"

"Oh, Michelle." Sandhurst closed his eyes for a moment as a warm rush of emotion swept over him. "I think I was lost when I first saw you on the staircase at Fontainebleau. I didn't even know who you were! I was standing with Anne d'Heilly. I asked her your name, and when she replied, I was stunned. Of course, I wasn't thinking in terms of love then. What drove me mad for so long was your seeming indifference! Every time you pushed me away and declared that you were betrothed to the Marquess of Sandhurst, I burned with jealousy."

"For yourself?" she murmured, swallowing irrepressible laughter.

"That's what Jeremy kept saying. He'd shout. 'But that's *you!*'" Andrew chuckled at the memory. "I didn't care. All I knew was that you were rejecting me for a stranger. It drove me mad, and I was determined that if I couldn't win you on my own merit, there would be no wedding."

All of Micheline's outraged anger seemed to be melting away, but enough doubt lingered to prompt her to wonder, "Andrew, how can you be certain that your feelings for me are rooted in love rather than in the challenge of winning me?"

"I'm not a boy; I'm a grown man. I knew real love when I found it." Leaning forward, his mouth grazed her cheek. "In any case, I could ask the same of you. You thought you loved Tevoulère, but in Paris you told me that you never knew love until you met me. How do I know that you are not merely infatuated?"

"Point taken." She smiled. "I suppose the time has come for both of us to listen to our hearts."

"Can we forget about the past," Andrew murmured, kissing her parted lips gently, "and make a fresh beginning?"

"Yes, Lord Sandhurst, I think we can."

His arms encircled her body with tantalizing slowness, until they were embracing. Micheline moaned with a mixture of relief and desire as their mouths came together. The past few hours she had felt like a ship cut loose from its mooring, but now she was home again.

"Madame?" A knock sounded at the door.

Sighing in frustration, Sandhurst got up to answer it. "Yes, Throgmorton, what is it?"

"Oh, excuse me, my lord, I didn't know you were here!" The old man actually appeared to blush. "It's just that—dinner is served... and Master Topping has arrived. He's already taken a place at the table."

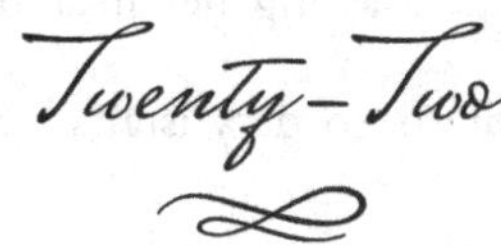

"FIRST IRIS AND NOW *RUPERT.*" Sandhurst groaned, throwing up his hands. "Why don't we just have a ball and invite the whole of London?"

Throgmorton coughed, uncertain whether a response was desired by the marquess. "My lord, I..."

"Never mind, Throgmorton. I appreciate the warning. We shall be down presently."

"Yes, my lord."

When the door was closed, Andrew rubbed tense fingers over his face. "Argh!"

Micheline couldn't help smiling. "Didn't you say that Rupert is a twit? Poor thing. He probably worships you."

Rolling his eyes, Sandhurst returned to the bed and threw himself back on it. "You don't know the half of it."

"You ought to make an effort to be kind to him."

"Don't say things like that until you've spent an hour in Rupert's company. He's absolutely—" He searched in vain for a word to describe his half brother.

The sight of him sprawled on his back across the sun-drenched bed was more temptation than Micheline could resist. Mischievously she hitched up her skirts and crawled over to rest her face against his neck, breathing in the clean scent of his pleated white fraise. His arm rounded her back, drawing her near until her breasts pressed his ribs.

"I don't want to go downstairs," Sandhurst complained.

"We must."

"I have all the sustenance I need right here." Turning on his side to face her, he slowly ran his right hand down Micheline's spine as they shared a sweet, lingering kiss.

"You have a guest, my lord," she reminded him, even as arousal coursed through her veins.

"The devil take my guest," he muttered. He kissed her again, then a third time. "As for dinner, you are infinitely more delicious than mere food."

Micheline pushed weakly at his chest. "I thought you said that we would not make love again until we were married."

"I've reconsidered my position on that matter."

His mouth seemed to scorch her throat, and her breasts were already tingling within her bodice, but Micheline summoned all her powers of resistance. "I would rather stay here with you, Andrew, but this is my first day in your home, and the impression I make could be lasting. I really think that we ought to go downstairs."

Sandhurst sighed heavily and released her, sitting up. "You're right, of course." He shook his head dazedly. "I must be going mad."

Crossing to the mirror, Micheline laughed and surveyed her radiant reflection. A quick application of her brush tamed the few wayward curls that flowed loose down her back. Andrew was waiting in the doorway.

"After you," he said with an ironic flourish, following Micheline into the corridor.

Minutes later, they were entering the parlor where Rupert Topping sat alone at a long table set for three.

Micheline smiled with an effort, for she was more inclined to gape. Was it possible that this thin, pasty, ferret-faced person could be a blood relation of Andrew's? The young man who approached them was barely taller than she, with lank brown hair, small nervous eyes, long teeth, and a receding chin. He wore a doublet of apple-green satin, rings, neck chains, sleeve brooches, and garters set with rubies below bony knees. His large feet, encased in spade-shaped shoes, pointed outward when he walked.

"Sandhurst! You're home! Everyone's been so worried about you! Where've you been?" he exclaimed loudly, arms outstretched.

Andrew extended his hand, avoiding the brotherly embrace Rupert sought. "Hello, Rupert. Allow me to present Madame Micheline Tevoulère, my future wife."

"What? What?! Did I hear correctly? *Wife?*" Letting out a rather manic laugh, he turned to Micheline. "Bunjar! Ha-ha, as they say in France, what? Well, well, I must say, this *is* a surprise!"

Somehow she managed to disguise her true reaction, smiling instead and replying, "It is a pleasure to meet you, M'sieur Topping."

"I say!" Rupert ejaculated, peering up at Sandhurst. "She speaks English! Well *done,* old boy!" He then turned to grab Micheline's hand and kissed it wetly. "None of this *mon-seer* folderol for us! I'm family, after all! You must call me Rupert and I'll call you Micheline."

At that point she could not resist a bit of mischief. "How sweet of you, *Roo-pair*!"

He stared, then laughed nervously. "Perhaps you ought to practice that a bit, Micheline. In England we say Ru*pert*."

Andrew wanted to turn and leave right then, taking Micheline with him, but the servants were entering with platters of food. "I'm ravenous," he said. "Let's sit down."

They took their places, with Sandhurst at the head of the table and Micheline and Rupert on either side, facing each other. Wine was poured, followed by mussel and fennel stew with dumplings.

"How different the food is here!" marveled Micheline after her first bite of dumpling.

Sandhurst smiled fondly. Her hair, set a-sparkle by the sun, tumbled down to frame an exquisitely lovely face. At that moment, however, his favorite feature was Micheline's right cheek, which bulged out because of the dumpling she could not bear to swallow.

"You look adorable!" he chuckled. "Try to get that bite down, fondling, and then I'd advise you to try a slightly less adventurous approach to any foods you don't recognize. You mustn't expect to become English in one day!"

"You mean to say that there are no dumplings in France?" Rupert appeared genuinely distressed by that possibility. "Lucky thing I hate traveling! Couldn't live without my dumplings!"

Remembering Rupert's nerve-racking French accent, Micheline wanted to say that his unwillingness to leave home was lucky for France as well, but she held her tongue.

Sandhurst, meanwhile, gave his half brother a sharp sidelong glance. "That reminds me. Why are you here, Rupert? It really wasn't necessary for you to come all the way from Yorkshire just to call on me."

A salad of purslane, tarragon, and watercress was served, then fresh pink shrimp, and pike with gooseberry sauce. Rupert tasted everything before replying. "I'd travel any distance for you, Sandhurst. You know that! I'd go to any lengths, suffer any hardship, if it meant that—"

"I know, I know. Spare me the discourse on your familial devotion and tell me why you're in London."

"Well..." Rupert shifted uneasily in his chair and darted a look at Micheline. "You see, the duke sent me south to find out what's happened to you. He was rather concerned that you might have, uh—flown the coop, if you take my meaning."

"Fine. Now you can return to Aylesbury Castle and tell him that I only 'flew' as far as France. I wanted to meet Madame Tevoulère before sentencing her to a lifetime of my company. Fortunately for me, the lady seems to like me well enough." When Micheline laughed softly and reached out to touch his cheek, he caught her hand before adding dryly, "I'm certain that Father will be vastly relieved to learn how pleased I am with the arrangement."

"Oh, yes, I'm sure he will!" Rupert said. "He's been brooding awfully about this, imagining that you were plotting some scheme to undo all his plans, but I did my very best to reassure him! I've always taken your side, Sandhurst, since you're never present to defend yourself."

"I've told you before that I'd rather you wouldn't."

"God's toes, I'll be so happy when Lent is over!" Rupert was exclaiming. "Fish, fish, fish! Not that you haven't got a fine cook, Sandhurst, but I'm sick to death of the stuff. The castle gamekeeper brought down a magnificent red deer last week, and we've all been salivating in anticipation!"

Sandhurst met Micheline's eyes, his brows flicking upward almost imperceptibly. A serving girl appeared with a covered dish of spinach fritters, one of which Micheline tasted tentatively.

"This is very good!" When Andrew gave her a look of dubious amusement, she smiled. "Truly!"

"At least they're not fish," Rupert put in.

Casting about for a topic that might be bearable, Andrew inquired, "How fares my sister Cicely?"

"Her health is fine." Suddenly he was intent on his half-eaten pike.

"And otherwise?"

"As you know, I don't like to carry tales, but I must say that Cicely hasn't been particularly agreeable lately. Patience, who is unwaveringly sweet-tempered, as you will remember, has tried to interest our sister in the coming wedding, yet the girl continues to sulk about the castle. She hasn't done your case with the duke any good, for Cicely continues to insist that you won't be getting married. She says that you didn't want any part of it, and that you were very angry about the whole situation." Flushing under Sandhurst's cold stare, he cleared his throat. "Don't suppose that was very tactful of me, what? My apologies, Micheline."

She gave him a charming smile. Dinner had begun to take on the proportions of a comedy as far as she was concerned, and nothing could dampen her amusement.

"Take heart!" Rupert reassured her. "There's at least one person at Aylesbury Castle who will be kind to you, and that's my dear wife, Patience. She has already begun airing her wedding dress in case you didn't bring one from France!"

"We will *not* be needing Patience's gown," Sandhurst stated flatly.

Looking offended, Rupert tried to thrust out his receding chin. "She wishes only to help."

"Please, tell your wife that I appreciate her kind thought," Micheline said. This fellow might be a twit, but clearly he couldn't help it.

Candied oranges and green walnut suckets, made by dipping the nuts in boiling syrup, finished the meal. After a while, Sandhurst suggested they take their spiced wine outside to the garden.

"I suppose you'll want to be on your way back to Yorkshire this afternoon, Rupert," he said when they were in the sunshine.

"I thought I might go to Hampton Court first. The duke would want me to pass along the news of your return to King Henry."

"Don't bother. I plan to take Micheline there myself within the next day or two, and I will speak to the king then."

Rupert glanced up at his half brother's face, about to protest, when he seemed to notice a telltale muscle flex in Andrew's jaw. "I meant only to save you the trouble."

"I have said this to you over and over, but it doesn't seem to sink in." Sandhurst stopped on the pathway and stared hard at the smaller man. "It's my life, Rupert. I'll take care of my affairs as I see fit, whether they involve my father, the king, or my marriage, and I would appreciate it if you would turn your attention to your own life."

For a moment Micheline was afraid that Rupert might begin to cry. His chin trembled as he nodded in reply and looked away toward the river. She found herself pitying him in the same way she pitied children whose high spirits were doused by hard-hearted parents. She wished she might appeal to Andrew, but he was walking away from them down the path, and the taut set of his shoulders told her that he would not soften on this issue.

In the next instant Rupert seemed to forget the unpleasantness. "Look!" he cried in a shrill voice, pointing downriver. "It's Anne Boleyn's new barge!" As if excited to know something Sandhurst didn't, he rushed forward to provide instruction. "You see, it used to be Queen Catherine's. Anne, I hear, grew so angry because the queen won't accept her new position as princess dowager that she had her chamberlain seize Catherine's barge on the Thames. The king knew nothing about it! Anne gave instructions that the queen's coat of arms should be erased, so the barge was then decorated in *Anne's* heraldic colors—blue and purple, with her own new coat of arms. Oh, my, how exciting! Can you see her at all? This has all happened in just the last two days. London is *buzzing!*"

Micheline shaded her eyes against the sunshine and tried to catch a glimpse of the barge's occupant as it passed Weston House. The boat was filled with liveried servants, but the one female sat in shadows—until she stood suddenly and waved to Sandhurst.

"I *say!* That was Anne Boleyn herself!" shouted Rupert. "I nearly forgot! You know her quite well, don't you, brother?"

"We're acquainted."

Micheline felt a twinge of jealousy when he raised his hand in greeting to Anne Boleyn. From a distance the Marquess of Pembroke appeared quite attractive. Jewels sparkled in her dark, her figure was fine, and she had a pretty smile that looked decidedly flirtatious to Micheline. When Andrew returned that smile, the twinge in her heart intensified.

"Is it true that Anne and the king were married secretly in January? I heard no confirmation in

France," Sandhurst said, wrapping an arm around Micheline.

"Oh, yes, it's open knowledge now," Rupert reported. "They say she's with child."

"I see." Andrew nodded, adding, "You'd better be on your way, Rupert, if you're going to take advantage of the daylight."

"Yes, of course. I'll go now. That reminds me—didn't I see Lady Dangerfield leaving here as I arrived at midday?" He attempted a conspiratorial wink. "I'll wager that's *one* person who didn't offer congratulations when told of your impending nuptials—though, of course, she won't be the only lady in London with a broken heart, eh what?"

Sandhurst closed his eyes for a moment and smothered an expletive. "Good-bye, Rupert!"

* * *

Andrew and Micheline spent the afternoon riding. He took her into the streets of London, which were so narrow and crowded with wagons, tumbrils, barrows, and drays that at times they couldn't move at all. The Strand had been so lovely, lined with the homes of the rich, that Micheline was rather unprepared for the filth and congestion that awaited her deeper into the city, but she viewed it all as an adventure, especially with Andrew next to her.

Cheapside was one of the few wide streets in London, and also the sight of the city's largest market. In a kaleidoscope of color and noise, country folk were wedged together behind trestle tables covered with baskets of their wares. The latter included everything from butter and eggs to sturgeon and shrimp. Micheline was fascinated by the sound of so many English voices as buyers and sellers haggled over the price and quality of the goods.

Sandhurst bought her a pretty box of comfits with a painting of London on its lid before they slowly wound their way back toward Weston House. Once in the Strand, however, he asked if she would enjoy some real exercise. Micheline smiled her assent and they rode on into the countryside below Charing Cross.

Before long they sighted a magnificent palace built along the riverfront, while new buildings had been erected covering acres and acres on the other side of the public thoroughfare.

"This is Whitehall Palace," Andrew explained. "It used to be Cardinal Wolsey's York Place, but he turned it over to the king five years ago. All of this"—he gestured to the sprawling profusion of galleries, towers, lodgings, and halls on their right—"has been built since then."

"Why would the cardinal give up such a splendid home?"

"Oh, it wasn't the first time. Hampton Court was Wolsey's too. This last gift, however, came at a time when the old cardinal had fallen from favor. The king expected him to efficiently arrange the divorce from Catherine of Aragon, and when that didn't come to pass, it proved Wolsey's downfall."

"Did he go to... the Tower?" Micheline had heard that a gruesome fate befell anyone sent to the Tower of London. English kings could condemn men to its dungeons on a whim. The prisoners were kept in dark rat-infested ceils to suffer horribly from the use of evil instruments of torture. Those spine-chilling tales had been confirmed that morning on the Thames, when she'd seen pirates hanging in chains from the Tower.

"No," Sandhurst replied, "but I'm sure Wolsey would have ended there if he hadn't died first."

A shiver ran down Micheline's back. "It seems harsh punishment for something that the cardinal may not have been able to control. I mean, the pope has final say, does he not?"

"You're right, fondling, but more than just the divorce brought Wolsey low. You know the intrigues that abound at a royal court. The cardinal was a shrewd, powerful man who made many enemies." He smiled grimly. "Be that as it may, I have never been intimately acquainted with the machinations of King Henry's court. I prefer to stay away as much as possible."

"Good." As they passed under one of the bridges recently built to connect the old palace with its new wings, Micheline reached out to Andrew and he grasped her hand firmly. "I never felt comfortable at Fontainebleau. I like a cozier home... and the company of only a few people whom I love and trust."

"We are of one mind." Sandhurst smiled, raising his eyebrows suggestively. "Twilight approaches. Why don't we return to my conveniently *cozy* home and explore this matter in greater depth?"

Twenty-Three

AFTER A LIGHT SUPPER, Andrew and Micheline adjourned to the second-floor library. A pile of letters and accounts due waited on Sandhurst's desk, so he sat down to review them while Micheline happily perused the bookshelves.

"What a wonderful collection!" she exclaimed.

He glanced up and smiled absently. "I'm glad you think so. The library at Sandhurst Manor is much more extensive, and perhaps I shouldn't allow you access to it."

She whirled around in alarm. "Why not?"

"There's always the possibility that you might bury yourself in books and forget about your husband."

There was a gleam in his eyes that made her blush. "You are wrong, my lord. That possibility does *not* exist if you are to be the husband in question."

"I do believe I am, unless the prospect of becoming Rupert's relative has given you second thoughts." Sandhurst spoke absently as he sorted through a stack of long-neglected business.

"Oh, no, I can tolerate Rupert," Micheline was replying. "I'm sure I'll deal perfectly well with your family. I must say, though, that it *is* difficult to comprehend that you and Rupert were sired by the same man!"

He broke the seal on a letter and smiled. "I'll take that as a compliment."

Deciding to venture forth a bit further on the subject of Rupert, Micheline said, "Actually I feel rather sorry for him. He seems to mean well, and although I understand why he irritates you, I can't help thinking..."

"Sweeting, at any other time I would love to chat with you, but right now I really must see to all this correspondence that's accumulated over the past two months."

Micheline turned to the books. A bright fire blazed in the white stone fireplace nearby, and there were beeswax candles in sconces on every vertical beam between the library shelves, affording Micheline enough light to read the titles.

There were volumes on every subject: philosophy, languages, proverbs, geography, medicine, chemistry, botany, and history. In addition, Micheline discovered volumes of poetry, songs, memoirs, drama, and even romance. Many she had already read and knew that English translations had been made, yet Andrew kept the original versions.

"I'm sorry to disturb you," she exclaimed after an hour had passed, "but I am so curious! Have you read all of these?"

"Hmm? Oh, yes, of course. Most of those books are duplicates of my favorites from the library at Sandhurst Manor," he answered without looking up.

Micheline was impressed. Her thoughts skipped back to the night they'd spent at Queen Eleanor's cottage, when she had been amazed to learn that the man she believed to be lowborn had been to school. Now it turned out that Sandhurst had not only attended Oxford but was apparently self-taught as well. They both had curious minds, and that was an important trait to have in common.

Another hour passed. Micheline settled down in a chair by the fire and looked through the large pile of books she'd chosen, trying to decide which to read first. A fifteenth-century romance by Olivier de la Marche, titled *Le Chevalier Délibéré*, piqued her interest. Leafing through the French text, she came upon an engraving that showed the chevalier outside a castle. The ramparts were lined with women, while on the ground a sad-faced young man held the reins of the knight's horse. Beneath the miniature a caption read: "How the Actor lost his way, and arrived in front of the Palace of Love, into which Desire bade him enter, while Remembrance held him back."

Micheline smiled. Less than a fortnight ago she had been faced with the same dilemma. Thank God she had made the right choice!

Pleasantly drowsy, she closed her eyes for a moment, only to open them a half hour later when Sandhurst knelt next to her chair and leaned forward to kiss the pulse at the base of her neck.

Micheline's heart leaped. "I must have dozed off."

He gave her an irresistible smile. "You are beautiful when you sleep. Vulnerable... soft..." He caressed the line of her cheek. "Warm... and fragrant."

"You must be finished with your work," she managed to tease as his mouth strayed downward toward her breasts.

"For tonight."

Andrew's warm, practiced lips were sending currents of fire through her body. She yearned to bury her face in his hair, to touch him, to surrender completely, but that morning she had made a decision that she was determined to carry out.

"I'm awfully tired, Andrew. It's been a long, exciting day."

"You're ready for bed," he supplied. "So am I. More than ready."

He helped Micheline up, looking slightly surprised when she brought the book from her lap along with them. Holding hands, they circled the library, extinguishing the candles, then emerged into the corridor. When Sandhurst stopped in front of a door down the corridor from her own, Micheline feigned surprise.

"This is not my bedchamber!"

"I thought you might like to see where Lady Sandhurst will sleep," he told her softly.

"With Lord Sandhurst?"

Andrew smiled and opened the door. "That is the general idea, fondling."

Micheline beheld a chamber even more spacious and splendid than hers. Beautiful arched windows nearly covered the south wall overlooking the Thames, with a grouping of chairs in front of them. The walls were paneled in golden oak, broken only by a brick and stone fireplace. Tapestry rugs covered the floors, and there were magnificently carved dressers and chests, but the focal point of the room was a huge bed hung with dove-gray draperies hand-embroidered in blue. The covers were carefully folded back to reveal plump, inviting pillows and a down-filled tick. Micheline's eyes strayed to the table beside the bed, which held a candle, a small vase of crocuses, a decanter of wine, and two Venetian glass goblets.

"Wouldn't you be more comfortable inside? This corridor is rather drafty," Sandhurst murmured.

Micheline summoned her resolve. "I'll be happy to

go inside, and happy to spend days on end with you in that wonderful bed… when I am Lady Sandhurst." Reaching for his hand, which was warm and strong, she looked up at him. "I've been thinking about what you said to me two nights ago at the auberge, and I've decided you were right. Our next act of love will be on our wedding night."

"But when I said that, it was because you didn't know yet who I was. I felt dishonest."

"The fact remains that you were right, Andrew," she said steadfastly.

"I'm a *fool.*" He closed his eyes as if he were in pain and muttered, "One day I'll learn to keep my mouth shut."

"Do not pout," Micheline scolded fondly. "You're a strong man; you can wait a few weeks."

Remembering the tempestuous nature of their lovemaking, Sandhurst groaned.

"Will you walk me to my door and kiss me good night?" she coaxed.

"Oh, I see! You plan to torture me during this enforced celibacy."

Micheline laughed and led him down the corridor. Outside her door she turned and reached up to twine her arms around his neck. It was torture for her, too, when he caught her up against his hard body and their mouths came together. The pressure of his lips, the taste and sensation of his tongue fencing with hers, and the evidence of his arousal, plainly felt even through the layers of her gown and petticoat, combined to make her tremble in his embrace. They kissed for what seemed an eternity until Micheline's strength and reason ebbed, replaced by a throbbing hunger for Sandhurst.

Finally his lips moved to burn her throat, then her

ear, and he was whispering, "This is ridiculous. I promise to forgive you if you've changed your mind."

Micheline very nearly yielded, but somehow managed to cling to her position and murmur, "You'll thank me in our marriage bed."

With a heavy sigh Andrew released her and took a step backward. "Perhaps—if I live that long."

* * *

Two mornings later Micheline rose early to prepare for their journey to Hampton Court. She was filled with excitement and also a measure of trepidation. King Henry, Anne Boleyn, and the English court were unknown quantities. What if they disliked her because she was French, or because of something she might say amiss? Andrew might contend that he wished little contact with the royal court, but the fact remained that he was an marquess and would someday be a duke—and, God willing, she would be his wife, with English titles of her own.

Little Mary, her maid, made up in enthusiasm what she lacked in skill. The girl prepared a lavishly scented bath and washed Micheline's hair so thoroughly that she had to be told, gently, that it was clean enough. Helping her mistress dress, Mary rhapsodized endlessly about the utter perfection of every color, ribbon, and jewel that Micheline had chosen.

The decisions had been difficult. Finally, the night before, she had brought Sandhurst in to elicit his opinion, and had been vastly relieved when he confirmed her own first choice. The gown Micheline donned now for her first introduction to the English king was made of soft spring-green velvet, parted in front to show a petticoat of pale yellow silk, and the sleeves were puffed and slashed to reveal more yellow silk. The square-cut bodice was set with emeralds, while a delicate girdle of filigreed gold rode just above her hips.

Mary helped to dress Micheline's gleaming hair, parting it in the center and smoothing it into a golden crispinette sprinkled with emeralds. She had just added two thin gold necklaces and turned to assess her reflection in the mirror, when there was a knock at the door.

"It's nearly time to leave," Micheline said nervously "That must be his lordship."

After opening the door to admit Lord Sandhurst, Mary made a speedy exit when he silently inclined his head. Across the room Micheline stood in a ray of sunlight, looking utterly lovely and charmingly skittish all at once.

"I am terrified," she announced.

Sandhurst went to her and lightly caressed her flushed cheeks with the back of his hand. "You look dazzling and I am convinced you'll be a huge success. My only worry is that the king will fall madly in love with you and decide he would rather wed you than Anne!"

"I fear I would have to refuse him," she replied primly, smiling at the thought of such a scenario. "And then, to keep our heads, you and I would have to run away and live secretly, as commoners. We could take the name of Selkirk."

"You would rather be Mistress Selkirk than the queen of England?"

"Even the idea of a choice is laughable, my lord," Micheline answered, "for no queen on earth has you."

She gave him one of her beautiful, radiant smiles, and his heart swelled with love. "How fortunate I am," he whispered.

"Once again, we are of one mind."

Andrew kissed her tenderly, marveling at the rich emotions that flowed between their bodies.

"I brought you a gift," he murmured at length. "Kindly turn around."

Although Micheline would have preferred to go on kissing him, she obeyed. In the mirror she saw his tanned fingers clasp a beautiful necklace of diamonds and emeralds around the base of her throat.

"But it's magnificent!" she protested, thinking that she didn't deserve anything so grand and costly.

"It was my mother's. As the future Duchess of Aylesbury, all of her jewelry will be yours, Michelle."

"I shouldn't wear this until we are married."

"These edicts of yours about what cannot happen until we are married are becoming tedious," Sandhurst said dryly. "This particular necklace was left in my care, and I am making it a betrothal gift to you."

Hesitantly Micheline raised her slim fingers and touched first the gems, which were cool against her throat, and then Andrew's hands, which were warm.

"Thank you."

He smiled. "Let's away. The barge is waiting, and the hour advances."

When Sandhurst crossed the room to open the door for her, Micheline suddenly exclaimed, "How handsome you look! It was very selfish of me not to have noticed immediately."

Never before, when he was pretending to be Andrew Selkirk, had she seen him so elegantly garbed, and still he looked absolutely masculine. Sandhurst wore a close-fitting doublet of rich blue velvet set with cut diamonds and rubies. The pleats of his white fraise nearly grazed his jaw. White silk puffed through the light slashings on both sleeves and breeches, and below his left knee Sandhurst wore a gold garter set with a ruby, sapphire, and diamond.

"I didn't want you to think that I owned no fine clothing." Andrew replied, "but I confess that I prefer the sort of things I wore at Fontainebleau."

Reaching the doorway, Micheline ran a possessive hand over his chest. "You will be the most splendid man at Hampton Court, and I shall be the envy of every female who lays eyes on you."

"Good Lord." He laughed fondly. "Next you'll be fighting a duel over me."

"I would certainly do so if it were necessary," she replied, walking ahead of him into the corridor. Then Micheline glanced back and added brightly, "And I would win!"

* * *

The journey by barge up the Thames was as close to paradise as Micheline had ever come. Although accompanied by Mary and Finchley, Sandhurst's valet, and two watermen, the two lovers were in a world of their own. They lounged on cushioned seats, talking softly, drinking wine, kissing, and sharing a delicious meal packed for them by Sabine, the cook. The banks of the Thames were a light bright green now, and budding leaves covered the tree branches where larks, finches, and robins sang tributes to spring. Meanwhile, swans, mallard ducks, and dabchicks followed the barge to feed on the bits of bread Micheline scattered across the water.

Eventually Andrew broke the spell by murmuring into her ear, "There it is."

Micheline sat up straight. Ahead of them, sculpted gardens spread across the right riverbank, leading to low walls, more gardens with trees, and a sprawling mixture of towers, ramparts, and buildings of red brick and white stone. Pinnacles and chimneys topped the palace, rising skyward.

Suddenly her palms were damp. "Must we?"

"I fear so." Sandhurst nodded. "Do not worry, sweetheart. What have you to fear if I am by your side?"

"Quite true!" After fending for herself for so long, it was difficult for Micheline to remember that she was not alone anymore. "You won't leave me?"

"You know full well that it is my ardent wish to remain with you constantly—day and night!"

His eyes crinkled at the corners, bidding her to laugh and relax. With Andrew next to her it was easy to pretend that what lay ahead was just an amusing adventure.

* * *

It wasn't Hampton Court that intimidated Micheline so much as the strangers who waited for her there. She was used to grandeur in excess, and this palace, though certainly splendid, did not outshine Fontainebleau. In fact, as she walked with Sandhurst up the pathway from the river, he told her that it was common knowledge that King Henry had begun to expand and improve his residences only to compete with François.

Richly garbed courtiers and ladies strolled about the grounds, many of them coming over to greet Lord Sandhurst and meet his future bride. Micheline saw not only curiosity but disdain in their eyes and knew the latter sprang from the fact that she was French. When the noblemen spoke to Andrew as if she were an idiot who could not understand, it delighted her to reply for herself in flawless English.

Learning that the king had just finished his meal and

had not emerged from the palace, Sandhurst headed there first.

"Do you want to see your chamber? Perhaps you'd like to rest for a while." Even as he said this, he sensed her reply.

"Chamber? Are we staying overnight?"

"Michelle, we must. It would be rude to leave so abruptly, and in any case, the journey back would take four hours at night."

Her heart sank. Sighing, she accompanied him through two brick-paved courtyards that were surrounded by buildings. Entering a third, with a fountain in the center, Sandhurst turned into a doorway and led Micheline up a flight of stairs. At the top they encountered a servant.

"The Marquess of Sandhurst to see the king. Is he available?"

A few minutes later, after passing through several other presence chambers, they were ushered into Henry VIII's audience chamber. Although Micheline had been impressed with the magnificent rooms, when the king appeared it seemed that all the palace riches paled in comparison to his person.

Huge and bejeweled, Henry held out his arms in greeting.

"Sandhurst! How long it has been since you deigned to grace our court with your presence!"

Andrew smiled, hearing the note of sarcasm in the monarch's jovial voice. "My apologies, sire," he murmured in mock contrition, and bowed. "It is my honor to present to you my future bride, Madame Micheline Tevoulère."

"So, for once you have done as you were told. I might flatter myself that it was because of *my* influence, but obviously that was not the case." The king held out a pudgy be-ringed hand to Micheline, who touched it and curtsied gracefully. "How fortunate we are to have stolen such a beauty from France! I'll warrant that my friend François was loath to let you go, madame." A smile spread over his beefy face at that thought. "I bid you welcome."

"Thank you, Your Majesty. I am happy to be here."

The king raised his eyes to Sandhurst. "One can't help noticing that you have a gift for turning every ob-stacle into an advantage."

"In this case, I have only you and my dear father to thank, sire," he replied, his tone gently laced with irony. "You have presented me with the greatest treasure of my life."

Noting the glowing smile the Frenchwoman gave to her betrothed, King Henry cleared his throat in dismay. "I must say, it looks as if the two of you are in *love!*"

Sandhurst bit his lip to keep from laughing aloud. "Positively, sire. In fact, I can't help thinking that God must have used you as his instrument to bring us together."

The king, at odds with Pope Clement VII over his divorce, was pleased at the notion that Sandhurst might consider him a link with God. Wine and sweetmeats were served, whereupon Henry declared that he must hear the tale behind this happy romance.

Andrew recounted his tale in an entertaining man-ner, interrupted from time to time by his radiant la-dylove, who could not resist adding an anecdote or two of her own. As the story unfolded, however, the king found himself far more intrigued by the fact that the Marquess of Sandhurst had spent two months at Fontainebleau in the company of King François I. As soon as he could do so without appearing obvious, Henry exclaimed, "My dear Madame Tevoulère, you have so charmed me with your wit and beauty that I insist you meet my own Anne immediately! I know that she will be as overjoyed as I am to hear about your betrothal to Lord Sandhurst. I'll own we never thought this rogue could be tamed by true love!"

Micheline clearly had little choice. Minutes later she followed a page out of the audience chamber, reassured by Sandhurst's parting whisper: "I'll be with you soon."

No sooner had the door closed than Henry VIII turned to his least tractable nobleman. "I would have speech with you, Lord Sandhurst. Sit down, and heed me."

Suddenly Andrew wished that he were anywhere but at Hampton Court. Biting his lower lip, he reclined against the uncomfortable carved chair back and waited with a sense of foreboding to hear what his king had to say.

Twenty-Four

HENRY TOOK a long drink of wine, then swallowed a sweetmeat. "I must be brief." His tone was deceptively casual. "There's a tennis match at hand. Will you play?"

"If you wish it, sire," Sandhurst replied affably, wondering what was really on the shrewd monarch's mind.

"How readily you acquiesce, my friend! It gives me hope! May I be frank?"

"That would be my preference, sire."

"You know, of course, that I met with the French king this past autumn. We have been striving to help each other in dealing with the Emperor Charles V and also with the pope, who has made my divorce such a difficult business. King François claims that his sympathies lie with me, and indeed he has promised to meet with the pope to plead my case. Unfortunately this was not accomplished as swiftly as I had hoped. I could wait no longer to make the Marquess of Pembroke my wife. You understand, I'll warrant, being eager to wed Madame Tevoulère?"

"Naturally, sire." Andrew sipped his wine to hide a smile. No mention was made, of course, of Anne Boleyn's obvious pregnancy—the real reason for their sudden secret wedding in January.

"I wish that you would do a great service for your king, Sandhurst. There are not many men I would trust to execute such a plan, but I have always admired your intelligence and ingenuity. Hearing of your masquerade at the French court, I am newly convinced that you could carry off the most delicate of missions."

"You flatter me, sire."

Henry's small eyes grew penetrating. "I would like you to return to France after you and Madame Tevoulère are married. I understand that she is a great favorite of King François, and once it becomes known that you are indeed the Marquess of Sandhurst, no doubt the two of you would be the toast of that court. I would have you cultivate the king's friendship, so that you might win his confidence... and travel with him when he meets with Pope Clement. There is much that you could learn through your various connections in the French court, and this service would earn you my sincere gratitude. As you know, I am quite generous with those who serve me well."

Setting down his goblet, Sandhurst met the king's stare unflinchingly. "I appreciate the compliment that you pay me, sire, but I am afraid that I must decline your request. My first concern at the moment is Micheline and the new life we are embarking on together. You know my family, and I am sure you will understand that they, combined with her adjustment to a new country, culture, and title, constitute a challenge that demands all our attention for the moment. I regret that we cannot consider returning to France at this time."

Sandhurst didn't add that, in any case, he would never spy on King François, nor did he care for whatever forms of gratitude Henry might care to show.

"What other Englishman would dare refuse his king?" Henry wondered in a voice that betrayed anger and grudging admiration. "I hardly know how to react! This time I'll let your rebelliousness pass, since you have, after all, done my bidding by agreeing to marry Madame Tevoulère."

"Your Majesty has a benevolent spirit," Sandhurst assured the king as humbly as he was able, adding an engaging smile for good measure. "Ascribe my foolishness to Cupid! No doubt his arrow has affected my reason. Let's away to the tennis courts, sire. Once you've beaten me soundly, your humor will improve."

* * *

Downstairs Micheline followed the page into a wing that was peopled with servants wearing blue and purple livery. Embroidered on the doublets was the legend "La Plus Heureuse." This made Micheline bristle before she ever met the future queen. How dare she proclaim herself "the most happy"—in *French,* no less!—when she was married to that pompous, corpulent man upstairs? Obviously the woman had no idea what happiness could be!

Gradually it began to occur to Micheline that she and Anne Boleyn might have different conceptions of the word. When she entered the bedchamber of the marquess, after being announced by a properly liveried page, Micheline found herself in a setting even grander than the one upstairs. All the wood was gilded, and carved with lover's knots that featured the initials *H* and *A* entwined. Golden vases filled with red and white roses reposed on every piece of valuable furniture, and the enormous, elaborately carved bed was hung with tissue of gold. In the midst of all this a young woman stood in a chemise, corset, and shakefold, surrounded by what Micheline assumed were dressmakers. Fabulous gowns that defied description were draped over chairs while Anne Boleyn chose from dozens of furs that were held up for her inspection.

When the page announced Micheline, Anne turned to greet her with a smile.

"Ah! You must be Sandhurst's little French girl! Do you speak English?"

"Yes. It is a pleasure to meet you, my lady."

"Oh, my! Andrew's good fortune has triumphed again! He's found beauty and intelligence in one package—and it was all by chance! Do sit down, madame. Would you care for some wine?"

Feeling rather overwhelmed at this point, Micheline accepted. A goblet of gold embedded with diamonds was presented to her. Anne Boleyn had returned her attention to the furs, and Micheline watched her with interest.

The future queen was not beautiful. Her skin was sallow, her face was rather long, and she had almost no bosom, yet there was a compensating loveliness about her black eyes, slender neck, and finely arched brows. Micheline had heard that Catherine of Aragon was sober and pious, so it seemed likely that Henry had been drawn more to Anne's vivaciousness than to her physical beauty. This thought gave her hope for the king's character.

"All right, I've decided." Anne turned to her guest. "What do you say, Micheline? Will not this gown of white tissue look best with ermine?"

"Oh, yes!" Enthusiasm seemed proper. "It will be lovely!"

"Well, then, good! That will be all for today," Anne told the dressmakers.

A maid scurried forward to help her mistress slip into a gown of deep violet that was encrusted with sapphires and diamonds. Anne sat down near Micheline while another maid brushed out her dark silky hair.

"I'll wager that you are a happy lady," she said to Micheline, sipping her own goblet of wine. "You're doubtless in love with Sandhurst."

"Truth to tell, I am."

"Who could resist him?" She paused to appraise the young Frenchwoman and pursed her lips slightly. The chit was a beauty. Anne had been surprised to hear from Rupert Topping that Sandhurst was going along with this forced marriage, but now it did not seem so unbelievable. There had been many moments during the years since she'd won the king's favor when Anne Boleyn had felt an almost overpowering attraction to the Marquess of Sandhurst. At times, lying in Henry's smothering embrace, she'd wondered what it might be like to make love with Sandhurst instead, and in her worst moments Anne had thought that if he showed even a hint of attraction to her, she would leave behind the prospect of becoming queen and go off with him. Of course, that never happened. Sandhurst was rarely at court, and when he was, he was unfailingly affable but he always kept a barrier up between himself and the rest of the world. Besides, it had all been a foolish fantasy on her part, Anne thought now. All women wanted Sandhurst because he was unattainable, and her own longing had grown out of the years of frustration that preceded this final month before she would at last become queen of England. Many times it had seemed that it would never happen, but now that she was growing larger with Henry's child, they had announced their January wedding, and in just a few weeks she would wear the crown of queen!

Micheline spoke, rousing Anne from her reverie. "It was exceedingly kind of the king to invite us to Hampton Court. I particularly enjoyed the journey up the Thames."

"We are always pleased to have Sandhurst among us," Anne said, smiling, "and, of course, everyone has been eager to meet you. But tell me, how is *your* king? I am very fond of François, and of France! You know, I lived at the French court when I was a child."

Before Micheline could reply, the door opened and a page announced, "Lady Dangerfield to see you, my lady."

"Ah, lovely! Show her in."

Iris swept into the chamber, her coppery curls ablaze in the sunlight. She wore a gown of blue and heliotrope satin, several necklaces of pearls, and a ring on every finger.

"Greetings, my lady, and congratulations!" she exclaimed.

"Thank you. Iris." Anne, her hair now caught up in a gold coif, rose to embrace her guest. "Do you know Madame Tevoulère?" Her dark eyes traveled from one lady to the other, well aware of the situation.

"We have not met," Iris replied coldly.

Micheline stood up. "Good morrow. Lady Dangerfield. I have heard a great deal about you."

Like everyone else, Iris registered surprise at the sound of the girl's perfect English. Her green eyes widened, then narrowed.

"I should offer you congratulations as well, madame," she said softly, "and I wish you luck. You'll need it to succeed where so many others have failed."

Lifting her chin with its tiny cleft, Micheline replied. "I appreciate your good wishes, my lady. And now, if you'll excuse me, I must return to Lord Sandhurst."

"You can't hide behind him just now, madame," Iris said. "He's gone to play tennis with the king, and they will probably be occupied for *hours*."

* * *

Micheline sat in her spacious Hampton Court bedchamber, her indignation growing by the minute as she waited for Andrew to return from his afternoon of male camaraderie. It was nearly time for supper, and still he had not knocked at her door. For her own part, she had bathed again while Mary aired out her gown, and now, with her hair freshly dressed, Micheline looked even more beautiful than she had that morning.

"Where can he be?" she demanded of Mary.

The young girl squirmed uncomfortably. "No doubt there's an explanation, ma'am. Lord Sandhurst is a very thoughtful man. Why, ever since I came to his household, he's always been frightfully kind. Most noblemen wouldn't even notice a common little kitchen maid, but Lord Sandhurst is very considerate."

Micheline rolled her eyes. "Mary, if you are going to be my lady's maid, you ought to have the decency to at least *pretend* to take my part at times like this."

"Yes, ma'am," she agreed meekly.

Remembering that Mary had said her sister was a pastry cook at Hampton Court, Micheline said, "I'm sorry if I seemed rude; certainly none of this is your fault. You're excused for the evening, Mary. I shan't need you until morning."

"Oh!" Her heart-shaped face lit up. "Thank you, ma'am!" At the door she turned, adding, "And I don't think you're one bit rude. I think you're wonderful!"

Alone in the huge chamber, Micheline murmured, "I'm glad someone does."

Then she straightened, listening. Were those voices on the other side of the connecting door? Had Andrew returned to his rooms without even stopping to apologize to her? Fresh outrage sent her marching to the paneled door. She thumped it once with her fist.

"Andrew? Are you in there? I wish to see you now!"

"Then by all means, enter." he invited her, sounding infuriatingly amused.

Micheline threw open the door and boldly entered his chamber. To her consternation, she discovered Sandhurst lounging in a steaming bathtub in front of the fire.

The ever-discreet Joshua Finchley was arranging his lordship's clothing on the bed, but the sight of Micheline's shocked expression made him swallow in embarrassment.

"You may leave us, Finchley. I won't be needing you again tonight."

Gratefully the older man made a hasty exit.

Micheline stood paralyzed on the far side of the room, unsure of what to do or say until her betrothed inquired casually, "What happened to you this afternoon?"

She gasped, incredulous. "What happened to me?"

"Didn't I just say that?"

The fact that he was naked in the bathtub suddenly meant nothing to Micheline as she crossed the chamber and exclaimed, "I was not the one who sauntered off to play tennis for hours on end after promising never to leave the side of my betrothed!"

"Am I to assume that you are angry?" Sandhurst tried with little success to look concerned, but his mouth twitched and his eyes twinkled.

She found this expression of his particularly appealing and tried to steel herself to resist. "How observant you are, my lord." ·

He had been soaping his chest but paused now and reached out to touch her hand with wet fingers. "Sarcasm does not become you, fondling. You must know that I had no choice but to play tennis with the king, any more than you had a choice when he decided that you must meet Anne Boleyn. Besides, I meant for you to watch our match. I bade Lady Dangerfield show you the way to the tennis court's gallery."

Helplessly Micheline felt herself soften. When he gazed at her and spoke in that low, masculine voice, anger was impossible. "Lady Dangerfield?" she repeated rather plaintively. "Why would you give that woman a message for me? She hates me, Andrew."

"The king and I passed her on the stairway, and she said she was bound for Anne Boleyn's chamber. It seemed a logical request at the time."

"Well, she never told me. Your precious Iris is a witch. How could you have loved her for so long?"

"I never loved her; I've told you that. In any case, she didn't become a true witch until you appeared on the scene."

"Do you know what she did? She *did* say that you had gone to play tennis, but merely indicated that this pastime would separate us for the afternoon. Then Iris and Anne Boleyn took me out to the garden and introduced me to a lot of strangers who stared at me as if I were very odd. It was horrible! After a few minutes the two of them drifted off to converse with their friends and left me alone with a boring man named Cromwell. I didn't even know I was allowed to watch your silly tennis match." She paused, thinking, and narrowed her eyes. "I don't suppose that Iris happened to turn up in the gallery?"

He began soaping his chest again, watching as if to make certain he didn't miss a place. "Now that you mention it... I do believe I might have seen her there."

Micheline paced angrily beside the tub. "I knew it! She is *worse* than a witch. I hate her, and I hate this place, and I wish we'd never come!"

"Fondling, come here. Sit down beside me." He indicated a low stool near the fire. After a moment she grudgingly obeyed, and Sandhurst reached out to take her hand, muscles playing over his shoulder and arm. "This is part of the reason I wanted to bring you to court *before* our wedding. I'm a marquess, and you would be a marchioness, and we should always have to spend some time at court, if only to keep the peace with King Henry. I have enough trouble as it is dodging his efforts to transform me into a faithful courtier."

"What do you mean?"

He sighed. "Nothing. I'll explain it all to you later, after we've left Hampton Court." As much as he longed to confide in Micheline, he did not want to add to her distress by detailing his potential problems with the king. She had more than enough to deal with on this first day with the English court. "All that's important now is that you understand that there are more burdens involved in becoming my wife than just tolerating my relatives."

She dropped her head, pressing her cheek to his strong, damp hand. "Sometimes I wish you were just plain Andrew Selkirk after all."

"No more than I, my love, I can assure you. However, fate dealt me a different hand. If I were a commoner, I would not only be free of royal obligations, but I could also close the door on my past. As it is, if you marry me, you shall always have to contend with women I knew before you and I met. I'm a decade older than you, Michelle, and I'm a man. Iris is not the only ghost from my past who will haunt us. Unfortunately the court abounds with females who once hoped to become the next Marchioness of Sandhurst."

"Must you boast, to me of all people?"

He smiled. "I'm trying to be honest. I want you to be aware of the possibilities, in case you should decide that the negative aspects of marriage to me outweigh the positive. It would devastate me to see you unhappy later on."

Now Micheline was ashamed of the harsh words she had spoken. She gazed at Andrew, achingly aware of his lean-muscled naked body so near to her. The firelight only accentuated his sculpted good looks, and suddenly she realized that this was the first time she had ever seen him fully unclothed in the light. Not that she was brave enough to look beyond his hard arms, tapering chest, and the handsome legs he propped on the lower rim of the bathtub. Sighing a little, Micheline thought that it would be wonderful if she could shed her costly gown and climb into bed with him, forgetting about the royal assemblage downstairs.

But Andrew was right. She had to make the best of their time at Hampton Court. Nothing would be solved if Micheline continued to alternately rage and sulk.

"I see your point, my lord," she told him sincerely. "I must learn to cope with Lady Dangerfield and her ilk on my own. I apologize for behaving like a spoiled child."

"No apology is necessary." Gently he drew her near until their lips touched, parted, then touched again. "Besides, I could never love a saint. You are never more ravishing than when you're angry."

Tears stung her eyes. Reluctantly she whispered, "I suppose I should leave you to dress."

He arched a wicked brow. "If you stay, I shouldn't dress at all..."

Twenty-Five

SUPPER PASSED PLEASANTLY ENOUGH. In the great hall, which had been recently rebuilt to feature a towering carved hammer-beam ceiling and a fanciful minstrels' gallery, the court feasted on fish of every description, from salmon and flounder to salted eels and whiting. Micheline, as the newest guest, was seated in relative security between King Henry and Andrew. The king was kind to her, though from time to time he gazed at her bosom in a way that made her vaguely uneasy.

The king's table was reserved for the court elite. It reposed on a raised dais, while the rest of the company supped at tables that ranged down the length of the hall. There was an open hearth in the middle of the floor near the dais; the smoke found its way up into the roof and out of an elaborate louvre.

Seated near Micheline were some of the luminaries of Henry's court: Thomas Howard, Duke of Norfolk; the Earl and Countess of Oxford; the Duke of Suffolk; Thomas Wyatt, the dashing poet who was said to love Anne Boleyn; and, most prominently, Thomas Cranmer, the newly consecrated Archbishop of Canterbury, and Thomas Cromwell, the king's dour-looking new chief minister, who was assuming the position vacated by Cardinal Wolsey. Micheline watched and listened carefully and soon began to connect names with faces and form opinions about their owners.

Finally sweets were served. There were jellies of all colors and shapes, plus sugared nuts and candied nutmeg and lemons. Then two liveried pages carried in an enormous rabbit made of almond paste and marchpane mixed with isinglass and sugar. The confection had been dredged with cinnamon to resemble a real, roasted rabbit. Anne Boleyn laughed in delight when the counterfeit hare was placed before her.

"My sweet Anne has been craving rabbit for several days," Henry whispered to Micheline. "Until Lent is behind us, this will have to suffice."

"Very thoughtful of you, sire," she said, smiling. Meanwhile Micheline was thinking that this wasn't so difficult. All she had to do was agree, smile, and compliment to get along in the English court. It was a small price to pay for loving Andrew, and she was comforted by the knowledge that he didn't enjoy the situation any more than she did.

It was late when the boards and trestles were removed from the great hall. Micheline stifled a yawn, hoping that she and Andrew could escape after a reasonable amount of time. However, everyone seemed to be leaving the hall, amid much laughter, and she watched in growing bewilderment.

"The king has planned a masque," Sandhurst explained, reading her thoughts. "We must go, too, and conceal our identities." His voice was sardonic.

"But that's silly!" she protested. "I have no other gown but the simpler one I must wear tomorrow. Everyone will recognize me!"

Laughing softly, he led her into the corridor. "We'll just don masks, and even those have been provided for everyone—in Anne's heraldic colors. The only person who must be entertained is the king. He imagines that he is anonymous in his costume and loves to make a game of finding his lady."

Once again Sandhurst was right. When they rejoined the rest of the court in the great hall, minstrels were playing gaily in their gallery, and blue-and-purple-masked dancers had begun to frolic. Before long another celebrant appeared in their midst. Clad entirely in green, from his jaunty feathered cap to his shoes, the man disguised as "Spring" was not only tall but barrel-chested and obese. His velvet costume was elaborately slashed and puffed, decorated with diamonds, rubies, and silken green leaves. Small eyes gleamed happily through an emerald-set mask, while their owner's ruddy cheeks contrasted with fair skin elsewhere and a reddish-gold beard.

"Hmm," Sandhurst mused, "I wonder who *that* could be!"

Micheline giggled. "I cannot imagine!"

"Spring" stopped before every female flower in sight, kissing hands and nuzzling necks as he inhaled various scents. When he reached Micheline, it was all she could do to smile politely and suffer his investigation. As if by design, Anne Boleyn stood at the opposite end of the crowd, now wearing an extravagant jeweled gown of cloth of gold, its bell-shaped sleeves turned up to display sable linings. Her hair was hidden under a gold gable coif, and her blue and purple mask was set with rubies. When the king finally reached her, he pretended to be unsure. He pressed kisses to her throat and ran his hands over her bodice, then caught her up in a crushing hug and let out a gusty laugh of triumph.

"How very peculiar," Micheline observed softly.

The musicians had begun to play and Henry led his future queen forward to lead the first dance.

Sandhurst was about to reply, when a stocky, well-fed-looking young man appeared before them. Like King Henry, he could not conceal his identity with a simple mask, for his yellow hair and flushed cheeks were clues enough.

"My lady, would you dance with me?" he inquired mysteriously.

Micheline was too surprised to play along. "M'sieur Playfair, is that you?"

"How ever did you guess?" Sandhurst laughed.

"Yes, that's what I'd like to know," Jeremy fretted. "What's the fun of these masques if everyone knows who one is? And, by the by, madame, my name is Culpepper, not Playfair!"

"My pardon. Sir Jeremy," she apologized. "I'll not forget again."

"Speaking of remaining anonymous," Sandhurst interjected, "how did you know who *we* were?"

"You're my best friend, aren't you? Besides, you two are the handsomest couple here tonight, and I've seen you wear that doublet before, Sandhurst."

This elicited a burst of laughter from Andrew. "It's good to see you here, Jeremy. When did you arrive?"

"Late this afternoon. I saw the two of you at supper, but I was seated at the other side of the hall. Not everyone is honored with a place beside the king."

"I'd have preferred your company, sir," Micheline told him sincerely. "And I'm awfully glad that you are Andrew's friend and not his manservant."

"You aren't the only one!" Jeremy harumphed. "I must say, though, that all the humiliation I suffered in France was well worth it if you two have worked things out. Word has it that you're getting married after all."

He smiled at his friend and shook his head. "Only *you* could have managed to escape successfully from that coil you were wrapped in two days ago, Sandhurst! Charm will out, eh?"

"Not charm, but love," he replied evenly.

"Well, I wouldn't know about that." Jeremy wore a rather wistful smile, watching as Micheline gazed at her betrothed. "What about that dance, then?"

The floor was crowded now. All the court seemed to be dancing, laughing gaily as they pretended not to recognize one another. Micheline found Jeremy very endearing, even when he made a wrong move from time to time and stepped on her toes. Across the room she glimpsed Andrew leaning against the paneled wall under a carving of Henry VIII's royal arms impaling those of Anne Boleyn. He watched her affectionately, and it filled her with delight when she saw him shake his head after a figure she knew to be Lady Dangerfield approached him.

Micheline's dance with Jeremy was followed by two with Sandhurst. Thomas Wyatt begged for the next, and as he led her into the crush, she felt something slip up her sleeve. It seemed to be a piece of paper, but she promptly forgot about it as she chatted and danced with the poet.

Long past midnight Sandhurst suggested that sleep might be in order, and they went to bid the king and Anne Boleyn good night.

"When will your wedding take place, my lord?" inquired Anne.

"In a fortnight's time, my lady," he replied, then looked toward King Henry. "I know that you had planned to attend, when first you and my father spoke of this marriage, but we realize that circumstances have altered in the interim. Doubtless the arrangements for the her ladyship's coronation as queen will prevent you from embarking on a journey to Yorkshire." His eyes added his understanding of the fact that the king might not be kindly disposed toward him since their conversation earlier that day.

Henry nodded slowly. "Certainly we shouldn't come all that way on *your* account, Sandhurst!" He laced his jest with an edge of steel so subtle that only the other man would perceive it. "And you are correct. There is much to keep us near London through May. However"—the king turned to beam at Micheline, lifting her hand to his small pursed lips—"we feel that the enchanting Madame Tevoulère deserves special consideration, and there are others from our court who have expressed a wish to attend your wedding. We can make no promises, but if it is within our power, we shall make a brief journey to Aylesbury Castle to join in the nuptial celebrations."

"As always, Your Majesty demonstrates exceptional generosity," said Sandhurst. "It would give us great joy to have you present at our marriage, and I know that my father would be equally pleased." Sketching a bow before Anne Boleyn, he added, "My lady, I hope to see you in Yorkshire. Your arrival would bring new radiance to that district!"

More courtly farewells were exchanged until, at length, Andrew and Micheline escaped, climbing the stairs to their quiet wing of the palace.

"How I despise such artificial conversation!" he muttered darkly, his mask dangling from his fingers.

"You seem quite adept at it, my lord," Micheline teased him. Away from the crowd, she was suddenly aware of her own fatigue. Voices, faces, music, and all the day's experiences continued to swirl in her mind; she would be glad for sleep if only to escape them.

"I need to be adept to survive, I fear. I can only hope that whatever charm I can muster will be enough to counteract the displeasure I've incurred when I could not bring myself to behave as an obedient subject ought." He glanced heavenward. "I've not the temperament for a lord of the realm, I fear. Obedience is not in my nature."

"Will you rebel against the bonds of matrimony too?"

They had reached Micheline's door, and he slid his arms around her slender waist. "This is the first time in my life I've faced a commitment to which it will be a pleasure to submit. Besides, you don't want to rule me."

"That's true." She opened her mouth as they exchanged a sleepy, sensual kiss. "And neither will you rule me."

"If I imagined it were possible, I couldn't love you as I do." he told her honestly.

They shared another sweet, drowsy kiss, then parted. Alone in her bedchamber, Micheline managed to unlace the back of her gown unaided. When she drew off the velvet sleeves, a small piece of parchment dropped to the floor, reminding her of that moment in the great hall when she had felt it slide against her wrist. Puzzled, she removed her gown, petticoat, and shakefold, then picked up the paper and sat down on the bed in her chemise to open it.

Printed in tiny, barely legible characters were the words: *"Leave England alone, or die."*

She blinked in confusion. As the message sank in, Micheline's heart began to pound and her hands perspired. Still, it didn't seem real. Mechanically she walked about the huge, chilly bedchamber, removing her crispinette, brushing out her hair, preparing for bed, all the while trying to block the ominous note from her thoughts.

Finally she blew out the candles and crawled into the enormous bed, but sleep would not come. Over and over again Micheline considered waking Andrew, but there seemed no purpose. Her door was latched. Who would be foolish enough to harm her with Sandhurst in the next room? Moreover, who would want to harm her at all?

An hour passed, and still her heart drummed against her breastbone. Occasionally there were footsteps and voices in the corridor. Each new sound made her start— and then, suddenly, when all was quiet, there came a soft scratching noise at Micheline's door. No sooner did she sit up straight in bed, wide-eyed and terrified in the darkness, than the scratching stopped. A full minute passed during which she neither moved nor breathed, then... *scratch-scratch*. The sound was all the more sinister because it was barely audible, but then it grew to alarming proportions.

Somehow, she made herself act. Scrambling off the other side of the bed, Micheline ran through the darkness, bumping into furniture. There was just enough firelight remaining for her to make out the shape of the connecting door to Andrew's room. Praying that no one had locked it, she found the latch, lifted it, pushed on the door, and it swung open.

"Andrew!" she gasped. In the glow from his fireplace, she could see the shadowed bed, and then a silhouette as he sat up.

"Michelle?"

In the next instant she was upon him, clinging to him, trembling violently.

"What is it? Did you have a nightmare?" He held

her tightly. "I can feel your heart beating against my chest! Tell me what's wrong. You're safe now."

"*C'est vrai,* I know." It was true; she felt a hundred times better in the shelter of Sandhurst's strong embrace. She buried her face in the taut curve between his shoulder and neck, shivering in reaction. He continued to soothe her, kissing her brow and temple, speaking to her tenderly until Micheline relaxed enough to tell him what had happened.

"Someone put a tiny piece of paper in my sleeve while I was dancing with Thomas Wyatt. I barely noticed at the time; I'd forgotten all about it until I removed my gown and the note fell out. It said—it said—"

"You're all right," he reminded her. "You're with me now."

"It said that I must leave England, alone—or die!" Her voice dropped to a whisper on the last word.

"What?" Sandhurst was incredulous. "Why didn't you bring it to me immediately?"

"I don't know. I thought you might be asleep, and it seemed so ludicrous and impossible. At first, I told myself that it was some sort of mistake... or bizarre joke... but I couldn't sleep, and then—just now, someone was scratching at my door!"

"Scratching!"

"To scare me, I suppose. It was a very tiny sound at first, but then it grew louder and louder until I felt terrified!"

"No doubt," Sandhurst said grimly. "Loose me a moment, fondling; I'll light a candle and have a look around."

Micheline nodded bravely and even managed a smile as he tucked the covers snugly around her. Her eyes followed him as he donned hose and a white shirt, then took a candle and went into her chamber. Barely a minute passed before he reappeared. After bolting the connecting door, he sat down beside her on the bed.

"Naturally whoever it was has gone." He held up a small square of parchment. "This is the note, I take it." He stared at it broodingly. "I can't make sense of this. Who would want to threaten you? And *why?*"

"I don't know!" Her voice broke on a sob. "There's only one person I can think of."

Andrew glanced over at her. "Iris? No, I would swear she's not capable of such a thing."

"Perhaps she hopes only to frighten me off."

"So you think Iris was scratching at your door tonight?" he countered in disbelief.

"Who else could it be?"

Sandhurst gave a harsh sigh. "I don't know."

Softly Micheline asked, "Will you let me stay here tonight? With you?"

"Of course you'll stay here. Tomorrow morning we leave for London, and until then I promise not to let you out of my sight—and this time I mean it. You can even hold my hand while I shave if you like."

He gave her a reassuring smile, but his eyes were on the menacing piece of paper he'd set on the table. Absently he drew his shirt over his head, then reached down to pull off his hose, unaware of the blush that was spreading across Micheline's cheeks.

Her gaze wandered helplessly down his long, tapering back and lingered on the hard curves of his buttocks. When Andrew stood to blow out the candle and place it on a chest, she caught a fleeting glimpse of his manhood in its nest of tawny curls. At that instant he felt the heat of her gaze and forgot about the mysterious note.

When Sandhurst drew back the covers and climbed

into bed beside her, Micheline was eager to put that frightening message out of her mind too. She snuggled against him, shivering, as if she couldn't get close enough.

"You're ice cold!" he exclaimed softly as her bare foot found its way between his calves.

"Andrew, I love you."

"And I love you, Micheline."

Glorying in the warm strength of his embrace, she sought his mouth with her own and kissed him passionately. She wrapped her arms tight about his neck and held fast, as if she were drowning and he was the shore. As they kissed, with Micheline's tongue the aggressor, he hardened fully against her thigh.

"Christ!" he gasped at last when she turned her hungry lips to his jaw, neck, ear, and eyes. "What are you *doing?*"

She laughed softly. "Don't you know?"

"What happened to your vow of chastity?" He knew, of course. She was trying to blot out the terror, and would regret it tomorrow if they made love now.

"Must we talk?"

"I can't believe I'm saying this, but yes, we must." He groaned and glanced heavenward while prying her arms from his shoulders. "Remember this next time you wonder how much I really love you."

"What's wrong? I thought you wanted to—"

"I did. I do! But not like this, Michelle." Turning onto his back, he held her cradled against his chest. The throbbing heat in his loins was torture. "You're just upset right now, and it would be selfish for me to press my advantage."

Embarrassed by her brazen behavior and the fact that she, too, was fully aroused and aching for release,

Micheline grew suddenly motionless. Tears stung her eyes.

Andrew reached up to stroke the soft hair back from her face. "Cheer up, fondling," he coaxed, kissing her brow with smiling lips. "You'll thank me, you know... in our marriage bed."

Twenty-Six

YORKSHIRE, ENGLAND

THE DAY that brought Andrew and Micheline to Aylesbury Castle began leisurely, for they had spent the previous night at the Starre Inn in York and were little more than an hour's ride from their destination.

Not only were they accompanied on their journey by Mary, Finchley, and squires for their coach and horses, but Sir Jeremy Culpepper had joined them as well. Micheline hadn't been surprised to discover that Jeremy had grown up on the estate bordering Aylesbury Castle. Since childhood, he and Andrew had been as close as brothers, and now he was eager to combine a visit with his family in Yorkshire with the opportunity to attend Sandhurst's wedding.

During the journey northward, Andrew and Micheline were rarely alone. Because of intermittent rain, he insisted that she ride in the coach with Mary. Mealtime conversation, which Culpepper cheerfully monopolized, was generally the only time the betrothed couple could be together.

On this last morning Andrew and Micheline rose

early by previous arrangement and met in the common room of the inn. When he put an arm around her waist and bent to graze her lips, Micheline flushed with excitement. It seemed that their moments of intimacy belonged to another lifetime, for now each casual touch sent currents of fire over her nerves.

He took her on a brief walking tour of York, and both of them were heady with mischief, like adolescents who had escaped the watchful eyes of parents. First, they walked up Stonegate, Andrew explaining that the oft-used suffix of "gate" in the city of York was derived from the Scandinavian word for street. It seemed that the Vikings had captured York in the mid-800s, and their influence was still felt.

"You're probably descended from a Viking yourself. It would be very fitting," Micheline said.

"That's the rumor," he said, smiling. "In fact, Aylesbury Castle stands on the site of a Viking fort. Unlike most of England, which was overrun with Danes, Yorkshire was conquered by Norsemen." Laughing softly, Sandhurst added, "My mother used to tell a story about a beautiful Saxon maiden from York who was taken prisoner by a handsome Viking and brought to the fort —now our castle—where he surprised everyone by making her his wife. According to Mother, the Westons sprang from that tempestuous union."

"That must account for your wild streak," she mused.

"If so, I take after my ancestor. Even he, celebrated as a heathen, was susceptible to the mellowing power of love."

Content just to be together, touching, they strolled north to Petergate, where Micheline viewed the great Minster for the first time. Sandhurst took her inside the cathedral for a proper look at the spectacular ninety-foot-high vaulted nave and the stained-glass windows that were justly celebrated. Andrew and Micheline knelt together, praying silently but with one heart, then lit a candle before leaving the cathedral.

On Low Petergate, Sandhurst stopped to buy warm sugared buns for them to eat, and then a nosegay of violets from an old flower woman. Micheline was wearing a gown of rose and lavender silk, and the violets made a charming accessory.

Petergate wound into the Shambles, an especially narrow street lined with butcher shops whose overhanging eaves nearly touched at some points. The sun was fully visible over the River Foss when they began to circle back to the Starre Inn. He chose a meandering route that eventually brought them back to their lodgings in Stonegate.

"I like York," Micheline told him, "and all of England."

"I'm glad," he said, pausing outside the Starre's doorway to hold her against him. "That was one of my chief concerns before we left France. There is so much for you to become accustomed to. A new country, new customs, a new family, friends, potential responsibilities dealing with a new king—it's a great load."

"I'm up to the challenge, my lord," she declared, amusement infecting her voice. "Why, I'm even learning to like dumplings!"

Laughing, Sandhurst led her into the inn, where they found Jeremy and the servants waiting for them and eager to compete the journey. So within the hour the band of travelers passed through the towered eastern gate to the city, bound for Aylesbury Castle.

Micheline looked back out of the coach window at the banks of daffodils that rose up to touch the magnificent walls encircling York, and wondered what sort of surprises the rest of the day held in store.

* * *

The sky grew darker as morning progressed. Still, Micheline found Yorkshire hauntingly beautiful. Gray clouds scudded over bright green vales dotted with trees and sheep and brightened with liberal sprinklings of buttercups. Especially interesting to Micheline were the intersecting limestone walls that seemed to snake endlessly over the windswept landscape. She chatted with Mary, enjoying the scenery, until her heart caught in her throat at the sight of a castle silhouetted against the swirling gray sky.

Sandhurst rode up alongside the coach, pointing, to confirm the fact that Aylesbury Castle was at hand. Unlike the charming, peaceful-looking châteaus of France, which were set amid parkland and gardens, this castle had a stark, wild look about it. The closer they drew to the cluster of bastions, crenellations, and towers, the more nervous Micheline felt. The place did not look welcoming, nor could she imagine it as her home.

Noticing her mistress's apprehensive expression, Mary soothed, "It's not so bad, ma'am, and his lordship hardly ever comes here. You'll like Sandhurst Manor much better, I'll warrant."

Micheline nodded bravely, but she was thinking that the austere appearance of the castle merely seemed to forebode the atmosphere within.

A chilling wind penetrated the coach as it climbed a twisting lane to the castle. Andrew led the way as they crossed a drawbridge that led them into the barbican with its surrounding curtain wall. Servants had already begun to appear, rushing to welcome the Marquess of

Sandhurst as he rode over a second drawbridge, through the gatehouse, and into the enormous inner courtyard of Aylesbury Castle.

Sandhurst swung down from his horse and handed the reins over to his squire, then made his way through the group of familiar happy faces, greeting each servant by name. Reaching the coach, he opened the door and helped Micheline down, holding her against him as he announced, "I want all of you to know Madame Micheline Tevoulère, who will become Lady Sandhurst just as soon as we can arrange the wedding." In response to their cries of excitement, he added, "There may be some extra work involved for many of you, but I'm confident that you'll understand my plight and take pity on me. Each day of waiting is torment!"

Sandhurst's exaggerated expression of agony drew laughter from the servants, followed by a rush to bow or curtsy before Micheline.

At length they were free to enter the castle. As they approached the mammoth arched doorway, a dark-haired young girl burst through the portal and ran forward to throw her arms around Sandhurst.

"Andrew! Oh, Andrew! You've come!" She was actually weeping with joy, her face buried against his shoulder.

He had to let go of Micheline to return the girl's fervent embrace, a fond smile warming his eyes.

"Of course I've come, child. Did you doubt it?"

"Don't leave me again. I couldn't bear it! Please, you must *promise.*"

"I'll do nothing of the kind. Loose me, Cicely, and meet your new sister, Micheline."

The girl pressed her lips together and reluctantly withdrew her arms from his neck. Micheline, who had been somewhat taken aback by the emotional scene she'd just witnessed, mustered a warm smile. Although Cicely kept her eyes averted, it was readily apparent that she was a beauty. Lustrous dark curls tumbled over her shoulders and the gently curving bodice of her rose satin gown, and her face was delicately enchanting.

"Greetings, Cicely. I'm happy to meet you at last, for I know how dear you are to Andrew."

Cicely raised wet sable-brown eyes and replied in a monotone, "Welcome to Aylesbury Castle, mademoiselle."

"I'm sure you two will be great friends," Andrew said. Silently he remembered the words his sister had spoken that night in London: "I hope that Mademoiselle Tevoulère is a toad!" Cicely was by far the most endearing member of his family. If she would not open her heart to Micheline, it appeared that there was little chance for a happy relationship between his wife and her new family.

For Andrew's sake, Micheline decided to try again. "Cicely, I have to confess that I have always wished for a sister. Much like you, I had only a much older brother. Perhaps we will be able to be the sisters that neither of us had before."

The younger girl shrugged and looked away. "Pretending's not the same, is it? Besides, I've been through this sort of thing before, inheriting fully grown family members. Rupert and Patience aren't exactly my idea of siblings."

Sandhurst gripped her arm tightly and said, "Micheline is nothing like Rupert or Patience, I can assure you of that. Let's go inside now. I can hardly wait to see the rest of my charming family." His voice was acid with sarcasm.

Cicely allowed herself to be dragged along into the

castle, and when her brother gave her a dangerous glare, she returned it defiantly.

The trio climbed a spiraling newel staircase in single file, emerging in a broad stone corridor that passed the family apartments. Micheline looked about as she walked, noting the fine tapestries displayed on the white walls and the woven rush mats that took the place of loose rushes. She'd expected the place to be gloomy, but in fact the castle's interior was remarkably clean and bright.

They came into the solar, which served as a private parlor. Its southern exposure and high arched windows filled the airy chamber with April sunlight, while the hall, in the adjoining east wing of the castle, was too large and shadowy for the comfort of a small gathering.

Seated in a velvet-upholstered chair was a bony old man who narrowed his eyes at Micheline. A fur-lined satin coverlet was draped over his shrunken frame, and his feet were propped on an oaken stool. Behind him stood Rupert Topping, while a pale, long-faced young lady occupied a settle near the windows. She put down an elaborate piece of embroidery and watched the proceedings with tiny, alert eyes.

"You're looking well, Father," Andrew said in greeting. Holding Micheline's hand, he drew her across the room until the two of them stood before the craggy-faced Duke of Aylesbury.

"Bah! I'm dying and you know it!" The old man briefly took the hand proffered by his son.

Sandhurst forced a smile. "Happy news, then. Perhaps it will improve your health to know that I've granted your request and brought Micheline Tevoulère here to be my bride."

Micheline stepped forward and dropped into a brief curtsy. The lavender of her gown and the nosegay of violets tucked into its bodice served to emphasize the vivid color of her eyes. Sunbeams burnished her hair and haloed her lovely face.

"I am so pleased to meet you at last, Your Grace."

"You speak English! Well, well. And you're a beauty. My son is very fortunate."

"Not so fortunate as I, Your Grace," she replied firmly

"Hmmph!" The old man arched his white brows. "That's a matter of opinion, but then, Andrew always has been skilled at charming the ladies." He turned his attention back to his son. "I suppose you're expecting me to lavish praise on you for doing as you were bidden."

Sandhurst's entire body was taut. "Far from it. I am marrying Micheline because we love each other, and I had hoped that you and I might declare a truce for her sake."

"I thought so. You couldn't resist telling me that you are doing this because *you* want to, and not because I wished it. As usual, you go your own way without any respect for other people—least of all your own father!"

"Are you saying that you'd be happy if there were no love between Micheline and me?" His eyes were dark with rage.

"Don't prattle on to me about love. It's beside the point. What I can't forgive is the way you disappeared for two full months! No one knew where you were; it was impossible to make wedding plans in view of your record of rebelliousness. Now you turn up unannounced and declare that you've been a good boy and expect me to smile and pat you on the head! April's nearly gone. It's too late to send word of your wedding to London. I wanted every nobleman in England to come to Aylesbury Castle for this occasion."

"In the first place," Sandhurst ground out, "the last thing I yearn for in this life is to be patted on the head by anyone, least of all you. Secondly, this is Micheline's and my wedding—not yours. If I'd had my way, we'd have been married a fortnight ago in London, but because you wished to have the ceremony here, I thought to comply in the hope that this might be an opportunity for all of us to make peace and a fresh beginning. As for your desired guest list, it doesn't matter who else attends this wedding so long as Micheline and I and the priest are there. It would be agreeable, but not necessary, to have family and friends present. If you want us to leave and be married elsewhere, just say so. Otherwise, I would appreciate it if you could endeavor to soften your tongue, at least in Micheline's presence."

The duke's face had gradually turned a shade of mauve. "I *knew* you hadn't changed. I heard that you were going to marry the girl, but I knew that you'd never admit defeat."

Micheline wanted to speak up and ask why a father would want to defeat his own son, but the air was so heavy with tension that she lost her nerve.

"I'm not broken, if that's what you mean," Sandhurst said, an edge of steel in his voice. "And as you know, I have no desire to continue these perverse little games of yours, the object of which seems to *be* the breaking of my spirit. I have more productive ways to spend my time."

"Oh, I'm well aware of that. You've always had something better to do than obey your father." The duke heaved a mournful sigh and dropped his head back against the chair, then glanced over to Rupert, smiling wanly. "Fortunately, not all my offspring are so arrogant." Now the old man turned his attention back to Micheline. "Let me assure you that you *shall* have your wedding here. I had hoped to make it a day that all of England would remember, but 'twould seem that is not to be."

"I assure you, Your Grace, that the ceremony itself is all that matters to me," Micheline replied as politely as she was able.

The duke shrugged and looked away from her again as if she were a child spouting nonsense. "The king himself expressed a desire to attend."

"Father, I spoke to King Henry," Sandhurst said flatly. "Micheline and I went to see him at Hampton Court. I had assumed that the preparations for Anne Boleyn's coronation next month would prevent them from attending this wedding, but he hopes to make the journey after all, bringing members of the court with him."

The old man merely turned his face toward the windows as if he hadn't heard.

In the silence that followed, Rupert cleared his throat.

"I haven't had a chance to bid you welcome!" he exclaimed loudly. Rushing forward, he shook his half brother's hand, then turned to Micheline. "Madame, you are looking more beautiful than ever! *Tress* bell, what?"

A bubble of amusement rose through her tension. "Hello again, Roo-pair. But no, that is wrong. Hello, Roo-*poort!*"

Even Sandhurst forgot his rage for a moment and smiled. Thank God for Micheline. What had he ever done without her? Slipping a hand around her waist, he drew her near and kissed her shining hair.

"You must meet my dear wife!" Rupert was declaring. "She's been looking forward to it so much!" He turned his head without taking his eyes off Micheline. "Patience, darling, do come and join us!"

Smiling shyly, Patience complied. As Rupert's wife drew near, Micheline saw that the poor woman was strikingly unattractive. Much taller than Rupert, Patience Topping had no breasts or hips to speak of, and her face was long, with thin lips, a sharp nose, and round little eyes. Her dun-colored hair was parted in the middle and tucked into an unflattering gable-hooded headdress, completing the picture of plainness. Micheline's heart went out to her.

"This is Micheline, dearest!" Rupert enthused. "Isn't she everything I told you? Aren't we fortunate to have her as our *sister?*"

Sandhurst winced slightly at that, but Patience was beaming. "We are indeed, dear husband. Hello, Sister, and welcome to our family."

"Thank you, Patience." Bemusedly she looked around the room, her eyes falling on a petulant Cicely; the shrunken, sour-faced Duke of Aylesbury; and gawky, overeager Rupert. Finally Micheline turned her gaze up to Andrew. There was wry humor in the set of his mouth and the way he lifted his brows as if to say, I *told* you they were different!

The warmth of his gaze melted her doubts. As long as they were together, she could surmount any obstacle. This resolve was put to the test minutes later when Patience kindly volunteered to show Micheline to her bedchamber so that she might wash and rest.

"You'll be safe from Andrew, just in case he should try to assert his rights before the wedding," Patience announced proudly. "His chamber is at the opposite end of the corridor!"

"Oh." Micheline nodded, feeling slightly ill. "How thoughtful of you."

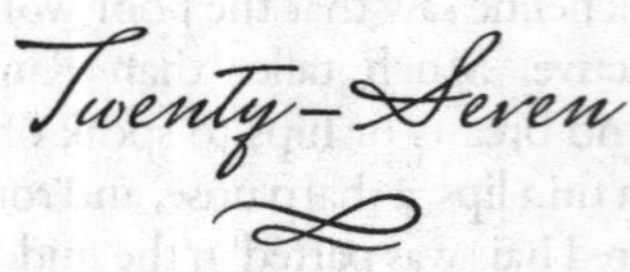

Twenty-Seven

SANDHURST WAS STANDING in his bedchamber, putting folded doublets into a carved chest, when Cicely appeared at the door.

"I've brought you some wine," she said hesitantly, holding out the pewter goblet. "And I came to say I am sorry for the way I behaved."

He was still tense with anger, but the sight of her looking so small and repentant in the doorway softened his heart. Cicely was still a child, after all, and deserved a second chance.

Stretching out an arm, Andrew smiled slightly when she put down the wine and rushed into his embrace.

"Say you've forgiven me," she begged, her face pressed against his velvet doublet. "You're the only person I love in all the world."

"Of course I forgive you, child. That goes without saying." He tipped her chin up and stared hard into her tear-filled eyes. "But you must never behave that way toward Micheline again. She needs your help to feel comfortable here, and, of course, you will be her sister and should treat her accordingly."

Cicely's lips tightened. "I don't see how you can talk that way. I heard you and Jeremy talking that night in London. You made sport of her! You didn't want to marry her! How do you think it makes me feel to hear everyone saying that you went along with the king's and Father's wishes to marry a stranger?"

"Who is everyone?" he interrupted coldly.

She dropped her eyes. "I went for a visit to our aunt Margaret's in Oxfordshire late in February. I was going mad here, and Rupert had to journey to London, so he took me to Oxfordshire on his way. I stayed until last week. We went to Hampton Court to watch a day of jousting in the tilting field. That was just after you and your *betrothed* were there, and the court could talk of nothing else. Of course, I'd heard already that you had decided to marry that woman after all, but I didn't really believe it until Hampton Court."

"Why didn't you come to visit us in London?" he demanded. "And how did you return to Yorkshire? You could have come with Micheline and me."

"Rupert brought me back. As much as I despise him, it was better than watching you moon over that Frenchwoman."

"I thought Rupert returned here earlier in the month."

"What difference does it make? I met him by arrangement at Hampton Court, and I must say that at least he remembered my existence, which is more than I can say for you!"

Sandhurst put other thoughts from his mind and concentrated on the problem of his sister. "Cicely, sit down." He went to fetch the goblet of wine and took a drink. "I confess that I am at a loss to understand your animosity toward Micheline. I know what I said in London, but that was before I had met the lady. In France everything was different. I fell in love, and *she* fell in love as well, not with the Marquess of Sandhurst but with a painter named Andrew Selkirk. Don't you see? Micheline turned aside the marriage King François had arranged for her in favor of the man she loved. Doesn't that convince you that she is a good person?"

Fussing with the folds of her satin skirt, Cicely would not meet his eyes. "You're besot. It's as if someone's put a spell on you, but it will wear off! As for Madame Tevoulère, she doesn't deserve you. It wouldn't surprise me if she knew all along who you really were."

He sat down beside her and gripped her arm. "Are you in league with our father to bring me misery? Cicely, you know how dearly I love you. We can deal just as happily together in the future as we have in the past, but first you will have to surrender all these nonsensical ideas you have about Micheline. She wants to be your friend."

"She can never be my sister," Cicely replied stubbornly. "You will always be my only sibling. I could never love anyone else as much."

Sandhurst felt as if he were beating his head against the wall. "You try my patience, child. You justly complain about our family, and now someone has come who would happily brighten both our lives. Once I am married, you can visit us at Sandhurst Manor and in London, for Micheline will be there to look after you when I cannot. Why do you turn away from her?"

Cicely whispered brokenly, "All my life I've loved you best, Andrew. After Mother died, you were so good to me, and lately I almost believed you might let me come to live with you." Tears spilled onto her cheeks. "It's not the same with that woman here. It seems you've forgotten there's anyone else alive in the world."

"Sweet child, the love between Micheline and me is

not the same as the love I feel for you. I am your brother; I shall always love you. Nothing can change that."

Cicely buried her face against him, weeping.

"If you love me," he continued gently, "you must wish me happiness. I implore you to share my joy and extend a hand of friendship to the woman I love."

She lifted her chin. "I cannot change my feelings, Andrew, any more than you wish to change yours. I will try to be polite to her, but I can't promise more than that."

His jaw hardened. "I begin to think that Father is wearing off on you."

"I will leave you, since we seem to have exhausted the only subject you are conversant with these days." Giving a frosty glance, Cicely stood and swept out the door. Rounding the corner, however, she nearly collided with Micheline, who was standing there as if frozen, her eyes swimming with tears and one hand covering her mouth.

"Eavesdropper!" Cicely accused.

"I didn't mean—" Micheline started to explain, but the girl had already turned away and started down the corridor.

Suddenly Sandhurst was behind her, enfolding her in his arms and drawing her into his bedchamber.

"I am sorry," he whispered against her hair. Micheline's arms were wrapped tightly around his neck as she wept quietly. "My sister seems to have been transformed into a vixen in my absence."

She managed to control the urge to make the same declaration she had at Hampton Court, that she hated this place and wished they'd never come. Somehow, she must find a way to cope with Aylesbury Castle and everyone in it. This was even more important than the challenge of dealing with the English royal court, for this was Andrew's ancestral home and these people were his family.

"Cicely despises me," she said. "What have I done to earn her ill will?"

"You have done nothing. It is time my sister learned that I do not belong to her."

Micheline raised her tear-stained face to his, and Andrew bent to kiss her. "Perhaps the problem is your mother's death," she mused. "It must have left a tremendous void in Cicely's life, and she's looked to you to fill it. When I put myself in her place and imagine living here with your father, Rupert, and Patience, it's easier to understand how she must feel."

"Believe me, I've agonized over this for the past five years, and my guilt has only increased as she's gotten older."

"I heard what she said about hoping that she might come to live with you. Andrew, couldn't she do that now? Is there any reason why Cicely couldn't make her home with us?"

He was stunned. "You can't be serious. As a new bride you would actually welcome the presence of that rude little hellion?"

"It might make all the difference for her. Certainly her attitude toward me would have to change, but I wouldn't expect miracles overnight. However, if I began to fear for my life, she would obviously have to leave!"

Micheline smiled a little at what she had meant as an exaggeration, but Sandhurst gazed absently out the window, his face grim. "I'll think about it. In the meantime, I love you for making such an open-hearted suggestion." To prove his point, he bent and kissed her long and slowly, groaning a bit when her lips clung to his as he raised his head. "This is torture. Did you come here solely for that purpose?"

Her smile faded. "No, I came because I found myself growing rather panicky at the thought of having a room so far from yours. Silly, I know, but after Hampton Court..."

"No, it's not silly at all. We'll arrange for Mary to share your chamber again, and I'll see that there's a proper lock on the door."

"I know that there's nothing to be afraid of here but I can't seem to quell these unreasonable fears. I'm sure that they'll pass with time, and once we're married, I'll be *much* better. What could I fear with you in my bed?"

Sandhurst pressed warm, smiling lips to her throat. "Your only worry then will be the threat of never sleeping again...."

"Andrew," she continued tentatively, "since I've mentioned the duke, I may as well ask you, is there anything I should do differently to win his favor? I tried to be tactful this afternoon, but he didn't seem to appreciate any of the things I had to say."

His body tensed. "For God's sake, don't even consider saying what you think he wants to hear. Go on just as you have, speaking the truth. It's a game! If he senses your weakness, he'll pounce and try to control you just as he controls that sniveling half brother of mine."

Micheline sighed. "I wish we were already married and alone at Sandhurst Manor."

"As always, fondling, we are of one mind." He paused, mentally reviewing all that had happened that day. "In fact, I see no reason to linger in Yorkshire. We shall be married as soon as it is humanly possible. I told the king a fortnight, so if he decides to come, he'll arrive in time. Why should we delay?"

Suddenly filled with joy, Micheline teased, "Patience

warned me that you might grow overeager to exercise your rights as a husband!"

Sandhurst grinned. His right hand slid slowly down to the base of her spine before drawing her body firmly against his. "For once, Patience is absolutely correct."

* * *

An interminable, tension-laden supper that night in the drafty hall only strengthened Sandhurst's resolve. He waited until everyone else had retired before approaching his father.

The duke had returned to his favorite chair in the solar, peering at a book under the light of a brace of candles. When Andrew walked over and sat down opposite him, the old man pretended not to notice.

"Father, there is something I wish to discuss with you."

A long minute passed before the duke glanced up. "A rare occurrence! How fortunate that you happen to be here at the castle rather than in London or Gloucestershire or France. One of life's happy coincidences, hmm?"

"Quite," Sandhurst agreed laconically. "Would you be terribly disappointed if I got directly to the point?"

"Not at all." These conversations with his son reminded him of the fencing matches he'd engaged in when he was younger. Certainly the rules were the same. "I am eager to get back to my book."

"This won't take long. I've come to tell you that Micheline and I would like to be married as soon as possible. There has been so much in her life that's new and I think it would be beneficial to get on with the wedding so that I can take her to Sandhurst Manor for a bit of peace. I said a fortnight to King Henry, which would be tomorrow. Why not have the wedding two days hence?"

The duke smiled wolfishly. "Next you'll tell me that this urgency on your part has nothing to do with your desire to bed that saucy French minx," the old man snorted. "Were you not man enough to spread her legs back in France?"

The scar that cut into Sandhurst's lip went white. It took every ounce of his control to refrain from striking his own father. "I'll ignore that vulgar speech this time," he replied in a tone quietly laced with danger. "I'll ride tomorrow to inform the priest and any friends that might like to attend of the wedding date. Jeremy traveled north with us so that he might be present, and no doubt his parents will come too. If there are others you care to notify, kindly inform me by tomorrow morning."

The Duke of Aylesbury pursed his lips. "As usual, you have taken matters into your own hands. Far be it from me to interfere."

* * *

Micheline slept fitfully in her comfortable feather bed. She would doze and dream, then wake to change positions, staring up at the two narrow windows that overlooked the Yorkshire countryside. Bright shafts of moonlight streamed into the room, annoying her until she finally scrambled up to close the bedcurtains on that side.

Mary occupied a little truckle bed nearby. It was good to have her there; since Hampton Court, Micheline dreaded the idea of being alone in the darkness. However, the little maid breathed loudly in her sleep.

Midnight came and went. Micheline dreamed that

she lay in Andrew's arms, soaking up his warmth, and listening to his heartbeat as he slept. Half-conscious, she turned onto her stomach and burrowed into the pillows, pretending they were Andrew.

A distant sound, a rattling, gradually brought her awake again, wondering fuzzily what could be making that irritating noise. It seemed to be coming from the door.

Her eyes opened and her heart began to pound. The rattling had stopped, and she reminded herself that she was safe, for Andrew had attached a heavy iron lock to the bedchamber door, not unlike the one that Henry VIII took with him from castle to castle to ensure his privacy and security.

Had someone been trying to open the door in spite of the lock? Memories of that terrifying night at Hampton Court returned in a flood.

"Mary? Mary, are you awake?"

"Hmmm?" the girl mumbled.

Micheline threw back her covers and rushed over to the maid's little bed. "Did you hear that noise just now? That rattling at the door?"

Mary propped herself on an elbow and blinked in the moonlight. "No, ma'am, I heard nothing! Was it like that scratching sound at the king's palace?" She'd been told that story the next day and ever since had felt rather uneasy about sharing Micheline's rooms. Now, however, Mary began to wonder if the Frenchwoman might have an overactive imagination.

"No—no, it was different, as though someone were trying to open the lock."

"Pardon me for saying so, ma'am, but I wonder if you might have dreamed this. You're still nervous after that other night."

"You're absolutely certain that you heard nothing at

all?" Micheline persisted.

"Nothing." The girl's voice was firm.

"Well," she sighed, "perhaps you're right, then. I'm sorry for disturbing you."

"That's all right, ma'am. I've had nightmares myself. You know we're safe with that lock Lord Sandhurst put on the door. Why don't you go back to sleep and order up a happy dream about your bridegroom?" The girl beamed in the shadows. "You ought to be far too happy to let a little rattle at the door disturb you!"

"You're right, of course."

"Good night, ma'am."

Micheline crawled back into her bed and closed her eyes. Silently she repeated, "It was only a dream," until sleep came at last.

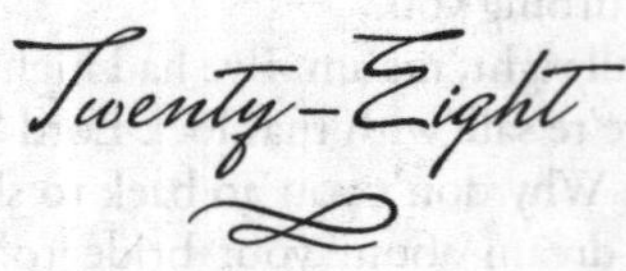

THE NEW DAY dawned so replete with buttery sunshine that Micheline was able to laugh with Mary about the noise she had heard during the night. Now she ascribed the entire incident to an understandable case of nerves.

After a refreshing scented bath, she dressed in a favorite gown of yellow silk. Mary was just brushing out her curls when a knock sounded at the door.

The maid opened it to admit Sandhurst. Looking rakishly handsome in the morning light, he was carrying a large orange and a bouquet of daffodils and bluebells.

"Good morrow, ladies! Have you ever beheld a finer day?" He presented Micheline with her gifts. "One thing is certain. No man has ever beheld a more beautiful woman."

She laughed as he bent to brand her throat with his mouth. "What accounts for this lighthearted mood?"

"Haven't you heard? I'm in love." Stepping back, he reclaimed the orange and began to peel it, smiling at Micheline as she buried her nose in the blooms.

"I've already heard that rumor, my lord."

"Indeed? Well, let me try another. Have you also heard that I'm to be married... tomorrow?"

She nearly dropped the flowers. "What? Do you jest? How can such a thing be possible?"

He took the daffodils and bluebells from her and stuck them into a nearby pitcher of water, then laughingly put a segment of orange into her mouth.

"It's possible because I made it so, fondling," Sandhurst explained blithely.

Because her mouth was full, she couldn't speak, and then he was kissing her, sharing the juicy orange. A wave of passion broke over Micheline's body as his strong hands slid around her hips and drew her against him. There were moments, like this one, when she thought her heart might burst.

"God's death," Andrew muttered while kissing her ear, "even one more day seems an eternity. I don't know if I can survive until tomorrow."

"You must," she warned shakily. Her skin was so sensitive that each brush of his mouth touched off lightning currents of arousal. "Tomorrow. Tomorrow!" She repeated the word in wonder.

"It may as well be next year for all the good it does me now." The ache in his loins had begun to annoy him.

"Andrew, what shall I wear? Will I be reduced to borrowing Patience's wedding gown after all?"

He drew back and stared at her with raised brows. "Now we're getting *serious*, I see." Suddenly remembering Mary, he looked over a shoulder to discover her pressed against the far wall, staring at them. "Mary, you're blushing! Compose yourself and show your mistress what she will wear for her wedding."

The girl bobbed her head nervously in response and darted out of the room. Sandhurst, meanwhile, released Micheline and perched on the edge of the bed. In the interest of his health, it seemed wise to avoid prolonged prolonged physical contact with Micheline.

"Eat your orange, sweetheart," he advised. "You need to keep up your strength for the marriage bed."

She offered him a segment of fruit and watched as he ate it, the picture of nonchalance in his fitted burgundy velvet doublet, breeches, and boots of black leather.

"You're wearing boots," she remarked. "Have you been out riding already?"

"I had a few calls to pay," Sandhurst nodded, "most notably to our parish priest. He'll be here tomorrow, which was naturally my only real concern. I also stopped at Greenwood, the Culpeppers' home, to alert Jeremy and his family, and I'll ride farther afield this afternoon."

"What does your father have to say about this plan?"

"Why do you ask such questions when you know you won't like the answer?" He sighed when she merely lifted her brows at him in imitation of his own favorite wordless response. "You can probably guess what the duke said. Since it's impossible to please him, I stopped trying years ago." His expression softened as he watched Micheline bite into the last piece of orange, her lips and fingers wet with juice. "Now, of course, I have your interests to consider, and they far outweigh any opinions Father might have."

"Well, you certainly know him better than I. All we can do, I suppose, is hope that one day he'll thaw. Does the duke like babies?"

Sandhurst shrugged. "I do seem to recall seeing him smile on occasion when Cicely was tiny, but he was different then."

"Did he love your mother?"

"I suppose he did. She was one person he never

found fault with, that much is certain. He thought Mother was the epitome of womanhood."

Micheline went to sit beside him on the bed. "Well, then, perhaps there's hope for him. We'll just have to be patient."

"Patient?" He lifted her slim, orange-scented hand and kissed each finger. "If you don't mind, I'll leave that to you."

"Have you given any more thought to Cicely?"

"Now I know why you crept over here next to me! It's a plot to weaken my defenses." Still, he was smiling, exploring her fingers and palm with his mouth as if this were the most intimate part of Micheline's body. "Frankly I thought you would change your mind about Cicely, but if you're determined that she live with us, I'll agree to a compromise."

His lips were scorching the tender inside of her wrist and her heart was pounding. "Why do I feel naked even though I am fully clothed?" she moaned half-heartedly. "Must I wear gloves as well?"

Ignoring her, Sandhurst went on. "I want a few weeks alone with you at Sandhurst Manor, but Cicely may join us in London in time for Anne Boleyn's coronation the end of May. She can return to Gloucestershire with us in June, on a trial basis. As long as she behaves and the two of you get along, she can stay, but I won't have her making life miserable for you in your own home. Your happiness is of greatest importance, fondling."

Andrew returned to her hand, kissing it once more as he raised his eyes to meet her own. Micheline sighed, thinking that his compelling gaze had the power in itself to arouse her.

From the doorway Mary cleared her throat loudly.

"I have the gown, my lord!" Her arms were laden with masses of ivory satin.

"Ah, thank you, Mary." Sandhurst went to relieve her of her burden, returning to spread the gown out over the dark green counterpane.

Micheline came to stand beside him. She stared, speechless, for a long minute while he watched her, waiting for her reaction.

"I realize it's not the current fashion," he said, "but I thought—"

"Oh, Andrew!" she breathed. "It's perfectly lovely! This is the sort of gown I dreamed of as a child!"

It was true. The gown was of an older style that Micheline adored. Fashioned of rich ivory satin, it had a very low round neckline edged with delicate embroidered flowers of gold and rose. A collar of lacy golden net, called a neck whisk, stood up in back, while a trail of embroidered flowers meandered down the length of the sleeves. The gown had a narrow, pointed waistline over a skirt that belled out to end in a long train.

Micheline leaned forward to brush her fingers over the romantic neck whisk. "It's absolutely exquisite."

"You wouldn't prefer a gown covered with jewels?"

"Oh, no!" She looked up in alarm and found him smiling at her. "I love these little flowers. I love everything about this gown. Where did you find it?"

"It was my mother's. I think Father may have forgotten it exists, but I never did. One day, when I was a child, I was helping Mother look for something in a storage room in the keep. She opened a chest and took this out to show me, almost as if she'd forgotten where it was stored herself. She told me that the rose-colored flowers were supposed to be bird's-eye primroses, which only grow in Yorkshire meadows, and the golden ones represented buttercups, for those were her favorites.

Then Mother stood up and held the gown against herself... I can still see her in my mind's eye."

"I'm so pleased that you remembered this gown and I'll be honored to wear it, but are you certain the duke won't mind?"

"Stop fretting about Father. I'll be surprised if he even recognizes it, and I know that it would please my mother above all things."

"It will feel a little as if she's with us after all."

"Well, now that that's settled, there's a great deal more to be done today, and I'd better be off."

"I'll go with you to the courtyard. I think I may walk on the hills for a while."

Arm in arm they emerged into the corridor. Glancing toward the solar, Micheline caught her breath at the sight of a tall slim woman with bright coppery hair.

It can't be! she thought wildly.

Slowly the woman turned, and Micheline met the icy green eyes of Lady Iris Dangerfield.

* * *

Feeling Micheline stiffen, Sandhurst followed her stricken gaze to the solar.

"Iris! What are *you* doing here?"

"Shame on you, Andrew." She pouted. "Is that any way to welcome one of your oldest and dearest friends?"

Since everyone in the room was watching them, he had no choice but to force a smile and guide Micheline forward to greet Iris Dangerfield.

"My apologies, madame." He sketched a bow, then lifted her hand to brush cool lips across it. "I was merely surprised to see you."

Another voice spoke from the settle near the window. "We weren't following you, Sandhurst." Timothy Dangerfield walked over to stand beside his wife. Very tall and thin, with dark hair and pale skin, he had a pointed nose and chin. "A party of us traveled up from London at the king's behest, arriving last night after you had retired."

"So I heard," Sandhurst replied. "I had to leave this morning before any of you had risen, so I wasn't aware that you were among the party. Your journey was pleasant?"

Dangerfield shrugged. "Overlong. We were all quite fatigued. Everyone's been looking for you. The others finally went off to wander around the castle. Doubtless you'll be pleased to learn that His Majesty and the Marquess of Pembroke will also arrive later today."

"Micheline and I are pleased you all could join us for this joyous occasion." His keen eyes met those of the younger man, remembering that Dangerfield had known of his wife's infidelity. There was only one possible reason for him to wish to attend this wedding, and that was to punish Iris and drive home the point that Lord Sandhurst was no longer available.

After introducing Micheline to Dangerfield, Sandhurst drew on soft doeskin gloves. "I trust you will understand if we leave your entertainment to the other members of my family. It's a busy time for us."

"Never fear!" Rupert piped up eagerly, rushing over. "Patience and I have a game of chance planned for the afternoon. I'm going to teach our guests to play passe-dix and lansquenet!"

Micheline wrinkled her nose slightly at Rupert's horrendous pronunciation of the French game, while Sandhurst glanced at him in mild surprise.

"Where did you learn passe-dix and lansquenet?"

"Oh, a Frenchman taught me one night in a tavern

in London." Rupert turned excitedly to the Danger-fields, gesturing with both spindly arms. "You can teach these games to the royal court when you go back!"

"We'll leave you to it, then," Andrew said dryly.

As they left the solar, Micheline could feel Iris's eyes burning the place where Sandhurst's hand rode at the small of her back. She couldn't help thinking about the noise she'd heard during the night, now that she knew Iris had been in the castle, but told herself that it was silly to imagine anything so farfetched. At any rate, Tim-othy Dangerfield was here to keep an eye on his wife.

As they emerged into the sunlight, Micheline felt drenched in bliss, but a shadow lingered. She watched as Andrew led his horse out of the stable into the sun-splashed courtyard, and when he asked if she might prefer to accompany him, she was tempted.

"I suppose you think I'm quaking with fear because your Iris Dangerfield is in the castle."

"She's not *my* Iris Dangerfield," he protested.

"Well, she used to be. And she'd still like to be."

Sandhurst left his horse and went forward to slide both hands around her slender waist, drawing her firmly against him. "She never was *my* Iris Dangerfield," he corrected in a low voice. "I was only passing time, waiting to find you." His mouth grazed hers. "My closest friend." Another tantalizing kiss. "My love... and, on the morrow, my wife."

His hand came up to frame her lovely face, his fin-gers laced through glossy hair as he stared down at her.

"My Micheline."

* * *

No sooner had Andrew ridden off than Micheline encountered the rest of the party from London as they entered the courtyard after inspecting the keep. Among them were the Dukes of Suffolk and Norfolk, Thomas Wyatt, and Robert Cheseman, the king's falconer. Richly garbed ladies of the court accompanied them, and Micheline went forward to offer greetings

Though she continued to feel that these members of the English nobility were inspecting and even looking down on her, it mattered little. The memory of Andrew's voice and touch lingered, infusing her with a dreamy glow.

The others went inside after hearing that French games were the order of the afternoon, but she decided impetuously to remain outdoors and ride over the Yorkshire hillsides. A groom provided a sweet-tempered mare who cantered past limestone walls, fat sheep, and black-stockinged lambs.

At length Micheline dismounted, deciding to pick a bouquet of exquisite bird's-eye primroses and tender buttercups to make a wedding garland for her hair. However, it was impossible to resist the other spring flowers that abounded on the hillsides. Soon her arms were filled with bright scented globeflowers, dainty yellow cowslips, and pale pink lady smocks.

The afternoon was waning when Micheline remounted the patient mare and started back toward the castle. Suddenly it occurred to her that the king and Anne Boleyn might be arriving shortly, and she ought to be present to greet them. Urging the mare into a reluctant gallop, Micheline tipped her head back, enjoying the sensation of the cool air against her face.

Her feeling of contentment was such that she barely noticed the odd flash of light from the trees on a hill above, but the mare was not so preoccupied. Caught by surprise, the horse reared back abruptly, sending the unsuspecting Micheline flying into the air. A lesser horsewoman might have been killed, but she instinctively curled up and relaxed all at once before striking the ground. When she sat up and tested her bones, she saw that she'd come inches from hitting one of the stone walls. Her heart pounded as she considered the flash of light. What else could have caused it except a mirror?

For a long moment she closed her eyes against the terror that washed over her, then made up her mind to put it aside. By the time she reached the castle and began to climb the spiral staircase to the family apartments, Micheline felt her fears dissolving. Perhaps it had all been a simple accident. Certainly it was better to believe that than to allow herself to be terrorized on the eve of her wedding!

She expected to find the living quarters of the castle filled with activity, and wondered at the absolute silence in the corridor. A need for distraction mixed with curiosity, and Micheline tiptoed down to peek around the corner of the solar.

"Hmmph!" grunted the Duke of Aylesbury. "What are you doing lurking about? Thinking to spy on someone?"

Micheline started at the sight of him, all alone in the sun-washed chamber. The old man sat in his favorite chair, wearing a nightgown faced with rabbit and overlaid with a worn gray silk coverlet.

She stepped into the open. "Of course not, Your Grace! I only wondered if the others weren't still enjoying their games. I confess that I tried to remain undetected because I feared they would ask me to join them, and I didn't want to appear rude by refusing."

His eyes twinkled almost imperceptibly in reaction to her frankness.

"In that case, I don't blame you for hiding, but it's safe. They've all gone to their rooms to prepare for the king's arrival," he replied gruffly, nodding toward her arms filled with wild flowers. "That's quite a bouquet you've amassed. I hope you left a few on the hillsides."

"Oh, yes, of course, Your Grace. One would never know I'd picked these, there are so many more. Aren't they lovely?" She selected a few blooms and crossed the solar to hold them out to him. "Won't you take these for your chambers? They smell wonderful! You know, I set out to pick just a few, to make a garland to wear for the wedding, but I confess I was carried away."

The duke clasped the flowers in his bony hand, his eyes softening. "So, madame, I suppose you consider yourself worthy to become Marchioness of Sandhurst, and one day Duchess of Aylesbury."

"To be perfectly honest, Your Grace, I haven't given much thought to my title. All I know is that I love your son better than my own life, and I shall do everything in my power to make our marriage happy and prosperous. I certainly will be proud to be Lady Sandhurst." Micheline took a breath and impulsively reached out to touch the old man's arm. "If and when your son inherits your title, I shall try to live up to the example your wife set as Duchess of Aylesbury."

The duke's throat worked as he looked away from Micheline. "Ah. That's good," he muttered, coughing. "Go on, then, child. I want to rest."

She walked away, but glanced back once before turning down the corridor. Andrew's father sat hunched over, staring at the wildflowers clutched in his gnarled hand.

* * *

Micheline's conversation with the Duke of Aylesbury drove all the dark thoughts from her mind. Perhaps there could be peace between Andrew and his father after all! Walking to and fro in her chamber, which was now decorated with vases of fragrant blooms, she waited impatiently for Sandhurst to return.

A soft, lavender-rose veil of twilight covered the sky when Micheline heard the sound of hoofbeats on the cobbled courtyard. Looking out her deeply recessed window, she beheld grooms wearing the king's livery.

Without a second thought Micheline went to greet King Henry and his entourage. The castle was no longer quiet. The sound of voices and footsteps followed her as she closed her paneled door and set off for the circular newel staircase. Her only wish was that Andrew might be by her side.

This spiral staircase was especially precipitous and Micheline had learned to take care with her footing on the treacherously narrow wedge-shaped steps. Today, however, her thoughts were on the arrival of the royal party and her impending wedding.

She'd descended just a few steps when a shadow seemed to spill down from behind her. A moment later, Micheline felt an abrupt pressure against her back and lost her foothold. She raked her nails over the smooth stone walls, searching in vain for something to grasp as she pitched forward, screaming, down the steep staircase.

<h1 style="text-align:center">Twenty-Nine</h1>

MICHELINE TUMBLED headlong down the stairway, but an instant before her face crashed into the sharp edge of a step, Sandhurst caught her. The impact of her falling body sent him reeling against the curving wall, and he very nearly lost his own footing. Through sheer force of will he remained erect.

A long moment passed before Micheline realized what had happened, that the abrupt horror of her fall into what seemed certain death had ended in Andrew's embrace. It was the harsh sound of his breathing and the thunder of his heart against her cheek that brought her out of her daze.

"Andrew! How—where—?"

"I had just started up the stairs when I heard you scream! Micheline, for God's sake, what happened?" Sandhurst's voice was as hoarse as if he'd just brushed death himself.

He was holding her so tightly she could scarcely breathe, and the muscles in his arms and chest were like steel against her face. "I don't know. I must have just lost my balance. I was thinking about you, about the wedding, and I wasn't paying proper attention to the steps."

"You aren't hurt?"

"No. No, I'm fine." Micheline tried to pry her head loose enough to look up at him. "Because of you. You saved my life."

Suddenly she was free of his embrace only to be grasped firmly by each shoulder. "My God, Michelle, if anything happened to you—" Tears glinted in his eyes before he crushed her against him once more. "I beg you to be more careful."

Micheline's reply went unheard as castle guests pushed past them on the staircase, hurrying to greet the king and Anne Boleyn. They had little choice but to join the assemblage in the courtyard, and, for the moment, Micheline's brush with disaster was forgotten.

For once, King Henry had traveled light. Only a dozen grooms and another two dozen assorted servants accompanied them, along with a large wagon packed with the necessary amenities.

Henry and Anne had ridden in a magnificent coach, and the sight of them emerging into the twilit courtyard was dazzling. The future queen was resplendent in crimson velvet trimmed with emeralds and ermine, while the king wore plum satin and cloth of gold. His fingers were a mass of jeweled rings, and around his neck was a gold collar from which hung a diamond as big as a walnut.

"Your Majesty," Sandhurst said, leading Micheline forward, "you honor us."

"Welcome, sire," Micheline added with sincerity. She dropped into a low, graceful curtsy before the huge monarch, rising only when he reached for her hand.

"It was worth the journey to gaze once more upon your lovely countenance, madame," Henry told her. Turning to Sandhurst, he boomed, "I am ravenous! I hope your cooks have prepared a proper feast for their king."

Andrew smiled. "My father awaits us in the great hall, where you may sup immediately if you like, sire. Shall we join him?"

* * *

Sandhurst wouldn't let Micheline out of his sight that evening, which pleased her tremendously. After supper the tired king and his lady retired to their chambers, so Andrew and Micheline were able to steal away early. He went with her to her room, where they played chess and piquet until midnight. When she began to nod over the cards, he bade her go to bed, averting his eyes as she undressed and slid between the covers. Although it was the eve of their wedding and he'd been randy as a stallion for weeks, tonight his mood was tense. Sandhurst was determined that nothing would stand in the way of their marriage.

Lying in bed, Micheline opened her eyes just enough to gaze over at his chiseled profile. Meanwhile, in the truckle bed across the room, Mary was making her usual variety of sleep noises.

Many times that evening Micheline had thought of telling Andrew about the riding accident and the brief impression she'd had of a shadow and of something touching her back before she fell down the stairs, but it seemed that those revelations would cause more trouble than good, especially on the eve of their marriage. She had been so preoccupied on the stairs that it was impossible to be certain now if there really *had* been a shadow, let alone identify it, and the pressure against her back might have been the wall. Unless she could point to the person who had pushed her, what was there to gain by upsetting Andrew?

Once they were married, Iris Dangerfield would have to face reality, Micheline thought drowsily as she closed her eyes. The woman would seek out another lover and leave them in peace.

* * *

At daybreak Micheline awoke to find Andrew sleeping in a chair next to her bed, fully dressed, his feet propped on the side of the bed. His handsome head was tilted to one side and sunlight glinted off the stubble of his beard. Birdsong filled the air.

Languorously Micheline stretched out a hand to lightly caress his cheek. Slowly Sandhurst's brown eyes opened as his brows went up. Catching her fingers, he kissed them.

"Good morning, my lord," she whispered.

"Go back to sleep, fondling. You'll need the extra rest to stay awake... later," he murmured with a wicked grin.

She smiled at that thought and dozed off again, dreaming that she was falling from a horse, sailing through the air, only to land safely in drifts of meadow flowers. Andrew waited for her there and both of them were naked. He smiled down at her, brushing aside violets and primroses from her breasts and belly, bending to replace the flowers with kisses.

"Time to wake up!" Mary was calling. "It's your wedding day, ma'am!"

Rolling over, Micheline opened her eyes. The chair beside the bed was empty. "Where's Lord Sandhurst?"

"Why, in his own rooms, I expect. Be patient, ma'am;

you'll have him next to you when day breaks again!" The girl sighed a little. "Just think, you'll be the wife of the Marquess of Sandhurst. A more fortunate lady never breathed."

Micheline had no desire to argue that point, nor had she time to wonder what had become of Andrew, for Mary soon had her out of bed and into a steaming, scented bath. It was nearly ten o'clock, and there was much to be done before the wedding that afternoon.

Midday found Micheline in her lacy silk chemise, petticoats, and shakefold, eating a plum while Mary finished weaving the coral-pink bird's-eye primroses and rich yellow buttercups into an extravagant garland for her hair. When that was done, the little maid helped her mistress into her gown.

Micheline was standing in her stocking feet before the mirror, ivory satin skirts flowing out around her, when Cicely came into the chamber.

Andrew's sister looked lovelier than ever, the budding curves of her figure accentuated by a gown of dark rose silk and gold brocade. Sapphires edged the square neckline and sparkled on the golden caul that tamed her curls.

"Hello, Micheline," she said. Color stained her cheeks. "I suppose I should wish you well."

Trying to ignore the rather backhanded nature of her blessing, Micheline crossed the room and gave her the warmest smile she could muster.

"Thank you. I promise to take good care of your brother... and I have some news that I think you'll like." She took a chair near the window and motioned for Cicely to sit beside her. "I know how unhappy you have been here at Aylesbury Castle, and also how much it means to you to spend time with Andrew. My situation was not so very different from yours when I was young, and I can understand what you are feeling. I've asked

Andrew if you might come to live with us at Sandhurst Manor."

Cicely looked torn between pleasure and wariness. "And?"

"He has agreed, with a few conditions. He says that you may join us in London next month, in time for Anne Boleyn's coronation. After that we will all return to Gloucestershire, where you will remain... providing you and I can live happily together. I would truly like to try."

At that moment Iris Dangerfield swept into the room.

"Well, if it isn't the almost bride and her almost sister! What a cozy family scene."

Micheline rose, gazing evenly at the other woman. She was certain that Iris was behind all the menacing events that had lately colored her life, but she was equally certain that this day's wedding would mark an end to those troubles. It still seemed to Micheline that Iris's main purpose had been to frighten her into backing out of the betrothal; failing that, she had tried to harm her in a moment of desperation. She was a human being, with an obsessive weakness for the Marquess of Sandhurst. Micheline could understand that.

"Good morrow, Lady Dangerfield," she greeted her calmly.

"So, the bride is garbed in her finery. I must compliment you on your gown, madame. That's a very subtle approach—flowers instead of gems." Iris herself wore a magnificent creation of cream satin and green velvet, studded with pearls and emeralds.

"I'm glad you like it," Micheline returned with a touch of irony. "This gown has special meaning, since Andrew's mother wore it when she married the duke."

"That's very sweet, yet so innocent. Rather misleading, isn't it? Everyone knows you aren't a virgin, after all."

Micheline lifted her chin. "It was Andrew's wish that I wear this gown, my lady." She turned away. "Now, if you will excuse me..."

No sooner had Iris Dangerfield taken her leave, than Cicely was on her feet.

"How dare you wear my mother's dress?" she cried. "This is outrageous!"

"I only dare because your brother bade me do so," Micheline replied as quietly as she could.

"You'll never take her place."

"Cicely, my only intent is to be Andrew's wife. As for your mother, I revere her memory. I would never think to replace her. I can only be myself and do my best."

The girl seemed not to hear. Eyes blazing, she vowed, "You may think you love Andrew, but you barely know him. You'll never understand him the way I do."

Micheline was saved from losing her temper, or answering at all, by the timely appearance of Patience Topping. She seemed to assess the situation immediately, and gave Micheline a sympathetic smile.

"The guests are arriving," she announced. "Cicely, dear, you'll have to leave our new sister so that she can complete her preparations."

The girl stamped across the chamber, pausing in the doorway to declare, "I have no *sisters!*"

* * *

The nuptial mass was held in the chapel, located in the castle keep. The wedding guests were the finest England could offer. King Henry and Anne Boleyn, glittering with jewels, were seated next to the Duke of Aylesbury and his family, and behind them were ranged the cream of British nobility. Every seat in the chapel was occupied, for friends and villagers had flocked from the countryside of York at Andrew's invitation.

As Micheline walked down the aisle, however, she saw none of the sumptuously garbed guests. All her attention was focused on the man she loved.

Even from a distance she basked in the loving warmth of Sandhurst's gaze, and thought that he had never looked so dazzlingly handsome. For his wedding he wore a doublet and haut-de-chausses of dove gray and blue velvet sewn with silver thread. White silk showed through the slashed sleeves and made a snowy fraise against his tanned jaw. His hair shone in the shafts of sunlight that poured into the chapel. He wore a smile, too, which grew more irresistible as Micheline neared.

As his bride drew closer to altar, Andrew beheld her beautiful face and gleaming cognac-hued locks. The garland of bird's-eye primroses and buttercups encircled her hair like a crown. To Sandhurst however, most lovely of all was Micheline's radiant smile. It called up all manner of fierce emotions within him, ranging from intense love to the burning ache of desire.

Currents of warmth flowed between their bodies as Micheline put her slim fingers in his strong hand. Dimly, they heard the voice of the priest, asking them to kneel. When they rose, Sandhurst's gaze held her near.

"I, Andrew, take thee, Micheline, to my wedded wife," he said.

"I, Micheline, take thee, Andrew, to my wedded husband," she vowed softly.

Sir Jeremy Culpepper, smiling broadly, stepped forward to present a band of solid gold to his friend. Sandhurst held it deftly between two fingertips. In a voice so intimate that it seemed they were alone together, he told Micheline, "With this ring I thee wed. This gold and silver I thee give. With my body I thee worship." He paused to smile almost imperceptibly. "And with all my worldly goods I thee endow. In the name of the Father" —he slid the ring partway down her thumb, then withdrew it—"and the Son"—now Micheline was staring at his fingers as they tantalized each of her fingertips in turn with the golden band—"and the Holy Ghost." Reaching her wedding finger, he gently slid the ring down to its proper place and concluded, "Amen."

Moments later, after a benediction from the priest, Micheline gloried in the sensation of being gathered into her husband's embrace. One of his hands came up to hold the back of her head, while the other completely rounded her waist, and then their lips met. It was a gentle, loving, sensuous kiss, filled with promise. Micheline felt weak with elation.

They stayed in the church to drink from a loving cup with wine sops, then accepted the first flurry of congratulations from Henry, Anne, and the other guests. Only Cicely, Iris, and the Duke of Aylesbury held back. The two females watched the bride and groom with resentment, but the sharp-boned old man was staring at his new daughter-in-law with tears in his eyes. Finally, when Andrew glanced over questioningly, the duke came forward. First, he extended a hand to his son, then turned to Micheline.

"You look every bit as beautiful as my Katherine when she wore that gown thirty-three years ago. Buttercups and bird's-eye primroses..." His voice was thick with emotion. "I'll wager she's watching right now and is as proud as I am to welcome you to our family, my lady. My son is a fortunate man."

Sandhurst felt a long-forgotten stirring of emotion as he watched his father. When Micheline replied by kissing the old duke's withered cheek, it seemed a symbolic gesture of peace. Somehow, Andrew managed to speak.

"I have you to thank, Father," he said softly. "You brought us together."

Part Four

Now welcome, night, thou night so
    long expected,
That long day's labour dost at last
    defray,
And all my cares, which cruel love
    collected,
Hast summed in one, and cancelled
    for aye:
Spread thy broad wing over my love
    and me,
That no man may us see,
And in thy sable mantle us enwrap,
From fear of peril and foul horror free.
Let no false treason seek us to entrap,
Nor any dread disquiet once annoy
The safety of our joy.

– EDMUND SPENSER
1552?-1599

Thirty

THE WEDDING PARTY adjourned to the great hall, a long, magnificent room with an oak-beamed ceiling, a huge fireplace, and white stone walls hung with priceless tapestries.

The marriage ceremony now seemed but a prelude to the real purpose of the day: serious gluttony and merrymaking. The next few hours passed in a blur for Micheline. She could scarcely hear the conversation at her table over the shouts of laughter. Meanwhile, dish after dish was served. There was oyster pie; lettuce stuffed with forcemeat; venison stewed in beer; salad of watercress, herbs, and cabbage; honey-glazed capon stuffed with apples, raisins, and almonds; and fried artichokes flavored with orange. Just when the feast seemed to be ending, bowls of juicy new strawberries and an assortment of cheeses appeared.

Micheline sipped fragrant Burgundy wine from a jeweled goblet, but the wine's effect paled next to the heady feeling of Andrew's lean-muscled thigh pressing through her skirts under the table. Every time their hands brushed, color stained Micheline's cheeks. Shyness mingled with excitement in her breast when she thought of what lay ahead for them that evening.

Dozens of toasts were proposed, including several by Rupert Topping, who appeared to have imbibed too freely. At one point he staggered to his feet and shouted, "I propose a toast to the most splendid brother any Englishman has ever known!" He took a hearty swig, spilling on his doublet of purple satin, while the similarly overfestive guests drank along with him. "And a toast to Lady Sandhurst, whose beauty and charm make her the only woman in the world worthy to become my brother's wife!"

"Hear, hear!" exclaimed the king, drinking heartily. He and Anne Boleyn were seated across the table from the bride and groom. There had been little chance for conversation, but now, as the toasts subsided, Henry leaned forward, his beefy face ruddy with wine, and addressed Micheline. "I can scarce find words to tell you how pleased we are that you are now an English marchioness, Lady Sandhurst! In fact, I wish that the two of you would consider traveling to France in the near future. What attractive ambassadors you would make! What do you say, my lady?"

Sandhurst intervened at this point. "We mean no disrespect, sire, but as I have already explained to you, Lady Sandhurst and I would like to remain in England for the time being."

The king's hands clenched, betraying his displeasure, but his smile barely faltered. "Will you not allow your bride to speak for herself?"

"I fear I must agree with my husband, Your Majesty," Micheline said clearly. "One day I might like to return to France, but only to visit dear friends. I've no desire whatever to linger again at the French court. That was part of another lifetime for me."

Henry's lips thinned. "I can only hope that you will reconsider." He gave Sandhurst a hard stare.

Anne Boleyn had been watching this exchange with increasing disquiet. "Can we not speak about something more cheerful? Pardon me for saying so, sire, but I think we should leave this couple to enjoy their wedding day!"

The king glared at her, but further conversation was interrupted by another toast from Rupert.

Watching his half brother weave and ramble incoherently, Andrew looked at Micheline, a smile playing over his mouth. "Have you had enough?" he whispered.

"Easily!" The mischief in his expression nearly made her giggle.

Sandhurst leaned over to speak to his father, who nodded approval, then waved away the servants who approached with curd and cheese tarts and orange pudding. Rising, he addressed the assembled guests.

"My wife and I would like to thank you all for being today to share in our happiness." He nodded toward King Henry, hoping to allay any ill feelings. "We'll stay for one dance, then I trust you'll understand if we take our leave." He paused, smiling. "I respect tradition, but today I ask that we dispense with the bedding of the bride... and attendant customs. I've waited a long time for this day, and I'd like to undress Lady Sandhurst myself."

* * *

The sun had just set when Sandhurst closed the paneled door to what had been Micheline's chamber but tonight would be occupied by both of them. The white stone fireplace danced with a freshly lit blaze, sending shadows capering happily over the walls while the sounds of music and dancing drifted in from the hall.

The first thing Micheline noticed was a delicate gold casket that reposed in the middle of the bed. "What's this?" she wondered, picking it up.

"Perhaps someone left it as a wedding gift."

Pleased, Micheline lifted the carved lid, but her expression changed to one of horror when she saw what lay inside the little box. Nestled in folds of white satin was a gold wedding ring, broken in half. "Andrew! What can it mean?"

Immediately he took the box from her and closed the lid with a snap. "A cruel joke, no doubt perpetrated by someone who desired to taint the joy of this night." Gathering her into his arms, he whispered, "You must forget about it. Forget about everything save the two of us."

Oddly enough, Micheline was able to obey with ease. Her bliss was such that nothing else could intrude.

"Let me dispose of this," he said. "I'll be only a moment."

In the corridor he had the good fortune to encounter Jeremy Culpepper.

"Take this evil thing and destroy it," Sandhurst said flatly, showing his friend the contents of the casket.

Culpepper's eyes widened and a cold chill ran down his spine. "Who would do such a thing? Iris Dangerfield?"

"I know not, and for tonight I do not care." His sculpted profile was hard with anger. "Later, though, I intend to find out. Too many sinister events have been taking place lately, and I mean to discover who is responsible."

With that he turned away and reentered the chamber, smiling at his wife as he closed the door. "Now, where were we?"

Curiously nervous, Micheline perched on the edge

of the bed, blushing like a maiden. She watched apprehensively as Andrew lit a candle and placed it on the table next to the bed.

"I want to see you," he said huskily, "the first time we make love as husband and wife."

"Oh." Her lips formed the word, but no sound came out.

"What's amiss, fondling?" Sitting down beside her, he raised one slender hand to his mouth and kissed the ring on Micheline's wedding finger. "Surely you're not afraid of me."

"No..." She gasped involuntarily when his mouth found the pulse at her wrist, then the tender heart of her palm, his gaze as intimate as a caress. "No, of course I'm not afraid of you." A tremor of arousal traveled downward to the place between her legs.

"I know." Understanding and playfulness mingled in Andrew's smile. Now he merely held her hand and looked into her eyes. "Try to remember that our love is all that really matters. This"—Sandhurst drew her against him and kissed her with frank desire, then murmured against her cheek—"this is just a physical expression of that love. As long as our feelings are genuine, we cannot disappoint each other."

Micheline warmed to his tender, eloquent words yet a part of her remained afraid. The responsibility of loving Andrew suddenly seemed overwhelming. Could she possibly make him happy? Already she feared that he might be disappointed on this first night of their marriage; how could she be enough for him year after year, for the rest of their lives? The future stretched out ahead of them in her mind, fraught with risks and possibilities for failure.

Inevitably Micheline thought back to the day she had married Bernard Tevoulère. It had become apparent to her that she hadn't known then the true possibilities love held, yet she had been more confident on that first wedding day than she was now. She realized that she had been far more naive at seventeen; that fact alone gave her pause. But if she hadn't been able to fulfill Bernard, how could she possibly be enough for someone like Andrew?

As usual, Sandhurst gazed into her troubled eyes and guessed her thoughts.

"Michelle," he said quietly, "put aside the past and future. Let us deal with the present, moment by moment."

She sighed heavily. "But—"

Putting a forefinger under her chin, he tilted her face up so that she could not avoid his penetrating eyes. "I love you." He touched his mouth to hers and their lips clung. "I want you."

Those poignant words were her undoing. Micheline's doubts fell away as she surrendered to the magic of his nearness.

"I want you, too, Andrew," she said shakily. Reaching out, Micheline caressed the muscles that tapered down to his narrow waist. Even through the velvet doublet she could feel the vital warmth of his skin. "I love you."

"Then there is nothing to worry about." His tone held a gentle note of finality.

Micheline watched as his fingers, strong and graceful all at once, unlaced her gown. She could feel the heat and moisture between her legs, and then she was reaching to unfasten his doublet. Andrew lowered the bodice of her gown with tantalizing slowness, bringing her chemise with it, until her breasts were bared, round and glowing in the firelight. Dark rose nipples stood out and he bent to kiss each one in turn, lingeringly, until Micheline moaned with pleasure.

Slowly he removed her clothing, savoring each precious inch of her as it was revealed to him. His fingertips traced the lines of her throat, the edges of her breasts, and down over her hips and belly, trailing fire. A hungering throb came then between her legs.

His doublet came off, revealing the powerful contours of his torso. Micheline slid her arms around him and drew near to press her cheek to his warm chest. An unexpected wave of emotion swelled within her and she blinked back tears as she listened to the beating of his heart. Andrew lifted her higher, into his embrace, and kissed her in earnest. His tongue told her all that he wanted to do. The last of their clothing fell away until they both were naked and he reached out to pull back the green velvet counterpane.

Micheline looked over to discover that the sheets were strewn with tiny colorful flowers: yellow primroses, violets, and lily-of-the-valley bells. Her eyes swam with tears.

Sandhurst drew her into his embrace and they knelt pressed together for long minutes, exploring and tasting each other's mouths. He fit himself between her legs so that she could feel the power of his need for her. Yearning broke in long, exquisite waves over Micheline's body as she melted against him, her fingers traveling over each taut muscle in his back and shoulders, then down to the hard curves of his buttocks.

Soon they were lying amid the fragrant spring flowers. Micheline loved this extra gift of sight, for in the past they had made love in darkness. She basked in the warmth of Andrew's eyes and gazed euphorically on his candlelit face, the corded muscles that joined his neck and shoulders, the strength of his arms, and the lean beauty of his chest. Even as Micheline gloried in the scorching kisses he trailed over her body, she was watching him move. Never had she imagined such a combination of strength and elegant grace.

Sandhurst knew exactly where and how to touch her. His mouth found the sensitive nape of her neck, the bend of her arm, her inner wrist, then lingered over her breasts before blazing a trail down her belly to the insides of her thighs. His fingers slipped into the nest of curls between her legs and she throbbed, aching, as he touched her in ways more intimate than she had ever imagined.

"So, so beautiful," he murmured, kissing her there.

Micheline writhed against him until the waves of sensation drew her up higher still and carried her to a place she had never known existed. She lay gasping, pressing against him. Sheer passion had burned away all intruding thoughts. As much as she wanted to touch and kiss Andrew's body, the need to feel him inside of her overrode all else.

"Please!" she whispered. Her eyes were drawn helplessly to his erect manhood. *How beautifully he is made*, she thought, aching for him.

When Sandhurst finally rose to deeply kiss her mouth, Micheline reached to wrap her fingers around him. His erection was hard yet warm, pulsating slightly against her palm.

"Oh, Andrew," she whispered, her voice breaking on a sob, "I love you."

He drew back to stare at her. "Michelle, you are more than my wife. You are my mate."

And then he came into her into her, filling her, moaning aloud at the sensation of her sweet, moist warmth tightening around him. They arched together, moving fervently, the sound of their gasps filling the room, until another wild surging climax shook Micheline's very soul. Sandhurst found his own shuddering release moments later. When his breathing slowed a bit, he lifted his face from the cloud of her hair and ran the backs of his fingertips over her damp brow. Their bodies were still united, and a slow smile spread over his face that said more than words ever could. Micheline felt as if she were floating on a cloud of utter bliss.

Later, after they had shared quiet caresses, Andrew poured one goblet of wine for them both and they lay against the pillows, sipping. She arranged flowers over his chest and he went a step further, putting primroses in the damp curls between her legs.

The sight of his smile ignited a fresh fire of love inside of her.

"I have never been so pleased to be a woman," she exclaimed. "A woman mated to the most splendid of men."

He laughed, basking in her radiance. "Life is sweet, indeed."

"I am so happy, Andrew. That's what frightens me. Does anyone deserve to be so happy?"

"You do, my heart," Sandhurst assured her. He reached over to set the goblet of wine on the table by the bed and returned to find Micheline's lips parted in anticipation of his kiss.

Thirty-One

GLOUCESTERSHIRE, ENGLAND

TO REACH SANDHURST MANOR, traveling as they were from the northeast, Andrew and Micheline had to pass through Stratford-upon-Avon, a quaint town of fewer than two hundred half-timbered houses. Accompanied as usual by Finchley, Mary, and two squires, they spent the night at a cozy inn on Chapel Lane.

Micheline slept little that night. Snuggled in the circle of Andrew's embrace, she thought about the first happy days of her marriage and wondered what life would be like in her new home. Three times she heard the watchman pass, calling out eventually, "Give ear to the clock, beware your lock, your fire, and your light, and God give you good night: three o'clock."

In the morning Micheline was radiant with energy and anticipation.

"Every day is an adventure," she told Andrew as they broke their fast, "because I am seeing places and things for the first time."

He paused in the midst of chewing a bite of plum to give her an affectionate smile.

"I would like to ride with you today," she said. "Then we can talk and share the experience together. I am so tired of that stuffy coach."

His brows flicked up. "People would find that quite shocking, my lady," he said with mock severity.

"How exciting for them," she laughed, coming over to perch on the arm of his chair and lean against him. "You must agree, my lord!"

Sandhurst fed her the rest of his plum, ignoring glances from the other people in the common room, "I yield to you, my wife."

It was still early when the group of six rode leisurely out of Stratford-upon-Avon. They kept to the river, which led them straight into the beautiful Cotswold Hills, one of the loveliest areas in all of Britain.

Above them the sky was vividly azure, dotted with snowy puffs of clouds, while the air was spring-sweet and warm. There were water meadows all along the River Avon, drenched in violets, wild thyme, and yellow oxlips. The Cotswolds themselves were green hillsides that were shaped, as Sandhurst remarked, "like whales' backs." The light was slightly hazy, almost iridescent, reminding Micheline of the Loire Valley in France.

"I've never seen so many sheep," she declared at one point, eliciting a chuckle from her husband.

"This is sheep country, sweetheart. The wool merchants are getting rich from them. You see, Cotswold sheep have lustrous wool that's really quite special."

Before long they turned south from the River Avon.

Micheline delighted in the rolling hills, and the secluded valleys lined with pollard willows and threaded with silvery brooks. The Cotswolds exuded a kind of magic that made Micheline feel content on another level from her happiness with Andrew. The softly undulating hills seemed to embrace her, welcoming her home at last.

When they rode into the village of Chipping Campden she was surprised to see all the buildings and houses composed of honey-colored stone. High Street curved ahead of them, tinted golden in the midday light.

"It's Cotswold limestone," Sandhurst explained, anticipating her question. "With time, it mellows from gray to the warm honey color you see here."

They wound their way through the market-day crowds of people, carts, and livestock. Down one of the quieter lanes of town they paused at the Crooked Billet inn for a meal of pigeon pie, asparagus with oil and vinegar, brown bread and honey, and stewed apples. To Micheline's surprise the innkeeper recognized Sandhurst and called his wife and children out to welcome "his lordship" home. When Andrew informed them that the lady at his side was the new Lady Sandhurst, they behaved as if she were royalty.

Later, outside the inn, he told her, "We're still two hours from the village of Sandhurst. For years our villagers have been pestering me to marry, so there will doubtless be another display of enthusiasm there."

Fortunately they came upon Sandhurst, a hamlet caught in a fold of hills, late in the afternoon, when most people were off the streets having a rest from the labors of the day. To the others who rushed forth to greet Lord Sandhurst, he merely said that he was eager to get home and would return soon for a proper visit. Micheline felt the curious gazes of the townspeople and smiled in return.

The buildings of Sandhurst predictably blushed a tawny hue, and there was a handsome church that struck Micheline as both dignified and primitive.

"It's Norman," Andrew told her succinctly. "No wonder you like it!"

South of the village, they rode through more sheep-covered hills as well as fields being plowed by oxen. Occasionally one of the farm laborers caught sight of Sandhurst's proud head and strong silhouette on horseback and called a greeting to him. Micheline's surprise grew when she heard him reply, invariably calling each man by name.

"These people work for me," he explained.

"But how can you recognize each one from such a distance?"

He gave a light shrug. "Instinct, I suppose. I've known most of those men all my life."

Finally they reached the curving brow of a hill and Sandhurst reined in his horse. "There it is," he said with feeling. "That's your new home."

Below them, in a deep, rounded valley, lay Sandhurst Manor. Micheline could see only that it was rose-colored, rather than golden, and sprawling, with an assortment of chimneys. Smooth, well-tended gardens spread out to the edges of the hillsides, and there were beechwoods to the north.

"Some people call it Sandhurst-in-the-Hole," he said with a wry smile. "You can see why."

Micheline was already mesmerized. "It's perfectly lovely."

As they rode down into the vale, Andrew explained, "The manor house was rebuilt during my youth and is exactly my own taste. It could have been created with me in mind."

Their horses slowed to a walk as they passed a lily pond and clipped yew trees. Ahead, an eccentrically splendid manor house of salmon-pink brick rose up, charming in its irregularity. The house was tall, turreted, and gabled, with decorated chimneys rising haphazardly above the battlemented parapet. The porch was not in the center of the facade, and even the spacious, square-headed windows seemed scattered at random.

Micheline stared, speechless, for a long minute, then turned toward Sandhurst, beaming. "I must be dreaming! Can this really be your home?"

"*Our* home," he amended. Andrew followed her gaze and the corners of his mouth turned up slightly. "Rather odd, isn't it."

"Rather wonderful!" Micheline corrected him adamantly. "It's a happy-looking house."

"Happy in its oddity," Sandhurst agreed. In spite of his offhand manner, he was immensely relieved by her reactions, not just now, but all day long. With some women, he might have suspected pretense, but never with Micheline. Since the moment she'd owned up to her ill-concealed feelings for him, he'd never had reason to doubt her word.

"I think it is very beautiful in its oddity." She was rising up to defend the house as if it had always been her own and Sandhurst were the newcomer.

"Pardon me." Laughing, he reached out to catch her hand. "Don't take me to task! We are in accord."

As they drew nearer the manor, Micheline finally noticed the long-legged horses silhouetted against one hillside, separated by dry stone walls from the sheep covering the rest of the valley. There were extensive stables to the west, and a long-suppressed thrill leaped inside Micheline at the thought of so many magnificent steeds.

Andrew felt his role as lord of the manor taking hold again. He could sense the house coming to life, and, meanwhile, he was wondering if the horses had been tended properly, if the gardens had thrived in his absence, and if anything had changed within the manor.

Stableboys were rushing forward to take the horses

as they neared the entrance to the house and dismounted. Sandhurst had no sooner lifted Micheline lightly to the ground than a plump, middle-aged lady with light brown hair drawn back tightly into a hood came flying out of the manor, arms outstretched.

"My lord, my lord!" she cried, tears dripping onto her pink cheeks. "Is it really you?"

"Of course it's me, Betsy," he assured her, holding her close. When the woman drew back to gaze at him, he reached out a hand to Micheline. "I have a surprise for you. This is my wife, Lady Sandhurst. Micheline, I want you to meet Betsy, otherwise known as Mistress Trymme. She's kept this place running smoothly for years. I couldn't leave in good conscience if Betsy weren't here."

"A wife!" Betsy exclaimed. "Our Lord has answered my prayers."

Micheline extended her hand, instantly drawn to the older woman. "It's a pleasure to meet you, Mistress Trymme."

"Oh, no, my lady, the pleasure is *mine!*" Looking up at Sandhurst, she nodded approval in a way that indicated a long-standing closeness between the two. "You've picked a marvelously lovely marchioness, Lord Andrew! And now you must know none of us will rest until there's a babe on the way!"

He feigned exasperation. "I'm doing my best. Nan Goodwyn had already begun bothering me on this very subject in London, a fortnight before Micheline and I were even married."

To Micheline's astonishment Betsy laughed and replied, "I hope you don't expect me to believe that you let a few simple words spoken in church hold you off!" She waggled a finger at him. "I know you better than that, my boy."

Sandhurst blinked, then chuckled. "Would you make me out a libertine before my sweet bride?"

"Your lady looks as if she has her wits about her, Lord Andrew, and I wouldn't expect you to marry less. Surely I haven't said more than she already knows!" Betsy beamed at Micheline, adding, "You all must be tired, and no doubt my lady is eager to see more of her new home."

The manor's buildings were grouped around a square garden courtyard. Inside, there were a bewildering number of rooms: twenty bedchambers, a private dining room plus summer and winter parlors, a high-arched, two-story great hall with its connecting chapel, and not only a pantry and buttery but also pastry, laundry, and linen rooms. There was also a magnificent library and a long gallery lined with windows on one side and Flemish tapestries on the other.

The great hall was bathed in sunlight and strewn with fresh herbs and fragrant hyacinths. Paintings lined the walls and Micheline was on her way to look at them when a liver-spotted spaniel came bounding into the room. The dog ran straight for Sandhurst, who knelt to welcome him, laughing.

"Meet Percy," he said to Micheline.

"That's rather an unexpected name." She came over to pet the spaniel's sleek head, smiling.

"I made the mistake of letting Cicely name him when he was a puppy. She was only five or so at the time and decided that he resembled a friend of mine called Sir Percy Buckthorn. As a result, I've had to hide the dog the few times Percy's visited. I don't imagine he'd be flattered to meet his namesake."

Percy let out a short woof of appreciation and licked his master's cheek. When Sandhurst stood up and walked over to the paintings with Micheline, the spaniel trotted along, attempting to insert himself between them.

"Oh, dear," Micheline whispered in mock anxiety. "I'm afraid your friend is jealous. I hope he's not used to sleeping on your bed!"

He laughed. "Rest easy, my lady. In fact, you'll discover a dog gate on the stairs to keep him in his place." Bending down, he gently but firmly dragged the reluctant spaniel over to his left side. "Speaking of places, *this* is yours, Percy. Don't look at me like that! The lady is my wife, and I won't share her with you."

Percy hung his head. "There, you see!" Sandhurst declared to Micheline. "It's not you he's jealous of, it's me. Obviously the beast was hoping to steal you away from me. Edging in between us, indeed. If Percy aspires to become a true rogue, he'll have to adopt a more subtle approach."

Although Micheline laughed, she felt a twinge of sympathy for the dog. No doubt he was used to having his master's undivided attention, for it seemed unlikely that Sandhurst had brought many ladies all the way to Gloucestershire. Instinct told her that he had kept his life in London apart from the quieter existence at Sandhurst Manor. Already, Micheline had begun to detect aspects of his personality that she had not seen before. It was exciting to realize that she would share in every phase of his life.

Gesturing toward a wonderfully executed painting of a dark-haired lady, Micheline queried, "Is this your mother?"

"How did you know?"

"There is a family resemblance. On the surface she looks like Cicely, but her eyes are yours exactly. Extraordinarily warm and compelling."

Sandhurst gazed at the portrait, momentarily far

away. "Odd that you should mention Mother's eyes. She was a very proper lady, quite restrained, yet one could gauge her mood by looking at her eyes. While painting her, they were the most difficult aspect to capture." He gave Micheline a sidelong smile. "The same was true when I painted you. Even more so, I'd say."

"That's because all my feelings were pent up inside —and when I was in the same room with you, there was a veritable storm brewing inside of me!" She laughed softly, remembering. "I didn't realize at first that you did this painting, Andrew. Don't tell me that you're responsible for *all* of these!"

"I confess, if you'll promise not to hold them against me," he replied a trifle ruefully. "In the past I tended to spend nearly every minute here either out with the horses or painting in the gallery. After Mother died, it seemed a good idea to hang this portrait, along with the one of my father. Betsy began complaining, quite shrewdly, that the wall needed 'balancing,' and soon she started bringing out all the other paintings I'd hidden away. I fear that the room's beginning to look like a shrine to my rather average abilities."

"Average?" echoed Micheline, "Not at all! You are very talented."

"I paint because I enjoy it. It's a challenge, and it relaxes me. The results are incidental."

Micheline had moved down to stare at the portrait of the Duke of Aylesbury. In it, he was younger and more contented-looking. His hair was sandy, threaded with white strands, and the angles of his face were softer.

"I did that a dozen years ago, just after returning from my studies in Florence. Mother 'commissioned' it for Father's birthday, hoping, I suppose, that the project would improve our relationship, but it all turned out badly, as usual. He was so critical of the finished product that I brought the painting back here and stored it in a cupboard. Years went by before I even looked at it again."

"Don't you think the duke has softened lately?"

"Perhaps. And perhaps you're responsible. Look what you've done to *my* well-ordered existence, sweeting." Putting an arm around her waist, he kissed her hair. "If he has changed, I'll be happy for his sake, not mine. I don't need his approval. At this stage in my life, all I need is you."

He spoke in a matter-of-fact way that warmed her heart long after they'd finished looking at the rest of the paintings. There were two village scenes, one of the Cotswold Hills at sunset, one of Cicely standing next to a beautiful horse, one of Betsy looking very proud, and lastly, a whimsical portrait of Percy the spaniel.

"Let's go upstairs and have a bath," Sandhurst said when they'd finished touring the hall. "Together."

Micheline pretended to be scandalized, then twined her arms about his neck and pressed her body against his. "I'd love it... if Percy isn't included in that invitation."

The spaniel stood on the other side of the carved dog gate, looking forlorn as they climbed the wide staircase and disappeared from sight.

Thirty-Two

AT DAWN, Micheline awoke to find herself warm in the circle of Andrew's arm, her face against his chest. The bedhangings of forest-green velvet were drawn back at the posts to allow the entrance of sunlight, and Sandhurst's body was golden brown in its glow. Wonderingly Micheline gazed at his sculpted face, the lips parted slightly, vulnerably, as he slept. His brows, so mobile when he was awake, were still, and long lashes closed his eyes.

These days, he slept with her and made love to her without reserve. Micheline gloried in the knowledge that he trusted her now, and acknowledged his need of her with equal ease. There was no reason to speak the words aloud in constant reassurance; both of them could comprehend each other's feelings with barely a touch or a glance.

Micheline's eyes roamed over Sandhurst's body, for the warm spring nights invariably caused him to toss off the covers in his sleep. In her years with Bernard, she had never been acquainted with him as intimately as she already was with Andrew. She knew every detail and contour of his body, from the shape of his ears to the sleek, hard contours of his rider's legs. She knew the texture of the crisp hair on his arms and legs—and elsewhere. In the past, her first husband's maleness had been a source of slight embarrassment. Neither it nor what was done with it was ever openly acknowledged by either Micheline or Bernard. With Andrew, all was new and different. They shared everything, every feeling and delight. In the bath the day before, Micheline had caressed him teasingly until Sandhurst called her bluff and lifted her through the water, impaling her on the length of his manhood. She'd felt no embarrassment, only overwhelming pleasure and satisfaction as they moved rhythmically in the water, her hands in his damp hair, his mouth at her breasts.

Now she stared down past Andrew's hard belly, thinking that his sex was as beautifully made as his hands. When she touched it lightly, it awoke.

"Good morrow," Sandhurst whispered huskily into her ear, then nibbled on the lobe. "My lady wife. What sweet words."

Although they'd loved twice the night before, Micheline found that her hunger for him could not be appeased. She turned on her side just as he did, her breasts and hips pressing against the lean lines of his body.

"I'm so pleased to be here," she whispered, smiling. "So pleased to be your wife."

His kisses scorched the curve of her throat while his agile fingers wandered down her spine to explore the satiny curves of her derriere.

"Mmm" was the only verbal response he could manage.

* * *

Later that morning Andrew took Micheline out to the stables. Already it was a glorious day. The sun shone brightly, wildflowers lent their fragrance to the breeze, and even Percy pranced hither and yon in high spirits.

The stables, built of honey-colored stone, were handsomely maintained. Grooms busied themselves exercising or caring for the horses outside, while a tall, raw-boned man with wind-blown white hair walked forward to greet the Marquess and Marchioness of Sandhurst.

"Welcome home, my lord," he said soberly, though his tone was belied by warm gray eyes. "'Tis good to have you back."

"It's good to be back." Andrew extended his hand, smiling. "I'd like you to meet Lady Sandhurst. Sweetheart, this is Trymme, the marshal here at Sandhurst Manor—and also Betsy's husband. Trymme is in charge of the stables, the grooms, and all the horses."

"I'm happy to know you, sir," Micheline said sincerely.

"Likewise, my lady. I hope you are pleased with your new home."

Her eyes shone with pleasure. "I love it!"

"My wife has a fondness for horses," Andrew confided. "I thought I'd let her choose one for her own—and I ought to say hello to Hampstead. He's well, I trust?"

"Quite! He serviced Willow, that young mare you approved of, and that went very well. He's just been groomed and is waiting to see you, my lord. I thought you might be along to exercise him."

"My thanks, Trymme. How fares little Stroller? Has she foaled yet?"

"No, my lord. Any day now."

Micheline listened with only half an ear as the two men continued to talk. They all walked along the stable boxes, where Andrew petted each muzzle and smiled into each pair of large, hopeful eyes.

"I've never seen such beautiful horses!" Micheline finally exclaimed. "Is this a breed you've developed yourself?"

Sandhurst couldn't repress a chuckle. "On the contrary, fondling. These are all Arabian horses. There's no finer horse on earth, in my opinion, and for the most part, I'm keeping the bloodlines pure. We have done a small amount of crossbreeding between the Arabs and some Welsh Mountain ponies, which, though similar in looks and temperament, are naturally smaller. The king threatens to decree that all stock under fourteen hands high must be eliminated, so we've been working to make those pretty ponies larger. We've also bred a few of the Arabians with Chapman horses from Yorkshire, to see what improvements might be made on some of the native breeds." He smiled ironically. "Make no mistake; I'm very fond of British and European horses, but once one becomes used to Arabians..."

"One is spoiled?" Micheline supplied, beginning to understand. Each of these horses possessed a lovely head, with large eyes and a small muzzle, carried on an elegant neck. Their bodies were compact, their legs long, slender, and strong.

Sandhurst nodded. "There's much more than beauty involved, though, as you'll discover. Arabs are intelligent, gay-spirited, and gentle. They're also extraordinarily fast, with great stamina and an ability to carry weight. The real reason I breed them, however, is their love for human companionship."

He'd stopped in front of an open box, where a young groom was putting a bridle on an elegant sable-brown stallion. When the horse saw Sandhurst, it neighed softly and nodded its head.

"This is Hampstead." He walked forward to greet his favorite steed and Micheline was touched by the scene. Andrew, with his own lithe strength, seemed to belong among such beautiful horses. "Come and say hello, sweetheart."

When Micheline reached the stallion, Sandhurst slipped a wedge of apple into her hand and she offered it with a few gentle words of greeting. Hampstead munched the fruit slowly, as if scrutinizing her, then he seemed to smile, showing strong white teeth.

Happiness welled up inside her as she stroked his sleek mane and coat. In the past there had been few people she'd liked as well as horses, particularly her Gustave, who must be languishing without her at Angoulême.

Andrew took Hampstead's reins and led him out of the box. "Have you seen a horse yet that strikes your fancy?" he inquired of Micheline.

"Each is more splendid than the last! I couldn't begin—" At that moment her eyes fell on an exquisite long-legged filly being groomed in the sunlight. The horse was a warm shade of chestnut, with white stockings and a long white blaze accentuating the beauty of her face. As if sensing Micheline's admiration, the filly tilted her head slightly, returning her gaze.

"Aha." Sandhurst's murmur was scarcely audible. He smiled in Trymme's direction. "I'd say we've just made a match."

* * *

During the next month Micheline settled into life at Sandhurst Manor as if she had lived there always. Indeed, she had never been nearly so happy in her childhood home.

Each morning Sandhurst and his bride rose early, usually sharing a piece or two of fresh fruit en route to the stables. Micheline was fascinated by the various aspects of horse-breeding and was never bored by the sometimes long conversations between Andrew and Trymme. Often she was there early enough to feed Primrose, her white-stockinged filly, a light breakfast of oats, timothy and clover hay, peas, sliced carrots, and apple peelings. Then she and Andrew would exercise Primrose and Hampstead, riding either south over the hills or north to the village. It was their habit to stop at some point, leaving the horses to graze while they lay down in the meadows.

Drifts of flowers blanketed the hillsides. Micheline was enchanted by the snakeshead fritallery, a flower mottled with light and dark purple that hung its head in the spring sunshine. One day she and Sandhurst lay kissing in a sea of cowslip and forget-me-nots while Percy chased elusive green-veined white butterflies and wobbly little lambs over the sloping hill. They were far from the manor, seemingly alone in a world of their own. When Andrew loosened her bodice to free her breasts, warm and pale in the sunshine, Micheline could only stretch sensuously and bask in the shivery sensations his mouth and hands evoked. Her own hands caressed him through his buff doublet and breeches, curving around the ridge of his arousal until her skirts somehow were hitched up and Micheline felt soft hay and wildflowers under her thighs. She unfastened Andrew's codpiece and their bodies joined in a torrent of sweet desire. Above her was a sky that Andrew called "heaven's own blue," and as they mated there in the sun-drenched meadow, it seemed to Micheline that heaven itself could not possibly surpass the life they'd fashioned together on earth.

Even when they were apart, she was happy. Some afternoons Sandhurst painted or looked after estate business while she rode Primrose alone or became acquainted with the workings of her new household. The servants adored Micheline since she refused to put on airs, and even the cook, a sturdy old woman called Lettice, welcomed her into the kitchen, where they worked at inventing dishes that combined the elements Micheline liked best in French cooking with the usual English preparations.

May Day came and the manor house wore garlands of flowers and hawthorn branches on its windows and doors. That afternoon Micheline put on a gown of white muslin trimmed with thin yellow silk ribbons, and Mary helped her secure a wreath of colorful flowers in her loose fire-gold curls. She and Andrew rode into the village to preside over the crowning of the Queen of the May, an honor bestowed upon a comely milkmaid called Meg. The townspeople danced and sang all day long, many of them cavorting in circles around a flower-decked maypole near the parish church. Everyone was delighted by the new Lady Sandhurst, who was as pretty and gay as any rosy-cheeked village girl.

As May progressed, Micheline's contentment grew apace. The absence of her monthly flow confirmed her happy suspicion that she and Andrew had created new life that spring along with the rest of nature's creatures. Sandhurst was delighted, but far from surprised.

The kind of reality Micheline had been forced to

deal with in Yorkshire couldn't be held at bay indefinitely, however. The third week of the month brought several days of rain, which refreshed the landscape but kept the couple indoors. One afternoon they sat side by side in a library window seat, sharing a volume of *The Book of Merlin*.

Sandhurst stretched out lean-muscled legs and propped them on a placet. Unused to prolonged inactivity, he was finding it harder by the minute to resist the distracting charms of his bride. As raindrops splashed the mullioned window behind them, his gaze wandered from the printed page to the display of Micheline's bosom above a low square neckline.

"What are you looking at, my lord?" she inquired primly.

"I find you far more absorbing than Merlin, my lady." His head dipped to kiss the tempting curve of her flesh.

"An interesting choice of words," she observed, shifting against the window seat in a way that told him she was already aroused.

He looked up and smiled boyishly. "Very apt." His eyes softened at the sight of her face, the picture of radiant beauty framed by a spill of brandy-colored curls. He couldn't remember the last time she'd pinned up her hair since arriving at Sandhurst Manor. "You know, you positively glow."

"Marriage... and your baby would seem to agree with me." She ran her fingers through his luxuriant hair, occasional strands gilded by long days spent in the sun, while his face was tanned and handsome.

Tenderly he kissed her mouth. "I'm glad you're happy here." Sitting back next to her, Sandhurst distractedly drew a pattern with his forefinger on the slim back of Micheline's hand. "I rather hate to bring this up, but you probably realize that we must begin preparations to travel to London. If it were anything except the coronation, I'd suggest we remain here, but it's just not that easy. If we don't make the effort, King Henry will remember."

"It's even more than that, Andrew. We're to meet Cicely in London. You hadn't forgotten, had you?"

He sighed. "I've been trying to. Are you certain you want to carry through with those plans, in light of the baby? I don't want Cicely upsetting you. I worry that you'll feel unwell and never mention it."

"You must *not* worry," Micheline insisted, aware that his anxiety was rooted in the knowledge that she had lost a baby during her first marriage. "The other time, I felt completely different right from the first day."

"Swear that you'll tell me if you have any pain."

"Honestly, I've never felt better in my life! You've seen how I've been eating. I'm thriving, Andrew."

"You must swear," he persisted, squeezing her hand.

"Very well, then, I swear."

* * *

The twenty-ninth of May fell on a Thursday. Dawn had scarcely begun to lighten the London sky when a knock sounded on the door of Andrew and Micheline's spacious bedchamber at Weston House.

Sandhurst slowly opened one eye to find his wife looking at him in bewilderment. "If that's Rupert, I'll kill him for certain this time," he muttered, his voice husky with sleep.

"Please, don't. I so deplore violence." She playfully pulled the covers over her head to escape his withering glance.

The knock was repeated and Cicely's voice came through the door. "Andrew, you haven't forgotten that you promised to take me downriver to watch the queen's entry into the city, have you?"

"I am not awake enough to even think yet." He fell back on the pillows and closed his eyes. "Come back in two hours and I'll let you know then if I forgot."

"Stop teasing me!" Her voice rose childishly.

"I assure you, I am quite serious. The procession of boats won't be leaving London for Greenwich Palace until midday. I'm not so old and doddering that I require an entire morning to dress and walk outside to the barge."

"But the river is already thronged with boats!"

"There will always be space for one more. I hereby close the subject, advising you to make yourself scarce until eight o'clock."

"But Andrew—"

"Leave us! If you want to depart for Greenwich now, get Rupert to take you. I want to sleep."

When there was no further argument from the corridor, Sandhurst burrowed under the covers and enfolded Micheline in his arms. "Actually that's not *quite* true. Mmm, you're warm." Kissing her throat, he caressed a breast, hip, and slim thigh. "And soft." His hand lightly traveled back up the inside of her leg until Micheline flinched slightly.

"Your sister still doesn't like me."

"I thought she'd been behaving rather well," he murmured absently. "Better, certainly, than in Yorkshire."

"Didn't you notice the way she failed to include me when speaking about the plans for today? It's as if she's trying to pretend I don't really exist."

"Oh, you exist, my love. I can certainly vouch for that."

His fingers were exploring intimately, expertly, and Micheline's thighs opened in surrender. Cicely was forgotten as Sandhurst's mouth covered hers. The love storm that dominated their lives was swelling to another crescendo.

* * *

That afternoon, while boats blanketed the Thames, the banks of the river were thronged with people. Everyone wanted to watch the magnificent procession for Queen Anne, though most subjects still judged Catherine the real queen. For, despite the Archbishop of Canterbury's recent decree that King Henry's first marriage was invalid, the pope himself had not yet spoken on the matter.

Micheline could not imagine a more sumptuous pageant than the one taking place around her on the Thames. Perhaps the procession had been made so overwhelmingly lavish in order to impress and thereby win over the skeptical citizens. The most incurably stubborn were said to crowd the dungeons of the Tower of London.

Music, cannon fire, and trumpet calls filled the warm air. Numerous barges had sailed down to Greenwich Palace more than an hour ago. Now they were returning. Cicely, clad in a pretty new gown of ruby silk, clapped her hands in excitement while Rupert shouted, "I say!" over and over again.

The first barge held Queen Anne herself, dressed in cloth of gold, attended by the colorfully decorated vessels of bishops and lords. The mayor even had a dragon on board, which thrashed about and spat fire into the river. More than two hundred other boats followed, embellished with tinkling bells and Anne's coat of arms paired with the king's. Streamers fluttered and danced in the breeze while musicians played with gusto from every craft.

When the queen's barge reached the water gate of the Tower of London, the mighty guns above her boomed in welcome. The constable and lieutenant came out of the crowd to greet Anne and take her to join the king, who waited at the postern gate.

"She'll spend the next two nights in the queen's apartments in the Tower," Andrew explained to Micheline. "It's a tradition. On Saturday there will be another procession—this time through the streets of London, bearing her to Westminster, where she'll be crowned on Sunday."

Nibbling at a sweetmeat, Cicely proclaimed, "I intend to be queen one day, but I suppose I shall have to be patient, for I would not marry King Hal!"

Micheline sighed. For the first time in her pregnancy, she felt the heat and was conscious of an enervating malaise, compounded by all the commotion and ceaseless music. "It's all very exciting." She gave Sandhurst a hopeful look. "Are we going home now?"

"No!" cried Cicely. "Please, Andrew, take us to join the celebrations! I don't want to return to that boring house!"

He had already given a signal that sent the oars dipping into the glittering water. As the barge glided upriver, he said, "Spare a thought for Micheline. She's with child, as I have told you, and deserves an extra measure of consideration."

The girl wore a petulant frown. "This is the most exciting day of my life! I don't see why we have to leave."

"No need for all this!" Rupert exclaimed, moving forward to clap Sandhurst on the back. "Patience and I would be happy to take Cicely out to enjoy the festivities, wouldn't we, my sweet?"

Patience surveyed them all with calm, tiny eyes. Her face was colorless in the sunlight. "Naturally," she said, smiling.

Thirty-Three

SATURDAY FOUND Micheline standing with Cicely. Rupert, and Patience behind one of the rails that lined the route of Queen Anne's procession through the streets of London. Although she felt better today, Micheline nonetheless missed Andrew's company, especially since she was surrounded by her new and less than ideal relatives.

The roads were hung with tapestry, velvets, and silks, through which traveled twelve Frenchmen, in blue velvet coats with sleeves of yellow, on horseback. Most of them Micheline recognized from Fontainebleau, but this was not the time for greetings.

Following the Frenchmen came all manner of officials in ceremonial robes. Knights of the Bath in their purple gowns, and finally noblemen in crimson velvet. There was Andrew, Marquess of Sandhurst, his hair ruffled in the breeze, standing out from the crowd as usual.

"Isn't he handsome!" cried Cicely, waving.

Micheline merely smiled. Sandhurst saw the hand in the air and winked, but it was his wife who caught the flash of warmth from his eyes.

"Crimson velvet would flatter any man, it seems to me," Patience observed quietly.

Rupert took up his half brother's defense. "Sandhurst is always the best-looking man in any gathering! Surely you realize that, my love!"

In the midst of more richly-garbed officials midst came Anne, perched in an open litter covered with cloth of gold. Dark hair flowed down her back so that she seemed to be sitting on it, and on her head was a coif set with jewels. She wore a surcoat and mantle of silver tissue lined with ermine. From under a cloth-of-gold canopy held over her by four knights, Queen Anne scanned the crowds, searching for signs of admiration.

The citizens might admire her beauty, but they withheld the approval she sought. Micheline noticed that few men removed their caps, and the sound of cheering was muted and unenthusiastic. The people seemed more curious than worshipful.

In an effort to rectify the situation, Anne's fool, capering at the edge of the parade, shouted, "I think you all have scurvy heads and dare not uncover!"

Stubbornly the crowd refused to take the hint.

"Why is it that you were not asked to ride in one of the chariots?" Cicely inquired of Micheline, referring to the crimson-clad ladies who followed Anne in decorated chariots.

"I'm not certain," Micheline replied honestly. "Perhaps it's because I'm French, and so new a marchioness. Or perhaps it's because they weren't certain we would attend. As you know, Andrew was told only last night that he would be required to join in the procession. In any case, my feelings are not bruised. I've had my fill of pageantry in recent months."

Cicely exchanged a look of disbelief with Patience but said only, "You are more forbearing than I, madame. I should feel quite insulted if I were you."

"I am too content with my life to take offense over trivialities."

After the procession passed, the crowd returned to its daylong celebrations. Rhenish wine flowed freely from London's fountains and music filled the air. Even the conduits of Cheapside ran with white wine at one end and claret at the other. Micheline watched as Rupert filled cups for himself, Cicely, and Patience. Now that the queen was gone, the mood turned festive, but Micheline had no taste for it. She could feel men's hands on her in the crowd, and her head had begun to ache.

"Have some wine, dear sister!" Rupert urged. "'Twill lighten your mood!"

"Thank you, but I must refuse. It's past seven o'clock, I'll wager, and the day has been a tiring one. I would like to go home and wait for Andrew to return from Westminster."

"My brother's wife seems intent on spoiling our fun." Cicely spoke to Patience as if Micheline were not there. "Next she'll insist that we accompany her back to Weston House."

"That's not necessary, my lady." Finchley stepped forward from his place behind them in the crowd. "I'll be happy to escort the marchioness home."

Micheline gave the manservant a grateful smile. "How very kind you are, Finchley!"

Farewells were made and Micheline set off with Finchley while her new relatives watched her go over the rims of their wine cups.

* * *

"Are you certain you feel up to this?" Sandhurst asked again. Seated in a chair by the window, he was watching

Mary dress Micheline's hair with diamonds and sapphires.

"Stop repeating that tiresome question! I've only been a bit fatigued lately. It's normal, considering my condition. Do you imagine that I'm the sort of female who takes to her bed at the least excuse?" She took a deep breath, hoping to ease the vague feeling of nausea that plagued her. "Besides, I wouldn't want to miss this coronation."

Andrew threw up his hands and sighed. "What am I to do with you?"

"That's easy." She gave him an enchanting smile, but he only narrowed his eyes in return. "You'll take me to Westminster, Lord Sandhurst, and allow me to enjoy the pleasure of being presented as your wife."

"You'll tell me if you feel the slightest discomfort?"

"Did I not swear?" Micheline glanced back at Mary, who was taking in the scene with wide eyes. "Don't you think that my husband looks magnificent today, Mary?"

"Oh—oh, yes, but of course, my lady!" This was a major understatement, for the girl had been casting surreptitious glances of awed admiration his way all morning. Lord Sandhurst was clad in a slashed, tailored doublet and breeches of rich amber velvet sewn with gold thread and set with diamonds.

"Do you imagine that you can change the subject by appealing to my vanity?" Sandhurst was asking his wife, half amused by such an obvious ploy. Rising, he crossed over to look down into her eyes.

"A valiant effort, you must admit." She laughed.

He shook his head, smiling. Mary had finished with her mistress's hair and now stood back to admire the effect.

"You look glorious," he murmured. Reaching out, he brushed the backs of his fingers over Micheline's cheekbone and smiled when he saw a blush spread under his touch.

Micheline glanced in the looking glass. Her gown, of soft violet satin set with sapphires and diamonds, parted in front to reveal a petticoat of sapphire silk lavishly embroidered with silver thread. "It is I who will be afflicted with vanity if you continue to stare at me so," she whispered.

"The jewels in your hair dim in comparison to your eyes, my love. You're the loveliest woman in England."

"My nose is too short," Micheline protested weakly.

This statement, combined with the sight of little Mary bumping into furniture as she attempted to back out the door, drew a chuckle from Andrew. "Nay. It is perfect." He bent to kiss it, then grazed her parted lips. "Perfect because it is a part of you."

* * *

The day passed in a blur for Micheline. She stood beside her husband in Westminster Abbey, watching as the new queen advanced up the aisle. Anne wore a robe and surcoat of purple velvet trimmed with ermine. Micheline recognized the man who walked in front, bearing the crown of St. Edward, as the Duke of Suffolk, high constable of England, who had tried with all his might since Cardinal Wolsey's fall to keep this event from happening. Anne's lips curved triumphantly as she stared at the duke's back.

No pains had been taken to disguise the queen's five-month pregnancy. Micheline had remarked on this to Andrew the night before, and he had explained that Henry VIII felt his subjects might approve the marriage because Anne would give England a prince. Apparently the king would not consider the possibility that he might have sired another daughter like Mary, Catherine's offspring.

At the high altar, Thomas Cranmer, Archbishop of Canterbury, spoke in Latin and anointed Anne on her head and breast. Slowly the heavy, jeweled crown was placed over her hair. She was given a scepter to hold in her right hand, a rod of ivory with the dove for her left. Victoriously, the newly crowned queen of England turned to face the assembled guests.

"Well," Micheline whispered doubtfully, "I hope she'll be happy. She's certainly waited long enough for this day."

"Six years." Sandhurst nodded. "Unfortunately, I have a feeling her troubles will worsen rather than cease. Our king is not the sort of man who finds contentment in the blessings of the present. He tends to want what he does not have."

* * *

The Lord and Lady Sandhurst were privileged guests at the banquet that followed the coronation. Cicely, the only other family member who had been invited that day, sat next to Lord and Lady Dangerfield at one of the four long tables that ranged down Westminster Hall, while Micheline had a place at the queen's table on the dais with other chosen ladies.

Although the king was not present, he watched the feast through a hole in the wall of a closet he'd had specially made in the adjoining church of St. Stephen. Lord Sandhurst was one of the marquesses designated to serve the new queen. He was the carver, while others executed the tasks of cup bearer, officer, and chief butler. Lords of the realm performed lesser serving duties.

Queen Anne, under her cloth of estate, with

Cranmer seated to her right, was in her glory. She allowed her old favorite Thomas Wyatt to pour scented water over her hands, and then the first course, consisting of twenty-seven separate dishes, was brought in. During the banquet the Duke of Suffolk and Lord William Howard rode up and down the hall on horseback, accompanied by the sounds of trumpets and hautbois to herald each new course.

Not for the first time that week, Micheline wished she and Andrew were back at Sandhurst Manor. She would have gladly traded all the rich food and titled company for a hard gallop on Primrose over the sunlit Cotswold Hills followed by an afternoon in Andrew's arms on a bed of meadow grass and wildflowers.

* * *

"Good morrow, my lady!" Betsy Trymme entered the spacious bedchamber carrying a tray of warm gingered bread and rosy peaches. "How are you feeling?"

"Sleepy, but so happy to be home." Micheline sat up in bed and smiled. "I've missed this house and all of you."

"And we've missed you, my lady." Betsy set the tray on a chest beside the bed and beamed down at her mistress. "It's as if you've lived here always. Even my husband agrees that it's hard to imagine those days when Lord Andrew was unmarried."

"Speaking of Lord Andrew—"

"He's gone to the stables. Didn't want to wake you. He's quite concerned about you, you know, and bade me bring you this food when you woke."

Micheline moved to get out of bed. "What is the time?"

"Half past nine, my lady." Firmly, Mistress Trymme

pressed her back into the pillows. "There's no hurry. Lord Andrew and your Primrose will wait. You've a baby to think about, you know. I've even brought you a mug of fresh milk. His lordship tells me you've not been eating properly this past week, and I mean to rectify that! Just have yourself a nice quiet breakfast and I'll have a bath sent up for you."

She sighed in surrender. "It would seem I have no choice."

"None whatever," Betsy agreed.

Before the housekeeper disappeared out the door, Micheline called, "How fares Lady Cicely—and Mistress Topping?"

"Lady Cicely went riding with her brother, and Mistress Patience is doing needlework in the gallery, my lady."

"Oh. Well, thank you again."

Alone, Micheline sipped the rich milk and stared up at the green velvet tester. It was a relief to be back at Sandhurst Manor, but there were worries at the back of her mind. Before they left London, Rupert had informed Sandhurst that their father wanted them to take care of some business there, then suggested that the women travel ahead to Sandhurst Manor without them. Andrew had refused, saying that his wife was his chief concern. However, Micheline guessed that part of him regretted cutting short their stay in the city, for she knew that he must have business of his own to look after. During their last two days in London, she felt so sorry for the restrictions her "condition" placed on Andrew's activities that she'd insisted he go about his affairs without her, even to the extent of pressing him to take Cicely to a masque at Whitehall Palace that Micheline felt too fatigued to attend herself.

Somehow, Patience had inserted herself into the

group traveling to Sandhurst Manor. It seemed the least they could do, inviting her there, since Rupert would be occupied in London. In spite of Patience's quietly gracious manner, Micheline felt doubly uneasy when left alone with both her "sisters." Instinct told her that Patience sympathized with Cicely.

Meanwhile, Lady Cicely Weston was on her best behavior. She was unfailingly polite to Micheline, especially when Andrew was nearby, but there was no real affection in her voice or manner. Cicely seemed to truly wish her sister-in-law did not exist. One day in London, when they'd found themselves alone in the summer parlor at Weston House, Micheline had decided not to initiate a conversation, just to see how her sister-in-law would react. A full five minutes had passed during which Cicely refused to look up from her book, pretending that she hadn't noticed Micheline's presence.

Micheline sighed now, staring at the tray of food. She felt drained of energy these days, though she continued to hope that the combination of rest and the Cotswold Hills would reinvigorate her. After all, they'd just arrived the night before, and it was a rather long trip, but tears came unbidden to her eyes as she thought of Cicely out riding with Andrew in her place. Was she even riding Primrose?

Betsy reappeared to direct the serving girls who brought in the bathtub and buckets of steaming water. After scolding Micheline for not eating, she stood over her mistress and watched as she managed to swallow a few bites of gingered bread. Mary came to wash her hair, then Micheline asked to be left alone for a soak in the tub.

Resting her head against the rim, she closed her eyes, helpless to resist the strong pull of fatigue. This longing to sleep was entirely new to her, and extremely frustrating. She wanted to dress and hurry out to join Andrew at the stables when he returned from his ride, but even the thought of so much activity made her wait to attempt it. Just a few more minutes of rest... Micheline sighed, and a tear slid down her cheek, but she did not stir.

"You look altogether too sad for one so lovely," Sandhurst's voice remarked from the doorway.

Her eyes flew open. "Andrew!"

"None other." He was leaning against a carved dresser, the picture of casual strength in the fawn doublet, breeches, and boots he'd worn that first night at Fontainebleau. His brown eyes watched her intently. "What ails you, sweetheart?"

Micheline searched for her soap in an effort to avoid her husband's gaze. "You know well enough what ails me—and how much I wish I felt otherwise... but after all, it *is* for a good cause."

"I wasn't speaking of your recent passion for sleep," Andrew said, walking over to sit back on his heels beside the bathtub. Gently he traced the course of her tear with one fingertip. "What's all this?"

Laying her cheek against his warm hand, Micheline sighed. She had no intention of burdening him with her insignificant worries. "I don't know what's wrong with me. I'm just not myself, and I don't like it any better than you do."

"Michelle, I *always* like you." Sandhurst flashed a grin and her heart melted. "I'm in need of a bath. Do you suppose there's room for me?"

Copying his tone, Micheline smiled radiantly and assured him, "My lord, there's *always* room for you."

Thirty-Four

EACH MORNING, Micheline would wake when Andrew rose at dawn, but then a tide of sleep would pull her under for more long, dream-filled hours. As if drugged, she would drift upward toward consciousness every so often, then sink back into oblivion. Her greatest challenge during early June was summoning the resolve to get out of bed to bathe and dress.

So when Micheline found herself outdoors in the garden before eleven o'clock one morning, her mood was self-congratulatory. Clad in a pretty summer gown of white and azure silk, she wound her way through the formal walks and shady alleys, past knotbeds and borders of damask roses, columbine, purple bugles, snapdragons, and red campion, cutting flowers and dropping them into the basket looped over her arm.

"My, don't you look the country gentlewoman."

Micheline glanced up to see Cicely approaching from one of the clipped expanses of lawn.

"I love it here," she replied simply, ignoring the hint of derisiveness in the younger girl's voice. "It's especially enjoyable this first year, since I am never certain what nature will unveil next."

Cicely selected a fragrant damask rose from the basket and held it to her nose. "You'll be happy to know that your filly, Primrose, is well. I've been exercising her in your absence and just came from the stables; they're going to see about mating Zachariah, the white stallion, with a mare who's in season. I don't imagine Andrew will be back for hours."

In spite of a twinge in the area of her heart, Micheline managed to smile. "I appreciate your help with Primrose. I'm sure this is but an interlude that will soon pass. Everyone tells me that the first three months are the hardest. I yearn to take up my usual routine again."

"But then your body will be changing," Cicely remarked as they walked toward a herb plot. "I mean, you may not be shaped for outdoor activity."

In the shadow of the charmingly mismatched manor house, Micheline bent to cut rosemary and flowering lavender, barely noticing the butterflies on the wing that flitted among a nearby shrub of honeysuckle. She couldn't decide what Cicely was getting at, or how to reply.

"I do not intend to become an invalid for the next seven months," she said at last.

Examining the folds of her soft pink skirt, Cicely murmured, "I hope, for your sake, that you will not. I mean, we both know how active my brother is. Already he's begun to show signs of restlessness, given your new habit of retiring early and rising late. I'm not suggesting that he doesn't care for you," she suddenly assured a stricken-looking Micheline, "but Andrew's always been a selfish man in that he's used to having his needs met."

A cold chill ran down Micheline's spine and her heart began to pound. "What are you saying?"

"I only meant to caution you. You weren't here in England prior to your marriage, and you may not realize how many ladies would happily supply my brother with female companionship."

"I'm not a fool, Cicely. I am fully aware that Andrew is immensely attractive to women, but I also know that he *loves* me. He would not stray just because—"

"Not without encouragement, perhaps, but he *is* human." Cicely started toward the manor, then turned on the path to stare at Micheline. "I'm not saying these things just to hear myself talk. You were not at Whitehall Palace the other night; I was. I may not have proved myself a very affectionate sister to you in the past, but I assure you that I would rather see Andrew with you than Lady Dangerfield!"

* * *

Waves of nausea swept over Micheline as she stood next to the herb plot, watching Cicely disappear from sight! No! she thought wildly. It could not be true. Not *Andrew!*

Staring down at the basket of flowers in her arms, she was reminded of the day in the gardens at Fontainebleau when she'd learned of Bernard's infidelities. Until that moment it had been impossible for her to imagine him capable of betrayal, but he certainly had been.

Were all men alike?

Her imagination burned with possible scenes that might have taken place at Whitehall that night. She saw Andrew in her mind's eye, bored and lonely, succumbing to Iris Dangerfield's entreaties that he dance with her. She saw him responding to Iris's open desire, imagined him putting his wife from his mind as Iris pressed her hips against his.

No. No, she must not condemn Andrew based on the words of a resentful fourteen-year-old girl. In the past the possibility had even occurred to Micheline that Cicely might have been responsible for the threats on her life, though she'd been quick to dismiss such thoughts. Still, in this case, it was easier to believe that Cicely might tell stories out of spite than accept the fact that Andrew had been unfaithful since their marriage. The mere thought seemed to stab Micheline through the heart.

She found a bench in the shelter of blooming apple trees and tried to calm herself. Finally it came to her that Patience and Rupert had also gone out to Whitehall Palace that night. Perhaps Patience could throw cold water on Cicely's horrible tale.

Bolstered with hope, Micheline went into the manor house through the kitchen door and discovered Patience herself working at one of the long, bleached tables.

"Hello!" she managed to exclaim.

"Oh, good morrow, Micheline. You've been out in the garden, I see."

"It's simply glorious, and a beautiful day too. There's no need to stay indoors, Patience. There are plenty of servants to see to the meals."

Lettice, who was chopping parsnips next to Patience, spoke up. "Mistress Topping's showing me her recipe for stewing venison in ale. Nothing like this in France, I'll warrant, eh, my lady?"

"No. No, I suppose not." Micheline was beset by a sinking feeling. Why was she beginning to feel like a stranger in her own home? "Lettice, I saw some lovely ripe cherries on the trees outside. Why don't you go out and pick them and we'll have tarts tonight?"

"Oh. Of course. As you wish, my lady." The cook cast a curious glance in her direction but wiped her hands and took a basket out into the garden.

Micheline drifted over to stand beside Patience, who was much taller and somehow intimidating in her horse-faced inscrutability.

"I'm nearly done trimming the venison, then it must marinate in ale for an hour."

"I see." The dish sounded particularly unappetizing to Micheline. She sighed. "Patience, may I be frank with you?"

"By all means, Sister. I hope that I've made it clear that I am your friend."

"Yes, certainly... you've been very kind. Now I wish that you will be honest as well." The eyes she turned up to Patience were liquid with emotion. "Forgive me for being blunt, but Lettice or one of the other kitchen servants might come in at any moment."

"What is it you want to know?"

"Will you tell me what occurred during the masque at Whitehall Palace... the night when I was too fatigued to attend? I am referring specifically to my husband's actions."

Patience dropped her eyes and returned her attention to the venison. "I don't know what you mean," she muttered in a way that froze Micheline's heart.

"I think you do," she replied huskily.

"There's really no point in going over it; you'll only be hurt. What Lord Sandhurst did at Whitehall was nothing personal against you. Men are just like that. Somehow they manage to keep the pleasure they take from women separate from their consciences." Patience looked at her sympathetically and touched her arm. "It doesn't mean he doesn't care for you. He was just passing the time."

Micheline shook her head in disbelief, tears stinging her eyes. "But—but Andrew is different." The last word came out on a sob.

"Every woman thinks that at first, and I certainly don't blame you for being beguiled by Lord Sandhurst. There's something about his eyes that compels one's trust. Still, he's human, just like the rest, and it's probably better you find out now and accept it rather than continuing in a dream world."

Tears spilled onto the table and Micheline wiped them away with the back of her hand. "Please—tell me —what did he do that night?"

Patience sniffed as if that were of no real consequence and turned back to trimming the venison. "How should I know? We all saw them together in the ballroom, cuddling in a corner. Mind you, he didn't behave as if he were besot by any means, but he certainly wasn't discouraging Lady Dangerfield. Her husband was absent for some reason. Everyone had had quite a lot to drink. I saw them kissing at one point." Micheline flinched at that and Patience touched her arm again. "And later they left together. Rupert and I brought Cicely back to Weston House before your Andrew reappeared. I've no idea what time he came home."

Numbly Micheline nodded. "Thank you. I appreciate your frankness."

"You would have had to face the truth sometime, my dear."

"Yes, I suppose so. Excuse me, won't you?"

In a daze she brushed past Betsy Trymme in the gallery and climbed the stairs to the bedchamber, where she and Andrew had been so happy. Lying far over on her side of the bed, Micheline shivered, dry-eyed, for a long while. Her mind seemed to wait, mercifully, before allowing thoughts to filter into her consciousness. When they did, her imagination was activated, and tears began to flow. All of Micheline's misery was compounded by memories of the heartache she'd suffered at Fontainebleau. Lately all of that had seemed part of another life. With Andrew she'd felt reborn, but now she knew such miracles were impossible. Faces and circumstances might change, but the pattern of life remained the same. Love was a cruel illusion.

When her tears were spent at last, Micheline allowed hostility to form a seal over her wound. Remembering every word of love and devotion Sandhurst had ever spoken, her outrage grew. Had it all been a joke to him after all? Had he been laughing to himself in Paris when she came chasing after him? She thought of his skill at chess and felt as if he'd played her like a pawn. She felt like the most ridiculous of fools for succumbing to Andrew's charm. Even Iris Dangerfield was wiser than she, for she dealt with the truth of the situation.

Micheline pressed a hand to her belly, which had begun to harden, and her eyes swam with fresh, harsh tears. This baby, whom she'd thought of as a child of love, now seemed fathered by a stranger.

* * *

Dusk was enveloping the valley when Andrew burst through the front door, laughing. Percy the spaniel, caught up in his master's festive mood, let out a long howl.

"Look who's come to visit," he announced to Betsy as she rushed into the entryhall.

"Why, Sir Jeremy! How good it is to see you! Are you here for long?"

Jeremy Culpepper shook his head of yellow curls. "Afraid not, Mistress Trymme. I'm off to London on the morrow."

"Then this is a celebration. You men will doubtless want some ale or wine."

"Your good husband has anticipated our needs already," Sandhurst laughed. "We've been toasting Jeremy's arrival at the stables for the past two hours, but I don't think it's possible to be too excessive at times like these." Leaning rather heavily against his friend, he sought Culpepper's advice. "Is it?"

Jeremy pursed his lips in a fair imitation of sobriety and shook his head. "Not t'my knowledge."

"What we *need*, though, is the company of my beautiful wife! Betsy, where's Lady Sandhurst?"

"Upstairs, my lord, but—"

"Ahhh!" He raised his brows in Culpepper's direction. "Her afternoon nap! Such a pleasure to wake her from those! Jeremy, find yourself something to drink and a comfortable chair. We'll join you directly."

Watching Sandhurst run lightly up the stairway, Betsy Trymme was relieved to see that he was less intoxicated than he pretended. Although she couldn't pinpoint the problem, Betsy was certain that something was amiss with Lady Sandhurst.

* * *

Entering the rose-shadowed bedchamber, Andrew made out the figure of Micheline, lying on her side at the far edge of the bed. He'd missed her that day, and would have returned long before if Jeremy hadn't appeared. Now, although he was dusty and in need of a bath, Sandhurst joined his wife on the bed, boots and all.

"Michelle," he whispered gently, caressing the curve of her hip, "are you awake?"

"Don't touch me."

He blinked at the sound of her voice. It told him that she was not only awake but angry. More than angry, in fact. "Sweetheart, you're trembling! What's amiss? Are you ill?"

Scrambling off the bed, Micheline cried, "Yes, I'm sick. *Sacrebleu!* I've never been sicker! Sick of men and their lies, sick of disappointment, sick of—"

"Me? Is that what you're saying?" Andrew sat on the bed, staring at his wife in disbelief.

"Yes. *C'est vrai.* I'm sick of you. Your charm and your eyes and your promises of love! You've played me for a fool, my lord, and I certainly was a willing victim. I, of all women, should have known better, but I succumbed to your spell just as you must have known I would. Has it failed you yet?"

This conversation was beginning to remind him of countless others in the past, when his father had fervently listed character traits that Andrew didn't recognize as his own. Instinctively he erected a familiar barrier. "Micheline, I don't know what you are talking about."

"I'm talking about your power over women. Your ability to make one believe and trust you implicitly with just a few words and a heart-melting gaze. Is it possible that you will now claim that you are unaware of these abilities you possess?"

Sandhurst was dumbfounded by this unexpected attack. He wished he knew what had set Micheline off —and further wished he hadn't drunk so much ale with Jeremy. Anger welled up inside him, but he tried to keep it at bay. Micheline was with child, after all, and her moods had been mercurial of late. Perhaps there was a rational explanation for this outburst. Sliding off the bed, he came around to look down at her through the lavender shadows.

"I won't lie to you, fondling," Andrew said quietly. "I'm aware that some women may find me attractive, just as you must know that you possess a beauty that makes men weak. But what does any of that mean now? We're married. The only lady whose approval I seek is here before me."

"Your tongue is as seductive as the rest of you," she answered stubbornly, and looked away from him.

He gripped her arms. "Don't talk nonsense! What is all this about? If I have committed some crime, name it and allow me to defend myself!"

"Your crime, sir, is that you are a man like all the rest." Micheline's eyes flashed with pain and rage in the shadowed room. "No wonder you are so happy these days. You have everything you needed and wanted. Your title and inheritance are safely intact, there's an adoring woman in your bed at night, and you've even managed to sire an offspring during the first weeks of your marriage. If I give birth to a son, all your problems will be solved and you won't have to continue this farce any longer."

"What the devil are you raving about?" Andrew's voice was a mixture of outrage and bafflement.

"You needn't pretend any longer. Your seed's been planted, hasn't it? I can't undo the marriage. Why not admit the truth?"

"*What* truth?"

"That nothing's changed. That you have no more intention of devoting yourself to me than you do to Iris Dangerfield! After all, it would be a crime to deprive womankind of your gifts when you can satisfy a wife and still manage to spread your talents around!"

The scar that cut down into his upper lip whitened. "I think you've gone quite mad, my lady."

"On the contrary, I've seen the light."

Sandhurst's frustration was such that he felt an urge to shake a rational explanation from her, but his love for Micheline ran too deep. Again and again love rose up, arguing for understanding.

"Micheline," he said hoarsely, "I beg you to tell me what's brought this on."

"If you knew, you would only tell me falsehoods." In the shadows, through her tears, there were moments when it seemed that Bernard stood there before her instead of Andrew—Bernard who had betrayed her and then died before she learned the truth. Remembering him made it easier to resist the urge to succumb to Andrew's pleas. "You know what you've done, my lord. There's no point in pretending innocence. I'm aware of the facts."

"*What* facts?" Sandhurst felt as if he were in the midst of a bizarre nightmare. Even this conversation reminded him of some awful garden maze. Each promising turn became a dead end.

Micheline presented her back and walked to the window. "I don't wish to discuss this further. Please go."

His entire body taut, Andrew raked a hand through his hair. Closing his eyes, he swallowed further words of appeal. "This is madness... and the time will come, my lady, when you will beg my pardon for each word you've spoken here tonight."

A moment later the door slammed, and Micheline was alone in the darkened bedchamber. A tremor shook her body, and she buried her face in her hands, sobbing.

Part Five

Western wind, when will thou blow.
The small rain down can rain?
Christ, if my love were in my arms
And I in my bed again!

– Anonymous

Thirty-Five

LARKS, finches, robins, and cuckoos began to sing before dawn, but Micheline could not be consoled as she lay alone in the bed that had been a cozy haven during the first weeks of her marriage to Andrew. It seemed that she hadn't slept all night. Where was he? His parting words, "This is madness," echoed in her mind, and she wondered if they'd been truer than he guessed. Micheline's world, which had been so happy just a day ago, was now turned upside down, and she felt as if she were falling down a dark, bottomless tunnel.

"Lady Sandhurst?" Betsy's voice came from the other side of the door, sounding unusually apprehensive. "Are you awake?"

Micheline almost smiled at the housekeeper's intuition. On a normal morning Betsy wouldn't have dreamed of asking such a question, for it couldn't have been more than six o'clock, and the sun had scarcely begun to rise over the rounded Cotswold Hills.

"Come in, Betsy."

The older woman entered slowly. "My lady, whatever it is that's bothering you must be resolved, for the sake of your baby."

Tears stung Micheline's eyes. "I don't know if that's even possible, Betsy."

Sighing, the housekeeper held out a folded sheet of parchment closed with Sandhurst's seal. "His lordship asked me to give you this."

She took it, trembling slightly, and whispered, "Where is he?"

"Gone to London, my lady. He left with Sir Jeremy Culpepper late last night."

"Oh." No matter how many times she told herself that she despised Andrew and didn't care what he did, her heart would not be convinced. "Please, stay for a few minutes, Betsy."

Haltingly she broke the seal and opened the paper, reading:

Michelle,

I have business in London, as you know, and this seemed a proper time to take care of it.

My hope is that you will resolve whatever it is that's troubling you while I'm away. Since you don't seem to want my help (just the opposite), I've taken you at your word and am leaving you alone.

Do, please, remember that I love you.

By your husband,
   Sandhurst.

It was very terse and to the point, right down to his signature. Micheline tried to dismiss the austere declaration of love, but a rush of emotion in her breast would not be denied. "Did he say anything to you, Betsy?"

"Very little, my lady. He asked me if I knew what might be upsetting you, and I said no. I can't recall the last time I saw Lord Andrew in so black a mood. At first I thought the ale he and Sir Jeremy drank at the stables might be the cause, but I soon realized that whatever passed between the two of you had rendered him utterly sober." She gave Micheline a searching look. "Do you want to hear the rest?"

"Yes. Please."

"He asked me if anyone had been here talking to you during the day. He seemed to think that someone had been putting ideas into your head, and quite frankly I had the feeling he was rather upset that you might accept someone else's lies over the truth from his own lips."

"I see you've taken his side, and I'm not surprised. You'd be wise, though, to think twice before accepting the word of so charming a man. I trusted him, too, until I learned of his infidelity from two different sources."

Betsy pursed her lips. "I don't know what you heard, my lady, but I've known Lord Andrew nearly all my life. Charming he may be, but he's never used it as a weapon—and he's never lied to me or anyone else here at Sandhurst Manor." She stood up, then paused to look back at the bed, trying to keep the anger from her voice. "There's one thing I do know, and you should too! Lord Andrew *loves* you better than his life. When he left, he asked me to look after you and I'll do so, but I must say I'm not very pleased at this moment to claim you as my mistress."

* * *

That evening Micheline dined with Patience and Cicely in the summer parlor. There was venison left over from the day before, plus mushroom and orange salad, an herb pudding, and almond soup that Patience had made that afternoon and now served with her own hands.

Micheline had come downstairs only because Patience had urged her to do so. She needed to get out of that bedchamber and eat a wholesome meal, Patience insisted, if only for the sake of her baby.

During supper Cicely stared at her new sister-in-law as if seeing her for the first time. Although she'd made up her mind before they ever met that she detested the Frenchwoman, she now found her heart softening as she regarded her poignantly sad expression. There were lilac-hued smudges under her luminous eyes, and her mouth turned down at the corners in a way that constantly threatened tears.

"I hope you're not worried about Andrew," Cicely ventured at one point. "He'll be fine on his own... and I know he will return soon."

Micheline nibbled at a wedge of orange, then pushed the food around her dish with a pearl-handled fork. "I suppose..."

"It's probably a good thing that he is away for a bit," Patience said, leaning over to put a bowl of soup in front of her. "You've had a shock, my dear, and can use this time to adjust."

Cicely's expression was troubled as she looked from one woman to the other. "Andrew's not a monster! I mean, there's no reason for you to stop—uh—caring about him."

Arching a warning brow at the younger girl, Patience agreed, "That will come in time, of course."

At that moment Betsy Trymme appeared in the doorway. "Pardon the interruption, my lady, but I don't seem to be feeling very well. The soup may have been a bit rich for me. If you don't mind, I'll go on to bed now."

"Certainly, Betsy. I hope you are better in the morning." When the housekeeper had departed, Micheline sighed. "I don't have much of an appetite myself. Will you both excuse me?"

"But you haven't touched your soup!" Patience exclaimed. "I ground the almonds and picked the herbs myself. Please, at least try it! Whatever ails Mistress Trymme has nothing to do with my soup."

Prepared to do anything to stop Patience's whining, Micheline obediently swallowed several spoonfuls of soup. Thick with ham, cream, sherry, and almonds, it was far too rich for her taste that evening. "It's delicious, and I appreciate your efforts, but I fear that I simply am not hungry."

"What do you think. Cicely?" Patience pointed her long chin in the younger girl's direction.

"I can't say, I'm afraid. I despise almonds. Sorry, but I won't taste it even for you, Patience."

They were still arguing about whether Cicely should try the soup as Micheline rose and slipped from the room. Upstairs, she shed her gown and petticoat, then walked over to the dresser and picked up her looking glass.

"*Mon Dieu,*" she whispered, "I look ghastly."

Still wearing her chemise, Micheline crossed the chamber and crawled into the bed that now seemed cold and uncomfortable without Andrew. His face swam before her, even after she closed her eyes, but at least tonight sleep intervened to provide an escape. In fact, Micheline found that once again she was unable to resist its seductive power.

* * *

In her own bedchamber Lady Cicely Weston lay wide awake, though the manor house was dark and she guessed it must be nearly midnight. Aside from the guilt she felt for causing her brother and his new wife so much distress, she also had the uneasy feeling that something else was wrong. Patience had been acting awfully odd lately. Of course, she'd always been odd, but there was a twist to this new mood that disturbed Cicely.

Why should Patience want to conspire to drive away Andrew's wife? When she'd suggested that they tell Micheline he'd been unfaithful, her explanation about sympathizing with Cicely and knowing that Micheline was wrong for Andrew seemed to make sense, but now Cicely had second thoughts. It had seemed rather a joke yesterday—until she saw her brother's face late that night when he was preparing to leave for London. She'd understood then just how deeply he loved Micheline. It was a love too real to be killed by an unkind prank. The thought of him in pain, because of her, had haunted Cicely ever since.

Complicating the situation further was the fact that Cicely was beginning to like Micheline. She realized now that sparks of affection had been struck many times, beginning the day in Yorkshire when Micheline had invited her to live with them, but all along Cicely had obstinately refused to open her heart. Tonight at supper, however, the sight of Micheline's stricken pale face had struck a chord within Cicely. She was starting to understand that this French girl Andrew loved so completely might become a lifelong friend rather than the enemy she'd imagined.

Sighing, Cicely turned on her side and closed her eyes, trying to relax enough to sleep. Tomorrow she resolved to treat Micheline with kindness. Perhaps overtures of friendship might be made... if it wasn't too late.

An odd, soft sound outside her door caused Cicely to lift her head from the pillow. Someone was out in the corridor! Who could it be—and why? She sat up, listening. It seemed to her that the person was moving down the hall, toward Andrew and Micheline's bedchamber. Moments later all was silent, but Cicely continued to feel uneasy.

Finally she climbed out of bed, donned a shift, and took the candlestick next to her bed. Strangely fearful, she stood next to her own door for a full minute before summoning the courage to open it and step into the corridor. At first, the only sound Cicely heard was the pounding of blood in her temples, and she was surrounded by darkness. Then she saw Patience emerge from Micheline and Andrew's room in a blaze of light. When the bony woman closed the door behind her, the hallway went black once again.

Cicely sniffed the air, terror-stricken. Could there be a fire? If so, why wasn't Patience screaming for help, sounding an alarm? A horrible thought occurred to her... almost too horrible to entertain.

She had no idea where Patience was, but she had no choice. It was imperative that she enter Micheline's bedchamber. The increasingly strong smell of smoke told her that all their lives depended on her actions now.

Cicely ran as lightly as she could down the corridor, hoping that Patience had gone downstairs—or outside, in search of safety. Her palm was wet clutching the candlestick, and it seemed that her heart would burst with terror, but she found the latch. No sooner had her fingers touched it than she was savagely thrown to the floor. Sharp fingernails clawed at her face and closed around her throat, squeezing, but Cicely was younger and stronger than her attacker. She brought up the candlestick, aiming for the shadow above her, and struck repeatedly with all her might. Finally she felt the fingers go slack against her neck as a body slumped over her own. She recognized Patience's cloying scent and shoved her aside with revulsion.

An instant later Cicely was scrambling to her feet and feeling for the latch. She pushed it upward, opened the door, and felt as if she had stepped into the sun. The entire room was on fire, it seemed. Blinking, she discovered that the flames were centered on the bed. The velvet tester and curtains were ablaze, but incredibly Micheline lay sound asleep and untouched in the middle of the feather tick.

"Micheline!" she screamed, shaking her brother's wife. "Get up!" When the girl merely moaned in response, she grabbed her arms and dragged her off the bed. Sparks dropped onto Micheline's chemise and caught fire, but she rubbed them out with her own hands. "Help!" she screamed. "Someone—help"

No one came. Cicely's heart seemed to be throbbing over every inch of her body as she ripped the fiery bedhangings down piece by piece and covered them with the Turkey carpet. She didn't feel the burns on her hands or notice the scorched smell of her own hair. When at last there was no more fire, Cicely collapsed beside the unconscious Micheline. Covering her face with her hands, she let herself sob.

* * *

"It must have been that horrid almond soup," Micheline murmured weakly. Propped against a carved chest, she surveyed the wreckage of her bed, then looked at Cicely. "Even the servants were drugged."

The younger girl nodded, glancing out into the corridor where Patience's body lay. "She's dead, you know."

"I'd say she deserved her fate, and that you have demonstrated incredible courage, *ma soeur*. We have to get you to a physician, though. Your face—and hands—" Micheline struggled to rise. She still felt as if she could sleep for days, and her limbs were like water, but whatever it was that Patience had put into the soup would have to be overcome. Staggering slightly, she reached out to Cicely, who warmly accepted her embrace. "I owe you my life," she whispered thickly.

They hugged tightly, tears mingling on their cheeks. "I am so sorry."

"No. The present begins now," Micheline said firmly.

"It wasn't true, you know, what we told you about Andrew." Cicely began to weep, in reaction to the night's events as well as the confession she was making. "Lady Dangerfield tried to seduce him that night at Whitehall, but he was positively rude to her. I couldn't really understand it at the time."

Micheline stiffened as her mind began to return to normal. "Andrew!" she breathed as if terrified. "He's in London—with Rupert! Patience must have been in league with him. Oh, *mon Dieu!* I must go to him at once!"

Cicely looked equally stricken. "Micheline, you don't actually think—"

"I'll tell you what I think. I think those two plotted all of this very carefully. They tried to dispatch me before the wedding, and when that didn't work, they worked out an elaborate plan whereby they could kill each of us separately. An accidental fire for me—"

"But if you're right," Cicely interrupted, breaking into tears, "Andrew could already be dead!"

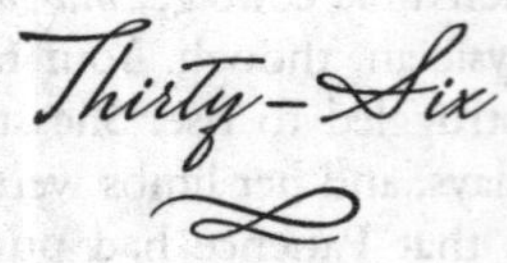

Thirty-Six

MICHELINE ARRIVED in London the next evening after a long ride on Primrose. Although it was pleasantly warm, summer also meant an intensification of some of the worst smells she had ever endured. She rode behind a groom through the city's impossibly cramped, twisting streets, following him to the home of Sir Jeremy Culpepper. Micheline feared that Rupert might be at Weston House, and she had no intention of alerting him to the fact that she was still alive.

They drew to a halt in front of a tall, narrow, half-timbered house in Drury Lane. Micheline dismounted quickly, handed Primrose's reins to the groom, and rushed over to pound on the door.

Jeremy himself opened it. Never had Micheline seem him looking so drawn and worried. Her heart, which had been pounding madly, seemed to stop for a long moment.

"Andrew—" she gasped, fearing the worst. "Is he all right?"

If Culpepper was surprised to see her, he didn't show it. Waving her into the entryway, he said, "Come in and sit down. Are you alone?"

"I came with a groom. We just arrived from Gloucestershire."

He spoke to a servant, ordering food and water for the groom and horses, then he took Micheline into a small parlor and poured goblets of wine for both of them.

"You've heard the news?"

A cold, sickening chill swept over her. "No. That is —I have news of my own, but you go first. I want to hear about my husband. Where is he?"

Jeremy ran a pudgy hand through his curly hair. "Sandhurst was arrested last night. He's imprisoned in the Tower."

"The Tower?" She drew a harsh breath, remembering the pirates hanging in chains from the Tower walls, not to mention the countless stories she'd heard about the rat-infested dungeons with their instruments of torture. "Andrew—arrested! On what charge?"

"It's not entirely clear to me. I went to Weston House this morning and Rupert told me the news. Apparently Sandhurst's been accused of attempted adultery with the queen, and there was something about treason as well. I gather someone overheard him making derogatory comments about King Henry."

"Adultery? Treason?" Micheline was livid. "This is madness. Perhaps you think I would believe the first charge."

"Why do you say that?"

"Didn't Andrew tell you what passed between us the night he left Sandhurst Manor with you?"

"Your husband does not discuss such things with other people, not even me. I nearly went mad at Fontainebleau trying to get him to tell me what was going on between the two of you." He flushed. "I wasn't prying, you understand, but my own life was affected."

"I must go to him at once," Micheline said suddenly, oblivious to what Jeremy had been saying. He'd opened his mouth to reply when she pounded her fist on the chair arm and exclaimed, "Rupert is behind all of this! I could kill him. When I think of the times I tried to persuade Andrew to be more generous in his treatment of that weasel, I am so angry at myself. He's been absolutely right all along."

Baffled, Jeremy gulped his wine and said, "I beg your pardon?"

Micheline spilled out the story of all that had transpired the night before at Sandhurst Manor, digressing briefly to add details about the threats she'd received since coming to England and the "accidents" while out riding and on the steps at Aylesbury Castle.

"I was such a fool. I thought Iris Dangerfield was behind it all! I took Rupert and Patience at face value, believing that act of theirs. Now I realize that those two would do *anything* to achieve their goal—and the first step involves killing Andrew, me, and our unborn child."

"And you believe that Rupert arranged Sandhurst's arrest?"

"Of course! He doubtless bribed people to go to the king and denounce Andrew. He wouldn't make the accusations himself, but I've no doubt that he's somehow taken credit for all of this."

"It's not hard to imagine Rupert standing before King Henry and mourning what he had to do for the good of the country," agreed Jeremy.

"The charges are awfully serious, aren't they?" Micheline mused.

"Life-threatening, I should think."

"Rupert made certain that Andrew would have no chance of reprieve. He's very smart! Rather than killing us both outright, he and Patience decided to take a more difficult route in dispatching Andrew. People might have been suspicious if we'd both died 'accidentally.' I'm sure, too, that he felt Andrew's disgrace would make *him* look better when he usurped his place as Marquess of Sandhurst."

Jeremy poured another goblet of wine, noticing that Micheline had not touched hers. "I confess, my lady, that all this has set my head spinning."

"We haven't time to discuss it any further, either. I must go to Andrew immediately, and then we have to concentrate on finding a way to free him."

"I don't know if they'll allow him a visitor at this hour," Culpepper said doubtfully.

"You'll let me stay here, won't you? You understand that I cannot let Rupert see me? Good. Then show me where I can attempt to repair my appearance sufficiently to ensure the guards' cooperation at the Tower."

Jeremy had to smile at that. The Marchioness of Sandhurst might be a bit dusty, and her curls were tangled, but her eyes sparkled with a new kind of passion. She looked simply dazzling.

* * *

The Tower of London was far more than just one building. The name referred to an entire fortress, with the turreted, whitewashed palace keep built by William the Conqueror at its center. This was known as the White Tower, but there were many other buildings within the ramparted walls, as well as many other towers, which were used for everything from housing the king's menagerie of lions and other exotic beasts to sheltering prisoners of the crown.

Exactly what sort of existence a prisoner suffered in

the Tower depended largely on who he was. If a man had rank and privilege in life, he usually was given fairly comfortable quarters. In Sandhurst's case, these consisted of a large stone room in the Garden Tower, with windows that overlooked the Thames, the moat, and the Traitor's Gate on one side and the Tower Green, where condemned prisoners were beheaded, on the other. He had a bed, table, and chairs, and a chest for storage. Best of all, if Sandhurst had been disposed to look on the bright side, his guard was unusually amiable and brought him adequate amounts of food. He'd barely touched it this first day, but realized that in time he would be grateful that he wouldn't suffer from starvation before meeting the headsman.

There was even a seemingly endless supply of candles. Andrew had too much on his mind to sleep, in spite of the fact that he'd lain awake the night before. Sitting in one chair, his booted legs propped on the other, he stared at the guttering candle flame and tried for the hundredth time to unravel the coil he was in.

"'Ey there, yer lordship!" It was Carson, the guard, his key clattering in the lock before he threw open the door to the tower room. "Look what I found wandering about on the Water Lane! Such a pretty thing, none of the guards've been able to resist her pleas t' see you. Almost makes me wish I was a prisoner!"

"What are you driveling about, Carson?" Sandhurst straightened, but his voice broke off at the sight of Micheline, haloed in the torchlight. "Good Lord."

"Against the rules, you know, havin' visitors at this late hour. The lieutenant'd have my head if he knew—" Carson paused here to guffaw at his own joke. "But this seems a special case. I'll allow you a quarter hour with yer wife."

The burly man took his leave then, eyes a-twinkle,

and Sandhurst stood slowly, scarcely able to believe that Micheline was real.

"Can it be you?" he wondered hoarsely.

Clad in a summer gown of apricot silk, her cognac-colored hair spilling over her shoulders, Micheline looked beautiful—and completely out of place in what were supposed to be surroundings of utter deprivation.

Meanwhile, her eyes were feasting on the sight of him. In view of all the trouble Rupert and Patience had caused within twenty-four hours, it seemed a miracle that Sandhurst was standing here, whole and strong, before her. He wore boots, buff breeches, and a white linen shirt without a doublet in the balmy June night. Micheline searched his face for clues to his mood.

"I'm very real, but do you want me?" she asked softly in reply to his first words. Crossing the floor, Micheline knelt suddenly on the damp stones a few feet away from her husband. "My lord, I beg your pardon and your forgiveness for every wrong word I spoke night before last. I was cruelly in error."

Sandhurst quickly lifted her up into his strong arms, burying his face in her hair. "Forget about it, fondling. I have." Their mouths came together and both of them were jolted by a powerful current of emotion. "God's death, Michelle, how can you be here?"

Tears glistened in her eyes. "How could I be anywhere else? Oh, Andrew, I wish we could spend this time mending the trouble I caused the other night, but there are more urgent matters to deal with. We'd better sit down. I have so much to tell you!"

Holding fast to his hand, she quickly related what had transpired at Sandhurst Manor, from the almond soup to the fire and the death of Patience Topping. "Your sister saved my life, and the manor as well, Andrew. She was extremely brave."

"It sounds as if you two are truly sisters now as well," he said softly while his mind sorted out all that Micheline had told him. "How is Cicely?"

"I saw to her burns as best I could and sent a page to the village to bring a physician. I also left instructions that Patience's body should be buried in the village churchyard. It was uncharitable of me, perhaps, but I didn't want her grave at Sandhurst Manor, reminding us..."

Rather distractedly Andrew pressed a kiss to her hand and answered, "No, you were quite right."

Micheline hurried on to more pertinent conversation. "You see how it was, though, don't you? I mean, the connection?"

"With Rupert? Oh, yes, I see," said Sandhurst thoughtfully. "It's perfectly clear now. I only wonder I didn't suspect him before. Remembering his unexplained absences from Aylesbury Castle these past months, a great deal becomes plain. Not just the incidents at Hampton Court and Aylesbury Castle, but also your riding accident and strange illness while we were still in France."

Micheline was rather taken aback by this deduction. Tiny hairs stood up on the back of her neck as the true extent of Rupert's villainy became apparent. "I was so obtuse! I completely misjudged him!"

"Not completely." Sandhurst gave her a grim smile. "He really is a bumbling fool, lucky for us, or he'd have succeeded in doing away with both of us long ago."

"He must be behind your arrest, though! How can we ever convince the king of your innocence, Andrew?"

"Rupert certainly aimed straight for Henry's weak spot... his possessive jealousy of Anne. No doubt the king's rage has blinded him to other considerations." Sandhurst stared into the distance for a long minute, his eyes hard, but when he spoke again, his tone was almost jaunty. "There's only one thing for it, I suppose. We shall have to maneuver Rupert into giving himself away in front of King Henry."

"We?" she echoed.

"I ought to be present, I think. I've a few questions of my own for that reptile who calls himself my brother."

A smile flickered over his mouth, setting off a wave of elation inside of Micheline. "But how?"

He pulled her onto his lap and kissed her deeply. "Are you up to participating in an escape from the Tower of London?"

Micheline blinked in the face of his amused nonchalance. Slowly a radiant smile lit her countenance. "I shall cancel my other social engagements on your behalf, my lord."

Sandhurst's brown eyes gleamed as he chuckled, "I rather thought you might."

* * *

"I do *not* believe I am *doing* this!" Sir Jeremy Culpepper muttered under his breath, glaring at Micheline as they approached the Tower of London's barbican.

She nearly giggled, as much from nerves as amusement. "I know you don't mean that, Jeremy!"

"You do?" Pausing in the moonlight, he scratched the false white beard wrapped around his double chin. "Sandhurst has coerced me into taking part in some bizarre adventures in the past—one of which involved you, my lady—but this is unquestionably the topper!"

"It was I who coerced you tonight, not Andrew," Micheline corrected him. "Stop complaining! Past experience should have convinced you to trust his plans."

"You're as mad as he is. Two of a kind!"

"Such lavish flattery," she laughed, then whispered more soberly, "You're certain the message was sent to Rupert?"

"Finchley took care of it this afternoon. He bribed a royal page to deliver the note personally."

"Good." They were outside the barbican. "Here we are. Behave yourself now."

At the sound of their voices a guard appeared. "Who comes there?"

"Oh, good eventide, Sergeant!" Micheline greeted the man as if they were old friends. "It's nice to see you again!"

"Lady Sandhurst?" he wondered doubtfully. The woman really was too beautiful; Sergeant Pease ached just looking at her. Her hair flowed loose, like liquid silk, and there were rosebuds pinned in it that matched her low-necked gown. The sight of the upper portion of her ladyship's delicious-looking breasts made him salivate.

"You remember me. How sweet!"

"I hope you haven't come to see your husband. It's past nine o'clock. Too late. We lock the gates at ten, you know."

Her face fell tragically and tears welled in her eyes. "Say that you will overlook the rules this time, Sergeant, please! I'm late only because I've brought my husband's aged father, the Duke of Aylesbury. He wasn't feeling well enough to go out earlier today. Won't you grant him a few minutes with his son? I promise that we shall take our leave well before ten o'clock!"

Lady Sandhurst's appealing tone wore away at Pease. "Well..." He glanced over at the bent old man who stood wavering in the arched doorway. "I can hardly say no, Your Grace. I have a son myself and can appreciate how you feel. I hope Lord Sandhurst will find a way out of this predicament." This last was spoken in a strained tone, for the sergeant knew there would be no reprieve for a man accused of trying to seduce the queen.

Micheline had taken Jeremy's arm and was already turning away when Pease said, "Pardon me, my lady, but you'll have to show me what's in your basket."

Her heart skipped a beat. "Just a few things we brought for my husband. Clean clothes, you understand." She lifted the cover and pulled out a shirt-sleeve. "Now that you mention it, though, there is something here that I'd like you to have—in return for your kindness." Reaching down, Micheline withdrew a bottle of wine. "It's one of my own, from France. I do hope you'll enjoy it."

The sergeant blushed in the light of her smile. "Very kind of you, my lady. I appreciate it."

"If you'll excuse us, then—time is short!"

As they walked hurriedly toward the Middle Tower, Jeremy pulled his soft velvet bonnet lower on his brow. "You're a little minx, Lady Sandhurst," he muttered, amused in spite of himself.

At the Middle Tower Micheline told the guard, "Sergeant Pease has given us permission, but we must be brief!" barely pausing to hear his reply.

They walked under the Byward Tower with equal ease and then arrived at the Garden Tower itself. The flaxen-haired guard met them with a look of astonishment. Briefly Micheline gave her explanation, punctuated with charming smiles and melting glances, and moments later the guard was letting them into Sandhurst's chamber.

"Dear Father!" exclaimed Andrew. Crossing the stone floor, he clasped Jeremy against him. "How good it is to see you!"

Culpepper's response was muffled. In the doorway Micheline stood beside Carson, the guard, and sighed. "You've all been very kind to allow this reunion."

"Rather touching, isn't it?" Carson allowed generously.

"Father, I would like you to meet my guard," Sandhurst declared, gesturing for Carson to come forward and join them.

Jeremy pasted on a feeble smile. "Eh?"

"Quite an honor, Your Grace!" The guard took two steps before Micheline walked up behind him and struck the back of his head with a brick she'd taken out of the basket.

Andrew caught the man in his arms and glanced up at Micheline. "Well done, fondling."

"No time for chitchat!" Jeremy exclaimed hysterically. "We'll all go to the block if we're caught!"

"Nonsense," Sandhurst soothed his friend. "Help me out, won't you?"

The two men dragged Carson to the bed, undressed and then covered him, positioned so that he was facing away from the door.

"Poor Carson. He was so nice to us," Micheline reflected while Andrew donned the guard's uniform. "I think he deserves a reward."

"Depends on what you have in mind!" Sandhurst laughed, lacing the guard's ill-fitting breeches.

Micheline took five gold crowns from the basket and held them up. "Perhaps these will ease his headache tomorrow." Reaching under the blanket, she put the coins in Carson's hand.

"Please!" Jeremy was beside himself. "Let's get *out* of here!"

"How do I look?" Andrew inquired, pulling on Carson's Tudor bonnet.

"Ridiculous," his wife decided, "but not ridiculous enough. You'll need some padding."

While Micheline stuffed wads of clothing up the doublet of his uniform, Sandhurst stared at her so intensely that hot blood rushed to her cheeks. When she had finished, she wrapped her arms around his expanded waistline and pressed her face to the hard breadth of his chest. The even beat of Andrew's heart nourished her spirit.

"God's bones! Are you two *ready?*" demanded Jeremy.

"Quite, but I don't think this is the proper time or place." Seeing his friend's eyes bug out with exasperation, Andrew walked over and patted him on the back. "Don't look so worried, old man. This is just one more escapade to recount to your children!"

"I'd like to live to produce them!" Jeremy shot back hotly.

"I think he wants to go," Micheline remarked..

"Lord knows *I've* been ready ever since I arrived." Andrew laughed again.

The comical-looking trio emerged onto the twisting staircase that spiraled down through the Garden Tower. Outside in the night air, Sandhurst inhaled the breeze off the Thames and gave Micheline a brief, meaningful grin. Then he put his arm around Jeremy, who sagged against his old friend as if he were ill.

Micheline was looking on with convincing anxiety as they came under the Byward Tower.

"The duke collapsed from the shock of seeing his son," Andrew muttered to the guard. "I thought it best to help him out before the ceremony of the keys."

The story worked until they came to Sergeant Pease. He heard Sandhurst out, then peered doubtfully at him in the darkness. Warm fog had rolled in off the river, making it difficult to see.

"Is that you, Carson?"

Fearing the worst, Jeremy let out a tortured groan. "I'm dying!" he gasped.

"Please, take my father-in-law to our carriage!" Micheline said to Andrew in an urgent tone. Turning back to the sergeant, she could see by the way his eyes followed the two men that he would wait only a minute or two for "Carson" to reappear. His distraction was such that Pease didn't notice her step back behind him and reach for the bottle of wine she'd given him earlier. An instant later he lay slumped against the stone wall of the barbican.

Lifting her skirts, Micheline ran to catch up with the two men. "We've only a few minutes!" she cried. "They'll find him when they lock the gates!"

Sandhurst clasped her hand as the three of them sprinted to reach the horses tethered at the top of Tower Hill. He lifted Micheline onto Primrose, then swung up on Hampstead, patting the stallion's neck.

"God's teeth!" Jeremy ejaculated. "Let's be away!"

Tossing his guard's bonnet into the street, Andrew laughed with relief. "You brought my sword?"

"No valet could be better!" cried Jeremy, brandishing the weapon.

"My thanks to you, old friend. Go home to the safety of your bed. My wife and I are bound for Whitehall Palace, where we shall effect act two of this drama!"

As the horses broke into a trot on Byward Street, Micheline looked over to meet Sandhurst's gaze. In spite of the danger that infused the very air they breathed, she had the sensation that he was kissing her with his eyes.

Thirty-Seven

MOONLIGHT SILVERED the King's Street Gate, which bridged the thoroughfare, allowing access from the river wings of the Whitehall Palace to the newer collection of buildings, gardens, tennis courts, a cockpit, tiltyard, and a bowling alley.

After tethering their horses in a darkened court, Sandhurst stripped off Carson's uniform and the added padding, revealing his sage-green doublet, buff breeches, and boots. To Micheline's astonishment he then caught her in his arms, and she found herself pressed up against the side of a building. His hands curved over her buttocks, aligning their hips as his mouth captured hers. They shared a long passionate kiss, hearts pounding in unison.

"You don't know how long I've been waiting to do this," he murmured finally, tasting the sweetness of her parted lips with his tongue.

He'd been hard the instant their bodies met. Micheline arched her hips suggestively against him. *"Mon Dieu!"* she sighed.

"I don't suppose you'd consider lifting your skirts....
"

"Shame on you." She couldn't resist one more intoxicating kiss, though, and her tone was less assured when she added, "I should think you'd have more important matters on your mind tonight."

"Nothing is more important than you, Michelle." His smile flashed in the darkness before he gave an exaggerated sigh. "However, I suppose we ought bring this adventure to a close so that I can take you home to bed."

"To sleep?" Her tone was playful. "It's late and you must be fatigued..."

Sandhurst's brows flew up. "Sleep! Oh, no, my love, I had in mind an entirely new adventure. The other events of the night will seem mundane in comparison."

Micheline laughed softly as he took her hand and pulled her off toward the turreted Palace Gate.

The watchmen were crying "Ten o'clock!" when Andrew and Micheline parted company in the gardens outside the royal apartments. To the east the River Thames glittered under the stars.

"You have half an hour before Rupert arrives," he told her softly. "I'll see you soon."

"But how will you—"

Mischief infected his tone. "It's a surprise. Now, go!"

She was pushed firmly toward the imposing palace steps, and then Sandhurst disappeared into the shadows, his sword hilt agleam in the moonlight.

* * *

It took nearly a quarter hour for Micheline to talk her way into an audience with King Henry. By the time she was admitted to his presence chamber, after passing through endless windowed, tapestry-hung galleries with ceilings wrought in stone and gold, her nerve was beginning to fail her.

In the cavernous presence chamber, Henry VIII sat on his throne of red and gold brocade. It crouched on a raised dais, with a canopy above, serving to make Micheline feel very small and insignificant.

Garbed in rich blue velvet and cloth of silver that was slashed, padded, and encrusted with all manner of gems, the monarch narrowed his tiny eyes at Micheline. Next to him sat Queen Anne, her rounded belly draped with violet silk. Her anxious gaze was fixed not on their visitor but on Henry as she waited to see what he would do.

"Good evening, my lady," he said in tone that made Micheline's heart sink. "I do not remember inviting you to Whitehall for this late interview."

She sank into a curtsy before the dais. "It was very gracious of Your Majesty to see me at this hour. I would not trouble you, but I am here concerning a matter of life and death."

"I thought as much." Henry sighed as if bored, and reached for his wine goblet. "If you've come to beg for Lord Sandhurst's life, you are doomed to disappointment. Any man foolish enough to make advances to my queen deserves to lose his head."

Anne spoke up imploringly. "I have told you, sire, that these accusations are lies! It is true that Lord Sandhurst smiled on me from time to time, but that was long before our marriage, and it went no further. He never touched me!"

Anger reddened the king's face. "Be silent! When you take his part, it makes me think that you encouraged him!"

"The queen speaks the truth, Your Majesty! This

plot against my husband was concocted by Rupert and Patience Topping. They meant to see both of us dead and Andrew disgraced, hoping that our titles would pass to them."

"What nonsense! Why, Topping could scarcely bring himself to disclose Sandhurst's behavior to me. His loyalty to his brother was nearly greater than his loyalty to me, but fortunately he saw that, morally, he had no other choice."

"I hesitate to contradict you, sire, but I think that when you hear what I have to say, you'll see things differently."

"This is a waste of my time," the king grumbled. "Go on, then. Tell your story, but be brief!"

Quickly Micheline related the various accidents and threats of the past few months and ended with an account of the events related to the fire at Sandhurst Manor.

"Rupert thinks that I am dead, Your Majesty, that Patience succeeded in her part of their plan. He can be tricked into revealing his true colors—if you will help."

Henry cocked a skeptical brow. "How do I know that *you* are telling the truth? And what part do you propose that I play in this scheme? After all, Sandhurst has refused to lift a finger to help his king of late! I really can't see why I should bother."

"I think you are wise enough to recognize the truth in my eyes, sire. In France I was told that you were both wise and just. Please help me now to right a terrible wrong, not only for the sake of my husband and me but for our unborn child and the Duke of Aylesbury. He would want his title to go to the proper person, a good man who will uphold the proud tradition of his family."

Henry shifted on his throne. The girl had appealed

to his vanity. If he turned away from her, it would look as if he was not fair and just. Also, her mention of France had given him pause. Henry had heard that King François was quite fond of the former Madame Tevoulère. Perhaps it would be better all around to humor her, just to be on the safe side.

"Very well, then, I'll go along with your plan. I've ever been one for exposing the truth. What do you want me to do?"

Micheline gave him an incandescent smile. "Thank you, sire! I must explain rapidly, for Rupert will be arriving at any moment."

"I beg your pardon!" King Henry exploded.

"It's part of the plan, Your Majesty. Please, hear me out!"

"Colossal nerve," he muttered under his breath while Micheline launched into detailed instructions of all that the king must say to Rupert Topping. When she was finished, Henry's mouth, which was quite small in his heavily fleshed face, curved upward slightly. "An interesting scheme, my lady. This may be more amusing than I anticipated."

At that moment a footman appeared to announce that Rupert Topping was waiting to see His Majesty. The king instructed him to show him up.

"Where may I hide?" Micheline asked anxiously.

"It's a warm night. Why don't you wait on the balcony," Anne suggested.

Quickly she curtsied and exited through the tall French doors. Micheline was backing onto the balcony, closing the doors in front of her, her heart pounding madly, when she bumped into a shadowy figure. Before she could scream involuntarily, a hand came around to cover her mouth. It smelled wonderfully familiar.

"Romantic, isn't it?" Sandhurst's breath was warm against her ear. "A moonlit June night, the Thames shimmering in the distance, the two of us alone on a palace balcony..." His lips grazed her temple. "The possibilities are intriguing."

Micheline heaved a gusty sigh of relief, turning in his arms. "Andrew!" She nearly laughed aloud in reaction. "How did you get up here?" The king's apartments were on the third floor of Whitehall Palace.

"I climbed."

Glancing down the sheer side of the building, Micheline ruefully shook her head. "I'm glad, then, that you didn't tell me beforehand. I'd have been worried sick."

He smiled down at her as she put up a shaky hand and smoothed his windblown hair. Then, out of the corner of his eye, he glimpsed Rupert Topping entering the presence chamber. Sandhurst laid an agile finger over Micheline's mouth and slowly turned her around. He kept an arm curved close around her and she leaned back against him as they listened through the slightly parted doors.

Rupert was wearing an ill-fitting doublet of purple silk topped by a green jerkin trimmed with rubies and fox. He looked very hot and very nervous as he bowed before the king and queen. Every so often the right side of his face twitched as though it had a life of its own.

"I have come, just as you commanded, Your Majesty!" Rupert declared grandly, his voice cracking. "How may I serve you?"

"I appreciate your efforts, Topping. I know what a strain you've been under, given Sandhurst's imprisonment."

"Such a tragedy," the spindly young man agreed. "I've scarcely had a wink of sleep, trying to deal with the misgivings I have about my role in his arrest."

"You were only doing your duty, weren't you? You were honor-bound to tell what you knew. I shouldn't feel guilty if I were you, Topping. After all, the crime was not yours but *his.* Correct?"

The twitch was spreading downward to Rupert's arm. Sandhurst listened to him blubber a reply, smiling to himself as he realized that the king was enjoying this little charade. He had the manner of a cat toying with a panic-stricken mouse.

"I hesitate to add to your trials, Topping," Henry was continuing smoothly, "but I received some news this evening that I thought you should hear."

"Oh, I say! That was very considerate of you, sire!"

"Sad stuff, I fear." The king leaned forward slightly in his throne, watching Rupert's face. "It seems that there was a fire at Sandhurst Manor—in her ladyship's bedchamber. Tragically she did not survive."

"What? Oh, my *God!* It can't be true! This is un-thinkable!" Rupert staggered back, clutching his heart and gaping at the king and queen. "She was so young, so *beautiful!*"

"Deplorable acting," Andrew whispered laconically out on the balcony, while Micheline swallowed a bubble of laughter.

"It certainly is a tragedy." Henry was saying soberly. "I was thinking that it might be best if *you* broke the news to your brother."

Rupert flinched in surprise. "Me? Tell Sandhurst? Oh, well, I don't know—that is to say—well, it's just that—"

"Good! You know, my sympathies are aroused by this calamity. I'd made up my mind that Sandhurst should go to the block by week's end, but now I'm having second thoughts. Perhaps the suffering he'll endure over his bride's untimely death will be punishment enough."

Perspiration rolled down Rupert's pasty face. "Very —uh—kind of you, sire, but—I just—that is, do you really think it would be *wise?*"

"It's not as if your brother is a dangerous man, is it, Topping? We needn't fear for our lives if he's set free!" The king chuckled at this, but there was a wicked glint in his eyes. "After all, there is quite a difference between a man who becomes awed by the queen's rare beauty and a *murderer.* Don't you agree?"

Rupert mopped his brow with a large kerchief. "It's only that, well, others might misunderstand your mercifulness. Your Majesty!"

"I have a moral obligation to justice, though. I must say, Topping, you surprise me! I expected you to rejoice at the prospect of your brother's freedom!"

"Oh, yes! Of course, of course!" His entire right side twitched convulsively. "It's just that, well, I didn't want to have to reveal this—family honor and all that—but the fact is, Sandhurst is not the man we believed him to be!"

"Is he not?" The king made a show of innocent surprise.

"No! There have been other crimes. The—the treason I hinted at earlier. It's been worse that you know! He mocks your stand against the pope at every opportunity! And—and—I've come to think that Sandhurst is quite *evil* beneath that charming facade of his."

"Is he indeed! Do go on."

"This is very difficult for me, you understand, but in the interest of justice—"

Out on the balcony Micheline pressed Andrew's hand to her mouth to smother the laughter that would barely be suppressed. Glancing up, she saw her husband bite his lip and cast his eyes heavenward.

"Courage, man!" King Henry was urging. "What is it you have to tell me?"

"This is the hardest speech I've ever had to make!" Rupert cried plaintively. "You see, the fact is—I already heard about Lady Sandhurst's death in the fire."

Henry started in astonishment and glanced quickly at the queen. "You *did!*"

"Yes, yes, I received word from my dear wife, Patience, who had been staying at Sandhurst Manor with her ladyship and Lady Cicely Weston. It seems that Sandhurst himself left abruptly for London following a terrible row with his wife." He paused here to sigh dramatically and wipe his brow again. The handkerchief was drenched. "In fact... Patience wrote me that Lady Sandhurst's death may not have been an accident after all. There appears to be conclusive evidence that the fire was arranged by—by *her husband!*"

"God's bones, that *is* a shock!" The king agreed. "So it's your opinion that the his lordship should not be released from the Tower? That I should speed his execution?"

"It breaks my heart to say it, Your Majesty, but... yes! I think my brother deserves to die! As quickly as possible!"

When Sandhurst himself emerged soundlessly from the balcony, King Henry barely blinked, though inwardly he was astounded. He cleared his throat to avoid an immediate reply to Rupert, watching with one eye as Andrew drew his sword and walked up behind his sniveling half-brother.

Rupert literally jumped into the air when he felt the prick of the sword tip at his back.

"Rupert, I am desolated to learn your true opinion

of me," Sandhurst said. "All these years I have basked in your devotion, only to discover that you really don't *like* me." His tone was laced with laughter. "I am crushed."

"Your Majesty! The guards!" cried Rupert. "Call the guards! Have this man arrested before he kills *me* as well!"

The king merely reclined in his throne, enjoying the show.

"I have some good news for you, Rupert," Sandhurst was saying. "My wife isn't dead after all. Aren't you relieved?"

On cue Micheline walked in from the balcony and made a wide circle around the two men, staring at Rupert with frosty blue eyes. Topping himself was too upset to speak. His entire body quaked against Andrew's sword point.

"However, the bad news is that Patience was caught in the act of setting fire to Micheline's bed. When Cicely intervened, your wife tried to dispatch her as well, but luckily Cicely had thought to bring a candlestick with her. Let us say that justice was done." He paused strategically. "What? No tears for your dear wife? Don't tell me that you're concerned only with your own survival."

"Don't listen to him!" Sweat dripped from the point of Rupert's nose. "He's lying, Your Majesty. He's always hated me!"

"That's rather a strong word," Sandhurst protested. "*Detest* might better describe my feelings. Why is that, do you suppose? I've often thought it odd that I never felt even the smallest twinge of familial affection for you. It's occurred to me, from time to time, that perhaps you're not really a relative at all." His sword cut through Rupert's jerkin and doublet, finding his bony back.

"Your Majesty!" Rupert begged.

"You're going to die anyway, Topping," Henry said

dispassionately. "Tell the truth or I'll allow Sandhurst to save the headsman the trouble."

"Very well," Rupert sobbed, cracking open like a walnut. "It's true, I'm not the duke's son! My father was the ferrier in Giggleswick. He was a drunkard, though, and wouldn't marry my mother, and so she began looking to see if the Duke of Aylesbury wouldn't like to have her back as a mistress. She hung about the castle to no avail, and eventually the frustration became too much. Mother decided to take control of fate. She pushed the duchess down the stairs one day, and after that it wasn't long before the duke weakened enough to take us in."

Micheline was stunned by these revelations but saw that Andrew wasn't. His chiseled face showed no reaction except for a gradual whitening of the scar above his mouth.

"Sandhurst wasn't much of a son, and though I hated the duke myself, I knew that my only chance for success was to court his favor. Everything was progressing according to plan until Sandhurst actually obeyed the old man for once and married this French chit."

"You followed me to Fontainebleau, didn't you?" Andrew demanded coldly.

"Of course I did! Not that I thought there was the least chance you'd fall in love—but it did seem wise to try to nip the thing in the bud. I did my best, but unfortunately madame was frustratingly resilient."

"It was you who shone that mirror and frightened my horse!" Micheline cried as the pieces came together.

Nodding, Sandhurst interjected, "And he doubtless put something in your wine the night you dined with Rabelais and became so ill."

She was aghast. "Rupert! You pushed me down the

steps at Aylesbury Castle! The same steps where the duchess met her death."

Topping merely shrugged in reply. Then, shocking everyone, he suddenly drew his own sword and spun around awkwardly to face Sandhurst.

"You think me a coward?" he cried.

Andrew coolly arched a brow. "Indeed."

"I am more a man than you know." He swung his blade up against Sandhurst's with surprising force.

"You make me a gift, mewling." Laughing, he caught the sword with his own rapier and deftly thrust the smaller man away.

Rupert wore a slightly crazed look as he began circling. He held the sidesword out and made an awkward lunge toward Sandhurst, who responded with a soft chuckle.

"Come here, little one," he taunted. "Let me remind you of the sharpness of my steel." In the next instant, he thrust his blade forward, just missing Rupert's chin, and cut the laces on his doublet so that it fell open.

"You mock me!" The smaller man's face was red and wet with sweat.

"At your invitation, good sir." Watching as Rupert hopped in an awkward circle around the room, Sandhurst merely stopped and raised his eyebrows.

Suddenly, Rupert summoned all the skill from years of practice and came forward with a flurry of thrusts that made Micheline cry out in alarm. Steel met steel, flashing, until Sandhurst drove him back. Then, unable to resist, he flicked his sword out once more to pare away three ruby buttons that decorated the front of Rupert's jerkin. They clattered to the floor and rolled away.

Rupert was panting hard now and his arm had begun to tremble. "Very well then, why don't you just kill me?"

"And put you out of your misery?" Sandhurst drove him back against a wall embellished with gilded panels and held the razor-sharp tip of his blade under Rupert's quaking chin. Torchlight from a nearby sconce threw shadows over the beaten man's face. "That sounds far too merciful for you, and far too messy for me. I've far better ways to spend what's left of this night."

The king had summoned guards who now came forward to haul Rupert Topping off to the Tower of London. Henry gave instructions that he should have one of the rat-infested cells in the Bell Tower rather than accommodations befitting a gentleman.

Micheline ran to her husband, clinging to his neck as he slipped his sword back into its scabbard.

"Quite an exciting entertainment, eh, my sweetheart?" Henry was saying to Anne as he heaved himself to a standing position.

"I'm glad it all turned out so happily," agreed the queen.

Wrapping a strong arm around the shivering form of his wife, Sandhurst said, "My heartfelt thanks for your help, sire. And I hope you'll overlook my premature departure from the Tower."

"Considering the circumstances, yes. And I won't even ask how you came to be out on that balcony! Now, if you'll excuse us—"

"Perhaps Lord and Lady Sandhurst would prefer to sleep here at Whitehall after their ordeal," Anne wondered.

"You are gracious, Your Majesty," Andrew replied, laughing softly, "But I mean to spend this night in our own bed."

* * *

Sandhurst was suffering from the kind of extreme exhaustion that made sleep impossible. He lay on his back in the great bed at Weston House, bathed in the moonbeams that come just before the dawn. The night was balmy, and all he needed to keep warm was Micheline. She curled against him, soft and trusting as a kitten, her rich hair spilling over his bare chest.

Andrew's left arm was bent behind his head, while his right encircled his wife's back so that his fingers rested on the curve of her hip. From time to time he opened his eyes, thinking about the events of the last few days, about his marriage, about Micheline, and what lay ahead for them.

It was difficult to realize that they had known each other only a few months. Life before Micheline seemed hazy to him. She was the center of his existence, yet the time they'd shared so far had been mostly fraught with turmoil.

The one oasis of peace had been the few weeks they'd spent alone in Gloucestershire following their marriage, and Andrew looked forward to returning to their home, to creating a life of contentment and adventure with his wife, and soon, with their child.

Caressing Micheline's silky hair, Sandhurst considered the urgency that often kindled their lovemaking. Tonight had been no exception. Passion had crackled in the air as they came together, expressing physically all the emotions that had no words. There was never time to linger. It seemed that whenever they touched, mutual arousal flared almost instantly into a storm of wild proportions, but now he found himself anticipating a time when they could slow down and savor one another.

Micheline made a soft purring sound in her sleep. Glancing down at her parted lips, and then to the creamy curves of her naked body, Andrew smiled to himself. Slowly he turned on his side, brushing his mouth over the satiny line of her neck and caressing her breast with exquisite gentleness.

"Mmm..." she murmured happily.

"My sentiments exactly, Michelle," Sandhurst whispered. "There's no time to begin like the present."

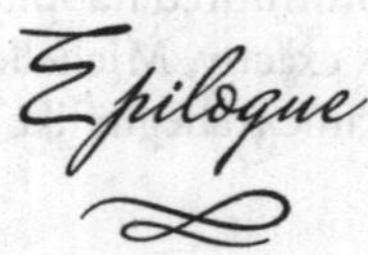

Thou walkest with me when I walk;
When to my bed for rest I go, I find thee
    there
And everywhere;
Not youngest thought in me doth grow,
No, not one word I cast to talk.
But, unuttered, thou dost know.

– MARY HERBERT,
COUNTESS OF PEMBROKE
1561-1621

GLOUCESTERSHIRE, ENGLAND, OCTOBER, 1533

MICHELINE, accompanied by Percy the spaniel, came over the brow of the hill and gazed down over the curving slope. The meadow grasses were still covered with daisies, wild marjoram, and pink clover. There had been a frost just three nights before, though, and the trees were turning yellow, crimson, and russet.

Winter would soon be upon the Cotswolds. It was a time to savor each fine day, like this one. The sky was a clear, vivid blue, the air was crisp, and in the vale below, Andrew and his horse, Hampstead, were one as they galloped and then sailed over a wall of golden limestone. Cicely, who was riding Primrose, appeared to challenge her brother to a contest, though there was never any real question as to which horse would win. They raced across the valley, jumping four successive walls, then retraced the course.

Smiling, Micheline settled down amid the wildflowers to watch. For an instant she was reminded of herself and Bernard, in the days when they galloped in unspoken competition through the woods of Angoulême. Her present was so rich and contented that she spared little time for thoughts of the past, but now Micheline remembered Aimée telling her that one day she would remember Bernard with fondness. At last she was able to separate the good memories from the bad. Bernard had not been a villain—only immature and misguided. And for a time he had loved her, and she had loved him. Who could say what would have become of Micheline if Bernard had not helped her bridge the gulf from adolescence to womanhood?

With a bittersweet sigh she looked down at the letter in her hands, rereading it. She was engrossed in the last few lines when Sandhurst called her name.

Looking up, she saw him leading Hampstead up the hill. Her heart contracted in a familiar way at the sight of his strong rider's body, clad today in slate-gray velvet. A soft breeze ruffled his hair back from his handsome face. Reaching his wife, Sandhurst gave Hampstead a light slap to send him back to the stables, Percy frolicking behind, then dropped down into the fragrant grass.

"My God, you're beautiful," he said in a low voice.

Micheline wore a simple low-necked gown of yellow velvet, cut high at the waist to drape over her ripening belly. The sun brushed her loose brandy-hued curls with fire, and her eyes shone as she smiled.

"So are you, my lord."

"Beautiful?" He frowned in mock consternation. "That's an opinion best kept in the family. Speaking of which—how fares my offspring?"

"Very well!" Micheline lay back in Sandhurst's embrace, watching as his hands curved expectantly over her belly, waiting. When the baby kicked, he flashed a grin.

"Three more months. It seems a lifetime!"

"Anticipation is half the fun," she replied, kissing the hard line of his jaw, then held up the parchment. "We've had a letter from Thomas and Aimée. She gave birth to their son last month!"

"So they had a boy. He's healthy?"

"Yes. And you know they lost a son a few years ago, their first child, so this baby is especially precious. They named him Étienne."

"Stephen," he translated absently. "Very nice."

Gazing up at his profile, she sighed a little. "Will you be disappointed if this child is a girl?"

"You know better. As long as it's either a girl or a boy, I'll be content." When Micheline didn't laugh at that, Sandhurst watched her for a moment. "You're not married to King Henry, you know. Just because he thinks that Anne failed him by presenting him with a baby girl last month—"

"Odious man. I could almost smell the queen's despair when we saw her at Greenwich after Elizabeth was born. The king was behaving shockingly, as if the birth of a lovely, healthy child could be cause for disappointment!"

Andrew continued to watch Micheline as she gazed out over the hills. "What of you? Has this letter from France made you homesick?"

"My home is here," she returned quietly.

"Perhaps we might visit the St. Briacs next year. Would you like that?"

A dazzling smile lit her face. "That's a wonderful idea! Could we take the baby? And Cicely?"

"I don't see why not."

Micheline buried her face against his warm neck. "Oh, Andrew, how I love you."

He took her back with him to lie in a bed of daisies. "And I love you, Michelle." He smiled into her eyes. "As always..."

"...we're of one mind!" She laughed.

"And one heart."

- Thank You -

Thank you so much for reading OF ONE HEART. I am honored that you have chosen my story and I sincerely hope you enjoyed it.

Would you like to be the first to know when I have a new book, a contest, 99-cent sale, or a giveaway? You can sign up here for my occasional newsletter: www.cynthiawrightauthor.com.

You're invited to join my most devoted readers in my private "Cynthia Wright's Rakes & Readers Group" on Facebook. You'll be the first to see my coziest posts, be included in special previews and giveaways, and have a chance to interact with others who enjoy reading historical romances. I hope you'll come by now to join us—just click HERE.

Also on Facebook: I post "Behind the Book" tidbits and news about my research, family adventures, and crazy pets at
    https://www.facebook.com/cynthiawrightauthor
    Or friend me at:
    https://www.facebook.com/cyntha.wright.98

You can also follow me on Twitter @CynthiaWright1 and on Instagram

If you enjoyed reading this book, please consider posting a brief REVIEW. It's the very best way to say thank you to an author, and your review will help other readers make a choice.

OF ONE HEART is Book Two in my *Crowns & Kilts: The St. Briac Family* series:

YOU AND NO OTHER (Thomas & Aimée)
OF ONE HEART (Andrew & Micheline)
YOU AND NO OTHER (Christophe & Fiona)
RETURN OF THE LOST BRIDE (Ciaran & Violette)
QUEST OF THE HIGHLANDER (Lennox & Nora)

Rakes & Rebels: The St. Briac Family:
THE SECRET OF LOVE (Gabriel & Isabella)
HIS MAKE-BELIEVE BRIDE (Justin & Mouette)
HER IMPOSSIBLE HUSBAND (Justin & Mouette)
HER SECRET ROGUE (Anthony & Frederica)

I'm excited to tell you that a fantastic audiobook of OF ONE HEART is available, narrated by Tim Campbell, who brings Andrew and Micheline to life more fully than I thought possible. Tim has also narrated audiobooks of ALL the St. Briac connecting books. He truly takes my books to another level.

If you enjoyed OF ONE HEART, don't miss ABDUCTED AT THE ALTAR (*Crowns & Kilts, Book 3*), starring Thomas de St. Briac's brother, Christophe, as a gifted architect. When King François sends Christophe to Scotland to restore Falkland Palace, he crosses paths with an irrepressible lass from the Isle of Skye and all his carefully-laid life plans are turned upside down. I'm thrilled to be writing a St. Briac series set in Scotland and I think you'll love it, too.

And Andrew and Micheline return as supporting characters in my new book, QUEST OF THE HIGH-LANDER, set in 1541!

I also invite you to read THE SECRET OF LOVE and HIS MAKE-BELIEVE BRIDE, which will reunite you with a future generation of St. Briac men and take you back to Château du Soleil. And Andrew's lookalike descendant, Geoffrey Weston, Marquess of Sandhurst, will steal your heart in THE DUKE AND THE COWGIRL.

Just after the Author's Note, you'll find an excerpt of ABDUCTED AT THE ALTAR, starring Christophe de St. Briac, in magical Scotland.

Once again, my heartfelt thanks for your support, encouragement, and interest in my books. I welcome your comments and suggestions, and I hope that you'll write to me at Cynthia@CynthiaWrightAuthor.com. I promise to reply!

Warmest wishes,
~ *Cynthia*

I truly hope you enjoyed reading OF ONE HEART (first published as A BATTLE OF LOVE by Ballantine Books in 1986).

To prepare for this book, I enjoyed a wonderful research trip to England in 1984, an adventure I shared with my friend, Kathy D'Huy. Together, we visited most of the English settings, including Hampton Court, York, the countryside around Oxford, and the Tower of London. It was my first trip to England, so everything we did was a magical adventure. I've been back many times since, but that time in England will always be special in my heart.

As with most of my books, the places I visited and the history I learned played the biggest role in the eventual plot of OF ONE HEART. Hampton Court really inspired me to bring in Henry VIII and Anne Boleyn as characters.

Most of you have already read YOU AND NO OTHER, Thomas and Aimée's story, and you know that I did a lot of research in France. These two books are two parts of a whole, and the stories of the two kings —Henry and François—also fit together.

A newer release, THE SECRET OF LOVE, brings

adventurous Gabriel St. Briac (a descendent of Thomas) into the lives of the Raveneau family in 1808. Gabriel's incorrigible older brother, Justin, stars in HIS MAKE-BELIEVE BRIDE, set in Cornwall in 1818. I think you will love both books!

OF ONE HEART is available as an audiobook, narrated by the fabulous Tim Campbell, who has also created a magical audiobooks of ALL the St. Briac Family novels. If you haven't tried audio yet, this is a perfect time to start.

Page ahead to meet Christophe de St. Briac in an excerpt of ABDUCTED AT THE ALTAR (*Crowns & Kilts, Book 3*).

As always, I am grateful for your friendship and support. I would love to hear from you at Cynthia@Cynthi aWrightAuthor.com and I promise to reply!

With heartfelt appreciation,
~ *Cynthia*

Cynthia Wright says: The hero of ABDUCTED AT THE ALTAR is Christophe de St. Briac, the brother of Thomas in YOU & NO OTHER, and you will reunite with many favorite characters. Join Christophe as he travels from France to Scotland and finds love when he least expects it. Please enjoy this excerpt...

Abducted at the Altar

CROWNS & KILTS: THE ST. BRIAC FAMILY, BOOK 3

Prologue

DUNTULM CASTLE

Isle of Skye, Scotland
May, 1538

TEARS welled in Fiona's eyes and filled her throat as she gazed at her mother, dozing fitfully under a tartan bedcover. Eleanor MacLeod had once been vibrantly lovely, but now, after years of slowly failing health, she was thin, pale, and weak.

"Yer da should be here," muttered Isbeil, the nursemaid. The old woman had looked after the three Mac-Leod offspring since birth, and now that they were grown she stayed on to help care for her bedridden mistress.

"Shh," cautioned Fiona. She certainly agreed that her father, Magnus MacLeod ought to be the one sitting on the edge of her mother's bed and holding her dry, hot hand, but it was difficult to hear the words spoken aloud. "Mama might hear."

Isbeil sniffed. "Nay. She hasna even opened her eyes for days."

Fiona ached with unshed tears. She was exhausted and numb after such a long, vain struggle to return her mother to health. The books Eleanor had taught her to read when she was a wee lass were stacked haphazardly near the bed. In recent months, their roles had been reversed and Fi had read aloud in Latin and French to her beautiful, bedridden mother. She'd acted out *The Complaint of the Black Knight*, written by the English monk John Lydgate, even jumping up to pace across the tower room and pantomime the action. When Eleanor laughed or grew tearful, Fiona had felt triumphant.

But now there was nothing more to be done. She could scarcely bear the thought that the end might truly be at hand.

Just then, Eleanor's eyelids fluttered.

"Praise God!" breathed Isbeil.

"Mama?" Fiona's heart beat faster.

"Darling lass," her mother whispered. "There is something...I desire to give to you. Isbeil knows..."

The old nurse immediately went to a carved chest and opened the lid. A moment later, she approached the bed holding a small silver casket, its top inlaid with enamel. "Yer ma has been waiting to pass this on to you," Isbeil explained, and put the box in her hand. "Open it, lass."

Fiona felt the warmth of her mother's gaze on her as she lifted the lid. Inside was a striking circular brooch, a ruby at its center, surrounded by four identically-carved sea monsters. "Mama!" she breathed. "It's wonderful! Why have I never seen this before?"

Eleanor looked to Isbeil. "Please...explain to our Fi."

"The brooch was part of a treasure buried by the savage Vikings who invaded Skye. Ye may know, the MacLeods are descended from Leod, the son of the Norse king, Olaf the Black." Isbeil spoke reverently, as if repeating an oft-told tale. "When our great Clan Chief, Alasdair Crotach, came into possession of the treasure, he shared some of it with his son...yer da."

"Aye, I knew that Grandfather had given Da some of the Viking treasure, but I have never seen this piece..." said Fiona.

"Magnus gave me the brooch on our wedding day. I tucked it away," murmured Eleanor, "saving it for the daughter I prayed we would welcome one day. It is right that you have it, my love, for you are a MacLeod and have ever loved the history of your clan..."

"It must be hundreds of years old!" A wave of emotion swept over Fiona as she allowed Isbeil to fasten the ancient silver brooch to her bodice. The ruby at its center seemed to glow in the soft light. "Oh, Mama, I love it. I believe the carvings must be the blue serpents who live in the Minch."

"I knew you would say that." Eleanor clasped her hand again, tears welling in her eyes. "Think of me, sweet daughter, when you wear it."

"Of course, I will. I will treasure it!" Fi stroked her hair. "Now you should rest, Mama."

No sooner had her mother drifted off again than Fiona heard a step on the stairs. *Please God, let it be Da*, Fiona prayed silently. However, when she turned, she saw two of her brothers instead. Although both of them were grown men, they stood with eyes downcast, twisting their wool bonnets in their hands.

"Fi?" whispered her older brother, Lennox. His powerful body was still as he waited. As always, he seemed to know that he didn't need to say more than her name, in the way he always had, trusting her to provide whatever information he needed.

"I...fear for our precious mother," Fiona managed to reply.

"Lads," Isbeil interjected gruffly, "make yer farewells." The old nurse gestured to them to come forward.

Lennox and Ciaran MacLeod both went white as Fiona stepped away from the bed to make space for them. She wanted to go into her brothers' arms, to take strength from them, but it was she who had been carrying the rest of the family through this long ordeal.

"Where is our da?" she whispered to Lennox.

His sea-green eyes widened. "Da? I—I think he's down in the hall. Having a cup of ale."

She knew an urge to scoff, "Our father is a big, strong *coward*," but it wouldn't help anything to say such things to her siblings. "I will fetch him then. Like it or not, he must be here by Mama's side now."

Stepping out to the spiral stone stairway, Fiona paused for a moment at the keyhole-shaped gun-loop that helped to light the castle's shadowy interior. As always, her spirits lifted when she beheld the sweeping view of sparkling sea and the small hump of Tulm Island. Duntulm Castle was perched high atop a stone pinnacle that jutted out from the north coast of Skye, into a wild channel known as the Minch. It was a fortress... but their mother always insisted that it was first a home.

When refined Eleanor Lindsay had fallen in love with Magnus MacLeod and agreed to live with him on the wild Isle of Skye, he had added a new tower to the old castle and brought new tapestries and furnishings from France. Magnus often said that he would do anything to make his bride happy, short of moving to the civilized Kingdom of Fife where Eleanor's family still resided.

Swept by yet another urge to weep, Fiona instead squared her shoulders and forced herself to deal with the challenges at hand. Where had Lennox said she might find their father?

Fiona descended the twisting stairway and emerged from the tower to pass into the rush-strewn hall. There she saw her father, sitting by the fire, drinking ale, and absently stroking the head of his great shaggy wolfhound, Dougal.

In spite of the flame of resentment that burned in her heart toward him, she also felt a wave of compassion. He was a man of rare energy and enthusiasm, capable (as his wife liked to say) of persuading the faeries to do his bidding. Yet now his broad shoulders slanted down-ward, as if he'd suddenly grown old. When Fiona drew near, she had to touch her father's arm to penetrate his reverie.

Even then, he glanced up at her with hazel-green eyes that seemed a shade paler than usual. "Oh. What do ye need, lass?"

"You must go to Mama," she said firmly.

"I dinna think I can bear it," came his faint reply. He drank deeply from the pottery cup.

"Da, it is your duty as her husband!" Fiona heard her sharp tone and drew a deep breath. "Would she leave *you* to die alone?"

Magnus shook his big head. "When I see her suffer-ing, it is like a knife in my heart."

She took a chair beside him and looked into his weathered face. "You would rather ride into battle, facing certain death, I suppose."

"Aye! It is the worst pain imaginable to not be able to rescue my bride."

"But you *can*. You can ease her way from this world, Da." Fiona squeezed his hand and said more forcefully, "You must."

Without another word, he blinked back tears and

heaved himself to his feet. It came to Fiona that her mother had always seen to their family's emotional challenges, sparing Magnus that discomfort as much as possible. More recently, as Eleanor's health declined, Fi had shouldered that responsibility.

She was weary.

"Come on then, I'll be right here beside you, Da."

Her father was a warrior, a trusted lieutenant to his uncle and clan chieftain, Alasdair Crotach MacLeod. He had never been afraid of anything, as far as Fiona knew, until now.

When they came to the top step and turned into the tower bedroom, Fi saw that her brothers were still there. Ciaran stood looking out the narrow window, his face an impassive mask of cold fury. Lennox sat on the edge of the big bed, holding their mother's hand, his tawny mane of hair agleam in the fading rays of sunlight.

"So, you've come," Ciaran said, turning as they entered. He was as tall as Magnus, dark and chiseled, silver-gray eyes glittering with anger. He and Fiona had both inherited their mother's black, rather curly hair.

Fi understood why he glared at their father, but she knew it was pointless. Da was oblivious to everyone except Mama, and he was doing the best he could in a situation that must have felt like unbearable torture.

As they approached the bed, Lennox gave a little start and looked up. His striking face, which Mama had always fondly compared to the Viking raider who'd built their castle, was wet with tears.

"Move aside," Da growled, and his younger son quickly obeyed.

Fiona felt consumed by pain and helplessness as she watched Magnus hesitantly take his dying wife's hand. After a moment, Eleanor opened her eyes and gave him the gentlest of smiles.

Magnus straightened his shoulders, his entire attitude transformed. He tenderly murmured what must have been private love names in the Gaelic tongue. She wanted to rush to her mother's side and take her other hand, but sensed that she must wait.

"Husband," Eleanor whispered. For a moment, she was lovely again, her violet-gray eyes soft. "How brave you are."

From the window, Ciaran made a disparaging sound, but when his two siblings shot him quelling looks, he fell silent. A muscle flexed in his jaw.

"Nay," Magnus replied. "I've been a coward. I couldna bear—to see you..."

"I understand. It's all right. I know well enough how much you love me." Eleanor paused to sip from the cup that Isbeil held to her lips. "You see, I have been waiting...to beg a favor of you."

"Name it!"

"Magnus, after I... leave, I would have you take our daughter to court."

Fiona gasped. It was the last thing she expected to hear.

Her father shook his big head. She knew full well what he was thinking. He had other plans for his only daughter. "'Twould be foolish, love, to take Fiona away, when she is needed here so desperately."

Fiona saw her brothers exchange glances.

"It is my wish for her, Magnus."

His tone turned soothing. "Perhaps ye have forgotten that she has taken on your duties since you fell ill, love. Our lass has taught Ciaran and Lennox to read and do numbers! Fi manages the castle staff, she looks after me... we canna spare her."

Through the partially open door, Fiona was startled to see Ramsay MacAskill lurking about in the shadows.

Watching, waiting. A chill spread over her. Even as she wondered who had given this man leave to visit during this family crisis, her sixth sense told her he had been summoned by Magnus. She feared that her father had plans for her he would never divulge as long as her mother was alive.

Eleanor waited until Magnus paused for breath, then whispered, "I think you know that it has always been my wish to take Fiona to Fife, to visit my clanspeople at Hilltower, to go to court at Falkland Palace so that she might taste my heritage...before she returns to her life here on Skye. Remember the Viking brooch your da gave to me after we were wed? It was always my intention to give it to Fi when she visited the royal court. I cannot take her myself, but I have not surrendered that dream." Her eyes closed for a moment, and Fi imagined she could see her mother's heart beating through the thin fabric of her nightgown. "You must take her in my place, Magnus. She has cared for all of us and deserves something for herself."

Fiona's father blinked, coming back to the moment. "Aye, then. If it is your wish."

Fixing her weary gaze on him, Eleanor pressed, "I would hear you give your word, Magnus."

"I swear." He lifted her pale hand to his lips. "But 'twill not be necessary. Ye cannot leave us."

As if conserving her energy, Eleanor made no reply, looking instead toward her sons. When she stretched out a hand, Lennox came to her first. In a tear-choked voice, he implored, "Ma, don't go."

"My beautiful lion, you will be just fine. Guard your tender heart, but do not hesitate to venture out into the wider world."

Ciaran held back, dry-eyed, when she looked to him.

After a long moment, he came closer but did not touch her.

"I know you fear opening yourself to love, dear son," she whispered as a tear rolled down her pale cheek. "But I can promise you, it's worth the pain."

He looked stricken and Fiona understood. A human heart could only hold so much, and who knew what might be the tipping point? Fi came around to the other side of the bed, taking Isbeil's place.

"Mama, you must rest. Will you have tea? Or a bit of food?"

Ciaran had backed away from their mother, while Lennox sat closer and Magnus wrapped her hand in his big one.

"All I need is right here," Eleanor whispered. "My family." Her eyes closed, her breathing slowed, and she squeezed Magnus's hand...just enough, it seemed, to remind him of his promise.

Fiona felt a draft of cold air in the tower room. Urgently, she said, "Mama, what about a warm biscuit with honey? I'll go and fetch you one right now."

"It's no use, lass," said her father. He looked as if he'd drunk poison. "Your beautiful mother is with the angels now."

In a daze of disbelief and exhaustion, Fiona backed away from the bed. She couldn't breathe. "Da... I must have a bit of air."

"Go on, then," he replied. "Ye deserve a respite."

She had to pass Ramsay in the arched doorway. He towered over her, attempting as usual to impose his will on her, but Fiona slipped by without meeting his eyes. Another day, she would have brooded about the plans the men were making for her life, but today she felt numb and longed only to get away.

"Do ye pretend I'm not here?" he asked gruffly,

blocking her path. "I bear a powerful regard for ye, Fiona Rose."

Fi saw him staring at the ancient brooch and raised a hand to cover it protectively. "Kindly let me by."

She squeezed past him and ran down the twisting stone steps, wishing she were not encumbered by skirts. When she emerged into the courtyard, the sun blinded her for a moment. Servants and animals were milling about, oblivious to the crushing blow that had just been dealt to her family.

In a quiet corner, near the ancient well, Fiona saw little Robbie sitting near her falcon's perch. Robbie was a stable boy who dreamed of being a real falconer, perhaps at Dunvegan, their chieftain's castle. But it was Fi who had the true gift for hawking. When the falcon was on her wrist, she felt completely alive—and free of worldly cares.

Just ahead, a flat-surfaced perch was anchored to the ground and on it waited her falcon. She had named the bird Erik, even though Da scoffed that birds shouldn't have names. He also liked to remind her that the stunning white gyrfalcon had no affection for her, no matter what Fi might imagine.

Robbie saw her coming and scrambled to his feet. Erik, wearing a soft leather hood decorated with feathers, turned his head this way and that, sensing Fiona's presence.

She donned a long, stiff leather glove on her right hand, a smaller version of the gauntlet men wore to protect their arms from a bird of prey's sharp talons. Fiona's heart lifted as she turned to Erik.

"Do ye mean to hunt today?" asked Robbie. "No one told me."

A sudden breeze from the Minch blew Fiona's black hair behind her like a banner. "Nay." She found, to her surprise, that she could smile. "I just needed a few moments with my friend here. Alone, if you don't mind."

With that, Fi pinched the tuft of feathered sewn to the top of Erik's hood and lifted it away from his head. She next unfastened the tether that held him to the perch and extended her arm to him.

He came onto the gauntlet and blinked at her, waiting.

Fiona started toward the curtain wall. She climbed the steps to the walkway that overlooked the Minch, holding her right arm out with Erik perched on the gauntlet. Gyrfalcons were the largest of the falcons, and usually reserved for men. Da had tried to give her a merlin, calling it a fitting bird for a female, but Fi would have none of it.

Erik looked at her now, as if he understood everything she was feeling. She loved his mood of serious calm, his beautiful white feathers with their flecks of black. It was a blessing to be alive in this moment with such a creature of God.

When they reached the battlements, Fiona went to the very edge. Staggeringly tall cliffs lifted Duntulm Castle high above the choppy sapphire-and-crystal sea. It was a mad place to live and she adored it. She breathed deeply of the tangy air.

"Fly for me," she whispered to Erik, then extended her arm upward in a signal to the great bird. With a whoosh of his white wings, he leaped free of her, into the air, and soared high above the Minch. He was scanning the water and the rocky shore, she knew, for signs of prey.

Watching him, Fiona was relieved to feel the hot tears come at last. "Fly for Mama," she added softly, her heart swelling as the gyrfalcon spread his wings wider and flew farther away, as if he were bound for a place unknown to her.

* * *

Manoir du Rêves
Near Paris, France

The hawk paused in mid-air, silhouetted against the pale gray sky, then made a sweeping turn and sailed back to land on Christophe de St. Briac's outstretched, gauntlet-clad arm. Christophe loved this moment, when he felt the powerful grip of the wild bird's talons.

"There are woodcocks over the next rise, in that thicket," said Philippe, his falconer. The wiry young man widened his eyes hopefully.

Nearby, Christophe's Grand Bleu hound, Raoul, watched them attentively, as if he could understand every word they said.

Christophe was just about to toss common sense into the soft spring breeze and agree, when he heard a familiar voice calling his name. Again. Wincing slightly, he turned to look back up the hillside toward his stately yet simple manor house.

Immediately he recognized the tall, powerful form of his older brother, Thomas, seigneur de St. Briac. As he drew closer, Thomas demanded in mock-outrage, "Have you been pretending not to hear me?"

Christophe laughed. "No, but I have been trying to escape from all responsibility today. The plans for the Madame Fouquet's new château are giving me a devil of a headache."

"Then you were right to ignore my calls. I confess

that I've been sent by the King to fetch you. He bids you dine with him at the Palais du Louvre."

"That is the last place I wish to be. All of Paris is celebrating the impending wedding of Marie de Guise to Scotland's King James V. Isn't our monarch right in the thick of it, since he arranged the marriage?" Arching a brow, Christophe turned to his falconer and extended his arm so that the well-trained hawk could hop to the other man's gauntlet. "I wouldn't be a bit surprised to find the palace filled with a lot of uncivilized Scots tonight."

As they walked back up the hill together, their long legs striding in perfect rhythm, Thomas murmured, "Perhaps a few... though the wedding will be at the Guise castle, Châteaudun, a good distance from Paris. And King James, her Scottish bridegroom, won't even be in attendance. He's sent a proxy, Lord Maxwell."

"Indeed? I beg you, remind me of that option if I am ever tempted to wed." Christophe arched an ironic brow. "Can I not send a proxy to answer this royal summons?"

"I'm afraid not. Will it help if I assure you that Aimée and I will be at the Louvre as well?"

Although Christophe was cheered by this news, he merely gave a slight shrug. "A little."

"Hmm. What if I tell you that Aimée believes Louise Rennault will also be in attendance?"

This drew a roguish laugh from Christophe and he threw an arm around Thomas. "My sister-in-law is an incurable matchmaker."

They were walking up the steps to the back of the stone manor house he had designed and built himself. Handsome doors set with large panes of leaded glass led into the study that stretched across the entire floor. Christophe opened one of them and ushered his brother into the room where he spent most of his days.

"How can you possibly find anything in here?" asked Thomas, looking around in mock dismay.

Christophe pretended to ignore him. He loved this room better than any place on earth. It was lined with shelves of his books, some of them stacked on top of one another, and there was a long desk in the middle that appeared to be cluttered with building plans. Some were rolled up and carelessly tied with bits of ribbon while others were spread across the polished wood surface, in no apparent order. There were special shelves and drawers built into the desk to hold his various measuring tools, ink, and quills.

"I don't know what you mean," he told his brother in a tone of wry humor. "I know *exactly* where everything is."

"The workshop of a genius," Thomas mused. "As I recall from the days when Leonardo da Vinci lived near the King's château at Amboise, that great man was the same. His mind was always running at a furious pace, and even at an advanced age, he was working on many projects at once."

The sun was emerging to shine through the many windows Christophe had designed to bring light into his study. As he drew off his leather gloves, he glanced longingly at the plans he had been working on, spread open in the middle of the desk.

"Couldn't I join you later? I've just had an inspiration for the tower in Madame Fouquet's new château."

"Absolutely not. And you'll need to wash up and change out of your hunting clothes before we go to the palace." Thomas crossed to a sideboard and poured himself a glass of wine.

"First, tell me what this is all about," Christophe demanded. "You wouldn't lead your own brother into a trap, would you?"

"No, of course not!" Thomas looked amused. "In fact, I think that you'll be pleased. The King's proposition may change the course of your life, but for the better."

This sounded ominous. Unlike his adventure-loving brother, Christophe had an aversion to *change*. He preferred to wake up in his own home, where he could arrange each day without surprises.

He glanced one more time at the plans for the château he'd been commissioned to build by Madame Josephine Fouquet. A flirtatious widow, she favored a design that was numbingly similar to all the other grand homes in the French countryside. Now that Christophe had conceived of an original approach, he felt excited and wished only to lose himself in a series of new sketches.

"You know that I despise the Palais du Louvre," he complained. "Almost as much as I dislike the rich food served at royal dinners, the overbearing palace décor, and the perfumed courtiers."

"You aren't referring your own brother, are you?" Thomas parried.

"Don't be ridiculous. You aren't one of those power-hungry sycophants. You have been the King's friend since boyhood and no one knows better than I how you've avoided accepting wealth or titles from him, so that you could retain your independence."

"That's true. And because I only do his bidding when I agree with his motives, please trust me." With a gleam in his eye, Thomas added, "Louise Rennault is waiting. It seems to me that you are overdue for an amorous diversion. Perhaps some feminine *affection* will soften your mood."

Christophe glanced over as Raoul strolled into the room. From his canine mouth trailed a silk stocking left behind by one of his master's paramours.

He didn't need Aimée or anyone else to arrange a romance for him; there were more than enough women angling to share his bed. The bigger challenge was getting rid of them in the morning.

ABDUCTED AT THE ALTAR is available on Amazon!

Find all of Cynthia Wright's titles here:
http://cynthiawrightauthor.com/books.html

— *Meet Cynthia Wright* —

Cynthia Wright is a *New York Times* and *USA Today* bestselling author best known for her *Rakes & Rebels* series, 13 intertwining historical romances starring the irresistible Raveneau and Beauvisage families. Her other acclaimed series are *Crowns & Kilts* and *Rogues Go West*. *Romantic Times Magazine* hails Cynthia's novels as "Romance the way it was meant to be."

Cynthia lives in northern California. She enjoys riding a tandem bike and taking road trips in an airstream trailer with her Colombian-born husband, Alvaro and their corgi, Watson. She is also devoted to her two adorable grandsons who live nearby.

You are invited to visit Cynthia's website (where you can sign up for her newsletter and peruse the Books Page):
http://cynthiawrightauthor.com/

You are invited to join Cynthia's private Facebook reader group here:
https://www.facebook.com/groups/986064468145940/

View her "Behind the Books" boards on Pinterest:
http://pinterest.com/cynthiawright77/

Books by Cynthia Wright

Crowns & Kilts: The St. Briac Family
YOU AND NO OTHER (Thomas & Aimée)
OF ONE HEART (Andrew & Micheline)
YOU AND NO OTHER (Christophe & Fiona)
RETURN OF THE LOST BRIDE (Ciaran & Violette)
QUEST OF THE HIGHLANDER (Lennox & Nora)

* * *

Rakes & Rebels: The Raveneau Family
SILVER STORM
HER HUSBAND, THE RAKE
SMUGGLER'S MOON
THE SECRET OF LOVE
SURRENDER THE STARS
HIS RECKLESS BARGAIN
TEMPEST

* * *

Rakes & Rebels: The St. Briac Family
HIS MAKE-BELIEVE BRIDE (Justin & Mouette)
HER IMPOSSIBLE HUSBAND (Justin & Mouette)